IN THE TENTH HOUSE

IN THE TENTH HOUSE

A NOVEL

LAURA DIETZ

CROWN PUBLISHERS
NEW YORK

Copyright © 2007 by Laura Dietz

All rights reserved.
Published in the United States by Crown Publishers, an imprint of the Crown Publishing Group, a division of Random House, Inc., New York.
www.crownpublishing.com

CROWN is a trademark and the Crown colophon is a registered trademark of Random House, Inc.

Library of Congress Cataloging-in-Publication Data

Dietz, Laura.
In the tenth house : a novel / Laura Dietz.—1st ed.
1. Mediums—Fiction.   2. Séances—Fiction.   3. Swindlers and swindling—
Fiction.   I. Title.
PS3604.137415 2007
813'.6—dc22   2006039188

ISBN 978-0-307-35284-2

Printed in the United States of America

Design by Lauren Dong

10 9 8 7 6 5 4 3 2 1

First Edition

For Jeanne Lauren Dietz,

my mother.

IN THE TENTH HOUSE

Prologue

FRIDAY, NOVEMBER 13, 1896

Drink, they said, and she drank and the women watched her. The hostess hugged her lapdog closer as she watched and waved her hand, rolling it like an axle to urge them to drink more. The hostess's daughters, thin but with soft pulpy mouths, each had a teacup growing cold on her knee while they watched, still as stones. Her cup was of wine. It was red and smelt of cherries and slipped down her throat so smoothly she wondered if it could really be wine at all. The drink she knew scraped the tongue raw.

St. Aubin moved to stand behind her chair. "The room will do well," he told the hostess. "I took the liberty of moving a few small objects the spirits might find vexatious. I have placed the photographs where they may do the most good. Is the company ready?"

Company, he said, as if it were another group of twelve or twenty, pressing elbows in the most cosmopolitan manner, voices splintering off the chandeliers. She found a safe angle as they moved to inspect the smaller room. "Too few," she mouthed.

"No, plenty of money. Rich as sultans," he mouthed back.

"Mother. Too recent."

"You worry too much."

A glance at the room made her palms damp. It was small and dim and stuffy with ornaments. The grossest mechanical tricks would go unnoticed. St. Aubin had crowded the table with photographs: a fair, small-eyed youth who grew tall as the pictures marched from left to right. Their silver ranks would obscure St. Aubin's hands when he sat. She would be inches from the bereaved mother and her overfed dog.

"When our medium has attuned herself to the vibrations, we shall begin."

"Please, Miss," one of the colorless girls asked. "How did you come to know the world of the spirits?"

"A very wise question," said St. Aubin. "Our medium was a prodigy among prodigies. In her earliest years, the spirits were drawn to her sympathetic aura and gathered around her cradle—"

Lily could still feel it when she shut her eyes: the japanned tea tray, glassy lacquer so like liquorice she had licked it when her mother wasn't looking. It tasted of hands. Carola's room smelled a bit of hands, beneath the smoke and incense, and candles and close breath. "Very good, my dear one," Carola would say, just the same every time her daughter brought in the tea. Lily had despised the women in their frayed bonnets and mended gowns, had wanted Mama to herself, but she knew why she was there: the sorry-bonneted strangers trusted more and pitied more when there was a child present, and when they trusted and pitied there might be meat for dinner. If she disliked bringing the tea, she hated the evenings behind the curtain. She had to stand straight to keep her white muslin clean until the curtain pulled to one side and the stranger at the table sobbed and called out some other girl's name. *Marian. My Alice.* Much better were the nights in the black frock, crouched under the table waiting for Mama's left foot to tap twice. Sometimes she rang a hand bell muffled between her knees and sometimes pulled a string that rang a bell sitting on the table. Magnets dragged along the underside of the tabletop moved keys and coins in patterns sketched by Mama's toe. The visitors screamed if Lily reached out a hand to stroke their knees. So much noise for just a tap on the shin! She would marvel at the bother she had caused with just a finger, and tap again.

"Spirits!" St. Aubin called, his patter done. There were joined hands, as ever, and the wires were where the wires always were. At the farthest edge of the row of portraits was a hand-tinted one. The small-eyed youth had hair painted in with yellow, cheeks with pink, while the coffin in which he lay remained white and sepia. Some of the best photographers specialized in funerals.

It did not matter that it was a mother, Lily reminded herself, or how badly the hand in hers trembled. And the weeping of the soft-mouthed girls did not matter, because however gross the trickery they were all placed there by fate. As long as she obeyed it fate would never play her false.

PART ONE

AMBROSE

1

FRIDAY, OCTOBER 2,
VICTORIA STATION

"THE MEDICAL SESSION. [At Middlesex Hospital] the inaugural address was given by Dr. W. Essex Wynter. He warned against the necessary effect of methodical teaching in developing too much uniformity in opinion and method, and encouraged them to assert their own individuality as early as possible. . . . Curiosity, he observed, was mental appetite; when it was aroused the utmost advantage should be taken of it."

—*The Times*, October 2, 1896

Soot landed and became grease, pungent and clinging, coating the inside of the nose, the throat—trains were a splendid equalizer, he had always thought. It was like an epic experiment. Representatives of every class and station, every gradation of intelligence, character, fortitude, and moral fiber exposed to a common irritant, responding accordingly, for the edification and pleasure of the informed scientific observer. He often came to Victoria Station when he was in want of inspiration. Sweat, noise, and dirt stirred the intellect in a way that quiet repose could not. Ambrose Gennett found that thought intriguing, and set a theory to simmer at the back of his mind as he watched.

He was ambling to catch the 8:19 to Liverpool Street, scanning heads as he always did when a crowd made scrutiny safe. He collected a nose here, a scabrous complexion there, a curiously deformed ear. He locked eyes with a nameless fellow regular, a man in striped trousers with a salesman's gaudy watch chain. The other man glanced away with sharp embarrassment. Gennett noted an ill-kept scalp and moved on to study others.

It was the women he was interested in. And not in that way, not in the obvious way.

He watched their shoulders and chins and their smooth gloved hands, dipping in and out of dainty net purses, dragging handkerchiefs across noses that dripped. He saw when they let their eyes trail slyly after a stranger and when they shied from the male gaze as if burnt. He did not linger over slender waists or even, as happened when ladies struggled with steps into carriages, the odd ankle, titillatingly exposed. Titillation was not his object. How long had men of science averted their eyes in fear of such puerile misunderstanding? How could one be content with current knowledge, the constricting limits of what could be done for patients and still call oneself a doctor? There, a nurse glanced with venom at an errant charge. Beside her, a flower-seller licked her lips when a well-fed young woman, her gait too loose for maidenhood and her gaze too frank, strode by in striped finery. A threadbare maid passed by and neither spared her a glance, wrapped as they were in their shells of self-satisfaction and envy. The maid—

He looked again. Perhaps that female was not a maid. She moved quickly as if she knew where in the station she should be—and Victoria was a large and unforgiving station—but also swiveled her head this way and that, as if searching. Yet was not looking at faces. He abandoned his covetous flower-seller and paid closer attention. His glove was on the handle of the last first-class carriage when he saw it. At the third-class end of the platform the woman collided with a man. From Gennett's vantage point it was difficult to tell who had been at fault. The man took the woman by the shoulders and half lifted her out of his path. The crowd made way the way city crowds did, shifting with their eyes averted to give the disturbance space but not attention. In the reordering, another man's suitcase, balanced on his shoulder, struck the woman's head. She went down as if shot. For a moment her hat bounced like a skipping stone across the roiling surface of the crowd before falling to the platform floor. Gennett was at her side before he was aware he was moving.

"Are you all right, Miss?"

She seemed not to hear him. She was on her knees, snatching her hat from the gauntlet of shuffling feet. A trio of artificial cherries sagged from the band at a defeated angle. She tried to stand, fighting for balance, but clung to the hat as if it were more precious than her head. All the while her fingers made a frantic circuit of the brim, testing for cracks. The sight moved him in a new and unknown way.

"Miss?" She had to crane her neck to look at him. She was really no larger than a child. "Are you all right? You should take more heed of obstacles. The blow was severe." The blow would perhaps explain the turmoil in her face, a hybrid of anxiety and confusion. Quite a tiny face, squeezed beneath a spectacular forehead: a perfect dome of alabaster, bulging slightly—from pronounced faculties of intuition and reflection—shockingly white against the gray and dun of coats. It was enough to make him wish that he still believed in phrenology. He felt an impulse, disturbing and unprecedented, to reach out and test her skull's messages with his own hands, pressing her luminous skin with his thumbs.

"Am I—you were sent?"

Her accent was not refined, but not overtly common, either. Perhaps a shopgirl half trained to ape the monied classes? He would need to draw her out into conversation. "The blow," he said deliberately. "Please do not think you can ignore such an injury. It would be most unwise."

"This is what comes of lying to your mother."

"I'm sorry?" He ventured the briefest glance over his shoulder but there was no one else to whom she might be speaking.

"She's in danger, however you pretend not to see." Her lip quirked. It was a very pink lip. "Because of the meddling. You try to help but you're a fool to think that there's anything you can do."

She hunched to hide her face from him as she stabbed pins to anchor her hat to her hair. He flinched at her careless aim, as if it were his belly at risk instead of her glorious brow. His eyes twisted away from her groping hands to her feet. . . .

She wore beaded evening slippers. Their soles were never meant to stray from parquet and were gouged now with gravel and glass. The needlework alone was five times the value of her headgear. And her dress—a silk hem, lush violet, peeped from beneath her cheap coat like fruit from a cracked rind.

"Miss, you must allow me to help, I absolutely insist." He had just enough time to escort her to a hospital, perhaps even a few minutes for questions. He was intrigued, obviously, but it was unthinkable that she be left on a station floor in her state of confusion. "Your thoughts are distressing to you, I believe? There are signs in operation here that you do not understand." She dropped a hatpin and met his eye.

He had seen every kind of fantasist and every kind of liar. He had heard families denying that anything was amiss while their daughters and sons screamed and tore at the restraints, ranting of plots and persecution and divine instructions, angels and demons that whispered in voices only they could hear. He had as fine a clinical sense as any for the borders between falsehood and delusion and truth. Her expression made his gut fold up like an envelope.

She knew him. He would swear to it. It wasn't censure; that he could brush off like mud from his boots. It was the sympathy in her face that pierced him through, as if she perceived in an instant his troubles and regretted them, even if she did not hate him for his failings. She spoke in the tone he used with patients when the news was bad. "The signs are clear. Your lies will catch up. It won't be year's end before the eclipse."

"Miss, your acquaintance, I have not—you must allow me to help you. I am a doctor."

Her eyes snapped wide, not in empathy this time but in fear. "The Cup—the messenger would be in disguise!"

She slipped like a needle into the crowd. Elbows that made way for her blocked his pursuit. He heard throats cleared and umbrellas rustled with emphasis; the crowd was not blind to everything. He knew how pursuit must look. He could defy it, but not pretend that he did not hear. It was only a moment that the freeze of disapproval held him but that was enough; he had lost her. It might have ended there, in the greasy soot of the station, an inexplicable moment, had she not turned back. It was the briefest glance. Her face appeared in the crowd on the stairs, unreadable in the distance. Then she vanished again behind the horizon of strangers. It was a crumb for him, a little raveling string where one moment snags on another, ready to be pulled.

She was gone by the time he reached the exit. He could have turned back to catch the next train, but he left the station and hailed a cab instead. "Belgravia, please. Forty-nine Eaton Place." He pulled a bit of paper from his breast pocket—it was the letter of invitation to this morning's conference, but no matter—to make notes on the back. *Lying to your mother,* and *she is in danger.* What else? His pen scattered ink in tempo with the ruts in the road. "And make haste," he called to the driver. Nothing had been wrong at his last visit, though he couldn't recall when that last visit home had been.

EATON PLACE was at its best in the autumn. Weak light softened the unrelieved white of the house fronts and made them intimate, like a duchess taking visitors in her retiring room. Cubitt's Georgian proportions were never better realized than here; each pillared portico just so, each lamp and window box placed by one master hand. Chopin had given his first London recital at Eaton Place. This was long before the Gennetts had bought, but streets had long memories, even in London. Ambrose's name was on the ninety-nine-year lease, his mother's widow's portion having been in cash, which he kept for her in the uneventful four percents. His name was on these investments as well. He paid her bills directly from the dividend accounts, including his half sister Ernestine's allowance and a bit of pin money for Ernestine's aunt, Emily Featherstone, and reinvested the remainder. His small constituency of women had come through the depressions of the early nineties with barely a hiccup of income. The house was maintained as scrupulously. *Her house,* he schooled himself, as he always did. The illusion of hospitality suited them both. He took the steps two at a time.

Violent squawking broke out even before he rang the bell. Over the din a voice barked "Quy-et! Quy-et!" in two staccato syllables. The woman who flung open the door was crisply aproned and capped, and held at arm's length a baroque wire cage in which a gray parrot stamped and whistled with energy. The woman spoke, once she knew herself to be heard, with ambitious diction. Her beady-eyed resemblance to the bird was nothing short of tragic. His mother had never in her life taken on a good-looking maid.

He was scarcely settled in the second-floor drawing room before his mother entered. The parrot was instantly docile, creeping up the side of its cage to poke its beak out toward the handle. It nibbled Ruth's fingers as she spoke.

"My dear! I knew it was you. I had a feeling, and Albert became quite excited, which he always does. He's so fond of you." Albert nibbled, indifferent. "But why didn't you send word? We would have kept breakfast out on the sideboard for you. But you'll want a cup of tea. Ernestine and Emily have already gone to make their morning calls. I know we're not on the telephone but surely a note—"

"The club's banned stationery completely, Mother. Hadn't you heard? All relics of print are an offense to progress." His cheek brushed hers in an abbreviated kiss as he drew her aside. "Tell me, are you feeling quite well this morning? None of those twinges in your ankles?"

"Ambrose?" She looked around her in case the servants may have heard her own son referring openly to her limbs. "You are very silly. Do come and sit. Of course you would like a cup of tea?"

"I'm just stopping in. That is, I was passing by, and I thought, why not? Or rather—you are quite all right? You have had no . . . surprises, distressing news, anything like that?"

"How had you heard so quickly?"

A seasick swimming afflicted his inner ear. He suffered it for an extraordinarily long moment before she said, "Your cousin's spaniel shows no improvement! None! And after such a sustained and disagreeable course of treatment! So shocking, sit down and I will tell you all about it. Unless you will be hurrying away to some engagement? You are always so busy."

He opened his mouth to agree, then stuffed the note-covered letter of invitation farther down in his pocket. "Not in the least. This is the King Charles spaniel with the respiratory complaint?"

The chat weaved erratically as the hour advanced. Ruth had not lived in Edinburgh since before her first marriage, but spoke as though she had moved from King's Way that morning. Even if he hadn't been listening for hints of danger his contribution would have been limited to polite noises. He understood that his mother spoke to know her own mind and each thought was voiced, turned over, and fitted to the jigsaw by hand. Gennett interrupted her only when the conversation swerved to the pets of unrelated persons. "How are the neighbors, then? The house? You haven't heard any vexing news about those new flats they're proposing?"

"No."

He studied her minutely but could see no sign of perturbation, even at his admittedly odd line of questioning. All at once his fears from the station fell away; she was perfectly well. Everything was well. Hard observation burned away anxiety but left him scorched and raw; exposed, had anyone the means to see his rank stupidity, listening to a strange woman babbling prophecy. . . .

His mother's good breeding would not permit conversation to falter, however distracted her companion: ". . . a pleasant day now that the rain has passed. It is most agreeable to see you before luncheon. I doubt that we have enjoyed your company at the visiting hour since you took up with that third hospital. How refreshing that at least someone there recognizes how improper it is to monopolize a gentleman's time."

She laid a touch of emphasis on *gentleman*. He was in no state to reopen that. "I'm on my way there now, actually." He kissed her again and busied himself consulting his pocket watch while the girl brought his coat. He could make the 10:57 if he hurried. The price of folly was one and three-quarter hours. He might pay in embarrassment but no one need be the wiser.

THE DOORMAN was taking another man's coat when Gennett arrived at the lecture hall. The servant bowed, passed the other man's coat to the boy behind the desk, took Gennett's coat himself, and bowed again. The other man opened his mouth to protest, saw for whom he'd been snubbed, and moved seamlessly to a welcoming grin.

"Dr. Gennett. What luck to catch you! The first speaker this morning reminded me, there happens to be a paper of mine that might interest you, so very germane to the talk of the day. Did you not arrive in time for the first lecture? Well, you'll be doubly keen to read it. You will? Splendid, splendid. I'll have it left for you at the desk, shall I? Just happen to have it with me."

The doorman bowed again in assent. They took their cues from each other, the staff and the members, the members and the staff. Across the lobby a man Gennett remembered from a conference on congenital deformity waved to catch his attention and started energetically across the floor. Gennett turned sharply for the stairs.

The second speaker was in full flow behind the podium. Gennett wanted to find a quiet corner and concentrate on the lectures. He crept along the aisle, squinting down each row of seats, but sprawled across every one were well-padded practitioners, chatting over the background drone of rising admissions figures in Canadian hospitals. To a man they asked: Would Gennett join them? Would he take a chair? Would he have an opinion on the latest board reshuffling at the Kensington? In his position he must have some insight into the matter. Gennett made his apologies and went on. He didn't usually mind the politicking. It was the price of status, and that status gave wings to his reforms. And no honest man could deny the importance of status to a healthy psyche. Gennett did try to be an honest man.

"Gennett!" The correctly muted hiss came from the back row. Gennett fell into the proffered seat with gratitude. Too late he noticed that his friend Booth was not alone. Platt made a great show of consulting the wall clock and waggled two digits in reproach.

"It was an hour and three quarters, not two. Can't a fellow be late without an inquest?"

"Oho!" Platt shifted to tap cigar ash onto the floor. "Far be it from me to press on a sore point. I'm sure that you were consoling the poor or visiting your aged mother. Proper manly appetites, what?"

"Very proper." Gennett sank back into his chair. It was best to get Platt off the subject of appetites. "What did I miss then?"

"Quite your kind of thing. Daftest lecture I've ever heard: all subconscious and unconscious and I-don't-know-what-conscious, all in the best gold-plated Kraut accent. You should be absolutely ill with regret to have missed it."

"It's excellent theory if you could be troubled to read it rather than sneering at it." Booth sounded like a scolding governess, but Booth was always a bit prim. Even at school, blue eyes, fair curls, and a pink rosebud mouth had given every pronouncement a lace-tablecloth niceness that was fatal to sarcasm. If the rest of his face hadn't saved him from handsomeness, he would never have survived past the third form. Gennett had few enough school friends in his social circle—squeamish of his work, most of them—but Booth had taken a route like Gennett's own, progressive Scottish and continental studies in preference to the Oxbridge orthodoxy. Gennett doubted that half of his papers would have been spurred to completion without Booth's generous offers to coauthor.

"You've never seen one of these neurotics?" Gennett asked Platt.

"No, and neither has anyone else." Platt was strictly old school: surgery and drugs, and a thick black line between soundness and disease. "Perfectly normal but for a whatsit-conscious wrapped around her ankles tripping her up? You'd love to get your hands on one, I don't doubt. In a metaphoric sense."

Neurosis! Gennett couldn't keep the quick burst of elation from his face.

Platt grunted and leaned forward to scrutinize Gennett. "Have your hands on one now, do you think?"

"Only a possibility . . . no, more than a possibility. It fits perfectly. This morning I was delayed because a passenger at the station was injured."

"How extraordinary that our branch of medicine was of assistance," said Booth.

"Interesting you should say that." Yes, it fit. He could feel his theory gathering speed, stripping the mystery from the morning's events, crushing the lingering eeriness under its wheels. "Because it was exactly that. It gave me the strangest turn. They affect one that way at times. Their certainty is almost mesmerizing; it's how one can tell them from malingerers, you know—and for a moment I almost thought—never mind that. But the injured girl went rather wild when I tried to help her. Spouted the most extraordinary nonsense, impending disaster and so forth. Either she mistook me for someone, as obviously I do not know her, or she was severely confused. Or—"

"Or she thought there was profit in making you think so," said Platt. "They're very wily, these street girls. What did she look like?"

". . . or she was, in effect, talking to herself if she but knew it. Her attire was not indicative of reason in the ascendant. She was about to board my train to Liverpool Street. I've never seen her before, but no one bothers with the peak-hour fares except commuters. She's certain to turn up—"

Platt dissolved into laughter, his jowls bouncing under side-whiskers slightly behind the fashion. "My God, you're not really going to slink about like Dr. Watson? Crouching behind chestnut vendors and combing her path for clues?"

"She would be very interesting simply as a subject. Do you suppose she has been a subject? She was so alarmed when I told her I was a doctor."

"The poor are always alarmed by doctors. If you're that hard up for a pretty girl, I can recommend a good house to you. I thought you made your way to Soho with healthful regularity, or is that all up?"

"Is it even possible for you to consider that animal instincts have nothing to do with it?"

"Your colleague in Vienna seems to think animal instincts have to do with everything. Any troubles at home you want to get off your chest?"

"I'm sorry, are you suggesting that I am lying or that I am confused? Do you think that I look at a female and do not know whether she appeals to me?"

"You accuse your patients of such."

"Accuse? Inquire, rather," Booth interrupted. "You must see that there is little parallel between a spinster, frightened and confused by the natural imperatives of her redundant reproductive system, and a doctor well acquainted with the causes and symptoms of repression. It is not pathology that manifests itself in the . . . fulfilled."

Platt raised his eyebrows. "Thought you were a bachelor, Gennett."

"He studied in Paris," Booth murmured.

"Ah, that sort of fulfillment. Just as well that our fair capital offers refresher courses. Five years is a hell of a time for a man to play the brave little soldier. You said this girl seemed to know you. What exactly did she say?"

"Quite the stuff of witches from the Bard. Concealed hatred. Terrible danger. Lying to women, or secrets about women—"

He choked off that angle of inquiry, but Platt's ears had visibly pricked up with interest. Gennett cursed himself. Sometimes avoiding a subject caused more gossip than indulging in it. "Perfect nonsense, nothing that could refer to anyone I know. Do you have the time? I recall that I have an appointment. I'll see you later at the club. In the card room, I think?"

"Bring cash," said Platt. "I have an intense premonition of a winning streak."

✠ ✠

THE OUTSIDE air was not refreshing. He slowed to a halt at a fenced spot of green at the end of the road. There was no reason for his restlessness, but it seemed that he could not force his feet to turn back to the conference.

Could not force them? Could not govern his own appendages? He gave a sharp rebuke to that absurd line of reasoning (unhealthy thought breeding unhealthy thought, that was the cycle) and made a circuit of the meager park at speed.

What had he been thinking, to take the girl's ravings seriously, even for a moment? Something about this was different. He rifled through the most neglected corners of his brain, an activity more familiar to him as guide than as subject, and could find nothing to link her to him. She fit no description he could match to a name, he could not place her accent or conduct or outlandish clothes in the character of a servant to his circle, and he had certainly never seen her. He could not conceive of having met her without marking the forehead and the huge unguarded eyes, or the dislocated dread he had felt in her presence, illogical as the certainty in a dream that one could not scream or run however much one wanted to. He rested one foot against a granite tribute to some obscure colonial hero and used his knee as a makeshift writing desk.

Subject: Name unknown.
Session, October 2ⁿᵈ, '96, 8:16 a.m.

He scribbled down details in shorthand, as he should have done when the impressions were fresh, instead of indulging irrational fears. *You were sent?* He was sure of that. But then? *You do not understand your women? You are blind to their danger?* And then cosmological events and something nonsensical about warnings from men in costumes. He struggled for the exact words. Without a verbatim record it was impossible to know the import of patient statements; the sane misheard deliberately, made allowances to deny the contagion of unreason. *You cannot help? Your efforts are impotent and resented?*

His own reaction was significant. If he found her case more affecting than usual, why should he ignore his instincts? This girl was more than usually disturbed. That was the explanation for his unease; her words had not been so very specific, after all, and if she had special knowledge of him he would have found his mother in mortal peril, not fussing over a poorly pet. If she did not know him, then his hypothesis at the lecture had been correct, never mind that Platt was too thick to credit it. She was ill.

Pity flowed out through his veins, cooling his head and clearing it. He could feel the ground beneath his feet again and it was steady.

That poor, poor girl. Somewhere she was at that moment condemning herself. *You try to help but you're a fool to think that there's anything you can do.* It was transference. She called him weak, impotent—looked at him that way— because she saw those defects in her own character. Her failings had driven her to the point of madness, to displacing her crimes to a stranger. It was madness indeed to accuse him as if she had some kind of unholy power left over from the Middle Ages, cramming her dirty fingers into the secrets of his home, flipping open his character like a book for all to see, to judge—

He tucked the notebook into his coat. There were not so many hospitals in the East End.

2

SPITALFIELDS

"Could you check again?"

The clerk breathed sharply through his nose. "We have had no admission of a young woman such as you describe, with or without a head injury, at any time today. Or ever, if memory serves. Have you tried any other hospitals? St. Anne's in Limehouse is more likely to cater to that sector of society."

"This was the last. I've tried everything within reach of Liverpool Street."

"She was hit by a train, sir?"

"No, but she may have boarded a train before seeking treatment."

"While injured, sir?"

"Yes, I know, but—there were certain circumstances—she may have been slightly confused."

"Confused!" The clerk smiled and took up his pen, ready to return to his duties. "Have you tried St. Botolph's, sir? Do you know of it?"

Gennett grimaced. "She's not there. I tried there first—I'm a consultant."

So many years, and he still found it shocking to see disgust. The public was one thing, but hospital staff should know that there was nothing frightful, nothing catching. The clerk came out from around his admissions desk to shut the door behind him.

⊷ ⊷

FOR EIGHTEEN months of dreary mornings Gennett had comforted himself with the same thought: He was seeing St. Botolph's at its worst. It was a Georgian box old before its time; for its flat-faced stolidity it might have been a converted bank or school. He thought now, as he looked at the rotting plaster, the long green stains drooling from gutters and eaves, that its undersized windows, high and narrow, gave it away. It was purpose built. Refuse pressed against the walls in drifts. More would appear before the dustmen came at dawn, but the immediate area would be clear when the senior staff arrived; the board of governors had that much influence. Inside, the wardens would be retrenching. Nothing that changed at night here ever changed for the better.

He mounted the steps. Framed within the lead gray double doors was a brief panel for entrance, now held by night locks. His keys were useless. Polite, and then insistent knocking elicited no response. The entry panel clattered like a horse cart when he kicked it. The stain his boot left on the paint seemed entirely out of proportion to his foot.

"Bobby?"

He lost his hat turning. Figures he hadn't seen were now looking up at him from the street with interest. The gutted wrecks of buildings to all sides were not empty; he supposed, now that he thought about it, that they never were. Spitalfields was not a place where shelter was likely to go to waste. Not two feet away a thin lad was pinching the brow of his cap in a cursory sort of tip, watching Gennett stoop for his bowler. "Police, Sir?" the lad enunciated. "Having a spot of trouble with your door, Sir?"

The entry panel inched open to reveal a porter Gennett knew vaguely. Call him *Smith*, Gennett decided. "Smith" was sweating and out of breath. His white smock sat oddly over thick boots better suited to a building site. "Splendid!" Ignoring the boy, Gennett smiled widely to put the man at ease. "I seem to be rather undersupplied with keys. Or do you bolt the keep after we all leave at night?"

In his experience, most volleys in life were exchanged automatically, as in tennis: warmth with warmth, candor with at least a show of informality. Hence the advantage of serving.

Smith merely blinked and worked his lips over his teeth. "It's after hours. All've gone."

"Might a patient or two be lingering?"

Smith looked ready to flee; the pickled breath assaulting Gennett's nose suggested that he had good reason.

"Do please allow me in. I'm only here to check if there were any late admissions."

"No admissions today."

"None? Well. I—well." As clearly as print on the page he could see himself in his bachelor's flat, staring at the ceiling with the hot water bottle going cold at his feet, chewing the day's events to pap until they choked him. Had he pressed? Had he asked the proper questions? Had he anything whatsoever to show for his efforts, or was no one the better for his having made an ass of himself, and in front of hospital staff, too? "There might have been an emergency," he heard himself say. "We were short-staffed today." This was true: Gennett had missed his rounds entirely.

"No trouble. That Coffley's down and settled now."

"Ah! Mr. Coffley had another episode? I'll see him."

"Not an, ah—"

"Inspection? Not at all." Gennett glanced behind to find the boy still intently following the conversation. "Good evening."

Too polite a dismissal; the boy moved to keep his eye on them until the door shut. Smith threw three bolts and dropped a bar of medieval proportions across the lot. Gennett had always wondered why they bothered locking up from the inside.

The halls looked the same: the windows, foot-square panels of clouded glass flush with the ceiling, admitted so little light around their bars that the time of day was irrelevant. Illumination came from the gaslights, each in its own protective cage, nestled at the junction of walls and ceiling like so many iron wasp's nests. The lamps were one of Gennett's innovations. He had threatened the board, cajoled;

regaled them with stories of advances on the continent and his hero Pinel (if he exaggerated or implied that secondhand accounts were miracle cures he had seen with his own eyes, it was entirely for the good of his patients), and in the end paid for them himself. He thought of it as a conditional victory. His gaslight, he noted with satisfaction, revealed no break in the gleaming blankness of the ceiling and walls. *"In addition to its other salutary effects,"* he had written to the board of governors, *"continuous light forestalls laxness on the part of porters, guards, and charwomen; those very squires in our crusade against degeneration who are, perhaps, most vital to a patient's recovery, and yet most susceptible to the temptations of sloth."*

Smith wheezed like an ox as they mounted the steps to the privilege ward. Here, families could supply small comforts: coal and counterpanes, tobacco and fruit. Gennett considered luxury counterproductive to the cure, but only the most rigid of traditional governors could object to a rag rug. At St. Botolph's class ascended no further than shopkeepers, skilled craftsmen, and the occasional clerk. Gentlemen went to private establishments (he could hardly dignify them as "institutions") in the countryside, and were cured when the money ran out. The stairs stretched on and Smith's sweat smelt of gin.

On the second-floor landing Smith paused and leaned heavily on the banister. Gennett saw his eyes dart down the identical corridors to the right and left.

"Right," Gennett supplied. "Do you know the room? I appreciate your effort—most conscientious—but I'd be only too happy to escort myself. If you would be so good as to loan me the key——" He was cut short by the hard, scratching dislike in Smith's glance. It was less like hate than profound irritation, but lasted only an instant before Smith's eyes shifted up to a spot just above Gennett's left shoulder.

"Catching my breath, Sir." Mindful of his lungs Smith led down the right-hand corridor with stately deliberation. His eyes flicked to Gennett's feet each time they approached a door. "Not far now, Sir, is it?"

Gennett hadn't the patience for a confrontation. Had the governor been there he would have invited a blistering rebuke on resisting challenges to his authority, because he dodged around the slowing porter and identified the door himself.

"Doctor Gennett?" a querulous voice answered. Gennett was the only doctor who knocked.

Inside, the high, barred window was limned in gray but its light seemed trapped in the glass. There was nothing for the senses to catch on but a constant, rolling scrape—dry, like paper on paper.

"Mr. Coffley," Gennett began, but faltered. Smith's alcoholic aroma was yielding to the stench of the room: bitter and sharp, like lye, with metal beneath. It seemed to pulse in time with the scraping. "Fetch us a light, please." Smith turned so smartly Gennett knew there was a catch. He said in time, "Leave the key."

"Can't leave prisoners with a key in the cell. The Head's right clear on that."

"I don't consider this patient," Gennett stressed the word, "to be a risk. I absolve you of any responsibility." He waited until the porter was well down the hall to lock himself into Coffley's room. He wouldn't hold out much hope for a light.

Once his eyes adjusted, the gloom wasn't quite so impenetrable. Moonlight just picked out the iron struts of the cot, an upright wooden chair, and the bald head of the man hunched in it. He still wore his spectacles. The other doctors didn't come near this one if they could help it.

"I was disappointed to hear of today's episode. I had hoped that we were beyond this." Gennett leaned on the edge of Coffley's desktop, bare and freshly dusted.

"I demand my papers." Coffley spoke fierce words flatly. He was coming down off of the mania. His hands were as dry and cracked as the sound they made and they rolled on, over and over each other.

"You know why they were put away and you know what you have to do to earn them back."

"Earn them. Earn my own books and my own pens. I really will go mad."

Gennett held his voice, disciplining it into smoothness. "You were abusive. You had a fit. When the staff tell you to stop, you must stop, or these are the consequences."

"By God, if I took a man from his home and locked him away like a dumb animal—"

"You bit Matron. Did you mean to do that? You are here to learn to manage those impulses. We are here to help you learn control."

"I can control anything I like to, thank you. If I don't wish to be ordered about by illiterate apes, that's something else. You are not even my regular physician, so what do you know about it?"

"You call biting a woman the action of a well man?"

"A well man in a bug house."

"Mr. Coffley, if you could simply give me a reason for this denial of your condition—"

Coffley's head snapped up. Gennett knew the shade of purple his face would be, and how his thin neck broke into cords like meat being torn from the bone, if only the light were strong enough to see it. It never varied. "You foul bastard. Do you know what I think you do at night, you—"

On it went, to Gennett's professional acumen, ancestry, personal habits, and sexual proclivities. The recitation varied so little that Gennett suspected it to be a speech, but he was the only one of his colleagues who had troubled to sit through it more than once. The inevitable, if repetitious, torrent of abuse had deflected questions for years. Coffley had thus avoided being committed until middle age, and this was the prevailing theory as to why the behavior modification was failing. However fiercely they forced him into normal conduct he slid back. No one could say why some took to the cure and some not.

"Mr. Coffley, why do you think that you are here?"

"Don't patronize me! I have the books. I have read the books. I know that I've had, I've had periods of ill humor at times. My

sister isn't a bad woman, only ignorant. Are you saying that no one has ever been committed by his enemies? You are pitifully undereducated in your so-called specialty, but not even you could believe that!"

It was always so difficult to know when to follow them down their twisting paths. One wanted to understand; one did not want to encourage, or give poisonous fantasy too much weight. "That is something for bad novels, heiresses locked away by scoundrels—"

"It does happen! What of Louisa Lowe?"

"It has at times been reported to happen. Usually when there is money involved. But there is no money involved here, is there? No one is off spending a fortune that is rightfully yours." If Coffley's family had any resources whatsoever he wouldn't be at a charity hospital, but that was best put gently. "Now let us think. What would you say makes a man . . . in need of help? Why do you think you are here?"

Confusion gave Coffley's voice a childlike lilt. The bright edges of his spectacles wove this way and that. "This is a trick? This is a filthy trick and you're filthy to play it."

"No trick. It could help you. That is all I want, to help you."

"I think it would not! And why would I need help? And why would I need it from you?"

Gennett could get nothing more from him. The patient sat twitching and flinching in the dark until Gennett departed, locking the doors for which he had keys. The bar on the main entrance could wait for Smith.

When he emerged from the building it was full dark, but a gibbous moon behind the clouds gave the impression of twilight. The street was like a scene from another century. Everywhere torches, lamps, fires in twisted metal cages spat in the rain. No streetlights, scant paving, nothing green. Every third house—if the warped structures lining the street could be so called—belched heat and cheap tobacco smoke from red-lit doorways. Men sauntered or paused to lean and converse with women draped over windowsills, limp as laundry. He was familiar with the neighborhood and consid-

ered himself quite unflappable, but at night . . . he couldn't reconcile the blackness of the scene before him with the luminous sky above.

"Sir?"

A shadowy heap in the corner of the steps was moving. Gennett took an involuntary step back and heard chuckling.

"Only me, Sir. Doctor, that is." It was the youth in the cap. "Right sorry to startle you."

"You've been here since . . . just sitting here?"

"Oh, about a bit, not far. Are you needing something?"

"Business can't be that slow!" He hoped that he sounded dismissive. The harshness in his voice could easily be mistaken for fright.

"Lot of the doctors here need errands doing, that kind of thing."

The lad wasn't in his way, exactly, but stepping down to the street would require brushing past him in a manner bordering on the rude. He wondered which of the staff were vulnerable to this maneuver.

"What sort of errands?"

"All sorts."

"Do you know what kind of hospital this is?"

The lad shrugged. "Mad doctors needs the comforts of life like everybody else."

His voice was hoarse and sandy. A juvenile tobacco fiend, no doubt. Gennett cut around him and made for the street.

"Doctor sounds like he has people he wants a bit of news on, wants to find."

Gennett stopped and half turned. The lad did not scurry, but wasted no time in coming close enough for whispers.

"Why would I want to find someone?"

"Or news." The lad smirked. "But as you do seem to have someone you'd like to find, well, doesn't everyone? You'd be a strange sort of fellow if there weren't someone or something you wanted."

"If one did," Gennett spoke low and, to an observer, would seem to be surveying the streets before him. "If one did, what would the, that is to say, how would one proceed?"

"Name?"

"No name. No address, either. One might know where to start, however. Places that this someone frequents."

The lad was pointing to the main road as if giving directions. "That's one for the experts, I'd say."

"Sadler's, Attwood's, that sort of thing?"

Whether he knew of those detective agencies or merely disapproved of the names, the lad made little effort to conceal a sneer. "I myself was thinking of the local experts, Sir."

"I mean, rhetorically speaking—" What was he asking for, professional advice? "Can you arrange it?"

"This way then, Sir."

Gennett had less than a moment to decide. It was a bit like an injection: no time for agonies once it's begun. "There," he had been known to say to his younger patients as he slipped the syringe free, "that wasn't so bad, was it?"

3

The Tavern

The tavern was as low, close, and smoky as any chronicler of London life could wish. A long rank of backs obscured the bar, stooped like stones in a woolen garden wall. Hooks jutted at intervals from the scarred beams though no one seemed inclined to relinquish his coat or cap. Cheap tobacco, stale breath, and coal smoke swam together under an overwhelming cloak of beer. Even as Gennett's professional eye marked dirt, rotting teeth, and the symptoms of syphilis and chronic dipsomania, he couldn't suppress a voyeuristic thrill. East End exposé was something of a national vice, at least among the gentle classes. Bedlam had been a tourist attraction for centuries—one of the reasons Gennett had left for a less-celebrated post—but it was becoming difficult to find a rookery not yet written up in the *Pall Mall Gazette*. Philanthropists and reporters dug for finds like truffle hunters. His generation had done its slumming, but he and his university cronies had never come up with something as authentic as this.

The crowd was dense but his companion led him undisputed to a corner table. Two cloudy glasses of beer were set before them; all Gennett saw was a beefy set of forearms, sweat beading in a pelt of ginger hair, before the barman was absorbed back into the throng. When he looked back there was a fat man opposite him at the table. The stranger seemed vast, but perhaps it was only his miniature spectacles and snug coat that made him seem so; his cuff links looked small as a child's fingernails. Having drained the foam and three inches of beer from his glass, the man folded his hands before him and, like any solicitor in his offices, prepared to begin his questioning.

Gennett cut him short. "I hope that I have not brought you here under false pretences, Mr. . . ." he waited patiently, but no introduction was forthcoming. "I have no name, no address, no identifiers of any kind. I doubt whether it is possible to find this woman again. But I suppose that, given the possibility, it would be remiss not to pursue even a slight hope. Don't you agree?"

"We've had worse." Taking out a minute pad and pencil he dabbed the latter against his tongue and said, "terms are a half crown in advance, ten bob to two pound on delivery, depending on the difficulty involved."

"I am concerned for her, you see. She's a patient of mine, in a way, quite disturbed, you can imagine how neglectful it would be to ignore—"

"That's your business. Description? Everything you know about her."

"A woman, as I've said. Small. Perhaps twenty years of age, dark with a pale complexion. I have reason to believe that she lives in the vicinity. High forehead; small, well-shaped ears; nervous in manner; given to nonsensical pronouncements, fate and that kind of thing. And large dark eyes. Rather unsettling eyes."

"Has she now?" Gennett fancied that the man's eyebrow quirked at that. "A Jewess?"

Gennett frowned. "Possibly. Not in the stereotypical mold— you know that hooked noses and grasping hands have no basis in science. Don't you?"

"If you say so, Sir."

"Good. Now, her voice is distinctive. . . ." Gennett took a long draught of beer, and then another. It was porter, thick and sour, like black bread. The harsh tobacco smoke was less bothersome now. He could see men at the bar greeting acquaintances with stately nods. Behind him a woman cried out piercingly, and then laughed. At his club, a game of faro would be starting in the ground-floor card room. Booth would try to hold the game and Platt would swear; where the blazes is Ambrose? He rattled off observations by rote— her hair, the length of her hatpins—even as he pondered the real question. How to describe that look? He could not put into words what had frozen him to the spot. Shock, obviously, at her unambiguous recognition of him. Fear, at her fear of what she saw. And perhaps a thrill, the cheap excitement of being singled out from a crowd, or an unsophisticated pleasure in being known—in the illusion of being known, that was. How strong beer could produce giddiness he couldn't say. But the room lifted and swung, and the pig-eyed man was his boon companion, and it was the most exhilarating of dreams.

THE BOY offered to catch him a cab. For the one service, a few pennies would do, but for the other Gennett had no idea of the appropriate tip. They stood now under the single working streetlight in the borough and he found it harsh, like waking. His feet didn't want to stay under him. It was fatigue, obviously, because he couldn't have got that drunk on just beer. On impulse, he brought forth a small handful of assorted coins and held them out in his palm, rather than pinching a single one for deposit into a waiting hand.

"Payment in advance."

If surprised, the lad didn't show it, but carefully helped himself to, not the largest denomination in Gennett's hand, but the second and third. When he came close Gennett saw that "lad" was a misnomer. His companion was no boy, but a very ill-grown adult, in his twenties perhaps but stunted and wizened like a little old man. His mouth, when not stretched into a matey grin, was pinched like an old woman's.

"Tidying up's extra, you know."

"Tidying up?"

"If matters prove unsatisfactory. Unless you're set up to take care of her yourself. Not many gentlemen relish the necessities." The little man squinted at him. "You won't want her on your hands then."

"On my hands." Gennett's hand closed around the remaining coins. They were warm and faintly greasy to the touch. "I shan't, I think—please inform your associate that I will need more time to consider his proposal. He is not to proceed without my approval."

"You gave it. You paid."

"I—you may keep the payment. If I do not return, the funds you have just accepted will compensate you for your time to date. You will not suffer for this." A cab ground belatedly toward their patch of curb. Gennett waved it down himself.

Whatever answer the stunted man had was lost in the rattle of studded wheels on cobbles. He stood watching as Gennett sped back to light and civilization.

4

BELGRAVIA

He rode home sick. The new, nighttime face of St. Botolph's squatted in the forefront of his mind; he could see it more clearly than the swagged upholstery of the first-class carriage or the inner suburbs flickering past his window: Dalston, Barnsbury, Chalk Farm. It made a stage across which Smith, Coffley, and the stunted man shifted and turned in ever more disagreeable patterns. He had the feeling of having stepped out of a boisterous party for air. As he sobered up and memory of what exactly he had said and done receded, the certainty that he had misstepped came ever more sharply into focus. The idea of returning for the information he had bought sublimed into an unreal fancy, like a pact made in a dream.

The thought of his bachelor's flat in St. George's Terrace was suddenly repulsive, the thought of Soho worse. He wanted a reminder of his responsibilities; a little tug on the fetters to bring his feet back in contact with earth. (He was not, he reminded himself, a neglectful man—wasn't tonight proof of that? Didn't he try to do right?) Rather than changing for Kensington, he rode through to Victoria Station and strode out to summon a cab. The foremost remedy for morbidly fanciful thoughts was a look at proof to the contrary: His mother was perfectly well. He would go and bask in the light of her perfect wellness.

He asked the cab to drop him at the corner. "I'll walk the rest, thank you." As he paid in full, the cabbie merely shrugged at the oddities of gentlemen and drove off without a word.

He rang the bell, then again and a third time. What was this? His mother's servants were excellent. The specter of the morning's foolishness brushed against him and he was sharper with the maid than he wanted to be.

"Of course, Sir. Very sorry, Sir, I'll fetch her, so sorry about your waiting. The mistress doesn't take so many visitors this hour." At second glance it was not the parlor maid he had seen that morning but rather a scattered girl from the kitchen, perhaps even the scullery, hair escaping her cap and striped apron lashed to her frame in great haste. It was not far past the dinner hour; the kitchen should have been at full tilt clearing up after the meal and preparing for breakfast, not taking off its cap to lounge in the housekeeper's snug. He did not suffer himself to be led to his mother's private sitting room but strode ahead.

"Ambrose?"

His first thought was that she was ill. There was no other explanation for wispy hair and a waistless Liberty garment in place of a proper gown. She had been attired with the most conservative taste that morning. He kissed her cheek and felt the flesh give like sponge cake. Her powdery lavender scent was the same as ever, but beneath it was a kind of dormant mildew, mold beaten down by lye and hot irons.

"Mother, you seemed quite yourself this morning. You haven't suffered any sort of shock?" He slipped his hand to her wrist to check her pulse. It was calm. Sluggish, even.

"What? I'm sure that I am just as I was. I often have a bowl of beef tea up here in the evenings. Six courses in the dining room do drag on a bit when one is alone—Ernestine says that without a gentleman's appetite they're never wanted—and it seems a waste to dress for dinner then. But of course when Ernestine and Emily are in we dine just as we do when you are here, and that is at least two nights a week."

"They are in only two nights a week?" Gennett settled automatically in the blue brocade armchair by the window while she took its threadbare twin by the fire. There might as well have been no other furniture in the room; the carpet was worn in tracks to these two, his mother's seat and her guest's. Neither spared a glance at the dusty leather chair cocked at the other side of the fireplace.

"Mother, have you been out today?"

"Oh, yes, or yesterday I'm sure. It's so very cold this week, quite unseasonable. Ernestine will be quite blue when she comes in."

"Where is Ernestine?"

The bird answered for her. A muffled thump of the front door shutting two stories below sent it into a frenzy of shrieks.

His half sister was rattling rain from her umbrella and stamping her long feet on the mat. "Ambrose!" She stood and dripped while he made his way down to the entryway, then flew into a torrent of squeezing, flapping, wringing demoisturizing. "I am so sorry. You must be having dinner, or perhaps a conversation with Mama but at any rate I won't disturb you for a moment, not one. I'll just get rid of all these nuisancy things—it's so beastly wet you wouldn't believe it—and make my way upstairs and by then I'm sure I'll be no use to anyone. I'm quite sure that I'll fall right to sleep." She held her coat like a shield between them and didn't meet his eyes. He might have left it had her aunt Emily not joined her in the entryway.

Emily saw him and squeaked. Ernestine had fended off his assistance but Emily was less protective of her coat. Her dipped chin and meek maiden-aunt posture made it difficult to catch her eye; she wasn't actually evading him, however, not when he required her assistance. She wouldn't dare. "Where could you have been so late? It wasn't raining a drop when I arrived."

Emily managed a breathless sigh. "Well, it was the most *interesting*—"

"—lecture," Ernestine supplied; just as Emily said, "—party!"

Ernestine had recovered her composure. "We were not expecting you." She took Emily by the elbow and steered her firmly upstairs.

"What am I to think if you refuse to say where you've been?" Gennett was standing like a footman with Emily's coat. It dripped lavishly.

Ernestine did not turn on the staircase, though she slowed. "It was nothing you forbade, I assure you. Your restrictions are inscribed on my heart like the Ten Commandments. But we really are very tired. Aren't we, Emily?" She gave the older woman's knobby shoulder a squeeze. "I myself am going directly upstairs before I catch cold and I do hope that you will leave it at that, Ambrose."

He returned to find his mother speaking softly to herself and the room nearly dark. Her fire was collapsing in on itself. He took the poker and stabbed at the withering pyramid of coals.

"Mother, where were they? Please don't tell me that they were safe with friends. Those friends are useless."

Ruth's murmuring trailed off as she gazed at the armchair at the far side of the hearth. He felt like a bully and this made him angrier still.

"For God's sake, why don't you stop them, Mother?"

Her eyes remained on the chair opposite. "Emily tells me it's nothing but a jolly party with some very wholesome scientific talk in the middle."

"Scientific? Oh, it's not—they're not going to some health-giving-energy-field quack jamborees now!"

Ruth fretted with her rings. "It's Ernestine's new friends, the local girls. They meet on Aldernay Street. There are no men, and no . . . professionals consulted. She knows she's not to deal with"—Ruth flicked her fingers rather than say *money*—"without your permission. Only the girls, all ladies. Is it really such a harm?"

He knelt before her on the ancient rug, interposing himself between her and the chair. Cinders dug into his knee. He took her hands and gently angled her body toward the firelight so he could see her face. "It is such a harm. It is dangerous and not just to them." He held her eyes and when they attempted to stray over his shoulder he kept them back, willing his conviction to appear on his face and persuade. "These 'specialists' who go from house to house spouting Latin at gentlewomen have nothing but profit in mind. It's indoctrination and it will end as the last one did, and then it will be vegetarianism or Roman Catholicism or God knows—once they're softened up with that, it could be spiritualism. You must try and prevent them."

"But she would never get into another disagreeable situation. She would never permit herself. She is an awfully clever girl and she knows better now."

"It couldn't have less to do with cleverness. And knowing better"—he cleared his throat harshly—"never kept anyone from doing wrong. Or making mistakes, I should say."

She dropped her eyes, but only to the unturned pages of the novel on her lap, which had been sitting open so long on the same pages the spine was warped. A Charlotte Yonge, he saw, and nothing like new.

"I'm quite sure that you are right, my dear."

There was a moment of awkwardness as he released her hands. The eeriness would not release its grip on his spine; he heard the voice of the girl at the station more clearly than his mother's. *You're a fool to think that there's anything you can do.* He busied himself rearranging the dishes on his mother's meager tray. "I'll need to be on my way rather early, Mother, but I have no engagements in the afternoon. What would you say to an excursion?"

She did not reply, but just before he slipped out of the room she said, "You are always right about these things, aren't you? When you were small and you heard a sound in the dark, you would tear the bedclothes from the bed to prove that there were no monsters underneath. So brave and conscientious. Although I suppose a boy with less imagination wouldn't have attached much importance to a noise in the first place. So like your father."

His head jerked, involuntarily, to the facing chair. It was not, of course, the chair; Gennett had had that moved to the back room, reupholstered, and finally given away. Wherever it was, he assumed that when the present owners glanced at it they did not see a gentleman, neither elderly nor stout and with only a modest compliment of spectacles and side-whiskers, pause beside it and clutch at his chest discreetly, and then with more force. They would not hear him fall. Gennett had heard the cry—"Ruth, my dear. Oh. I am sorry," he had said, with remarkable clarity—and the crash. It was a narrow footman's chair from the hall and it had creaked sharply under the impact, skipping sideways on the stone, shrieking like fingernails on a blackboard. Gennett had fixed his eyes resolutely on volume two of Wernicke's *Manual of Brain Diseases,* determined not to witness an embarrassing scene or even acknowledge it. It was Ernestine, coming down the stairs, who saw that it was not an accidental fall. She tried, in her way, snatching at her stepfather's clothes to keep him from caroming off the chair onto the floor. She did no good and perhaps some little harm. But she did scream for the parlor maid and summoned help, when Gennett's circumspection would have left his father dying in a footman's chair. As it was, he died on the Italian marble floor.

"Mother," Gennett said, "I need to concentrate on my work. Isn't that important to you?"

"You could concentrate here, in your own home."

"I can't. But I can come here, and I can spend as much time as you like here. Haven't I been here more, since? And my calling cards. They still give this house; I haven't had a single batch made for the new flat. It's only that I'm extremely busy this month, and that won't last long."

"It won't?"

"It won't. Good night, Mother."

Gennett paused in the hall; already the murmuring had resumed. It rose and fell gently, conversationally. It was her way of setting out her thoughts, he reminded himself; simply how she relaxed in the comfort of her private room. It was entirely coincidental that she spoke in the direction of his father's chair.

5

SATURDAY, OCTOBER 3,
THE BREAKFAST ROOM

"The taste for knitting and crochet is never
likely to diminish so long as there are constant novelties to tempt workers in the way
of wools and clear directions for making
these into garments of all sorts."

—*Lady's Companion, For Wives and Daughters,*
October 3, 1896

The next morning was sharp in a way that London almost never
was. The bluntness of moisture and coal smoke had given way
in the night to dry air; the blacked iron spikes atop the garden
wall were paper cutouts against a perfect sky. The bare vines
shrouding the breakfast-room window, which would in spring
block out the light in an avalanche of clematis, struck his eyes with
the etched perfection of botanical drawings. Warmth and activity
would smudge the crispness as the day wore on but the moment
itself was individual. He would call it a morning meant for new
beginnings, if the idea were not next door to fate and omens and all
the other nonsense to which his half sister was so prone.

He had been determined to catch her before she had time to craft
an excuse; this meant catching her before she left the house. He had
taken up his post at the breakfast table when the morning shadows
were still long. The beauty of the day helped to still his temper as

the hours crept by but Ernestine did not. She had never been an early riser—to be fair, by nature neither was he—but her object was clearly to hide upstairs until he was called away by other obligations. A woman could usually wait out a man. But he had some authority and in this instance, because he deemed it necessary, the world would wait for him. It was almost like the world waiting for her.

He had half expected her to start and shriek at the sight of him waiting, but she took her customary chair with a resigned look. Ernestine had dressed for the meal in unrelieved lilac. Her morning gown was such a monstrosity of squashed-violet rosettes and ruffles, the effect on her complexion so dire, he wondered if she'd chosen it to punish him, like a child chopping off her curls to spite Nanny. Her pompadour and leg-o'-mutton sleeves framed her face like a horsehair-stiffened shell.

"The tea is stale. Let the girl bring a fresh pot," he said, though she hadn't reached for it.

"I don't think I care. Do pass it here."

Rather than leave the situation to deteriorate into a symbolic tussle over the toast rack, he set down his cup and brushed his lips with a linen napkin. In its corner a small gothic G was picked out in white thread, beautifully. "It is extraordinary to me how you underestimate your influence."

That caught her attention. He could feel her eyes on him, warmer than the weak sunlight from the garden window. He looked closely at the vines as if in study and kept his tone light. "Who do you think you are in this house, on this street? I don't wonder that Aunt Emily is upstairs right now waiting for your verdict on the fate of her new hobby. If she goes to another of these execrable meetings, it will only be with you."

He didn't need to look up to see Ernestine blinking, trying to make sense of this new development. He dropped his eyes to his cup and rattled it about his saucer as if fidgeting sullenly. He let a crease appear between his brows but knew that a sigh would be overplaying

it. "With you, you see. It's not my judgment she's waiting for, nor your friends on Aldernay or at the Ladies' Institute or anywhere else. Nothing is more corrosive to reason and to the moral sense than superstition. It eats away at the faculties like rot. It weans you off of the evidence of your eyes and leaves you blind and dependent on a charlatan's word. Perhaps the strong-minded can afford to dabble, but the less strong? The followers?"

He risked a glance across the table. She was gazing off to the side with an unfocused look, her mouth twitching in a series of aborted frowns. Dropping his cup, he reached across the table and pressed his hand to the tablecloth a hairsbreadth from hers. She would recoil at having her hand taken; she was not their mother.

"Ernestine, I cannot very well board up the windows and station guards in the back garden. All I can do is ask you to think about the broader consequences." He tossed down his napkin and busied himself with his cuffs and tie to give her time to compose herself. His tongue was sour from more than cold tea. Home had once been a haven from strategy and tactics. But an error on her part, however disastrous, was by definition the fault of her guardian, and who but he was to blame for that? "I think I would enjoy a show this week. I don't suppose you might join me?"

"What, in front of all of your friends?"

"If you think that of me, I don't wonder that you ignore everything I say."

Chatter rose up, as it typically did, like a cloud of smoke from her embarrassment. "Yes, unfair of me, I agree. Friday? We can go and strut about like those vulgar little nouveaux riches from Pimlico in our best clothes, and your doctor friends can compare us like Mr. Darwin's finches." She turned to the window as she spoke, capturing her profile in the worst possible light. They both took after their mother, but Ernestine had inherited the nose without the balancing chin. Gennett took great care to keep regret from showing in his face when he looked at her.

"Friday. I'll fetch you at eight."

HE WAS extravagantly late for the hospital but no patients were waiting. Two committees had been ignored, but a meeting with other doctors was not in his estimation a sacred trust, and his colleagues had shown patience before.

His rounds were brief, by his standards. A delusional poet was prescribed purgatives. Two phobics were responding well to desensitization treatment, although Gennett thought that the merchant seaman with a dread of rats should be looking into a change of employment. The sooner he left the hospital the better, if only for the sake of the staff tasked with carrying in baskets of rodents for each session. Mrs. Mecklenberg, suffering from shakes, shooting pains in her hands, and intermittent blindness (the authenticity of which they had tested by waving leftover desensitization mice before her eyes, and making rude gestures, none of which provoked a reaction) was the really interesting case. Disappointingly, she seemed quite herself this morning. He winced as he sent away the visiting scholar who had stopped by for a look. "Charcot's girls never let one down like that," the man commented. "When one came to see neurosis, neurosis one saw."

Gennett had a stack of the latest monographs from Paris and Vienna waiting at home, and Booth was pressing him about their piece for the *Asylum Journal,* already past due. The compacted business day left him little time to ponder. The question of his half sister still bubbled up among the files and notes and swabs. He bit into it, stoking his temper and cooling it down by turns. It was good for pushing aside more confusing questions.

He had allowed himself to be distracted by coincidence.

Coincidence was, of course, the wrong word; there was no system in the random concatenation of events, only in the spurious patterns the mind made of such juxtapositions. It was all too obvious: Subject neglects the women to whom he has responsibilities, then meets a strange woman and attaches undue importance to her predicament. A first-year student could see it. Platt could see it. (Perhaps

Platt had seen it. That was not a pleasant thought.) His own women were at risk and having been shown this (not *shown,* that implied design), having discovered this, however odd the means, that risk was his concern.

He hurried his pass through the chronic ward: mercury for the tertiary syphilitics, bromide for the boy with seizures (whom Gennett wasn't certain should be in a mental hospital in the first place), and little more than sympathy for the old man with shakes. The psychotics were deadly dull. With no change and no improvement, all he was required to do was sign off on more medication and wait.

He had been negligent, he saw that now. He wasn't sure which was worse: that his sister was pickling her brain with codswallop or that she disrupted the household routine so often to do it. It had to be taken in hand. He would call by Eaton Place more often, take a more active interest; he would curtail his Soho visits; and there would be no more midnight pursuits through the East End. He was resolved. He would have no truck with the stunted man from the Botolph's steps. If the girl from that station appeared now, waving her troubles like flags, he would tip his hat and walk by.

He accomplished little, even for the short workday before the Sabbath. Rather than stay on he locked his office at five minutes to two with his thoughts half on the irritating bureaucracy of modern hospitals and half on the irritating customs of Ernestine. They seemed to him to share an essential obstinacy. Moving either required a tedious ballet of ceremony that, should any finicky point be forgotten, forced the postulant back to zero to begin again. They were as bad as Coffley. How different it would be if just one of these mules would accept his help; what a spur it might be to the others . . . that girl, but he was no longer thinking of the girl, that was settled, he was not tempted to reconsider . . . but if she did not know him, she was mad, and she had to be mad, because she certainly did not know him. . . .

Gennett stopped. Lying women and *secrets from your mother.* Platt had suggested that the girl had tried a fiction on him, to imply knowledge in the hopes of profit. But if there was even a chance that the girl knew of his sister's misdeeds before he did (not that this was confirmed; there was still such a thing as a lucky guess), what else might she know? Gennett ducked into a colleague's unoccupied and, fortunately, unlocked office, borrowing a sheet from the store of cheap and anonymous stationery. (Gennett would be doing him a favor when he repaid the loan with his own superior stock.)

We must not meet, he wrote. *No contact until I send word.*

Gennett stuffed the note into an envelope and went to the mailroom for a stamp. He would post it from a box far away from gossiping mailroom boys.

"There's a letter for you, Sir," said one such boy, betraying excessive curiosity as he handed over Gennett's stamp. "Forwarded from another hospital. A St. Botolph's, I think."

It was a dirty foolscap envelope that he opened without thinking. DOCTOR A JENET was block printed across the front. There was nothing inside but a slim white card.

ELDARD AND RAMSAY
BIJOU AMUSEMENTS FOR THE REFINED
9 ABINGDON STREET, KENSINGTON

On the opposite side was scrawled in a crude hand:

DOES LILY RING A BELL?

6

ABINGDON STREET, KENSINGTON

He would walk by once. Plans rattled past quicker than the cabs on the High Street to his right. One pass, and after that . . . He could pose as an inspector of some kind. He could send a spy. He slowed and the crowd bullied him forward past the shop fronts. Less than a mile from his flat and he knew nothing of what to expect.

Like every other shop on the street, number nine bore a modern plate-glass window and flamboyant gold lettering sailing across the eaves: *Eldard and Ramsay.* Some jewelers still advertised with hand-lettered panels swinging beside the door, but not in this enclave of up-and-comers. From across the street he could picture their wares: warped abstract motifs, scarabs and diamond-pavé frogs, whatever the latest was in stones and enamel. The smartness stung his eyes like saltwater.

He had come here fearing—what? A frisson ran through his vitals, an eeriness like the worst moments at the station, but he banished that from his mind. There was nothing unnatural at work. It mightn't even be her. If she knew something—it was impossible that she knew anything of his affairs, but if she did know, he could master that situation just as he could master a wayward patient. If she needed help, she would have it; he would balk at nothing to root out the cause of her neurosis. He knew precisely how he would begin each conversation as well. It was guessing which conversation it would be, crafting some interchangeable opening, that kept him pacing.

On his fifth pass the shop door swung inward and there, rattling free the tangled vanes of her umbrella, was the girl. The pathetic hat was gone, replaced by a severe item in brown felt. Beneath it her face glowed like polished stone.

He stopped and her eyes found his as she looked up, without searching. His plans deserted him. Shifting his walking stick under his arm he tipped his hat to her in a frank greeting. She nodded in an equally unambiguous reply.

"You don't know me," he challenged.

"I do."

The street swam in his vision for a moment. Though she remained on the step their eyes were on a level. Her mouth was tight with emotion but she looked neither surprised nor expectant. He knew such looks from waiting rooms, where the character of the news made waiting attractive by comparison.

"From?"

"Yesterday morning."

"Not before?"

"Should I know you, Sir?"

Coats shuffled to either side of them, heads so engulfed in umbrellas and scarves they looked like hat stands gone for a stroll in the light rain. The gaslights were just beginning to assert themselves in the gloom.

"This is no fit place to stand." He thrust out his elbow as if daring her to ignore it. She did not.

THE THIRD floor café of Derry & Tom's was moderately busy. The big department stores of Kensington were always crowded in the late afternoon, when workingmen ate their main meal at home and the idle held out for a more elegant hour. There was a sprinkling of men—not the kind of men Gennett would know—but in the main it was women, delicately staving off appetites with cakes and tea. Their gloves lay folded beside saucers like pale moths.

He paused at the doorway to survey and then led her to a choice table by the window, ignoring the throat clearings of the waiter. She unpinned her hat and secreted the hatpins, straight and plain, fastidiously into the band.

"You look very white. A cup of coffee might be of help."

"I would prefer tea."

"Tea is the worst thing for you; it's a hopeless drink. It has no worth but a kind of nursery comfort, and that's no more than habit. A hot coffee will give you your strength back. With sugar, or perhaps a biscuit."

"I am quite all right."

And so she was. He would tip his hat to her in the street if he met her like this, a respectable woman like any other, and yet it was her, she said so. She tucked trim black boots beneath skirts of sober tweed. But the tension was there if one looked beneath the surface. He could feel it scratching at him like an insect crawling on the skin.

His coffee and her tea were brought by a dull-eyed girl. This provided a moment's distraction. The thick china seemed to have been chosen with the café girl's gracelessness in mind; the scrapes and stirrings that took the place of conversation were blunt, like spoons tapping on clay. His companion poured her tea without using the strainer and waited for the leaves to settle to the bottom of the cup.

He watched her holding the cup in both hands while it cooled. She managed to give the impression of ease, as if there were nothing out of the ordinary and this meeting were governed by convention like every other. Even excepting the proper day dress, the tidy felt hat, she was still not quite as he remembered her. Recollection had pulled at her features like a caricaturist. In the flesh she was not quite so small, her hair not quite so thick, her eyes not exotically black but merely a cool deep brown (though they were large eyes, and her skin fine). Except for the eyes and that impressive forehead her features were small and regular, lacking the Junoesque quality that fashion preferred, but pleasing enough. And yet *pretty* would not adhere. Perhaps it was her eyebrows, straight and severe as pen strokes. She looked out from under them warily—or rather, watchfully. She observed one so keenly it seemed that she knew something that one didn't, which was never calculated to please.

"You were frightened of me. At the station."

"I wouldn't say frightened."

He waited, but no elaboration came. "Is that your home, above the shop?"

"What? Oh, no. Those are an accountant's offices above."

All the questions he had composed piled up in an impenetrable snarl. He wanted to ask everything at once, from the dimensions of her childhood home to how she ate her breakfast egg. He had to force himself to approach the problem systematically. "Work on gems must be quite absorbing."

"I work on some pieces. As often as not it's sitting behind the cases with a book. Some days no one comes in for hours at a time."

So she was employed at the jeweler's. It was easy to envision. He could see the fragile thin fingers wrapped around her cup—child's hands—coaxing gold wire into place around a ruby. He could see them stringing pearls. He must have been staring because she set down her tea and smoothly tucked her hands into her lap.

"You have never worked in Soho, have you?" He meant only to determine whether he might have seen her before; the implication came to him too late. "As a jeweler's assistant, I mean." Worse and worse: she had pushed away her cup; the rasp of china had a deadly finality to it. "Or in Belgravia? Or—I am sorry. I have forgotten everything important." He delved through his waistcoat pockets, mixing up his cases and nearly giving her a cigarette instead of a card.

She studied it with open brows and a mouth looking very ready to turn up at the corners. Strange, how friendliness and mockery were twins in the early stages. "Doctor Ambrose P. Genet," she said, pronouncing it in the French way.

"Gennett."

"A doctor of what?"

"The usual kind."

"There are all kinds of doctors, aren't there? Of science, or of divinity, things like that."

"That last would typically go by Reverend or whatever his office was, but—" he thought again of her vaguely contrived vowels, and the odd tics in the way she took her tea. "Are you from England? Originally."

"Yes."

"Ah." His cheeks felt warm and were probably going red under his side-whiskers.

She gave herself a barely perceptible shake, as if admonishing herself for a fault. "But I see that it's not obvious. I find that sometimes the best judges of Englishness are foreigners."

"I was born in Scotland, myself. I haven't been back but for a bit of time at Edinburgh University. It's very good for medicine, you know, and much more advanced than the London societies."

"Is it? I have heard the same said about . . . Germany?"

"One does one's time there, obviously. And Paris, and Vienna these days." This was ridiculous; he sounded as though he were showboating, and to a girl who probably couldn't afford a day out to Vauxhall Gardens. (If this were a real session, he would have more control. It was the bustle of diners and thudding step of the waitress that broke his concentration.) It was exceedingly awkward, conversing across the boundaries of class. It would be easier if he could place her. She was quite as far from the awkward waitress as she was from the gentlewomen with their handmade gloves; further still from the apparition on the platform, who was gone as completely as if he'd imagined her from the first. "Travel is of inestimable value to one's education. It sharpens one's awareness of detail. Have you found it so in your own schooling?"

Her eyes dipped sharply to her lap. "My mama taught me."

He smiled—getting somewhere at last. She was self-conscious about her learning. It was obvious enough: Her speech was unfashionably plain, quite without the flourishes and classical allusions that characterized sophisticated conversation. Even ladies could be counted on for a reference to the novels and personalities of the day. And yet, the working-class subjects he knew led him to expect either a show of vulgarity, music-hall cockney bravado with a put-on contempt for books, or a sense of inferiority so strong that it demanded complete withdrawal. She was neither cowed by the gaps in her knowledge nor at pains to display them.

She seemed to be always looking down into her tea, but he sensed that she was studying him. The scrutiny was somewhere between flattering and invasive. "If I were Scottish, then perhaps London would be as instructive to me as to you."

How odd that she worked at a jewelers yet wore no ornament herself. She had piercings for ear-bobs but the scantiest lobes, narrow as if they had been pulled back and pinned. "I can scarcely boast of being Scottish. My father inherited factories in Glasgow but came down in late '72, when I was still in school."

"That's difficult for children, moving house. How old were you?"

"Six or seven years, I suppose."

"So you were born in '65?"

The question was too odd to parry, and he couldn't think of a reason to when he'd asked so much of her. "I was, yes."

"In late summer?"

"July twenty-ninth."

She had sat placidly, letting her tea grow cold, but now she made one firm sound of assent, a closed-mouthed hum.

"At the station, when you were struck," he ventured. "One might say odd things. Without quite meaning to. That is, the words have significance, but not in the way we expect."

She looked him in the face. He suppressed an impulse to flinch. "We are surrounded by significance we ill understand. We are not made to understand the influences at work on us."

"I framed that badly. It may have been, not so much the pressures in the moment, but . . . something in yourself, if you follow my meaning."

She looked at him again, almost startled. "Of course. Others would not have done the same in the same instance, but no one but we would have found ourselves in that instance in the first place. We all act according to our private laws."

She couldn't have surprised him more if she had whipped a stethoscope from beneath her jacket and revealed herself to be a lady doctor, or some other equally fantastical creature. "But, can't we manage our natures? Appreciate their prejudices and compensate accordingly?" he tested. "Read signs . . . symptoms, I mean; not in the way of symbols in so-called prophetic dreams—"

"Very few dreams concern the future, but they tell us a great deal about the dreamer. And why would we presume to understand ourselves? So much happens"—she frowned, searching for a word—"offstage."

His mouth hung open for a moment; then he smiled. He leaned across the table and she did not pull away. "Did you read that? I didn't know that the popular press had any interest. There is a Krafft-Ebing theory that I think you would find fascinating. A brief sketch—have you a bit of paper?" It would be easy to delay brutal questioning and give himself up to the flow of surreal conversation. Really, it might be best. She might reveal herself without thinking of it; they might speak for hours, perhaps repair to the Connaught for a meal if the hour grew late. He looked again at her cool, broad forehead and her eyes and felt that slipping sensation, the sense that his feet were on glass. He remembered it from the station and wondered what in himself was causing it. Such things always came from inside. A woman could no more plant such sensations in a man than look into his mind. "What were you doing at the station?"

His directness was a mistake. They pulled apart to lean back in their chairs; he realized how closely they had been knotted over the table.

"I had been on a visit," she said.

"That explains it. I was en route to a visit myself. But really, as we both have regular business in Kensington, the surprising thing is that it took so long for us to become acquainted. There was no coincidence in our meeting, none at all."

"*Coincidence* is a very silly word for—"

"At the station," he pressed. "When you said those things. You did not mean them, did you, in the sense that they were said? Because you don't know a thing about me. You were referring, perhaps"—he groped about for a guess; she had spoken of threats and danger and women, the obvious, surely—"to your mother's illness?"

Blood flushed two small rounds on her cheeks as if she'd been slapped. She looked almost freakish with her large eyes so wide, twin holes in her face. Then the shock was gone as if it had never been. But rather than defeated she looked strangely . . . replete. His own satisfaction, sharp as a knife cut at her reaction, dulled a bit at this unexpected denouement.

"Thank you for the tea." She rose and settled her hat en route. Each pin found its place in a separate feat of dexterity.

"You haven't finished. And we have so much more to say. Stay."

"I prefer to go."

The other diners were politely avoiding direct looks, which told him that they were following every word. He couldn't match her grace with outer garments and was struggling to catch up as they descended to the street.

"What did you mean at the station? When you looked at me— don't tell me it was nothing." He made an impulsive grab for her elbow but stopped himself in time, before he was standing in the street detaining a woman who gave every appearance of decency. His brush with gaucherie—lewdness, even—left his guts reverberating as they did when he woke from a dream of falling. "Miss!"

She was almost running. She slipped around a corner so sharply he nearly lost her himself. He caught up to her as she skirted a knot of strolling old men.

"Miss, I must insist. I am quite certain that you are in need of help."

"I—thank you, I know. But we can't force it."

"Force what? Don't leave with that! When may I see you?"

"I don't know. I'll have to find out."

"What do you mean you'll have to—wait," he interrupted himself, "you're not running all the way to the train station?"

"If you try to follow me I'll call a policeman."

"For God's sake." He waved his cane like a standard and in moments a cab pulled up to the curb. He hopped up on the running board to hand coins to the driver. "Take this lady wherever she wishes to go."

"I am capable of walking."

"Ah, but are you capable of avoiding me? I'm a fairly good tail, you know."

After a moment's indecision she gave a hint of a shrug and stepped into the carriage. "Finsbury Park," she said so quickly he was certain it was a false address. He passed another handful of change to the driver.

"Meet me here on Monday, five o'clock," he shouted to her through the cab window. "And tell me what you've found out."

He was certain that he'd seen her nod through the porthole window. But she wasn't there to meet him; nor the next day, nor the next.

$$\mathrm{\ ==\!\!\!=\ 7\ =\!\!\!==\ }$$

Friday, October 9,
the Kensington Hospital

AVENUE THEATER,
Licencee Mr. Chas. Hawtrey
Every Evening at 8:15 (Doors Open 7:45)
A MUSICAL COMEDY,
by Sidney Carlton, Harry Greenbank, and
Howard Talbot
MONTE CARLO
THE GENUINE SUCCESS OF
THE DAY

—Advertisement, *The Times*, October 9, 1896

The patient was led in and strapped down to the chair of restraint: buckles for the ankles, padded bit, a board wrapped in clouts to steady the head, strait-waistcoat. He resembled a robe-swaddled king carved into the vaults of a medieval cathedral, down to the furious bulging eyes. Gennett glanced at his notes: until recently a significant figure in the Bank of England. That was no sinecure. Gennett jotted—*Responsibility—rows of figures—imprisonment by figures—involvement in a major scandal?* As one of the seniors spoke:

"Imagine a sedate gentleman, staid in his habits and having no custom of eccentricity, tearing the clothes from his frame and racing down Pudding Lane as bare as Adam." The senior addressed his fellow doctors as if the students were not there. The students scribbled notes in tiny booklets.

"Previous episodes?" asked another senior.

"None reported by witnesses, but the likelihood is high," replied the first, "as there has been no improvement since he was committed. The patient does not cooperate with procedures and shows continued violence of thought in his resistance to treatment." Amidst the bit and head restraints the patient's face swelled and purpled. "If released from this chair, he would undoubtedly engage in similarly unsightly outbursts—"

"Hi heaver hid!" bawled the patient around the bit.

"*I never did!*" wrote Gennett. *Exhibitionism—perversion in Krafft-Ebing mold?* This very interesting new thinking from Vienna said that the "how" was in the "why": that each dose of madness was singular, that there could be no cure without an understanding of its cause. Concealed within thickets of irrelevancies were details that held the key. Gennett thought of the girl and the questions he would ask—would like to ask, if he could find her again.

"Intractable," said the senior, and gestured to the guard. "We'll try again next week. The students may be interested in the potential of therapeutic terror. The dripping of hot sealing wax on the palms, or immersion in a tub of eels, has in some cases—"

"A moment." Gennett waved aside the guard and pulled a wooden chair toward the patient, resting one foot on the seat and leaning forward on his knee. "You never did what?"

"Dr. Gennett," the senior warned.

Gennett ignored him. "The vocal restraint, please."

The guard undid the straps. The patient regarded Gennett with wary fascination, unbound lips vanishing under his mustache.

"It's an uncomfortable necessity, the chair. King George III was in one very like it. That was a very long time ago, of course, but it was instrumental in his recovery."

Temporary recovery, but the patient wouldn't note that as long as Gennett kept control. He willed his breath to slow, his eyes to keep from blinking as they held the patient's in a steady, confining gaze. The calming effect was evident. The patient's face subsided to a healthy pink. What was it that she had said, *not made to understand our private laws?* "The chair spares the mind the distraction of movement. And the mind has so much work to do." He let sympathy color his voice just a trifle. Not so much that authority was undermined; healing required above all else that the frayed, unruly psyche have a place of safety in the doctor's care. "It's difficult to know what to say, isn't it? Words sound different here."

The patient's eyes widened. He glanced from side to side and licked his lips. Beneath the mustache the corners of his mouth were cracked and reddened from the bit. "I know, I know what they say. But I didn't, I would never . . . I didn't mean to."

"Of course not. No, there are reasons why it happened. We will discover those reasons. We will prevent this happening again and then you can go back to your wife and children, that is what you want, isn't it? Unless there is trouble in your home. Were you under strain there? Were you under strain at the bank?"

"Dr. Gennett!" the senior barked.

"We will speak of all of this. My colleagues and I will listen to whatever you have to say. Will you speak to us?"

The patient choked himself trying to nod. The guard applied a swift thump to the chest. "Yes!" the patient wheezed, sputtering for breath.

"Dr. Gennett, you will join us?" The doctors and students clustered at the far end of the room. With no anteroom for retreat they stood in ridiculous silence while the patient was unbound and lead away.

"I'll see you tomorrow?" the patient asked.

"Or one of my assistants," said Gennett. The case appeared straightforward and a junior could manage it now that the breakthrough was achieved. The man was well outside Gennett's research interests. "Tomorrow if not sooner." He turned to watch the senior's face contort in a series of repressive sneers.

"Listen? It is most interesting; I do think I may have heard you say that you intended to listen to the mad."

"We've discussed this." Gennett directed his comments to the students, who had some small chance of taking in what he was saying. *So much takes place offstage.* His nerves were still taut; patients could smell fear like animals. Concealing his agitation from a brace of wide-eyed undergraduates was simple by comparison. "It is not untried. What they say is deranged, yes. But it is the only clue to what transpires in their minds."

"Dr. Platt says that nothing transpires in their minds," a student supplied. "Not until they're well. Whatever they say is just noise, with no more meaning than the grinding of a broken cartwheel."

"How does indulging their unwholesome fantasies do anything to cure them!" the senior interrupted. "Yes, we have discussed this, Dr. Gennett. We wait, we show patience, and when they begin to respond and behave rationally, then communication may begin."

"This patient spoke sense as soon as sense was spoken to him. He hasn't been cured with a wave of my hand, you know. This is the merest beginning."

"You reinforce their delusions and prolong their detachment from reality. Not even you"—the senior caught himself hissing and moderated his tone—"can be so arrogant as to think that you can talk them out of madness. The doctor must assume control."

"You throw control away when you decline to penetrate their thinking. I do not put the scalpel in the poor soul's hand. I merely examine before I perform the surgery myself."

The other doctors were exchanging looks. The nods told Gennett that the consensus was with him. Where persuasion failed, status bought, if dearly.

The thwarted senior found the manners for a tight smile. "I . . . bow to your certainty, Dr. Gennett. Let us give it a month. No one would be happier than I to see a cure effected."

Perhaps the patient was not so wealthy after all, Gennett thought, then chided himself for cynicism.

The students chattered their way out into the hall. The gossip would be through the staff rooms by evening. "Listening to the mad!" one whispered. Did the boy mean to be overheard? "Dr. Platt says that if he's not careful he'll end up mad himself."

8

AVENUE THEATER

The theater was vile. Leaving it until Friday afternoon (haunting Derry & Tom's at five o'clock each day was remarkably time consuming) Gennett had been forced to make do with a musical comedy that wheeled from tepid romance to tedious low humor. Ernestine sat beside him stiff-backed for an interminable three hours.

"I'd meant to get that new Russian play," he whispered to her during a particularly slow-moving duet.

"My friend Flora saw that with her father a few weeks ago. I believe that there's a very good production of *The Tempest* at the Garrick, with a ship and artificial wind, and an actual cannon."

Simply getting her out of the house had been an ordeal. His plans for tea at the Dorchester had been trampled under the feet of the maids still rushing from room to room with the elements of Ernestine's toilette, pins clenched in their teeth and false hairpieces coiled in their palms like sleeping rabbits. He had been forced to wait with his mother and Emily in the drawing room while the chairwoman and secretary of some committee droned interminably about a slight from the editor of some philanthropic newsletter. Courtesy demanded that his mother overlook his attempts to take her aside for a quiet word about Ernestine's recent conduct. He had risen with alacrity when his half sister appeared at last, stifling any comment on her oppressively brown ensemble. She invariably took his comments the wrong way. "There is just time," she said, fussing with a brooch, "to stop at the benefit before the curtain—it is so tiresome, the number of things one has to do—Ambrose, did I possibly forget to mention the benefit?" Then he, his mother, Emily, Ernestine, the chairwoman, and the secretary had made their untidy way to some gala in aid of some society in aid of some cause he didn't have the patience to note, except to reassure himself that it was not positive-thinking cures for tuberculosis.

"How unlucky!" their hostess had exclaimed as he appeared as rear guard to their unwieldy party. "You have just missed poor Mrs. Stone. I had told her that you might be here with your family but she had other engagements. She would have been most pleased to discuss progress with you, I'm sure. Or have you met recently regarding her husband's case?"

"The judge was still at that institution in Kent the last I heard," the secretary supplied.

"Poor Mrs. Stone," the chairwoman murmured. "I cannot imagine. And she was such a leader in society. It is so much worse than being a widow, I think; no one knows how to treat her."

"Well, she looked as enchanting as ever this evening; the tragedy doesn't show on her face." The hostess's voice dropped to a conspiratorial pitch. "With her coloring I can't say that half mourning doesn't suit her as well as the latest from Paris. Nothing is as good for red hair as black. Is something the matter, Dr. Gennett?"

The women surveyed him quizzically, thin eyebrows disappearing beneath their hat brims. Gennett wondered how his face had betrayed him. "Do forgive me," the hostess said, stricken. "But the judge's case is I'm sure progressing as well as can be expected. I hadn't imagined that it might be a sore point—"

"My son treats his patients with the utmost seriousness," said Ruth.

"Each one is as dear to him as, as family!" said Emily.

"God help them," murmured Ernestine. No one heard her but Gennett. Perhaps he had only felt those words, light as her dry breath on the back of his neck.

AT INTERMISSION Ernestine would not consent to being bought so much as a lemonade. Gennett decided that the health of his nerves depended on a whisky and shouldered his way to the bar alone. There, with his foot on the rail, was Platt, supporting on his arm a gaily attired woman whom he did not introduce.

"Gennett? Thought I saw you down in the stalls. Hardly seems your sort of thing, but the female must be appeased, must she not? Who was that whispering to you, by the way?"

"My sister. Half sister, actually."

"Oh, thank God!" Platt shot droplets of gin onto the unfortunate beside him in an animalistic fit of snorts and hooting. "What a catastrophe!" He dabbed his eyes on a silk handkerchief and passed it to his companion, who tucked it into her sleeve. "Couldn't be more glad."

"That's my sister you're talking about."

"Half. Scarcely closer than a cousin, hereditarily speaking. Isn't that right? Well, a drink to my error," Platt said, availing himself of a long swallow. He was speaking again before Gennett had done more than sip. "I thought that might be your mystery woman. I wouldn't have been the least surprised to catch you, you know. I think I have her number."

Gennett swallowed in haste, sputtering to clear the burning in his nose. Platt laughed delightedly. "Come now! I hope that you haven't been doling out the guineas to her while she sings her sad, sad song. Quite sane enough to tell the kind doctor what he wants to hear, I'd wager. Quite the kind of thinking her line of work requires."

"Line of work? She's—" He had been about to say that she was a jeweler's assistant, which would mean explaining how he knew. "I don't know her line of work."

"Don't you want to? Don't tell me that you've conquered curiosity at last. And you must at least wish to know whether you've been made a fool of."

"How would my concern for a poor girl's welfare make a fool of me?"

"Consider it more deeply. If she wasn't a servant—and I never in my life knew a maid to have Friday as her day off—what was she doing leaving Kensington at eight o'clock in the morning?" He fixed Gennett's watering eye with his own, suspiciously sober. "Returning from a regular client, do you think?"

Gennett observed the anger in his voice as if it were someone else's. "I believe that she is in danger."

"Not unlikely. If a doxy crosses her fancy man, she has grounds to fear for her life."

9

SATURDAY, OCTOBER 10,

KENSINGTON AND SHOREDITCH

"A FALSE CHURCH: Matt., vii, 15; x., 16
When a false church is marked as a true one,
The one thing it fears is public opinion."
—REV. T. G. HEADLEY

—*The Times,* from the "Personals" column,
October 10, 1896

He rehearsed before attempting Eldard and Ramsay again; improvisation was a failed experiment. When he had his plan he ambled over, briefly perused the display window, and stepped inside. A heavy brass bell rested on a table by the door, but a man emerged from a back room before Gennett had rung it. He was stooped, with arms too long for a torso folded up like a penknife, and when he saw Gennett his thin face lifted in a beatific smile.

"Ah," Gennett said, taking one of the shop cards—a match for the one sent to him anonymously at the hospital—and waving it as a prop, "perhaps you can help. I'm looking for a young lady employed here?"

"Are you a regular client of hers?"

"Am I what?"

The shopman's expression didn't change, but something behind it shifted; a different man spoke from the far side of that mask of servility. "Is she expecting you?"

Gennett was thrown off stride. He couldn't think of how to regain control of the situation. "I was told to ask for her—Miss Lily, or perhaps Mrs.? She's a young woman, very pale, dark. It's about a piece of jewelery."

"Miss Embly does most of her work on commission. Clients, you see."

Embly. "Surely there is something of hers in the shop. I would very much like to view it."

"Perhaps you have the wrong Lily Embly."

There was nothing to do but turn for the door. His suit was from Poole's and money whispered from every bespoke fold, but no amount of glaring budged the shopman's bland obstructiveness. "I doubt she would be pleased to find you so unhelpful to her friends."

"Perhaps I could be of greater assistance," the shopman smiled as he ushered Gennett out, brushing his elbow almost insolently, "if she had shown her face here since Saturday last."

Behind him, the shopman threw the lock.

THERE WERE directories and he tried them; even the registries of the three hospitals with which he was affiliated. He thought of formal detective agencies and even the police, but when he did his thinking on the steps of St. Botolph's he knew that he had chosen his course. There were five stamped-out cigarette stubs on the marble steps when the stunted man appeared, tipped off by some passerby or idler to whom Gennett was news with market value. It was mad to think that he passed unnoted. Men here descended to the crumbling sewers in search of lost coins, women sorted saleable bones from the refuse heaps, children and crones sorted worse. In his half of the world candles burned in empty rooms but here nothing was left to lie; if it had worth, it was passed from hand to hand until it fell into dust. Gennett saw the jaunty avarice in the man's face and knew that his need to find her was one of many things to rescue from a gutter, dust off, and pass on.

"You sent the note, didn't you? On the jeweler's card," Gennett said. "How did you find her so quickly?"

"Trade secrets, Sir, trade secrets. Nothing's too much trouble for a paying client. Speaking of . . . home address is extra, as I'm sure you'll understand."

LILY EMBLY opened the door herself.

Shoreditch at night was, to his mind, very like Hell. He felt eyes everywhere. The streets were filthy, the air worse—the cobbles beneath his feet seemed alive in the unwholesome damp, shifting eerily. The downpour, having passed through ten shrouds of pollution, left trails like grease. He stood at her doorway wretched with suspense and stinking rain. His hopes had risen on the long walk. No one with an ounce of influence in the world could live here. But then the door opened, and the room behind framed her in a noose of guilt.

Red. Plush red, with tassels; candles and lamps, the fumes of wine, distilled, borne out on waves of heat from a merry fire spitting in the background. She looked as alien to the slums as he. A dark shawl was gathered under her chin but her hair curled—had it always been curly without his noticing?—from a suggestively wild knot. Her eyes, wide with shock, looked wider still from charcoal rings.

The heat of the room made him dizzy. He felt like a baited dog, mad to bite. "You didn't have to lie to me."

"When did I lie?" she asked. And she even looked as though she believed that, her wide eyes all innocence. "I've done everything that's been asked of me. You think about what I've done and said and you'll see."

He sucked hot, smoky air through his nostrils. "I will still help you. I can take you away from this—" He could not bring himself to say *whoredom*. "It is not too late. We can leave tonight, right now."

"This isn't what I need to get away from."

His hand closed like a vise on her arm. Instead of reaching flesh his fingers sank deeper and deeper, drowning in fabric. A slight wrench and her shawl parted, exposing more red, satin glistening like water. Her throat was bare. A stark blue vein snaked across her breast just below the collarbone. It seemed strange to him how still it was, not pulsing. "Please, don't be a fool. Whatever hold these fiends exert on you, I will protect you."

"You can't protect anyone." Was she angry, or frightened? Could she be either when her voice was so resigned? "And that's not your purpose here."

A man's voice, tense, called out from an inner room. "Miss Lily, how long are you going to keep us waiting?"

She pulled away, leaving the shawl dangling from his fist. The garment beneath could scarcely be called a gown. It hung in stiff panels like a cleric's robes, crazed patterns of gold scratched across the scarlet like a nightmarish Klimt. She looked less like a body than an abstract pillar topped by a severed head. She turned her back on him and threw open two carved wood doors with a theatrical flourish.

Inside were five men and four women, of Gennett's class or higher still, crowded around an ebony table. A stone board in its center was etched with letters and numbers arranged in whorls. Eighteen hands rested lightly on its edge, and nine faces turned to Lily with hungry awe in their eyes. A man in a dark suit rose from the far side of the table and came to stand behind Lily. His face was in shadow and only his fingers, resting lightly on Lily's shoulders, caught the light. The elegant voice sank into Gennett like a branding iron.

"Ladies and Gentlemen, just one more guest to join us on our latest voyage with the spirits. Now, if you will join hands, our young medium will summon guides, and entreat them to aid us on our explorations of the Great Beyond!"

PART TWO

LILY

10

THURSDAY, OCTOBER 1

Strings

"In this age of morbid church activity, when armies are sent to bring people to civilisation, when men and women—mostly women—provide blankets to be sent to Equatorial Africa, where they are useless . . . Wanting is what? Modern spiritualism, with its facts and philosophy, to prove every death a resurrection."

—*Wanting Is What?*, "trance discourse" given by
G. H. Billings for the Collyhurst Society of
Spiritualists, October 1, 1896

The Page of Cups and the Magician. The Three of Cups and the Ten, crossed with Pentacles, crowned by the Chariot. Perhaps there was more to this than money, after all.

Lily stopped herself. Her hands had clenched themselves in fists and she found that she was pressing them together over her heart. That was too much like praying, which was too much like asking something of the cards, as if they granted wishes instead of revealing truth. She had never approached divining in such a childish way. She wouldn't now, no matter how much they needed a sign.

She breathed out until her lungs were empty, clasped her hands behind her back like a child in a museum, and leaned close to study the Page.

This was one of the new cards. Her mother's pack was, in theory, a chain that bound them to an endless line of mothers who had long since crossed. "Passed down through generations of diviners," Carola had whispered many times over the candles and green baize, "entrusted to me by my own dear mother on her deathbed. She guides me even now." If the customer was receptive, and most were, she would elaborate, folding in crises, expulsions, flights from Egypt. This was in the old days, when Lily had only to open the door for clients and carry in the tea. "No one wants a good old fortune told anymore," Carola said often. "Well, roll with the times, or they roll over you."

The core of the tarot pack, perhaps thirty cards of the seventy-eight, was transparent with age. The colors were mere suggestions on vellum as brittle and yellow as old fingernails. The balance of the cards were new, or rather, replaced as they went missing, a butterfly collection of the past hundred years. Somewhere along the line the figures of the deck had stopped evolving, hardening into tradition with a single step. Painted in 1680 or 1880, they were all in the same entrenched style: medieval and crude, with thick, sexless hands and feet, flat noses. All but the Page. This she had bought not six weeks ago. The loss hadn't been through damage or mishap; one morning, when she opened the lead box under her bed, the Page wasn't there.

The Page was a messenger, and in Cups one who would render service. He meant news but also application, reflection, meditation. He—all figures in the tarot were male, unless otherwise specified, but this one she truly wasn't sure about. This figure was so slim and androgynous, with a garter rounding one shapely calf. It reminded her of a stained-glass Joan of Arc she had once seen in a window. The Page knelt with its arms open, welcoming, or presenting the golden chalice it held aloft, or simply flourishing this beautiful thing to the world. It was in the latest style, Nouveau, they called it. "Raw and natural, the essence of the medieval," supposedly. She couldn't imagine anything more modern.

The Page could be saying that the turning point was near. There was reason to believe it was; Mercury was on the verge of a new house, for one thing. Barren places would become fruitful and empty hands would run over with gold. The messenger she needed to watch for would be a man and a stranger, she suspected, but perhaps in disguise. Unless—might he have crossed her path already? One had to be alert to recognize omens for what they were. And yet, she couldn't imagine a true sign—this stranger?—having slipped past unnoticed, not when she was looking so carefully.

Habit kept her face expressionless, even in private, which was just as well. She could have chewed her lip until it bled. The stars had affirmed that their luck was due to change. They needed it so much——

"Lily!" The thumping of Carola's canes echoed up the stairwell. "I hate these house calls. Where is the spare slate? We're running late already."

"I have it, Mama." Lily scanned the pattern once more and slipped the pack back into its box. The fortune was tainted anyway. Reading one's own was not good practice, and she'd read her own future too many times in the past days. One couldn't extort answers from the cards like that. If pushed, the vision came apart in one's hands like separating cream, peeling into layers in the heat. Now there was nothing to do but put aside the overpalmed cards and wait for the vision to cool and come together again. Beside her their collected equipment, including the slate, was strapped down in its fitted case. Her coat was already buttoned. "The coach will be here in five minutes. Get your cape and we'll go downstairs."

Cups never had been her suit.

THE VENUE was some miles away, in a still-smart corner of Islington. The client had offered her own driver for the journey. Lily preferred as little recorded traffic at their address as possible. They had compromised by meeting the coachman in the garden of the

Wesleyan mission on City Road. Lily was officially, for the evening, just an assistant; no one attending knew her as Carola's daughter. They had more freedom that way. Carola patted the quilted upholstery as they rattled past Old Street, running her thumb approvingly along the unfrayed seams.

"You've got to give them the chance to show that they value you, dear. You can't be too accommodating. But you've got to give them something for their trouble. I don't like house calls, either, but it's worth it. Think of them as beaux and you'll have the right balance." Carola smiled blandly. An onlooker would think that the subject of suitors was an entirely innocuous one.

"They paid in advance?"

"Don't worry about them paying. They're not grand enough to ignore their bills." Carola laughed. "Unlike ourselves. Think of the look on our poor butcher's face when he gets our account settled at last."

"If all goes well tonight. We promised a payment tomorrow morning."

"Why would it not go well? This is the right level: a few more coins in their pockets and we can make the same return on fewer sessions." She wheezed. "Fewer sessions. And you won't have to slave away in Kensington every day. It's seen us through but you can spend your time on better things. Then the money from tonight to our delightful lender, all with perfect timing. Haven't I always told you that things balance out for the best? One spring goes dry but another wells up behind you; then the first one recovers when you least expect it."

The house was decently sized, one of a terrace graced by its developer with modish Egyptian motifs. Two servants were waiting before the carriage had rolled to a stop. One assisted the driver in unloading their case from the roof while the other ushered them indoors, glancing anxiously up and down the length of the street. Lily followed her mother's example and kept a studiously straight face.

"You had no difficulties?" Their hostess made no pretense at detachment; she stood, hands clasped, in the center of her drawing room like a maid at attention.

"None, Mary." Carola sat on the most robust of the finicky davenports and settled her canes by her right hand. Lily watched critically. The art had long since begun. Carola sighed slowly, lowered her shoulders slowly; Lily could see the settling, fiber by fiber. When Carola looked up to her hostess at last, her unhurried smile had suspense to break. "No difficulties of any kind."

Mary Brewer closed her eyes and sighed.

THEY HAD plenty of time to arrange the room before the guests arrived at ten o'clock. Mingling was to Lily the most tiresome part of an evening with her mother's clients, but Carola was adamant that if they lurked in the wings until showtime, they came across as hired help. Besides, an unsupervised hostess left the mood too much to chance. Carola held court from the settee while Lily circulated with a glass of burdock cordial in her hand.

"Truly?" A plump blonde woman with a string of comically large false pearls hung on Carola's words with an open mouth. She was pop-eyed from some combination of surprise and corsetry.

"Indeed," Carola whispered. The lower she spoke, the more tightly her marks gathered in; those out of earshot were visibly angling toward the settee. Only the two men leaning on the mantelpiece were too intent on their conversation to heed the guest of honor. Lily shifted with her back to them, settling her face in blank attentiveness toward the settee while she listened behind. It was not difficult to follow. The younger man was a good half head taller than the elder and too polite to stoop closely.

"No, I was here once before, but Mary had some mincing Frog who fiddled about with the table all night and then told us the 'vibrations' weren't right. Is this one genuine?"

"I've heard of her."

"She's not the one just caught out in Brighton? A glove filled with paraffin on a bloody stick . . . had a stagehand hiding in a cupboard, they said."

"No, that was the Moldavian. If you can't be bothered to check the room, what do you expect? Even Mary must see that. Kept a decent eye on this one, I hope?"

"Says she never let this Carola out of her sight. We might be in for the real thing."

The men's voices became clearer, as if they had turned to scrutinize Carola over Lily's head. "Well, the proof of the pudding is in the eating—"

They didn't trouble to laugh quietly. "She is a bit of an ox, isn't she? Still, you'd be a fool to judge on appearance. I don't see the point in that Eva C, or the new crop who look like music hall stars. Do you think that supernatural forces care about an eighteen-inch waist?"

"I care. But a toothsome young assistant is the next best thing."

Lily slipped away.

BY THE time the guests filed in all was in readiness.

"Whatever you prefer," Carola said when one woman stood lingering in the doorway, glancing from chair to chair. Another man, overhearing, nodded significantly to his companion. Lily bit her lip to keep from grimacing; the most trivial liberties could be taken as proof against trickery. Somehow choosing one's own chair obviated the arbitrary table, the lighting. Active debunkers aside, most marks favored an indolent sort of questioning that only made them easier to fool. At times it made her angry. They were so furious if they found they'd been had, but so credulous it took active effort to keep from having them.

The hostess took her time in settling Carola in the grand armchair set aside. A respectful hush dropped over them all. Lily took her own place at the foot of the table like a straggling parishioner slipping into the last empty pew. There had been no danger of anyone taking a chair so narrow and hard and generally unappealing. This is what they did with their freedom of choice. They took what was presented them as obediently as if she'd written out place cards.

"Welcome," Carola began, as if the shiny new room and expensive bric-a-brac were hers. "I sense a strong positive force for this expedition; we may be successful. We must apply ourselves. I enjoin you all to clear your minds of distraction. Cast your eyes to the objects in the center of the table."

Cast your eyes was her cue. Lily detached from the rolling monologue and began to count. At one-hundred-twenty she pulled the first string, and it was dark.

The guests drew in their breath in unison. "I believe," Carola said slowly, "that spirits may be gathering. They dwell in shadowy places, you see, and are not fond of light." In the darkness her rich voice was more compelling, the wheeze of bad lungs departed. "We shall see if they are eager to cooperate with us this night. Spirits!"

Lily flexed her index finger, and a lamp in the corner of the room flickered cautiously. The wire ran from the lamp's damper switch, the leg of the faux marble pedestal serving as a pulley. Even with the added support her palm spasmed under the strain. One voice piped, "Oh, my!" and Carola did not silence the resulting titters. Casual visitors couldn't take the hushed aura of danger that most mediums preferred. More and more of the visitors were casual these days.

"May we take this as a sign?"

Lily tugged again and the light rose. One guest laughed delightedly, like a child. Another—Lily couldn't spare the attention to determine which—shifted noisily. Lily slipped her fingers from the padded rings affixed to the underside of the table and massaged her wrists. It was too soon for fatigue. It was a bad sign, and one that cast doubt over the success of the evening. She pictured the cards and the shape they had made that day and searched for warnings. Mary Brewer had been there to watch as they settled the room, but misdirection had dealt with better sentries than she. The equipment for a house call was best kept as simple as possible. Lily mentally reviewed the positions of her various wires and props and scrubbed her damp palms on her gown. It was the plum, not the black. Carola thought black better for setting the mood. Lily found black too redolent of other things.

Lily knew of the cards and the charts on a level deeper than memory but the beginnings of the spirit work she could recall: Mama looking at her with a plump finger tapping her lip, and cold air seeping up between the floorboards because the rug was at the pawnshop again. Then she had two new frocks at the strangest of times, when dinner was bread and drippings; one of white muslin and one black worsted. Mama had made her a black petticoat and filled their teacups with slippery concoctions: fat and ashes, wax and soot, flour and violet face cream. Lily had stood on a chair to see her experimental cheeks in the mirror, one black and one clamshell white.

Carola was gathering momentum. The single lamp was placed to carve dramatic shadows from her roundness; it caught her jowls and the bags beneath her eyes, dragging age out into almost ghoulish disfigurement. Even so, Lily saw the girl in her mother at these times. It made her want to put aside her worries about the direction of the evening, about Eva C and eighteen-inch waists and their future, because she could see children emerging from behind still faces all around the room.

The guests were glancing up at each other, furtively, as if spying. She could only really see them in a darkened room, and wondered if it was the same for them—in the parlor her eyes had skipped over commonalities, registering only small differences that denoted rank. Now she could see the lace trim at the throats of the women's blouses and the face powder settling in the creases around their eyes. She could smell their rosewater, the men's macassar oil, the stale tea on their breath, and the woody smell of a liquorice comfit from the tongue of one with something to hide. The man beside her, the tall young one from the mantel who fancied himself a good judge of figures, had a signet ring too small for his littlest finger. It bit, and left pillows of reddened flesh on either side.

"Concentrate," Carola said. "Build the energies that will draw the influences we need. The departed are drawn by strong feeling, and tasks they have left unfinished. With luck, we will encounter the shades of those we know, or admire. There are, however, malevolent spirits; these would wish to confuse us with nonsense, or even cause us harm. If we do not marshal our thoughts, the forces gathered here may attract the wrong element. Focus yourselves.

"My spirit guide is a girl called Mar. She lived in Egypt at the time of the Pharaoh Akhenaton. She was a slave." Lily stifled her amusement as the women, their faces warm with interest, gave identical simpering frowns of pity. No hard-hearted ones here, all the sympathies in place. Their reactions to the story were always telling. "She was body servant to the wife of the grand vizier, but had the misfortune to catch her mistress in the company of a common soldier. She—" Carola broke off and squinted; Lily had sniffed twice and tipped her chin toward her left shoulder. "But after a short and sad life of servitude, she now aids us out of choice. She will be our intermediary. Through her, the messages from beyond will be translated into sounds, or actions, that we can understand."

Lily scanned the rapt faces. Compared to what other mediums invented for their guides the Mar story was a model of restraint. She had only recently convinced her mother to retire a one-legged Tibetan circus performer who died saving the life of the Emperor of China. It was slightly surprising that Carola had even heeded the signal and cut short the melodrama. Perhaps she felt the same unease. If they doubted themselves the session was lost.

"In the center of the table," Carola said, "is a slate, a simple child's slate as one might see in school. Sir"—nodding to the young man from the mantel—"would you examine it?" He pursed his lips but did not excuse himself from the task. He ran his hands over the two squares of chalkboard with their wooden frames, the hinge that held them together like a book with a space between the pages, and the latch that held the book shut. It was not, in fact, a slate as one might see in school; those were typically flat. But this model was better for the show and, when Carola pronounced it typical, it did sound true.

"Nothing of note," the man said.

"Look carefully!" Carola said. "Come now; take the boards from their mountings, look under them. No hidden panels? No writing to be seen?" He blushed. That was what any sensible person would be looking for, but it always seemed to the marks that Carola had seen into their thoughts. "Very well. Oh, do put the chalk back there in its holder where you found it. Our guide will need chalk! Would you seal the slate, please? Our hostess has kindly provided wax from her own desk. If you have your seal with you?" For a moment Lily didn't think that the signet ring would come off. The man closed his eyes, winced, and half dislocated his finger. Worry worked on Lily's stomach like a shot of brandy. But then the ring was off, and a set of initials sat jauntily atop a rather messy pile of crimson wax over the latch. "You see yourselves: No hands will touch those surfaces until the seal is broken. No human hands." She set the slate down just so, lining up the bottom edge, where the wooden sides gapped very slightly, with the almost invisible slit in the tablecloth, velvet damask a quarter inch thick and so wildly patterned that a nest of eels could writhe beneath it unnoticed. Done, and safely. Lily let out another clasped breath.

The women were all right. So was the man beside her, but his diminutive elder, near Carola, was beginning to scan the walls. Further delay could be a risk. She tilted her head and looked at the door for a half minute.

"Mar!" Carola barked. The short man jumped. "She is near, I believe. Join hands! Focus!"

There was a brief scramble; contact with strangers was titillating or distasteful, or both. The signet ring was directly beneath Lily's thumb. She could feel a tiny trapped pulse drumming in the squeezed flesh. Beneath her other hand, the woman with the pearls and protuberant eyes was limp and clammy.

"Mar, can you hear us?"

Lily pressed her knees together and released them, fast. The snap of wood on wood was like a gunshot in the quiet room. She was prepared, but the sudden clutch on both her hands was still painful. She schooled her face into an expression of shock, and clutched back.

"Mar, is there someone waiting to speak to us? Would you give us a sign: one signal for yes, two for no?"

Lily squeezed again, more slowly this time. The spring slapped the strips of balsa wood together more gently and the resulting sound was more of a papery click.

"Mar, please bring these spirits closer." Carola contorted her face as if in pain. "Everyone, please concentrate! Mar, to whom does this spirit wish to speak? To Mrs. Brewer?" The noisemaker cracked twice. "No?" Mary Brewer, at Carola's left hand, who had been glancing about with excitement, flushed to the roots of her hair. She stared at the center of the table, blinking, like a girl snubbed by a dance partner at a ball. "Who, then? Someone to my left?"

Click. All eyes swung to the thin man in pince-nez beside Mary Brewer. His Adam's apple jerked up and down like a net float in the surf. *Click.* The woman to his side smiled eagerly and opened her mouth to speak. *Click.* The short man from the mantel blinked, waiting for the next sound, but it didn't come. Carola raised her eyebrows fractionally, but Lily stuck to her choice. Unlike his companion, he was now attending closely, in spite of his mockery. Lazy skeptics made some of the best marks.

"Do not tell me your name, Sir," Carola said when he opened his mouth. "I know nothing of you, not even your nation of origin." (This last was slightly disingenuous, as he was wearing tweed.) "The impressions must come directly from Mar, without interference." Even the young man in the signet ring nodded sagely at the wisdom of this. The older man blinked.

"Well, yes. I see. Quite."

"Mar, what do you perceive? The kingdom of the Nile that you knew, so sensitive to the power of the unseen . . ." Carola would continue in that vein, swaying and rolling her eyes as if inches from a fit, for as long as Lily needed. Ten minutes was usually ample. Lily shifted her hands with care to bring the index and second finger free.

Her companions would have noticed had Carola's antics been less absorbing. Lily slipped her fingers through a slit in the velvet cloth and found the wires. With one for each hand she had sufficient control over the shared loop at the end. She worked the far ends of the wires out the second slit in the tablecloth, through the gap at the bottom of the slate, and hooked the wire loop over the enclosed chalk. Too slow, they would become suspicious. Carola's acrobatics concealed Lily's ragged breathing. She let out a breath, stilled herself, and began to draw. It was closer to fifteen minutes when she eased the wires free, pulled her fingers from beneath the cloth, and signaled with a loud sniff.

"Mar, where have you brought us?"

Mary Brewer snatched at the slate. The untidy seal flapped crazily as she pawed it open, and bounced free when she dropped the slate with a shriek. Carola smiled as the guests leaned forward to gape. "In life, our guide knew no letters but pictographs, and her English remains a bit uncertain. You see that she sometimes prefers to draw her messages."

It was a crude sketch, but recognizable as a house on a hill with a winding path to the front door. With the slate technique one picture took hundreds of hours to master, so they had chosen one that could mean anything. Lily had added a semilegible *papa* along the top, the limit of her wire penmanship. Despite the gasps it elicited the sketch was just another effect. Effects on their own were no more remarked upon than clever street jugglers. It was what Carola did with their trust that mattered.

Carola tilted back her head until it rested on her hunched shoulders. "You will know the import of this message better than I. But my long partnership with Mar gives me some insight into the symbolism of the spirit world. I see . . . green. Green grass. Great fields of it. Or . . . lawns. Rolling lawns. There is a building in the distance, with stables. Could it be a rectory?"

The elder man, who did look rather like a rector, made a show of considering. "In gray stone, with a long, straight drive under trees?"

"No. I believe that she means to suggest brick, a great deal of brick. The path I see curves. A man walks along it."

"There you are, Edgar!" the man in the pince-nez crowed. Now that he was confirmed as a spectator he was puppyish in his eagerness. "Your place oozes brick; I've never seen a building like it for sheer brickishness. And you never used the main drive any more than your son does. The back road curves," he added in an aside to Mrs. Brewer.

"Why Edgar's son? Isn't this supposed to be about ghosts?" Lily's pop-eyed neighbor asked. No one bothered to answer.

"A man walks the back road, and meets . . . a woman there. They stop. They are conferring in the shadow of a wall. About *papa*, perhaps? Mar! Is this who is here to speak to us?"

The table, a substantial chunk of cherry wood, jumped several inches into the air. The guests gasped. Mrs. Brewer jerked her hand from Carola's and clutched the arms of her chair. "Do not break the circle! Mar will—" Lily, concentrating on managing the lever with her feet without letting the tension translate to her arms, failed to register the trembling in the pop-eyed woman's hand until it was too late.

"It's blasphemy! How dare you, how dare you!"

Lily caught just a glimpse of her face as the woman lurched away from the circle: red, with the whites showing all around her pupils, shining like her pearls. It was only a moment before chair, skirts, and a side table behind tangled fatally, and she went down like a capsized ship.

"She's hit her head. Let me by!" Edgar's command of the situation lasted a few moments before he tripped over the upturned table and fell to the carpet himself.

"Get a doctor!" cried the man with the signet ring. Mary Brewer was screaming. "Christ, pull yourself together. Who's your doctor? We need some light!"

She had a minute at most. Lily slid under the table like a ferret and yanked the lever out from under the base. Above, Edgar was shouting. "Where is that blasted lamp?" Lily grasped the wires and pulled. There was breaking glass, more screams, and darkness.

A DOCTOR examined them separately in an upstairs bedroom. The fainting victim had not, after all, struck her head, but the falling side table had bruised the foot of the man in the pince-nez, and Edgar had put his hand down directly in the center of the broken glass. In the parlor, he sat stiff as a preacher and supported his whisky with two bandaged hands.

"I just had no idea," Mrs. Brewer sobbed. "Sophia swore to me that she'd been to séances before and that everything had gone splendidly. I can't imagine what it was. No one was even bothering with her."

"We all knew there can be risks involved." The man in the pince-nez had his sore foot propped on an ottoman, and leaned down to touch it often as he sipped a second whisky. "I don't think one should run experiments in the field if one isn't prepared for that."

"If I want hysterical females I can shop on Upper Street on a Saturday." The man in the signet ring stood and turned to Edgar. "Another washout. Coming?"

"I think that's quite unfair," the man in the pince-nez rejoined. "We saw some very remarkable things before this unfortunate interruption, which can hardly be called our guide's fault. There's always a danger, isn't there?"

Carola was back on the davenport, but this time cut off from the chattering circle. She drank deeply from a glass of hot milk and brandy and breathed with worrisome labor. Lily sat with an arm around her shoulders, rigid from both panic and the coiled wires jammed awkwardly under her overskirt, wondering how she was going to get back into the room and fetch the lever mechanism from behind the sideboard.

"Yes," Carola replied wearily. "There is always some danger involved."

The ailing Sophia was dispatched in the carriage that had brought Lily and Carola. Supported down the stairs by two servants (the gentlemen calling their apologies from the settee), she was seen off with many kisses from Mrs. Brewer and the other women, and did not acknowledge Lily or Carola with the slightest reference. The remaining guests took their cue from her. No one turned to them until Mrs. Brewer had waved the last down the street. She stood in the door to the front hall pressing her hands to her waist. "I suppose you want to stay the night now?"

"The arrangement was to return home tonight," Lily said. "I see no reason to change it."

"You'll have to wait until the carriage gets back. The coachman will probably want tomorrow off." Lily held their hostess's sour gaze. "Well, come upstairs to wait, then. You'll want to gather your things before you go."

Carola lasted until the first landing of the staircase. Lily saw her hand tighten on the banister. "Mama!" There was time to maneuver her to the top step before she crashed down to the foyer. The coachman's boy was sent running down the street after the doctor, who was already halfway home.

11

Friday, October 2

Redness

"JERUSALEM, my happy home!
When shall I come to thee?
When shall my sorrows have an end,
Thy joys when shall I see?

"PARK—when will you be in London?
I have not forgotten.—I.P"

—*The Times,* from the "Personals column,"
October 2, 1896

The doctor arrived flushed and exhausted, and recommended patience. Mary Brewer, made hysterical by the idea of a swarthy medium dying in her guest bedroom, was overcome. Servants ran back and forth with hot compresses and cold towels, as often as not taking an item from the room of one invalid to deliver to the other. The doctor prescribed to Mary Brewer sedatives, rest, light food and barley water, and a long stay in the country, and to Carola immediate relocation.

"She doesn't want to go to a hospital," Lily said. "It won't help."

"Young lady, that is a decision for the family, but I can tell you with certainty that she hasn't any choice."

Carola's fingers were waxy and cold in her daughter's hand. Nurses in striped blouses and long white aprons, like cooks, mistook them for ladies, and a private room was found. The room was like a pencil sketch. The lines were there, but in iron, and ironed cotton, and white paint and bare wooden boards. Lily sat with her mother on the edge of the white bed watching the sun rise. When she left, she promised to return sooner than Mama would think possible, with clothes and books and food. "I'll bring the clock from the mantel, and a candle, in case you wake at night."

"Bring me some proper medicine instead. I want a doctor who knows his place, not a popinjay who thinks he understands my poor bones better than I."

"Mama"—Lily rose and shut the door—"if they hear you and decide that your head wants treatment along with the rest of you—"

"As if they knew what a right mind was!"

"If they think you lack one they can put you away. Please, Mama. They're ignorant, but being told so won't make them wise."

Carola snorted but accepted the warning with a nod. "The apothecary bill will be at least two bob a day over the standard. Budget for that."

Lily nodded obediently. It was likely to be a great deal more than two bob.

A nurse was waiting just outside. Lily had hoped to make it out and back in at least once. The nurse was gray haired, with what on a grander woman would have been called a majestic bosom rather than the ruins of a figure. Her hands were clean and broad and red. Lily could imagine this woman's children, done the best for that could be expected, because she was gentle with the practicalities of the hospital, and didn't even charge her for the name of the man she needed to see.

"No exceptions, I'm afraid." The roundish man wrote without pause as they spoke. He was brisk and, if his manner made it clear that there was one of him but many of her, he didn't wield this roughly. His spot on the back steps was directly below the offices of the official administrator, who would not be on duty for some hours hence. By the start of the business day Carola would be whomever her daughter could afford, and Lily could remain anonymous.

"Payable weekly in advance. I can give you two days grace for the first week, but only with security. There's always the public wards."

Lily could hear the coughing and wailing of the public wards. Her coat with the collar of gray rabbit fur was not enough; she added her new black hat. "Pheasant," she said when he pursed his lips and tickled the end of a feather.

"Looks a bit like green dye to me."

"Well, it's not."

He shrugged and added a note to his ledger. "Full payment today?"

"This morning. That coat there will do." She pointed to a tatty article from the pile behind him, payments in kind from Lily's fellow mendicants.

"Do for what?"

"My trip to get your money. I'll need a hat as well."

He grudgingly supplied the most risible old bonnet within reach. It was a disheartening thing, black straw with artificial cherries, and clashing fabric flowers. But really, she reasoned, the more out of character for her, the better.

"This goes on your bill."

"Use of them only, please. I'll be back today with your money."

"Next time, bring your husband. I don't much care for a woman doing business."

Suitably disguised, she set out for Abingdon Street to ask for help. Mr. Eldard was not in.

SHE STOOD on the pavement far longer than was sensible. Even in her tatty hat, she was conspicuous. A woman staring up at the bare velvet necks of the empty window display would be seen and noted. People would talk, and someone would guess Miss Embly—who "looks after Mr. Eldard's shop, or so he'll tell you," as she heard whispered. A stray shot was as good as a bull's-eye for losing your place.

It was impossible that this morning, out of all mornings, he was missing. He routinely stepped out at nine to speak to suppliers but at seven he should be with his stock. He slept guarding it like a butler with a plate. But there you were. There were reasons, certainly: Saturn was sesquiquadrate Mars, with Jupiter in opposition, an unusual combination that was certain to cause quarrels between well-meaning people, accidents . . . particularly household accidents, now that she thought of it. The doctor wasn't sure yet, or refused to say, what might have caused Carola's collapse, but staircases were a classic Saturnine pitfall. Carola was prone to impulse. She was born in a fickle hour, with Mercury in the fifth house.

How Lily could have permitted Carola, assisted Carola with a house call when the stars were so inauspicious . . . she might as well have pushed her mother down those stairs, and knocked her over the head with a brick to finish the job. That carelessness could be a sign of something worse: some previously overlooked conjunction of the planets driving them to calamity, some subtle flaw in her character making itself known at the worst possible time. The future was elusive but the sight had never failed her quite so badly before.

Lily was suddenly frantic to get back to her cards and charts. If she could retrace her steps, identify the moment she had strayed from the path, might there be time enough to find her way back?

She clamped down on that urge with vicious energy. She was not going back to the flat, not yet. She needed ready cash, today, and if Eldard was not available, she would return to the hospital and wait for another opportunity. Something would turn up. She had drawn the Page of Cups last night. She pulled her borrowed hat farther down around her ears and set off for the station. She might catch the 8:19.

His GLOVES were the first things she noticed, and every impression that followed was smoothed by that perfect gray kid with stitches so tiny they must have been sewed by the shoemaker's elves. How could she have noticed the stitches? Still, she had, the way in the throes of her migraines she could count the feathers in the pillow beneath her head. His coat and gleaming leather shoes, beetle hard, were not gaudy, but rather breathlessly up to date. Hard collar, felt hat, a ring on his smallest finger, gently distending the soft hide glove. His hair was brown, but his whiskers had a reddish tinge and those were what told. Redness sat on him like a luxurious perfume.

His lips moved. She had only been tapped and she knew how to roll with a blow, but she couldn't attach words to the shapes his mouth made. Flat like a line, round like an *O,* then flat over his teeth, again and again. Hissing. *Miss,* he was saying.

"Miss?"

The Page of Cups was a messenger and fair.

"Miss—please do not think you can ignore such an injury."

She shook her head—he knew too much of her; he knew her trouble.

"It would be most unwise."

Mama was going to die. She had brought it on them with her deceit, she had failed to play her part and be the cautious one. For a smooth-tongued man to appear, as stereotypical a Leo as she'd ever seen, poured too much fuel on Carola and the failed séance. She wasn't certain when the thoughts had wriggled free, but he stared at her in horror—she had been speaking aloud. And he had blanched and stared as if she had been speaking of him rather than herself.

"Miss, your acquaintance, I have not—you must allow me to help you," the vision had said. "I am a doctor. . . ."

A doctor . . . Jupiter covered and Venus crossed. His hand on her forehead. She knew that a messenger was not dodged or outrun, but she, Lily, had fled. That was the real signal, the fuse on it. The sign.

It was so blatantly symbolic that the moment she was swimming through the crowd she began to wonder, had he been there at all? She turned back on the stairs, though she knew it was a mistake. One couldn't be importunate. The doctor didn't appear again. Already his face was hard to recall—a strong nose, but then what? Only the redness. She was glad, suddenly, that she had no time to stop in Shoreditch. The redness would have followed her home.

12

Debts

"Every man or woman must find out spiritual truths for themselves. In Spiritualism, as in other scientific provinces of study, there is no royal road to its fountains."

—E. B. Jackson, *An Hour with Modern Mystics*, 1896

M ama, you'll make yourself ill."

"But two pounds and five shillings! I've never seen a hospital so grasping. Why didn't you get it from Mr. Goldfarb? He remembers the letters I found for him. He'd be more than fair."

"He's retired from lending. It's not much. We can get it back pawning the carpet, and perhaps a few of my dresses, and that can be done at any time. We needn't build up more than a week's interest."

"Why haven't you gotten it back already, then? Pawn the carpet and pay the grocer and the rent at least."

Lily tucked the blanket more closely around Carola's knees. They were in the hospital sunroom. Conservatory glass with black iron struts sprouted from the walls where the ceiling should be. Carola was one of dozens of patients laid out on low wicker chairs, immobilized with wrappings, lying back with their faces to the rain-painted glass. They looked like passengers from the deck of an ocean liner around whom a box had been dropped. Like sponges, their somber blankets soaked up the space between bodies and made it crowded. Lily didn't have enough air.

They spoke low from deeply ingrained habit. Lily continued her ministrations, unhurried. She met her mother's eyes fleetingly before joining the rest in looking up to the glass. A long look was excessively sincere, and gave away fibs. "We must give them some interest. There will be trouble later if we don't."

"Well, at least the debt's not been sold upward. A speculator will have his twenty percent or blood."

Lily concentrated on the proper fold of the blanket as if it were that on which their future depended.

"Lily," Carola said. She looked like a stranger. It made Lily cold with fear. People changed, they said, when they had glimpsed the end. "Lily, the debt hasn't been sold?"

Lily looked her mother in the eye. "No," she lied.

"I don't suppose you've had a messenger 'round from Mary Brewer, with the balance due?"

The tension was broken. They had a refreshing laugh over that.

MR. ELDARD paced dolefully, sparing the worn areas of the rug. "I shan't blame you, my dear. Lord knows you have your burdens. We are none of us perfect." He gave her a long, mournful look, studying her for signs of remorse. "I sat behind the counter yesterday with a full-day's work sitting idle in the safe. I had the shock of my life when I came back from my doctor's at eleven and found the shop closed. The one morning, the one morning in eight years I sacrifice to my digestion. Who knows how many customers won't trouble to try us again? I couldn't even get out for a crust to eat. By the time a telegram boy could be found to fetch something my dyspepsia was so violent I couldn't get a proper mouthful down. And then no one to help me close up."

"It was an emergency. I've never disappointed you before."

"Indeed not." He shook his head, gazing down at his tortured path along the carpet. "And what does it matter? Perhaps one lost customer. We'll be skipping our lunches for more than one reason, to be sure."

Lily felt another door slamming in the hallway of her options. She had not expected anything beyond a short-term loan from Mr. Eldard anyway. His chart showed no improvement in business. They were collaborators, supposedly, professionals in a mutually beneficial partnership. There was no Mr. Ramsay. When Mr. Eldard had begun selling small items through shops on Hatton Garden thirty years ago, he had grafted on the extra name for effect. Frederick Eldard, sole trader, suggested a lone artisan, a craftsman, and he loathed the image of the workbench. When one of his well-heeled ladies lifted a butterfly brooch from the velvet, he had wanted her to picture a small, elegantly appointed boutique in the best part of town, with sumptuous fabrics quilting the walls behind a rich but witty window display. He wanted them to see the Eldard and Ramsay of today. Perhaps they had, because his rings and pins and earbobs had sold. He placed pieces in more and more venues and, at last, amassed the capital to open the true Eldard and Ramsay boutique, where devotees could buy in the proper setting. This was when the bottom had dropped out of the business. Mr. Eldard now spent less and less time setting diamonds (the cases were distressingly full) and more and more lurking behind the curtains, sizing up the adornment needs of passersby and muttering darkly to Lily about the state of the Imperial economy. All morning he pulled aggrieved faces as he passed like a lanky ghost from workshop to office and back again, while she kept her spine correctly rigid and laid her cards beneath the counter, out of his sight. She didn't know which was more painful: the angle of her neck or the muddy neologisms she read.

She had only one appointment that afternoon. For the season business was remarkably slow; on this point, she and Mr. Eldard were in perfect agreement. A glance was enough to tell her that this was another day trip by a spiritual tourist who wouldn't be back. She was a short woman, tending toward the stout, in a fresh-looking brown piped ensemble very ill chosen for her figure. Her hands

were held together at her waist, pinched, as though she were clutch-
ing a slip of paper.

Even a one-off was income. Lily rang the bell for Mr. Eldard,
who sighed from the depths of martyrdom as he took her post,
despite the fact that he was apprised of her appointments in
advance. She led her client to the room in back and offered her tea.

"Mrs. Brown?" Lily asked, for her guest was looking to twiddle
the fringe right off the tablecloth.

"Ah, I must tell you. My name. I had to give you something in
the letter, but—absolutely no offense to you, my dear—you know.
I don't suppose that you might mind too, too much if I leave it at
that?"

"Cut the cards," Lily said. They were seated at her octagonal
table in her small, octagonal room. The faux Mrs. Brown's mouth
hardened as she glanced about. The shop always gave people the
wrong impression. Most mediums, Lily's mother included, worked
in a kind of blood-warm dimness, and clients assumed that diviners
preferred the same. Wide windows and robin's-egg blue walls
seemed incongruous at first, but most came around to Lily's room
quickly. The connection between light and honesty was too deep.
This one looked more skeptical. She had counted, Lily inferred, on
an air of concealment.

"Why?"

A troublesome one, indeed. "When you handle the pack it
becomes attuned to you. Your psychic vibrations will allow them to
tell your future."

"I don't need my future. I have a question, that's all."

"That's not the best use of this kind of divination. The cards will
reveal the forces surrounding you, and the true nature of the difficulties you face. With that deeper understanding, you will be better
able to face the choices ahead of you."

"Can't I just ask—I mean, ask to myself my question, and those
cards can tell me if the answer is yes or no? Mary said—" She
sucked in her breath like a child who has just scorched her mouth on
soup. Lily filed that away.

"I can help you to interpret the patterns," Lily's voice was gentle, but Mrs. Brown looked more horrified still. "I'll perform the reading. You'll see what it is that the cards can tell you, and then you can decide what to do."

"I don't want to pay for rubbish."

"You're already here. You can decide whether to pay when I'm finished."

She forced herself to lay the cards gently instead of slapping them down. Mrs. Brown was at least quiet. Lily watched the pattern form with a tightening chest.

She could get no feeling from this woman. The cards were over-handled; without that still center of certainty, truth never came. She used a variant on the traditional configuration. The first card, representing the self, should have struck a match as soon as she turned it over. Then the second, laid atop the self card to form a cross, revealed the most immediate influences working on the subject, and the scrim of circumstances that were likely to distort their perceptions as they looked out into the world. If the head of the card pointed to the left, it was inverted, as the self card was when it pointed down. Inversions indicated opposites, the reverse meaning of the card. For an inauspicious card, inversion was in theory a positive sign. In practice, they were slippery, unstable elements that Lily never welcomed. Meaning turned inside out wasn't obliged to return to its original shape.

She laid the next four in a diamond above, beside, and below: distant past, immediate past, present, and future. At this point the reading should have been taking shape. In a successful reading impressions radiated out from the core of the two central cards: from the self and the past, threads of speculation crisscrossed and began to add up to something more. Suppose the Emperor, insight and power, sat beside the World, divine balance and harmony. Strength exercised with wisdom was an excellent conjunction. But the Emperor and the Fool, blind naïveté, suggested dangerous, self-aggrandizing delusion. The strands ran together like water choosing its path down a hillside. Some petered out, but others reinforced each other, validating the same few directions, and revealing the true path.

Now, she felt nothing. The Moon, the Chariot, various Wands and Swords. The parts were just parts with no sum. Mrs. Brown eyed the pattern with wariness. It was time, as Carola said, to busk it.

She hated this. There were times when it happened, and she wondered whether it was at all akin to what husbands felt during the bedroom incidents, or rather nonincidents, that a few of her clients related to her in highly opaque terms. To her long-term visitors she could admit when the impressions weren't coming. If anything, it increased their trust in her. To this sniffing, grudging tourist, such an admission was impossible. She did guess when she had to. But this was not a matter of assisting her mother with parlor tricks. It was a lie, and an innocent woman would act on it. But there was her mother to consider, and she of all people knew that honor could be pawned as well as sold.

A middle-aged woman experimenting with new styles, petulant rather than patronizing with a younger woman. Lily watched her twist her wedding ring in an endless circuit. If she couldn't give truth, common sense applied to everyone, and always sounded as though it were made for you alone.

"You have a deeply loyal heart," Lily said, "and do not always note the signs of dishonesty in others. But there is someone around you whom you cannot trust." She made a vague pass over the core of the pattern, the seven of Wands crossed by the five of Pentacles, without indicating what pertained. "I see a strong influence, one with a silver tongue. This is not necessarily a force working on you. This could be influence exerted on others."

Mrs. Brown's fidgets were gone. She was not looking at the cards now. "Yes, yes there is."

"But the way is clouded. Can you be certain of what you see when mendacity is everywhere? We are warned against rashness," she said, with another empty gesture. "You must watch and listen, weigh the evidence unclouded by emotion, and wait for proof before you act. The next four cards deal with the path ahead of you." Lily reached for the deck again to lay four more cards in a vertical line to the right of the main pattern. "This will help you to judge the best—"

The string of fulsome invention stopped dead on her tongue.

The first card she turned up was the Page of Cups.

Hairs rose on the back of her neck and down, as if a finger dipped in ice water had been dragged along her spine. She looked again at the larger pattern, and saw. The seven of Swords: thwartedness, agency blinded and made impotent. The five of Pentacles: careless profligacy, here pressing down on the seven like a curse. Around it ranged the Moon, the Queen of Wands, reversed, the Chariot, and the Fool. And there on the threshold of time was the Page, waving flags in her face lest she miss the obvious.

Mrs. Brown never had cut the deck.

"The way, the best way forward." Lily knew precisely what this meant, and who was the nexus of her predicament, but not his exact place in the pattern. He might ruin her, or he might be the mechanism for her salvation. Time would tell. But she would be ready when she met the smiling red doctor again.

Mrs. Brown had seen the shock in Lily's face, and the awed recognition, and was nearly hysterical. "Tell me!" she cried. "Is he?"

"He is exactly what you suspected. Exactly."

Lily spoke to herself, but her client would hear it however she chose to. Universal predicaments always feel unique.

13

WEDNESDAY, OCTOBER 7

Shells

S/he stopped four times along the way. Stepping sideways into the arches of doors, or behind pillars crowned with ornamental urns, she slipped the directions from her sleeve and checked again. Yes, the street names were correct, all spelled out in iron signage smart with paint, at that. There was the graveyard she was to turn at, and there a house in curious pink stone, shiny as a boiled sweet, that would tell her she was nearly there. But this was like seeing her mother's shawl and pillboxes brought to the hospital room to make it homely. The points of reference were there, but everything in between was wrong.

Why had no one mentioned? If she could have given herself the directions, she would have been clear. *Lily, every house will be a palace, with a wall so high it has battlements, and space around enough*

for a traveling fair. Look for trees like in a painting of hunts in a forest.
When you hear footfalls on the street it will be so rare as to surprise you.
A quarter hour's walk from the station and she was wondering how
she could be in London. She knew terraces, flats. If asked to guess
who lived in these, these country-things, she might have said,
Lords? Parliament men? She had thought she had known the man
she was on her way to see. She stood behind her pillar and waited
for facts to settle around her new spot of ground. It was fine for
people to change, truly. She only asked that there be some path
between the person she had known and the present.

That morning Lily had run up the back stairs, out of sight of the
nurse-guards. The slick leather of her boots afforded little purchase, but little sound, either. "You'd best get up to your mum,
quick," her contact at the door had said, holding out his hand for a
penny. "There's news."

A doctor was in the room and Lily had to wait in the hall. Sweat
was cooling under her arms, curdling in the cotton chemise under
her corset, beginning to itch. The doctor who emerged was a tall old
man, colorless, who glanced at her with little interest before making
his shuffling way down the hall. It was not the crisis she had been
dreading. The swarm of fears in her head cleared even before she
saw her mother's face. That fullness, a look of being topped up with
life, meant a scheme.

"My darling."

"Dear Mama."

Cheeks were kissed and hair patted. Lily surreptitiously tested
her mother's hand for clamminess and searched her eyes for cloudi-
ness or glaze. Carola chuckled and looked her hard in the eye.
"Good gracious, do you see something wrong, Doctor? Something
frightening? Look again. Look closer."

Lily dropped her hand and moved to sit at the foot of the bed.
Carola clucked and patted the wool blanket, as her daughter was too
far away. "You can stop your worrying, darling girl. The answer is
here in front of us." She gestured to the lockbox beside the bed—
another costly purchase from the hospital's second economy, but

one they both had deemed necessary. Lily found a new letter inside, torn open untidily in Carola's way. Her pulse seemed to stumble for one beat. He had communicated so soon? But it was a false alarm. It was not the smiling red doctor at all.

Carola waved it for emphasis as she spoke rather than reading from it. "This is from Monsieur St. Aubin. You remember him? It's been years. I didn't write to him, of course. We have our friends, you and I. So I have not been seen for some short while, and news goes from ear to ear, and Monsieur St. Aubin would very much like to see you and discuss some small matter. He wants to know how we are, of course, but I do divine that he would also like to talk business."

"Mama, I'm glad. But I'm not worried about finding friends to loan us. I'm worried about paying it back."

"Loan! Monsieur St. Aubin isn't speaking of a loan, my dear, and neither am I. I did not write to him. But he is a friend—has shown himself to be a good friend—and if he would like you to call by I must say that I think it a fine idea."

The house was very much in line with the neighborhood—so much in line that in the event of collapse, it could have been rebuilt with covings and cornices and sash windows borrowed wholesale from the rest of the street. It was quite ostentatiously discreet. Lily had some idea of how much discretion cost.

M. St. Aubin had once been a frequent visitor to their flat near Brick Lane. Like them, he had suited, fitted in like a knife to its own place in the block. Brick Lane was a place for any newcomers, Hugenots to Hindoos, who found the homegrown cockney inhospitable. St. Aubin was of mixed nationality, and introduced himself as French with a dash of Italian, or vice versa, as it suited him. No one knew where he came from, except that it was clearly not from a divining family like theirs. He had come to spiritualism in some other way. But like Carola, he had had the good fortune to begin his career as a medium soon after the death of Prince Albert, and had risen on the lucrative waves of grief. Lily had never heard that he was in difficulty, but one never did. Friends just faded off into the wings at times, nursing cracked shoes or wet coughs, and were not asked after. Luck intervened. But she was reminded, lifting the gleaming brass knocker, that Luck was not always a euphemism.

He was fatter, with hair grown mysteriously thick and black, but otherwise as she remembered him. He kissed her hand and kept hold of it as he surveyed her. She would have liked to stare back and see what he made of that. Instead, she thought of her mother and the money they owed, and dipped her chin demurely.

"My very dear Miss Embly." He gave a deep and satisfied sigh. "You are like the first rays of morning sunshine, breaking through the clouds of my melancholy, and making me believe in beauty again."

She supposed that, having begun to pay her bathetic compliments when she was fifteen, he felt obligated to continue. Few men of her acquaintance found poetry in an unmarried woman of twenty-five. She smiled regardless. "You look very well yourself, Monsieur. Truly, you have not aged a day."

"And kind as well. You do me a great compliment by calling. I always use this house when in London. The duke is a most devoted friend." His eyelashes fluttered to his cheeks modestly, the way churchgoers' did when they mentioned the Lord.

He took her on a brief tour of the house. There were an implausible number of servants hurrying by with brooms or pots of beeswax. "The dining room sits perhaps thirty, but with the table removed there is more than ample space for dancing. Do you still dance? The chandeliers work rather well for social gatherings. All modernized, of course, but they look very much as they did with the original candles. The paintings are what can be spared from the main residence in Hertfordshire." He waved his long fingers at the bewigged aristocrats. She tried to picture him under a carpet of Restoration curls, with a spaniel under his arm instead of an amber-headed walking stick. If he wanted to pass the ancestors off as his own, he might.

"The library." Here he sat, and gestured to another chair when she hesitated. She felt strangely exposed without chintz and knickknacks about her. She had spent her life in the front rooms, parlors, drawing rooms, receiving rooms, of the quality or rather less. She was flattered in spite of herself.

"Miss Embly—Lily, if I may." He waited for a sign of approval before he spoke again. How rare that was. "Lily, I have no intention of insulting you with charity. You may be sure that my offer is made with my own interests in mind." He lit another cigarette. "Have you ever assisted any medium but your mother?"

"I—help my mother, in whatever way I can. That's all."

"I know about your fortune-telling business on the side. Your arrangement with that jeweler is a shrewd one, I must say. Do you pay him for the premises?"

"I look after the shop when I'm not working, and do a bit on the jewelery. Easy things. Quite a number of my clients have bought from the shop as well. I do advise them on the best stones for their charts, and adjust pieces now and then to improve the resonance. I certainly don't tell them to buy an emerald when peridot is what they need. But if you send people through a shop often enough, some of them are bound to buy."

"I suspect it's rather more than that."

"You flatter me."

"Please don't take offense. Would I criticize success?"

She looked, as she was meant to, up and around, forced to admire. She could see how the sight dazzled him even now.

"Lily, this fortune-telling, it will take you nowhere. Some have caught the ear of a Romanoff or Bonaparte and risen that way. I do not think that that life, the prophet life, is the place for you. Oracles are a thing of the past. They want now what they can see. Give them the pieces and let them think they puzzle it out for themselves; if Alexander sacrificed a goat now, he'd thrust the soothsayer aside and read the entrails himself. Try to, at any rate. You can seek truth as you always have, my dear, but not in the same way."

A servant came in to arrange the fire. Another took away their teacups and brought sherry, in cranberry cups of Bohemian glass.

"What do you propose?" Lily said at last.

"If you consider your future—"

"I am concerned with the present. The letter you sent to Mama went to the hospital. You know all about it."

"Your present is precisely the matter under discussion. Really, you're not much of a fortune-teller if you don't see that. I need a new practitioner with whom to collaborate. My audience is not one of paupers. You help me, you help your mother, you help yourself."

"I'm not a medium."

"Not yet, no."

She finished her little draught and looked through the glass to see her host refracted through the crystal. He looked like a giant behind his cup and a dwarf under the shelves that rose like the arms of a cathedral, under the tapestries, and it seemed very foolish to take offense when she could walk out now or in a moment or in an hour as she chose. It was all very far from her flat with its bare floor.

"I lied to Mama. We have old debts. It was a bad year even before Mama's health deserted her. I told her I was making more from the tarot readings than I was. All the indications were that our luck was about to change and I didn't want to worry her so I borrowed more. We're behind on the payments. When I tried to give an installment to our grocer he told me that the entire debt's been bought by a speculator, I don't know who. She needn't ever know as long as I get the money soon."

"I understand, my dear."

They sat together and watched the fire. The sherry had left Lily's tongue furry and thick. "The last session went wrong," she said. "Then I had trouble at the station. It would have been worse, but a man helped me."

"A client?"

"He doesn't know about any of that; he's a gentleman. But an odd sort of gentleman. Very stylish and modern and up to the minute, but then earnest like a Methodist preacher. He seems to watch and see things, but then he gets swept up in his conversation and is too busy talking to listen. I haven't told Mama."

She never kept anything from Mama. She would tell her of this as soon as she found the right way to describe the sensation, stepping from Mr. Eldard's shop to see him there, his mouth round like a startled little boy's, and then tipping his hat with such emphasis that even his pose cried out its symmetry with the Page of Cups. She had known he would appear eventually, so it was not surprise that rushed over her, nothing to make her hand tremble as she slid it through the crook of his arm. The pleasure she felt was the perfect satisfaction that came from feeling one's trust in fate rewarded.

Mama might misunderstand. She saw Lily and men intersecting at only one junction. When business was up, no man was good enough for her daughter, and when business was down, no man who would have them was good for anything. Mama sometimes saw things in the thinnest, cheapest way.

"Please don't tell Mama."

"My lips are utterly sealed."

"I'm not sure why I told you. It's nothing important. It's only knocking about my head, you see, but——"

"You are under terrible strain, my dear. Think no more of it."

"I won't. I won't."

14

SATURDAY, OCTOBER 10

Mirrors

It won't work," Lily said as the carriage squeaked to a halt near the stairs to her flat. "They'll never come. Why can't we hold it at yours? They'll hardly have to cross the road."

"Exactly my point."

It required practice to disembark without becoming acquainted with the contents of the gutter. St. Aubin negotiated the jump better than a gentleman should, but no one was watching. "We are introducing you as a new addition to the scene. Reintroducing you, I should say. Your appearances with your mother won't be a problem.

You've only been seen a handful of times. She never identified you as her daughter, did she?"

"No." Something worrying was tickling at the edge of her memory, but if she told St. Aubin, he would put it down to nerves. "What about my clients?"

"There shan't be much overlap, I daresay. This is rather a different level."

"If they do hear of it?"

They were nearing her door. He paused until she had put off the chain. "Now, there is a slight possibility that you would lose one or two. There are some shocking prejudices to be found. Where astrology is concerned—I don't mean the least slight to you, my dear, not the least—there are some, shall we say, lay practitioners whose ignorance damages the entire profession. They cannot grasp the natural progression to clairaudience and astral projection. With such a childlike view—yes, some might not be capable. But as for the rest, when they hear of the circles you move in now—well, my dear, you'll never want for custom again."

They didn't bother with refreshment, which at any rate she would have had to send for. St. Aubin walked from room to room, comparing the lighting and dimensions.

"This might do, if you moved the bed out. And they will come! Think of it: risk, adventure in Darkest England. If they want a comfortable day out they can go to Tunbridge Wells. You'll be a find."

"I can't quite claim to be a 'learned practitioner celebrated the world round.'"

"Learned? Oh, no, you'll be a natural, as we say. Much better for women—closer to Nature, Sibyls at the foot of Apollo, that sort of thing. That's where Blavatsky went wrong, trying to be bookish." He took up a declaiming pose, presenting her to a phantom assemblage: "'Mademoiselle Embly herself!' No, better to say, 'Miss E, a conduit between our world and the next since she was a babe in arms. She was first sought out by the spirits in infancy. Saved from drowning, agent of the miraculous rescue of trapped miners . . .' " He shrugged. "That sort of thing. Try to look dewy."

"Are they really going to buy that from an old maid?"

"Say that you're twenty. You look twenty."

"What did I look like when I actually was?"

"You looked fifteen. It's a shame we didn't start sooner. A child who speaks for angels—that would have brought in the Prince."

They wasted no time. He showed a refreshing lack of false reticence when it came to shifting the small necessities of feminine life: mirror, basin, powder box. Much of it had already been packed off. They took the bed between them like stevedores. "Why on earth do you have such a monstrous bed? I doubt that Nero had a bed like this."

"It's Mama's."

He nearly dropped his end. "On reflection, it's rather stuffy in here, isn't it?"

"This is the biggest room in the flat; the table won't fit anywhere else. I don't like it any more than you do. She wouldn't mind, you know. She's not petty that way."

"She'll need somewhere to sleep when she comes back."

"I spoke to the doctors. She won't be back soon."

They wrestled out the bed in silence. The room looked oddly smaller without it, quite the opposite of what she expected. But she would not brook any remorseful asides. This was the best course. She would give Carola her bed and sleep on the hard floor if it came to that, but it wouldn't come to that. She would have the bed back in place, and the carpet and all the rest, and this was the way to do it.

"It is quite a fine room," St. Aubin ventured. She thought he sounded oddly apologetic. "The proportions are a bit awkward, but the door makes up for that. It has, how should I say it? It has the right energy."

"You're concerned with that?"

He looked at her sternly, the mentor once more. "I find your cynicism very closed-minded, Lily."

She pulled a key from her petticoat pocket and unlocked the wardrobe. The contents sprang outward like silk from a milkweed pod, but silk in a riot of peacock blue, garnet, and bottle green. From behind the layer of gowns and robes peeped indecorous things: white linen shifts, garters, voluminous drawers enlivened by a strip of lavender ribbon. St. Aubin cleared his throat prodigiously. Lily ignored him, heaving aside layers of feminine sediment, heavy with the musk of wear, from which nicety would have forced away a stranger. Beneath was the compartment, and from this she took a handful of wires. They were badly mangled from their hurried extraction at Mary Brewer's.

"Mama taught you to use these. You're better than I am. I've seen you write in Greek and Latin from an armchair ten feet from the slate."

"Lily," he said. She could hear the oil spreading through his voice, and stared. Not hard, but looking into his eyes and seeing his silk handkerchiefs and costly watch fobs, and making clear that she was seeing them. He faltered, of course. The oil sounded ready to break and let his other voice out from beneath. She remembered another side to him, one that wasn't all flattery and paste, even if it was rarely in evidence these days. She pictured an orange, emerging fresh as its greasy rind fell away.

"I learned all of your mother's methods. I still use some of them, at times. But so do you." He held up a hand to forestall protest. "Indeed you do. Everything you've learned of stagecraft you learned from her, and do not pretend that you don't notice the lighting, or read your client's moods. Think of us like that. You have every gift to become a great medium, whether you like to hear that or not."

"It is absolutely different. It is in every way different."

He shrugged extravagantly. "There is space to be found between the stark truth and a lie."

They left the bed in the front room until somewhere could be found to put it. Lily sat on it after St. Aubin left, with her cards laid out beside her.

⇒ ⇒

AND THEY did come. That night she sat at the window with the lights off and she was watching as the first arrived. Just the carriage was enough to draw the residents out onto their stoops. So her neighbors knew something had changed, but that would do her no harm, not if she managed it properly. The guests—fellow seekers, St. Aubin had cautioned her to call them, never customers, never clients—would never know they were marked. They came up her stairs and laid their feet like landlords. She saw them tipping their heads together before they were even inside. Their drab coats sat crookedly on their shoulders, costumes. The riches beneath them took her breath away.

They seemed just as awed by her. She wore a patchwork of her clothes and Carola's, held together by loose stitches and basting tape. She could feel their eyes tracing over the arcane symbols embroidered across the smock in gold. They could stare all they liked; those signs meant nothing that she understood. Carola sometimes said they were traditional, and sometimes told Lily, laughing, that they told the story of a poor, impatient seamstress working in bad light. Now Lily wondered if they did have a story of their own, and if her ignorance and the guests' was all part of the tale.

They were sirs and marquises and hon.s. Their voices seemed incapable of quietness. "You are Miss E? You truly did raise the spirit of Wellington on two occasions? Perhaps my great-uncle had a look in; he went down with the old fraud. Can you say who you'll get? Aubin says not. Do you know that they are who they say they are? Aubin says yes, mostly."

St. Aubin worked the crowd in an orbit around her, touching elbows, admiring disguises. "You must have been a second-story man in a previous life, old chap. I'd never have known you in that cunning scarf." She was quiet, as advised. She knew patter when she heard it, but this was different: St. Aubin spoke earnestly of planes and projections, of the physics of psychic energy, and how emanations could be amplified by electrical means. She noticed how studiously everyone avoided the word *dead*.

They gathered in Carola's room with no names spoken. It was a tremendous table. They had had the tabletop in storage for years (it was profoundly unpawnable), using the massive pedestal to support a more practical surface of pine. The stone was what gave it the weight. Inlaid in the mahogany were panels of slate, bridged by ebony and a beech so light it was sometimes mistaken for ivory. The symbols cut into the stone were more familiar: the zodiac, prominently; numbers; letters in Greek. The arrangement was obscure even to her, but the guests needn't know that. The chattering stopped abruptly when they saw it, and then rose to a pitch more heated than before. She also caught the faint curl of St. Aubin's lip. After his Royal Society act, she wasn't surprised, but she wasn't going to apologize for a contradiction she found spurious. He might think himself above the old ways, but they still worked. If he looked around him he could see it. They liked technical terminology the morning after, when they recounted what they'd seen over the sideboard at breakfast, but that didn't speak to the blood.

St. Aubin arranged them, alternating men and women—was that standard practice, she wondered?—and settling their hands flat on the table with small fingers touching, rather than clasped. He had some justification for this innovation involving psychic circuits. She could see how much easier it would make it for the medium to slip her hands away. She took the head of the table—Carola's chair. St. Aubin had suggested it. She rattled in it like a stale nut shriveled in its shell. Her voice sounded odd to her; cracked. "Please, cast agitation from your minds. Cast violence from your minds." She let a long, deep pause open up between each line. "Let the spirits speak through me, if it pleases them. That is all I will say."

She cleared her own mind. This is what she would do if there were cards before her, or long tables on the positions of the planets. It was not looking closely, or looking or hearing at all. It was like pressing, to let her palms take the shape of what was beneath them. It was opening, and letting herself take an impression, like sand. If there were cards, they would be alive to her when she opened her eyes.

The crash made her scream.

"Good Lord!"

Was that one of the guests shouting or St. Aubin? Her heart felt pierced through. It beat like waking from a nightmare, so hard it was a wet pain. Was this what Mama had felt? The crash came again. Now she could tell it was only knocking, though violent. The door sounded ready to give way.

"What kind of spirits are these?" a woman shrieked.

"You said this was a private affair," barked one of the men. St. Aubin wagged his head but Lily spoke first.

"Unexpected, sir, but I'm sure it is nothing. Wait here." Lily shut the carved doors to Carola's bedroom behind her and latched them. The front door shuddered again. Outside the warmth of the inner room, the draft slapped her throat like icy water. She touched her neck: slick. She snatched a shawl from the hooks by the door. That was just a person outside, doing violence to her door. Short of sticking her in the belly with a knife, what could he do to her?

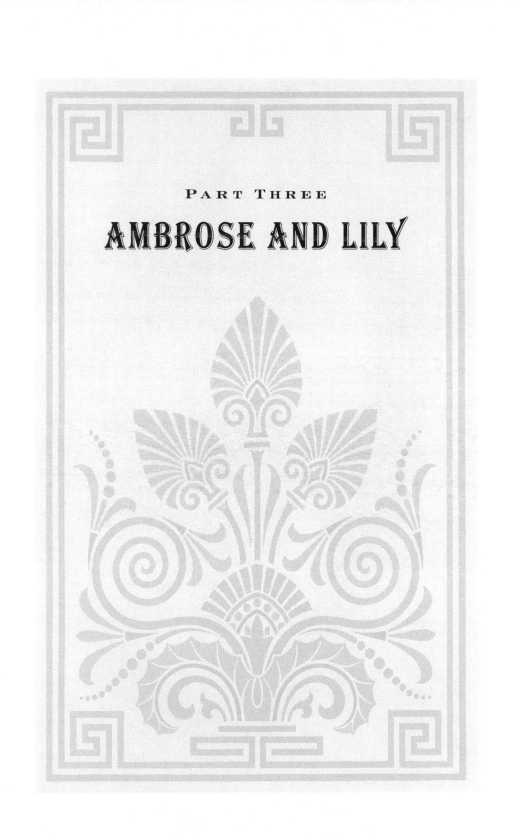

PART THREE

AMBROSE AND LILY

15

Expectations

Aconsummate professional," St. Aubin said afterward, first to her and then to a succession of fellow practitioners. "I was unconcerned," St. Aubin also said, of the intrusion, "as it was clear that her mastery of the situation was undamaged." This was false on all counts.

The doctor had said nothing, staring at the assembled party from the doorway with his mouth stretched wide with shock, before lurching back out to the hall. They heard him thudding down the stairwell like a drunk. Lily had the strangest urge to run after him. A viselike hand on her elbow—chill, not hot like the doctor's—brought her back from the echoing stairwell to the room. St. Aubin tilted her face to hide his from the guests. "What a bizarre manifestation, and we haven't even begun the communication! It will be a lively night!" His eyes, fixed on Lily's, were a snake's. She jerked her chin upward, which could mean anything to him, except that it was not a gesture of defeat. "Are you quite all right, Miss Embly? Your receptive faculties are not disordered?"

She returned to her place at the head of the table, met the gaze of one of the unsettled gentlemen, and smiled. She knew then that something was so changed that even the dull guests could sense it. The gentleman, who had all but patted her head in greeting, as if she were a child, now flushed, wet his lips, and looked away. She closed her eyes but could feel them shuffling, trading looks. Feel them?

Yes, she concluded, that was more than a convenient word. It was as though the air between them were suddenly thick, and when they pushed on it, even with their eyes, the echo came through to her on the other side. Her silence was alarming them further. She thought of coolness and receptive serenity, and laid her hands out palms down once again. They followed. They had no choice but to follow.

St. Aubin, she understood, was down at the foot of the table, crackling with tension and, though he would not call it that, fear. She was not insulted. His belief in her only stretched as far as the first sign of trouble, but this was no surprise, as his faith in himself went no further. His task was the effects. She put him from her mind, and the vibrations from that quarter faded into the general ripples of the background.

It was the doctor again. Before his entrance this had been another session, more tense than most. The stakes had served to deaden her. Nerves, like St. Aubin's rattling like a wasp in a bottle, closed her to anything but the ricochets in her own head. This new feeling was the opposite of that tense imprisonment, and the doctor was behind it. *Let me help you.* This was stripping the mercury from the back of the mirror. For the first time she could see through.

The guests were still now. She knew this from the quiet air, but through her small fingers there was another current. It was taut, but not yet humming, like a guitar string between notes. One of the men cleared his throat with a House-of-Commons flourish. "Now then," he said. His voice was wrong in the room, to the point of comedy, like human speech issuing from the muzzle of a dog. "Miss E, do you intend to summon the spirits as we were led to expect?"

"Speak to them, Sir. They are here."

This caused some consternation. Heads swiveled and feet ruffled up and down under the table. No matter, any of it, even St. Aubin's sweat, because the current was growing in strength. She could feel it ready to leap out and crack like a whip.

"Ah, ah hello? Spirits?" It was a measure of the tension that no one laughed. "This is Sir—well, never mind that. We were wondering, could you perhaps consider giving us a sign?"

"What was that!"

"What?"

"Do not break the circle," St. Aubin warned, when the first man looked ready to point with a finger. Sighing in frustration, the man pointed with his chin instead.

"There! I saw—there was something moving."

At this moment a clear bell rang out. All the guests began speaking at once.

"That was right over our heads! It definitely came from the ceiling!"

"Spirits! Oh   may I speak to them, too?"

"Spirits! Who is this? Are you here to speak to a specific person? Knock, I mean ring the bell once for yes, twice for no! Or you could ring out the alphabet. One for *a*, two for *b*, and so on. Or you could write! Do we have any paper?"

"Look at my hands!" One woman was staring down at the liver-spotted backs of her hands. "They're floating. I'm not lifting them, they're floating. I can't force them back down to the table."

"Don't force them!" whispered St. Aubin. His low voice snaked through the panicked excitement and pulled them all back to the table. He focused on the woman's hands and the guests' eyes followed his as if yoked. "But do not break the circle. Now, Milady," he whispered, rather than Madam, "can you feel a presence?"

"Yes," she said, tentatively. "But I can barely feel anything, I think."

"Is the presence cold? Like cool hands holding yours, so that the feeling in yours is deadened?"

"Yes! That's it exactly." She flexed her fingers experimentally. Her neighbors had hooked their small fingers about hers to keep hold, and now clung for dear life.

"Do not alarm them; they will not harm you. Does anyone else feel anything?"

"Ah!" The first speaker, the politician-man, jerked upward as if pulled with a marionette string. "On my knee!"

"Eek!"

"There it is again!"

While the politician and the woman next to him exclaimed over the hands touching their knees, the man who had seen the moving shape cried out again. Some watched the woman with the floating hands, some the general direction of the spectral vision, while the others twisted comically to peer under the table without losing contact with the circle of hands. Most glanced from time to time at Lily, seeking what she did not know. Proof, or proof of deception, perhaps, or ridicule. No one at all watched St. Aubin. He had to cry out twice to regain their attention.

"Do not break the circle!"

Whether someone had or not (Lily was sure that the circle was intact) they had to debate later, for a hideous, sickening crack came from the center of the table. Most jumped, and the circle broke for certain. Lily's circuit was gone. She blinked, bewildered, glancing from face to face. Her contact with them was gone as if it had never existed; the air was just air, thin and supporting of nothing. Without it the faces looked flat and distant, like people in a cinematograph. For long moments faces turned to faces all around the table. She half feared that they would be scandalized to find her as they were, struggling to get her feet beneath her. Instead they were solicitous. They patted her arms; one woman stroked her back like a mother. They asked if she required a restorative.

"You must be terribly drained. Where are the servants? Whose hovel is this, anyway?"

"Quiet, dear," someone said in a whisper. "It might belong to someone she knows."

"Brandy, perhaps? Tea? You're frightfully pale, Miss E. Monsieur St. Aubin, what exactly is the physiological impact on the medium?"

"I say, St. Aubin, cracking! I've been to my share of these, certainly, but—well!"

There were nods of assent. Excited comparisons kept them occupied until the cabs and carriages arrived. "Oh, absolutely. Much better than Maude's last. Not quite so many manifestations, but charged, absolutely charged with psychical energies. Like the air before an electrical storm, wouldn't you say?"

"Oh, but it was nothing at all like a storm! Spiritual powers are far softer, more subtle than that, traveling in waves, according to the latest research. The latest monograph from Mr. Myers puts forth——"

"It was tiny hands, like a child's."

"Oh, no, much larger than that. A man's, if not superhuman in proportion."

"A man's! They were so soft. There wasn't a line or a crease on them."

"Well, that just proves it, does it not? Adult hands that are also newborn hands; that's just quite exactly what one would expect from the other side, after we are reborn!"

"Name the place," a man was saying to St. Aubin, pumping his hand up and down. "There must be another session. Can she call up specific spirits? Would she be willing to try? I wanted to see for myself first, but my mother would be most interested in a private session, if Miss E could just pop up to Derbyshire. It's hardly even a hop by train."

"My sister . . ."

"My cousin . . ."

St. Aubin was like a waiter, gathering up the orders. "Absolutely. We'll see what we can do. The fifteenth? Perhaps we should discuss that over a drink; your club would be fine. Now, Miss E, she is exhausted." Somehow they all lapped out onto the street and took their noise with them. Air came in to fill the space they left. Not the powerful, living air of the séance, but neither was it the air she'd known before.

St. Aubin sat down in the wing chair Lily had occupied, Carola's chair. Even he looked shrunken in it. His face still set in an ingratiating grin. Perhaps that was the natural expression it fell into when not monitored; perhaps he slept with it. "What did you do to get that terrific noise? I thought the ceiling was falling in."

Lily traced her hands across the table. "It's one of the slates. They're not glued in very tightly." She prised the shattered panel out with her fingernails. Symbols of Gemini and Virgo now had their own flakes, and Cancer was split in half.

"So it burst where it lay? How on earth did you engineer that?"

"I didn't."

"Lily," he said slowly, still smiling, as if asking her how many lumps in her tea. "I admire your nerve, truly I do. I can't think of anything better for spectacle than a good atmosphere of unpredictability. But do you realize how close we came tonight to ruin? I don't mean a duff session, my dear. I refer to the undesirable position of having to make for Dover with one's life in a hand valise."

"I swear to you, I wasn't up to anything in the session. I hadn't prepared. I couldn't have mounted any stunts if I'd wanted to. When I sat back down at the table, I had the strangest sensation, rawness, like my skin had slipped off, like—"

"Let me tell you something about the rich: They never get so rich that they don't care about their money's worth. You gave them a blazing show, my girl, so they forgave you the intrusion, but that's the only reason. By rights, your beau should have been the end for us."

"My what?" She was trying to return to the atmosphere of the séance, but St. Aubin had hoisted her, wriggling, back into the cold air. "I beg your pardon?"

He didn't shy away but met her eye coldly, as he would a man's. "Don't faint with outrage, please. I will have my answer."

Standing, she still didn't quite have the advantage. "You presume far too much, Sir. I would indeed be in the wrong had a friend threatened our undertaking. But for the unwelcome intrusion of a virtual stranger I can accept no responsibility."

"Do be honest. What a lady does not actively repel, she invites. Uncivilized, perhaps, but even a gentleman with such admirable tailoring as that is uncivilized in matters such as these."

"Matters such as these?" Lily had not been raised in the proverbial gilded cage; she knew what happened to women who threw themselves away on untrustworthy men. Or any men. She didn't need her mother's warnings to be wary. But even if she had thought that risk worth taking, Venus did not feature in her chart, and that was that. "Please attend; I have not given that man my address, or so much as my district. I did not even give him my name." All strictly true. She would tell the rest when she knew the full pattern. St. Aubin was not in a frame of mind to listen rationally to the evidence.

St. Aubin's face softened, but with alarm, not warmth. "That is the man from the station?"

"It's not worth panicking over. I'll take care of it."

"You'll get protection is what you'll do. I know a few men. And we'll find you another place to stay."

She swept an arm over the lurid salon that had been her mother's bedroom. "After all that?"

"We've made a splendid start. I would never wish to go through the last hour again, but you have a foothold and that's all that matters. And do not tell me what you think happened to the table." He waved a hand delicately, as if wafting away a distressing smell. "Do not speak to me of it. You are a natural, as I told you. Do you believe me now? It's nothing to do with paraffin puppets or how clever one is with one's hands." He smiled devilishly. "It is all in the mind. Keep it there."

He took the shards of slate from the table and examined them briefly. He gave a moment's effort to piecing together the flaking edges, then tossed them into the fire with a shrug. "Of course, you'll never perform here again. That goes quite without saying. Onward and upward, my dear. Onward and upward."

16

"A few testimonies will show that when one gives himself or herself up to the control of the spirits, such ones take a most perilous position. The spirits insist on their victims becoming passive, ceasing to resist, and yielding their whole wills to them. . . . Mesmerists gain control of their subjects in the same way."

—Uriah Smith, "The Dangers of Mediumship,"
*Modern Spiritualism: A Subject of Prophecy
and a Sign of the Times,* 1896

Had he thought he was sick before? Gennett could laugh at that. He could go back and advise that queasy passenger unsettled by an East End pub that *sick* was falling into a gutter on Brick Lane, throwing stones at the rats to work off some measure of disgust. That, and stopping the cab, when he'd finally found one, so he could be physically sick on the curb. Pneumonia was little enough to expect. He only wished it had brought more fever and less clear-headed leisure for introspection.

"Couldn't really be pneumonia, though," Platt said. "Aggravated chest cold, more likely. Three days with a bad head isn't infection.

Did you have any proper nursing? Probably just sat up with an uncovered pate stewing in brandy, which only makes a head worse."

Gennett was reminded why he so rarely invited Platt to St. George's Terrace. It might be a block of bachelor flats, but even bachelors had standards.

"Don't even answer that. You'll end up in fisticuffs, and in your condition even he could lay you out in a half minute." Booth tapped the sugar spoon fastidiously over his cup before turning to Platt. "I'll have you know that Ambrose's condition was no laughing matter. I've been 'round myself several times and prescribed mustard plasters, plus an opiate for sleep. I only consented for him to remain at home because his man is quite good; a model of well-trained service, really. And his sister was there for the feminine element."

Platt raised his eyebrows in a parody of concern. "Was that of use?"

Gennett grimaced into his hot whisky. When he was a boy, hot, spiked lemonade had been his consolation prize for his infrequent days of illness. When his governess's back was turned he would sink his nose as far as he could reach into the glass, blocking off air to drown in the winey, sticky steam, and then dip his tongue to the surface and lap like a dog. Interesting that he thought of that now. "Swing by Eaton Place and thank Ernestine for my continued presence in your life," he said. "Truly, she was a great help. She has quite a talent for nursing."

This was true. The sight of her plumping pillows and scolding his man Wilson for bringing the soup too hot had been surprisingly soothing. She was an unlikely candidate for nursing but did it well. She still refused to have a serious conversation with him—"I could not countenance tiring you with vexatious talk, I could not"—but the bland talk and mild bickering were as peaceful as he could remember them being since before the trouble. The more irritable his complaints, the more forbearing she became, but this wasn't that she was pleased to see him low, of course. A woman did like to be useful. And they had been very close, once.

"I myself would say that females are almost invariably a nuisance in the sickroom, but Miss Gennett is unusually capable," Booth said. "I spoke to her several times. A most practical woman."

"Yes, well. Some women are more welcome than others." Platt fixed Gennett with a look of sympathy suitable for a music hall stage. "Any progress on that score?"

Gennett flew into a violent fit of coughing. Booth took his tumbler before it hit the floor and thumped his back expertly.

"I'll be off," Platt said. "My sympathies, Gennett."

When the door shut behind him Gennett allowed himself a vicious, if watery, glare. Booth reached for his bag but Gennett waved him off. "Just a glass of water, thank you."

Booth pulled the service bell. "Would you like to tell me what that was about?"

"Never mind. Platt is disgusting. How a man with a mind that filthy is meant to help the disturbed I have no idea." Gennett took a moment to marvel at the acid tearing in his stomach, a counterpoint to the pounding in his head. He had felt stronger having put *her* from his mind for a few moments. It interested him the way any pathological response would. "Maurice, what are your thoughts on superstition?"

Booth steepled his fingers. "Perhaps you could give me some further context?"

"What about it attracts, and what about it makes ladies particularly susceptible?"

"Incapacity for rational thought," Booth said, as if surprised to be asked.

"No, I mean something in the female psyche. Is it their known affinity for religious faith that makes them easier to dupe? Their elevated moral nature? Would those fellows in Vienna, Breuer and Freud, have any experimental data on the subject?"

"I see. If you put it that way, I suppose that all superstition is mental illness of a sort. Overreaction, making a meal of dumb coincidence." Booth nodded. "Yes, I think you have something there. Are you planning to write it up?"

GENNETT LAY back on his bed and breathed, noting the quick rapier nicks at his lungs, and listed his symptoms.

"Muscle contractions," he said as he wrote, as if dictating to his secretary at the hospital. The flat was empty, Wilson having departed for his half day off. Gennett had never before stayed in on one of these off nights. Wilson had laid in food enough for six ailing neurologists, plus instructions with the doorman to have a meal fetched directly from the restaurant across the street if necessary. Ernestine and his mother thought him attended by Wilson. Booth thought him attended by Ernestine. In solitude his voice sounded brighter, rounder, and he spoke to fill the corners.

"Persistent and intrusive thoughts on unpleasant recent experiences, disturbing sleep." He lay propped up in bed in his nightshirt, hair wild and soft without oil to tame it. It was five in the afternoon. "Restlessness. Insomnia. In—SOM—ni—a!" It rolled around the walls like wine swirled in a goblet. "Debilitating headache, perhaps a result of sleeplessness. Hampered digestion. A general and persistent feeling of unease."

He reviewed his list with the satisfaction of the sorely aggrieved. It could be added to. He was determined that no injury should be omitted. When he was finished this would be tighter than a legal brief. He smoothed down the leaf with his fingers and strove for a dispassionate analysis. He could hear his own voice as in a lecture hall. "What is the source of this man's discontent?"

"Our subject is displeased by what he has found, as anyone would be displeased. Rank superstition. Craven chicanery. But is his reaction appropriate? Was his conduct appropriate? He has been wronged." Gennett stopped there. True? Yes, but—he made another run up to it. "He has been wronged. To impose upon his irreproachable desire to be of assistance—it was worse than spurning his help, it was mocking him. And to exploit the trusting nature of females . . ." But what of her own trusting nature? To what degree was a woman responsible for what she believed, if this one believed anything of what she peddled? "She . . . pursued . . ." He frowned. "No, she *drew* the subject, *lured* the subject, with methods—" He stopped. "Half meanings. Vocal techniques." He thought again of her voice, worn and smooth in the café, hoarse and thin at the station, that accent lurking like soot in the corners of a clear pane—vibrant and liquid and sinuous at the Shoreditch flat—and the baroque spirals of her hair that lay smooth when he saw her in daylight. And her forehead, and pressing in at all corners her white fingers, her little white fingers like bones. . . .

There was scratching by the door.

Something papery whispered against carpet. His gut curdled with mortification; there was someone in the hall. He sat in bed propping the counterpane up on his hands like a tent until the sound was long gone. It took him some minutes to remember that anything under the door would be staying there unless he picked it up himself.

He somehow felt as exposed in his own reception room as he would wearing his nightshirt on the street. His dangling equipment shriveled in defiance of the central heating. A square envelope projected from beneath the front door. He snatched it and retreated to the bedroom. The stationery was unfamiliar, sumptuous, and addressed only to *A.* What further business could she expect to have with him, unless it was to apologize, to plead for his help in reforming her ways—

But it was not her, of course it was not.

It could only have been left with the assumption that he would find it when he came in after dinner, by someone who knew it was Wilson's day of rest. There was nothing in the envelope but a square of blank paper. It was so impregnated by a familiar, luridly feminine scent—tuberose, spice, and light musk—that his nose twitched. He tossed the reeking item into the basin and doused it in cold water. Henrietta had grown to love gestures like this. She thought them very continental.

Governor,

Yes, I am recovering quickly, and remain most grateful for your patience. I am afraid that I have reason to impose upon it once more. A new patient—I should say, a potential patient who did not prove suitable for treatment or study—has nonetheless thrown up an intriguing line of inquiry. I understand your concern that I apply my mind first to the present caseload, but this is entirely in my own time, and productive thought will be conducive to health. (Before you ask, I am not brooding, and I do not know how Dr. Platt came up with that absurd idea.)

I am considering various vulnerabilities of the female psyche and suspect that current research may throw some light on the matter. I have a new tack for the Asylum Journal paper I'm preparing with Booth. You dismiss the Austrian school too easily. I missed Freud at the Salpêtrière (he studied with Charcot some years before I did) but I wish now that I had met him. He is one of the few taking a properly firm line on superstition. The more I consider the matter the more I see that this is the fundamental thing. His approach, dedication to observable phenomena, has a boldness and integrity of which the pure theorists can only dream. (You do Freud a disservice when you lump him in with the metaphysical set—it is the ones with a mania for intellectual systems who put theory before experimental data.)

Might I ask if your influence can procure translations of the latest Freud and Breuer materials, in particular The Psychical Mechanism of Hysterical Phenomena? I am the first to admit that my German is not what it was in my student days, and the only conclusions I can draw via Wörterbuch are rather peculiar. I'm certain that there is a version in French. Maurice Booth is meant to be running that to ground for me but he's taking an unpardonable long time over it. My thanks I intend to give you in person.

Best regards,
Dr. A. Gennett

17

THE NATIONAL GALLERY

The night was unseasonably warm for autumn. The cab was stuffy as a result. There was no way to leave windows open in Soho; the noise and street smoke and dirty fog stole in like burglars, followed by the real thing if one became known for carelessness. Gennett had paused on the way for a drink, toying with his wine until the landlord asked if there was something wrong with it. He doubted that he cut the figure of a man en route to his assignation point.

Gennett's frequent jaunts to Soho were no great secret, at least not to the likes of Platt, who made other men's weaknesses their business. A gentleman made his arrangements. If there was discussion, it would only be of whether Gennett was one of those who kept a single woman, or kept a series of women, or (very French, this) kept a way station for the use of women of no fixed itinerary. It was, at least, an ideal explanation for his evenings away from society. No one suspected the truth. Such things were not done in their circle. On D'Arblay Street Gennett stepped out onto the curb in front of a particularly notorious bordello. The driver winked as he accepted his fare. Gennett tried to inject a measure of swagger into his step as he rounded the building before engaging a second cab to convey him to his actual destination.

Late as he was she made him wait. He made a circuit of the eighteenth-century galleries (she had a weakness for the rococo) and found them occupied only by tourists and idlers. The docents policed these discreetly to ensure that no one grubbied the Gainsboroughs. He wandered from frame to frame. A series of classical subjects, Dianas and Phoebes with bare breasts as rigid and pearly as upturned teacups, left nothing to the imagination save coyly draped loins. The name on the placard might be Boucher, but the subject matter would have been the same at the premises he had walked past on D'Arblay Street.

Gennett had not been inside such an establishment in six months. He was not unfamiliar with them; he had, after all, studied in Paris. A gentleman made his arrangements. His last had been a particularly satisfactory one, a woman of such brisk efficiency and impeccable hygiene that he would have considered her for a job in nursing, were it not for her moral unsuitability. The abrupt cessation of a service that a gentleman took as much for granted as the shining of his shoes had left him faintly . . . distracted. In many ways—the Austrian school was persuasive on this point—maintenance of this kind was successful if it inoculated one against base thoughts in the other twenty-three-and-one-half hours of the day. Gennett's maintenance always had.

All that was done with now, of course. The request had been clear. When asked (circumspectly, and with lowered eyes—how he regretted being the agent that brought such coarse subjects to her lips!) that his needs be met by one woman alone, he had concluded the transaction with his last mistress, via a sum she had not been sorry to accept, and not replaced her. He was highly relieved, of course. He was grateful to have been prompted to end a state of affairs that, however commonplace, was hypocritical.

He was sitting in contemplation of a turgid Mars-conquered-by-Venus when he heard her. He kept still. He did not need to look to identify the delicate rustle of French silk, or the measured step (graceful, almost languid) that was as familiar to him as the sound of his own breath. She settled on the bench with her back to him, ten inches of pregnant air between them. They spoke low.

"Did you say it would be half past rather than on the hour, my dearest?"

"I'm sorry," he said.

"Sorry for what? That we've not been together for a month? I think it might be a month, something like that."

"A few weeks. I've been ill, and you know that I have responsibilities."

"How unfair, all these duties that keep you from where you wish to be."

"I've told you, it's the hospitals. I'm wretched with work. Not that I can persuade the Boards to do much of anything; no money at Botolph's and no nerve at the Ken. I'm completely disillusioned with the Parisian school. Now, the Austrian—" He cut off that thought. Henrietta was the last person with whom he wanted to discuss his latest researches. The slightest details could tell much. Was Henrietta on her guard as she should be? "I need to spend more time at home. At my mother's home."

"I thought that you might have new distractions keeping you away."

A docent floated through, silent as a ghost or good servant. They studied their respective walls until he was gone. "My mother is not a new distraction. Please don't be jealous, darling. The new flat was too abrupt, that's all. I haven't moved back to her house, have I?" He didn't blame Henrietta; she was in an impossible position, an intolerable position. Why should a woman as vital as she be denied love? The unfairness made him fume if he dwelt on it. Fuming, he could feel like a champion, a liberator, as though he were striking a blow for freedom by setting a false trail to Soho, creeping to assignations in secret. He dwelt on the unfairness as often as possible. "There is no one else."

"And yet you are different towards me. You have so little time. And there are temptations, I am sure. Your work—"

"That is absurd. That is—my work is as devoid of temptation as waking hours can be. I see patients. They are not—many are women but they are not and can never be women to me. Forgive me, but the idea is disgusting." The idea would have been unthinkable a week ago, laughed off without a qualm. Never mind the articles he'd been reading about the inevitability of transference and a patient's falling in love with her doctor. They were only theories. *Patients* and *women* were as cleanly divorced as patients and doctors, or the mad and the sane. "Have you any news from Kent?"

She pulled her arm from his field of vision. "He can have no effect on us any longer."

He did not touch her—that would be importunate—but leaned toward her, hissing from one side of his mouth. "You cannot lose hope! His case is not a simple one but many a man has recovered from neuralgia. Your old life isn't gone forever."

"And what about all of this?"

"This will not be an obstacle to you. I will not let it. How can you be asked to pay—" He gulped air, but could not call back the word. If there was paying to be done, the woman always did it. "We need to stop meeting for a time, anyway."

"What?" He could feel her eyes on the side of his face like hot sun.

"I have a project, something to which I owe my full attention. I would never insult you by coming to you distracted. And there could be danger. I may be forced into contact with persons of very low morals. What if I were followed? Not today, I was careful today. What if they bribed a doorman, made off with my post?"

"We don't send letters. You ordered that long ago."

"I didn't order anything! This is for your sake."

"You're trying to be rid of me."

"Are you suggesting that I do not understand my own motives? I am cut to the quick, the very quick. What have I not done for you? You mean everything to me. Your safety means everything to me—far more than my own needs." As he shifted their bench creaked like bedsprings. "We share a pure love. I had seen that as the only consideration but I was wrong."

"We could meet at my home."

"My dear, nothing has changed since we last suffered through this conversation. A doctor and the patient's wife? They will think

it a"—he dashed a look at her turned face before blundering in—
"forgive me, they will think it a physical arrangement. The world
will question your husband's treatment. They will accuse us of col-
lusion, of committing him to the mental hospital solely to get him
out of the way. If anything were to happen to him you, or I, or the
both of us would be all but accused of murder."

He could hear her breathing rapidly. He worried that she might
faint; her lacing was at the chic end of what was medically possible.

"We could meet . . . we could meet in hotels. We could go
abroad. Spa towns. You must know them."

"Hen!" The blood rushed to his face as if his previous impure
thoughts had leapt out to parade lewdly about the gallery. "I would
never demand such a sacrifice from you. I will sleep with a lock of
your hair under my pillow. I will think of you every hour."

He could still see her as he had first seen her, rigid and cold in
the corridor of the Kensington hospital, an anguished Dido, her
tragedy as arresting as her deep red hair. A hand in sympathy had
led to words, and when she had asked him to take over her husband's case personally, it had been only fitting that they speak often.
Walks taken and meals eaten, later and later in the evening; it had
been only too simple for nature to take its course. There was nothing more understandable. Women did not merely desire love; they
required it for health and sanity. If his studies had told him anything, it was the futility of denial. But honesty was not the same
thing as being ruled by animal impulses. He and Henrietta met each
other's true needs and gave each other strength to resist the illusory
ones. It was pure with her.

He paused. Was that how it had begun? He instructed that thought
to wait in its dark corner until there was time for a properly rigorous
examination—he had bid it so before—but it worked itself loose.

Yes, walks and meals. Those he would have taken with any
patient's wife. He had conveyed himself virtuously back to his
mother's house at the end of each, well pleased at having discovered
a new way of exploring a case history, via the family. But gradually,
the talk came to range further. She had her own griefs. It was not

only for the case that he met with her so often, and over such elegant and modish dishes (she presented a dinner as handsomely as she did everything else. She dithered a bit over decisions, he had noticed, but once she had chosen, she was committed with no second thoughts). He saw a way to help her as well, and took it. It was something of a bargain, healing two lost souls at once.

He wanted to go back and horsewhip his former self for that arrogance, and blindness. It went on for months before his eyes were opened.

"Superb, Mrs. Stone, even by your high standards." He must have said something foolish like that, as he'd dabbed his lips with his napkin. Compliments had flown like confetti all evening. The dinner had been as succulent as it was stylish—oysters, and fruit from the West Indies—but the hostess strangely distant. She had worn a new head-dress with a spray of jet feathers over one ear. The further she withdrew into her beguiling silence, the more energetically he found himself pursuing her, throwing down trestles of words with which to cross the water. "How vile it is to tear myself from your side!"

"Are you leaving?" She had set down her cordial glass. She looked so exquisite, so like a painter's masterly improvement on reality, it was startling to see her move. "I had thought that perhaps"— the house was so quiet (where had the maids been dispatched to?) that he could hear her swallow—"you might not leave."

She had sent away the servants, he had realized. They were quite alone. Then, naturally, there was no other course. He saw in an instant the pattern as it appeared to her, every question and glance and word of concern and gentle touch to her elbow turned at an angle, assembling like stars when a constellation is pointed out. He knew then why she had never backed away. It was not that, like him, she scorned the crude conventional strictures on a man's friendship with a woman. It was that friendship was the furthest thing from her mind. She had no reason to think him any different. And when he considered the matter, he was not different after all. He did not know where their romance would lead them. If she were free? But she was not, and he knew the difference between a lady and a whore.

"You will . . . think of me?" she said.

"Constantly! This will not affect our love, which is all that matters."

"Just until this little project of yours is finished?"

"Yes!"

She rose. He followed her to the rank of cabs on the curb. Despite the public setting he saw her slender hand beacon him from her open window; he responded before too many people could see. It was full dark and as safe as it could be. They would have perhaps a quarter hour. He fought to look in her eyes (sleepy gray, as beautiful now as when she was a debutante) even as she slid her fingers down the lapel of his coat. It would play out as it always did: a bit of heavy breathing, a few buttons undone, but stopping short of what a lady, even one in love, could consider.

"Whoever she is, I'm sure that I can occupy you better."

Pure and consistent, he repeated to himself. It was enough.

18

"Many engage in charitable work fitfully, but
a great number give a portion of their time to
it regularly. . . . Such work, it is now generally admitted, requires a knowledge of good
methods . . . as well as consideration and
self-discipline."

—Letter from the Charity Organisation Society
to *The Times*, October 19, 1896

The matron saw him coming from the far end of the hall, and
they had long moments to examine each other's polite discom-
posure. "Doctor," she said, adding quite gratuitous import to
the word, he thought, "they've long since begun the staff meeting. I
did a round of the hospital myself to be sure you hadn't been kept
back on a case."

"What a shame. I'm sure it would be kindest to let them proceed
without me." He circled around to the left, but she stepped to cut
him off.

"If I am not mistook, they have proceeded without you for some
number of regular, scheduled weekly meetings. This is most
remarkable, as I have seen you in the hospital many times."

"I'm only here to see my own patients. Overtaxing one's strength
is a very foolish thing to do after a protracted illness, is it not?"

She somehow ignored the invitation to pontificate on medical matters, a temptation that, given her faith in her diagnostic abilities, was rarely resisted. Her lips quivered with suppressed anger. One would think it was her hospital. "I will see to it that the complete minutes of this meeting, and every other regular, scheduled meeting you have been unable to attend, are delivered to your office for your immediate review. I am sure that time spent reviewing these in detail will be most rewarding to you, and help prevent your falling behind on the business of the institution."

"Matron, you are kindness itself. If you will excuse me, I will endeavor to follow your good example by being punctual on my rounds."

His blandly pleasant rice-pudding smile didn't even last to the door. It was his own fault for giving her the opening. Three meetings—at the Kensington Hospital—was too much. He'd have to make it up with long evenings in the saloon bars of the senior consultant's choice. There was no penalty in a touch of hooky here any more than there had been at school, so long as one climbed up on the stocks later to do one's time, showing willing as the butt of jokes. The hours had to be made up somehow, and risqué anecdotes over port could be more onerous than a staff meeting. But he needed the time to coax his creaking German back into service. Freud was entirely sound on superstition, but the rest . . . he had at first thought the ideas intoxicating, and they were, in a more literal sense than he had realized. *Repressed memory. Inversion. Transformation of impulses.* The first giddy draughts had given way to nausea, but all he could think to do was keep drinking.

He was locking up his office when a nurse trainee came breathless around the corner. "Dr. Gennett! You're wanted—there's an attempted self-murderer brought in. They didn't ask for the attending, they asked for you."

Reception was a bawling mass of shouting relatives and weeping friends, a cub reporter nosing around the edges. "Clear this lot out before they upset the patients," Gennett said. Two ponderous male nurses were unpacking the arrival: a girl, swaddled in canvas and rawhide restraints, a foamy garland of gauze wrapped tight around her neck.

"Miss MacAndrew?"

His patient met his eyes for an instant, and the odyssey of despair Gennett glimpsed there kept him numb even as her father rounded on him with venom.

"THE GOVERNOR is sorting out the family," the senior consultant said, pulling up another chair to the desk. He and Gennett were alone in the office. The MacAndrew case file lay open before them. "He'll cool them off. The father's a lawyer. Be thankful that he can't sue you for a relapse. Now, what was the history?"

"Melancholic," Gennett said. He didn't need to consult his notes. "Discharged ten weeks ago. Went up to Cambridge to start her term, I believe."

"Symptoms entirely relieved, it seemed," said the senior, flipping carelessly through prescription slips and quarterly summaries. "Uncommon for depressive tendencies, no? Her house chaperone found her. Botched the hanging; just as well she wasn't an engineering student. Atypical, though. Females tend to use poison or throw themselves off bridges. The academic environment warps these lady scholars, masculinizes them. Gennett, how did you manage to bring her back on form in the first place?"

Gennett swallowed. "The talking cure."

The senior's hands stilled. "I wasn't aware that we had any experimental treatments under way."

"The family approved it. That is, they approved a trial—all we had projected was a trial—but her response was phenomenal. There was a poetess in her father's parish, you see, whom she looked up to as a bit of a heroine, but this idol died of spinal tuberculosis. Very slow and painful. No one marked it at the time, but Miss MacAndrew formed a deep dread of the future—a sort of desire to get it all over with and end the suspense—with the attendant fantasies of death, of course. But once this was out in the open it was possible to confront and rationalize her fears. All of this came out under hypnosis. I took the idea from some most excellent case studies coming over from the continent. M. Charcot—"

"Charcot. Hasn't he had some rather dramatic reversals recently? Since he passed away I have heard that a number of his cures have relapsed."

"That is rather overstating the case, sir. In every instance there were extenuating circumstances. The child-murderer, for one—"

"Yes, I'm sure. We shan't allow that to slip out to the family, shall we? More traditional therapies might suit this case at the moment. A good solid somaticist would serve here. Dr. Platt, I think. I'll refer this to him. He'll keep you updated on the patient's progress, Dr. Gennett. That will be all."

But rather than dismiss him, the senior let his hands roam about the desk, disarranging papers, toying with a pen. "Bad publicity blows over quickly enough. I hope that you shall not take this setback to heart. Patients travel ridiculous distances to be seen by the renowned Gennett, and when they're mainly women . . . well, you're sure to get a few hopeless ones. The female psyche is a capricious thing. In fact, you might do well to spend a bit of time on more conventional cases."

"Sir, with respect, feminine psychology is my chosen specialty. I know that I've fallen behind a bit in the past weeks. I have a campaign—a project, I should say—to pursue. But give me a few days to catch up on the journals and I'll make a fresh attack on the MacAndrew case. I hear that new research—"

"You made your reputation on conventional cases. It would be a great shame to fritter it away on imprudent experiments. Come back to this when you find yourself more settled." The senior lifted the pen as if it were made of glass. "So many matters of delicacy about it. Feminine psychology is not the best choice for a young, unmarried man."

To the Editor of the Morning Express
Dear Sir,

A recent letter to your publication (purporting to comment on a recent article referencing my own work in the field of alienism) made a number of outrageous statements regarding spiritualism and its relation to the study of the mind. In the interests of scientific accuracy I am forced to correct these statements with the force which their potential to harm requires.

Spiritualism, Lady Reader, is not the 'natural and enlightened extension of science' that you suggest. It is, as far as anything can be, the opposite of science. No experimentalist should forgive himself for soiling the scientific method with proximity to the irreproducible results seen in the parlors and music halls that you so inaccurately term 'spiritual laboratories.' You refer at length to the physicist Mr. Crookes's experiences. It is true that no less a figure than Mr. Darwin has expressed interest in the so-called Society for Psychical Research. It is also true that Mr. Crookes never gave up hope that his measuring devices would someday conclusively prove that spirit activity can defy the laws of thermodynamics that he himself helped to define. His 'ambiguous' results are not reason to explore further, but rather virtual proof that the great man was hoodwinked.

I refer you to Mr. Podmore (himself a former member of the Society, before the scale of the deception became obvious). Like so many enthusiasts, Crookes was recently bereaved—in this case, a brother cut off in the earliest flower of manhood—which is hardly the ideal foundation for dispassionate inquiry. So-called mediums seek out not necessarily the weakest minds, but minds at their moment of weakness. Hence, Mrs. Elizabeth Browning's and Mr. Conan Doyle's accounts of the impossible things they have seen, rendered as eloquently as only those celebrated authors could make them. Every personage respected for learning, station, or sense is held up like proof. However, the phenomena they describe are far from inexplicable.

Unconscious muscle movements can account for 'rappings'. Where there seems to be no surface to knock against, as in the frequent experiments where investigators immobilize the limbs of a suspected fraud, small bones might be made to percuss against one another, quite possibly without dishonest intent. (These concessions, offering error as an alternative to trickery, are most soothing to those who have succumbed to the courtesan's charm that charlatans deploy so cunningly, or cannot bear to admit that they had been swindled.) Stories are warped. Even the freshest personal account is likely to be tainted when tales of a particular encounter were compared and, again unconsciously, embroidered to fit each other, and to fit the inflated reputation of the player. Mr. Podmore is a Platonist at bottom, and appreciates that the eye can be more easily deceived than the mind.

In short, spiritualists are inherently parasitic, they cannot, as you suggest, empirically derive genuine insights into the mind or human condition. Any 'help' they provide is accidental. To remove them is not an equation of 'measuring their benefits', as they have none. They at best empty your purse and at worst inflict intolerable mental damage as they do so.

Respectfully yours,
Dr. Ambrose P. Gennett

19

> "Canon Watson said that the subject of cul-
> pable luxury was not without its difficulties.
> What was and was not extravagance was not
> always an easy thing to define. . . . Luxury
> was a relative term."
>
> —Proceedings of the Church Congress
> (C of E), October 1896

What do you mean, they've all gone? Where?"

The maid was impressively bland. The stereotypical kitchen shrew was nowhere in evidence; for her bloodlessness, she was almost like a female butler. "Church, Sir. If you were a visitor, Sir, I'd have said that that was none of your business, you understand."

"It's Wednesday."

"Yes, Sir."

He felt a fool standing on the stoop like a thwarted brush salesman. Before he reached the street, he turned and called after the maid. "Have they been attending weekday services for long?"

"Three weeks, Sir, if you count this as the third week."

His worst fears proved false. They were there at the first place he looked, which was nothing but the usual St. Mary Evangeline's, a very correct and tasteful local house of worship that had enjoyed the Gennetts' Sunday patronage since the nearer place had gone so dreadfully Low Church. They sat in the front pew. Gennett had to nudge for a space on the back wall. The contrast between the ladies in front and the workingmen and their wives in back was astonishing. There was a shortage of churches in the newer, poorer districts of London, he reminded his mother when she looked distressed coming home on Sunday mornings. This made her speculate as to the advantages of a residence in the country.

The vicar was droning on about modesty. Gennett stole circumspect glances at his fellows in the back, comparing them to the heads and necks of the quality. Amazing what a quick business it was to find one's own in a crowd. He had scarcely entered before his gaze landed, as if drawn by magnetism, on his sister's neck. Was it some kind of vestigial primitive instinct, good for picking one's own blood from a hunting pack? He studied her shoulders: rigid, seemingly ready for a leap over the pew and onto the podium. It could be her posture that he recognized. Certainly Ernestine's concentration was unmatched in her pew. Most shoulders there, capped by neat jackets, were suspiciously rounded. He doubted that fierce religious feeling ever coincided with a slack neck. Not that Ernestine was exceptionally religious, of course. Gentle right feelings were a credit to a woman—or a man, of course—but fervor traveled too often with fraught marriages and bad lungs. The incident earlier that year had been an anomaly. Beside Ernestine, Emily showed more conventional deportment, garnished by the occasional nod when the vicar made a particularly affecting point. She probably sighed as well.

On Ernestine's other side was Ruth. This would have caused him another shock had he not been warned by the maid. His mother's faith was not the insecure kind that made a spectacle of frequent observance. But there she was, glancing about as if slightly surprised to find herself there. But she wouldn't be there had she not been honestly persuaded to alter her habits. No, she was not so malleable as that.

He wondered about meeting her after the service, where to stand and what to say to cause her the least upset. It needn't be awkward if he handled it properly, avoiding any suggestion of following, or spying. He thought of mingling with the crowd, of paying his respects to any friends of theirs among the ladies, what to say to the vicar. He left before Communion.

21 Oct 96

Booth,

Of course I gave him the Breuer article; he asked for it. Said it was about superstition. Whence the sudden concern over what he reads? Everyone wants to know his business lately. If he plans to make a prize ass of himself he will, and it won't be the first time in my opinion. If he were concerned with his reputation he wouldn't be advertising his newfound allegiance to the Austrian school. Did you know that this Freud is an atheist? Says you can't be a scientist and believe in God, which I can't say will catch on in England. And that's before one gets to the racy stuff. I assume you've heard the rumours about the newer theories. If Gennett gets himself tangled up in funny dreams with phallic symbols he'll have himself to thank. (Who'd have thought it from fish-blooded Teutons?) If Gennett's nailing his colors to the mast—so to speak—I hope he's ready to defend the whole ship.

Platt

"It's very late to call," Ruth said, while Emily poured the tea. Gennett declined Emily's offers of milk, milk and sugar, lemon and sugar, or plain lemon, in turn.

"I lost track of time. Where have you been out and about this fine day?" He winced at the last. While his mother's rooms made him expansive, the upholstered propriety of the drawing room inspired fatuity and speeches suited to a hero from Scott.

"Nowhere at all, I think. Perhaps to the shops. Did you find something suitable?" she asked Ernestine, who shrugged delicately.

"Her new gloves," Ruth said gravely, "were entirely ruined by a railway carriage handle so filthy with grease, I don't know how to tell you. Can you believe that the trains should be neglected so shockingly? One is safe nowhere."

Was that a muted rebuke? Gennett could see no hints or signals in his mother's placid consumption of tea. It was difficult to discern anything over the wailing siren of Ernestine's hostility. "There are indeed dangers. Many seek to take advantage of a woman should they think her without support, without people who care for her and her welfare."

"Oh, some ladies, yes, but not our dear Ernestine!" said Emily. "Some ladies take the most extraordinary risks, going to the shops without companionship and frequenting restaurants, which is virtually an invitation for strange men to address one, but Ernestine is simply never troubled by strange men."

"It's heiresses and widows, Emily," said Ruth. "A woman without . . . without," she shook her head, looking irritated and bewildered to the same mild degree. "How did Herbert put it? He was so very firm on the subject, and said so often . . ."

"A woman without a man's protection can never be secure, and if she is of independent means, it is infinitely worse," Emily supplied. "Herbert was ever so clear on the matter. Her status is a positive temptation to gentlemen who might otherwise show better judgment. And of course there are men who are not gentlemen, and the less said about them the better. It always ends the same way. He would never have forgiven himself had he allowed a daughter, or a beloved stepdaughter, of course, to fall into such an invidious position, with stocks and deeds and a bankbook all in her name and just waiting to be snatched from her by some scoundrel."

"But of course, not every woman is as fortunate in her family as we," said Ruth, smiling at her son.

"I am always careful, even if I have no reason to worry," said Ernestine. Gennett watched with amazement as she set her teacup in its saucer with a delicate *click*. The smallest reference to financial settlements usually made her wild with wrath. She had some other reason to be satisfied with herself today.

The hours limped past. All Gennett could think of was the stacks of reading on his desk at St. George's Terrace, but he couldn't leave without confronting Ernestine in private. Ruth retired at her usual hour. Emily sat at her tapestry frame and made what she described as excellent progress on a faun. Gennett leafed through an album of landscapes. Ernestine sat with something from the lending library. The air between them was so alive, quivering like a rope drawn to the point of breaking, it seemed that Emily and her needlework would be twanged through the molded ceiling if one of them dropped an end.

"Are you tired, Auntie?" Ernestine asked, not looking up from her book.

"Not a bit." Gennett could hear the silk thread drawing in and out of the linen: one, two, three stitches. "Oh, now that you mention it, I suppose that I am rather fatigued. Quite exhausted, really. I don't know how I've kept awake this long."

"I'll put away your work for you."

"Oh, how kind you are, dear girl."

Gennett watched while Ernestine folded the frame away. She couldn't be faulted for care; its cherry wood legs were tucked in place with delicacy befitting the limbs of a baby. He watched her slowing, dragging it out. He counted in silence to keep his temper.

"Out with it. If you say 'Out with what?' I'll call Mother down and ask her."

Ernestine set the frame beside her on the floor. A tiny, insipid smile suggested some minor saint in a stained-glass scene, but her posture fizzed with triumph. "I don't believe that you have much right to ask me questions. I believe that you should be looking to your own conduct before you dictate to me."

"One Wednesday at church and you're blameless. Don't deny it, the maid told me. What do you think you're playing at?"

"I have been surveying," Ernestine said primly, "various centers of spiritual education to compare their views on certain points, not that that is any of your business."

"Which certain points would these be? And what 'centers'? You go from one year's end to the next without getting on a train if you can."

"You can pick at me with questions all night if you like. I have no obligation to answer you."

Gennett rose to stand over her chair. He had the firelight behind him; Ernestine was eclipsed. Their voices dropped instinctively even as the venom coiled. He was reminded, intrusively, of whispering in the dark of the nursery, of their secret pacts and betrayals after bedtimes, of hoarded mint humbugs downy with pocket lint.

"There's some personality behind these visits and views and 'certain points,' isn't there? I've had a warning of sorts regarding these parasites."

"What a lucky chance," snapped Ernestine.

He couldn't keep his voice low any longer. "This is disloyalty and a disgrace to you. If we are a family, we stand together. You, and Mother, are my responsibility and by God, I won't be turned aside from your welfare by a childish whim!"

"Ah!" she shrilled, as in victory. "Do you call deceiving Mother, cruelly deceiving me and leaving me standing outside your flat when I'd come to offer you comfort in your illness, loyalty? Or were you out indulging a *childish whim?*"

His mouth sagged open. This was riposte enough for her.

"Oh, I gave you the benefit of the doubt at first. I assumed that you were at your club. But then the next time I came to you I found out. Your servant wouldn't say where you were—I wonder why that might have been, hmm?—and would have put me out of the flat had I let him. There in with your papers were your bills——"

"You went through my desk?"

"I could have fainted, I felt so sick! I could have screamed! Perfumed love notes! Bills for gifts bought in Soho! Gifts of jewelery! The *expense.* I may not be a woman of the world—unlike certain other women of your, may I say, highly inappropriate acquaintance—but I am capable of seeing when I have been made a fool of. Oh, I was blind for some time, but you are not as discreet as you might like to think. You virtually hurl it in our faces. You may write our letters to the bank, but you will not be presuming to dictate our morals any longer."

She took advantage of his shock to make a dash for the door, as much as she could dash in a full complement of feminine drapery. He could not block her bodily and was forced to snatch at her elbow like a beggar. "Who is behind this? Explain yourself."

"You may do so! If your private life, however unsavory, is to be a closed book, then so shall mine be." The housekeeper was passing by on her last patrol through the house and gave them a puzzled look. Gennett dropped his sister's arm. Ernestine would have grinned, had her face been capable of such an expression.

"This is not concluded. You cannot end every argument by running out of the room to have the last word," he whispered.

"No, it is not concluded. But you'll see that for yourself soon enough. Mrs. Allen," she said to the housekeeper, who was twisting the life out of her keys in frustration. Mrs. Allen was usually adept at skirting domestic incidents. "Please don't bolt the front door just yet. My brother is leaving."

"Do you require a cab, Sir?"

"Oh, no. I'm sure he could do with a long walk. There's nothing better for soothing one's temper, don't you think?"

20

THURSDAY, OCTOBER 22

Upward

"Medical investigators of eminence have for-
tified the case for temperance by discovering
subtle, hitherto unsuspected, consequences
of drinking to excess carried on for several
generations."

—*The Times,* October 22, 1896

And mother-of-pearl buttons on the back as well? Quality
always comes out in the detail. Turn around, turn around!
Let me see how the mantle falls."

Lily spun obediently, holding her arms aloft like wings.

"Absolutely splendid." Carola leaned back to her cushions with
a contented wheeze, but was up again in moments, examining, comparing, theorizing as to the origin of the fine braid at the gown's
hem. "Is it really a gift?"

"Partly an advance on my share of the takings, but also a present. The session did go so well. And we both agreed that I needed
better gowns for the calls I'm making."

"This, and takings as well?"

Lily smiled and nodded toward the new feather bed, the curtains
on the hospital windows, the oil-burning stove in the corner bringing the room to ovenlike temperatures. Lily had bargained those
from the man on the back steps with the half crown she had from

St. Aubin. Carola needn't know that they were hired rather than bought, or that the gown had eaten such a share of the takings. The residue hadn't seemed very much to her, but St. Aubin had explained that the first priority in a new venture was always to reinvest.

"And fastening up the back again, thank goodness," Carola said, turning Lily to admire her line. "You looked like a little Toby jug in those front stays. Who laces you now?"

Lily bit her lip; she had prepared for this. "Monsieur St. Aubin has invited me to—you know that he is the guest of a very grand friend? He keeps his own house abroad, he says. But now that I'm out West every day it is so very far from our flat . . ."

Carola's eyes narrowed.

"It is in a separate wing of the house, in a guest suite. It's so large there is a separate team of servants. And there is a lady's maid, and it is easier to dress."

Carola's look was more thoughtful than displeased. Lily shivered. She was wary of her mother's temper, but not nearly as wary as she was of her mother's questions.

"More private, hmm?" Carola said at last. "When you owe money you get a lot of cheek. Your creditor somehow thinks he may call in at any hour of the day or night. Better that he not be coming in to see you in curl papers."

Lily swallowed. "Quite." She had meant to start cutting back on the main debt by now, though she didn't know for certain to whom it had been sold. The likely candidates ran from unpleasant to unthinkable. She could delay as long as she avoided the Shoreditch flat. Only a very few there knew about Ramsay and Eldard's, and none about the duke's. But she hadn't meant for her mother to know about the need for subterfuge.

"I knew that letter would be the making of us," Carola said, changing tack with her usual speed. "And our kind friend Monsieur St. Aubin. It's the Jovian factor. Was there ever such a time for new beginnings?" Carola flicked through the dominant influences: Jupiter returning to the ascendant, Saturn in retrograde; the natural progression from the fourth planet of the Zodiac to the fourth day of the week, the fourth card of the tarot—the Emperor—and the fourth letter of the Hebrew alphabet, Daleth. In the old days, when the horoscopes had done better, clients had been struck dumb with awe by Carola's memory for the charts. Her confidence was such that, if there were perhaps a few mistakes or omissions in the recitation, who would take note? "And a man, magnetic fellow and not quite a stranger, at the heart of it? You must have noticed that, when you checked your chart this morning. A Leo, I think. Our Monsieur St. Aubin is a Leo, did you know?"

Lily shifted uneasily. "A charismatic man, yes." The man wasn't as prominent in the charts as it was in the tarot. Why had her mother fixed so readily on that? It was the smiling red doctor to whom those signs referred. She herself would think it pointed to St. Aubin if she didn't know better, but she did know. The doctor had appeared from nowhere at her first séance and it had been a success. That was proof.

"You must tell me everything, everything of Monsieur's methods. Tell me the patter. It's the new scientific talk that I find so bewildering, but it must be mastered. Vulgar, but one can't wait for punters to develop taste!"

"But there's no . . . hurry." Lily felt a chill graze her spine. "We have plenty of time to work with St. Aubin. Don't we?"

Carola laughed. "Plenty of time, just no time to waste. You never know when a spot of independent operation is called for. Think of the new crowd you'll run across in Kensington and Chelsea! You might already have prospects in mind. All of these rich men must have mothers and sisters and aunts. Just the one introduction, if it's the right one, and we'll be rescued even without Monsieur St. Aubin."

Lily's hand stole to her pocket, moving before she had a conscious thought. She had his calling card with her   and why should she have it with her at this moment, but for the fulfillment of a purpose, the rescue that the cards had foretold but she had not until now understood? There was hardly a feeling in the world, she decided, more sweet than relief from doubt. She could see the card's bold script with the pads of her fingers. It grew warm from handling and seemed to print its shape on her petticoat like an iron.

To the editor of the Morning Express
Dear Sir,
Your kind decision to print my recent letter (appreciated) has engendered an unfortunate consequence: far from quenching further interest in 'spiritualist' confidence artists and their sickening pretensions to healthful or scientific ends, it appears to have invited an avalanche of ignorant comment from the lunatic fringe. (I fear that your decision to excerpt my letter rather than printing in full may have contributed to this regrettable circumstance). Certain responses protesting the 'benefits' conferred by spirit-contact and psychic-healing only serve to emphasise the dangers posed by frauds. I hope that an amended policy will bar such noxious nonsense from the pages of respectable newspapers. The public must be protected.
Yours,
Dr. Ambrose P. Gennett

⇥ ⇤

Ambrose,
Draft enclosed, my comments are in the margins. I have taken the liberty of toning down a few of your more <u>original</u> thoughts. You will forgive me if I say that it needs a trifle more work before it sees print? Your ideas are becoming so very unconventional. The Editors at the Asylum Journal can be quite timid, and it would not do to be blacklisted, would it? You must be more careful with people's sensibilities.
I confess myself somewhat confused by your line of reasoning in paragraphs twelve to eighteen. Believe me when I say that you are making work for yourself in trying to carry through the earlier argument—when we discuss women we do not mean <u>ladies</u>. If you wish to argue that mental illness has its roots in childhood

trauma, we may, although I remain unconvinced (why is it that some individuals emerge from similar experiences without discernable pathology?). I could almost countenance this <u>unpleasant</u> *theory regarding the sexual aetiology of neurosis, provided that you make clear that the sort of illnesses rooted in sexual trauma (I beg of you, stop saying 'child-rape') are the sort primarily found in the lower orders—imbeciles, slum dwellers sleeping ten to a room, etc. Where I must object is in this allegation that unsavory impulses are to be found in the average, asymptomatic woman. Females suffering erotic manias become prostitutes or seek treatment. Ladies of good character do not 'require an outlet' for some kind of 'fulfillment' aside from childbearing, and they certainly do not have reservoirs of thwarted passion concealed even from themselves. Think of the ladies in your own circle to whom you extend this analogy! I know that you like to be consistent but perhaps it is not necessary to assimilate every current theory. Leave the Freud / Breuer alone, and leave a bit of clear blue water between the instinctive sexual animal and the modern British female. What you call a logical conclusion I call very bad taste. There are certain contradictions in our research but a sensible man prevents these interfering with useful work. Everyone else ignores it and until recently so did you.*

Another thing: I would give myself a few weeks' holiday where these letters to the editor are concerned. You cannot respond personally to every crank in England and you're already becoming known as the fellow who's a bit funny about ghosts. You used to be known for your work.

Sincerely,

M Booth

21

SATURDAY, OCTOBER 31, ST. GEORGE'S TERRACE

"The spiritualist tells of manifestations of power, which would be the equivalent of many thousands of 'foot-pounds,' taking place without known agency. The man of science, believing firmly in the conservation of force, and that it is never produced without a corresponding exhaustion of something to replace it, asks for some such exhibitions of power to be manifested in his laboratory, where he can weigh, measure, and submit it to proper tests."

—Sir William Crookes, "Spiritualism Viewed by the Light of Modern Science," *Quarterly Journal of Science,* 1870

Gennett's study was submerged, though it was paper, not brine, that lapped over the desk and engulfed the carpet. Reports, journals, circulars, clippings, and files were shored up by books, and concealed the odd nest of forgotten crockery. The staff had long since cut the room off from their rounds. Booth's posture registered his distaste.

"I would dismiss every servant in my employ," he said, shifting a stack to perch uncomfortably on a stool. He waved his hand vigorously at the threat of refreshment. "God, no. Who knows how long the cup would be here to torment you?"

"They don't come in here any longer. If I leave so much as a note card in the bedroom it's tossed in the door when I'm not looking. I don't see any point in protesting when the rest of the flat is spotless." Gennett swept aside a stack of recent calling cards, ignored too long already. In passing, he glanced down at the card now resting on the edge of his wastepaper basket, bent into a cone by rough handling: *Mr. Henry Bettering, Referrals for Professionals and Gentlemen*. Never heard of him.

"Where does it all come from?"

"I'm working," Gennett said, stung. He stood to snatch back the copy of *The Two Worlds* that Booth dangled between his fingertips. Gennett stuffed it back into its stack between Kensington meeting minutes and yesterday's *Times*.

"I never had you down for this sort of distraction."

"It's for a patient. And my office at the Ken is a complete loss. It's nothing but a crow's nest over the staff disputes—they seem to want me to be policing the juniors instead of tending to my patients."

"You've tried the club?"

"You know how the club is. Endless chat."

Booth shifted his narrow backside fractiously. He took another draw on his cigarette and looked about with anxiety.

Gennett fished an ashtray from beneath an old *London Daily Graphic*—some scandal rag still raking over the eight-year-old Ripper murders; Wilson must have brought it in—and pushed it across the desk. "If you're that offended, the sitting room is pristine. I don't know why you wanted to come in here, anyway."

"I wanted to see for myself where you were holed up, old boy. One asks at the club what you're up to and the answers are a bit funny."

"Funny."

"Yes." Booth tapped ash twice. "Don't be thick, Ambrose. I shouldn't have to spell it out for you."

"What do you suggest, then?"

"Smarten up, for God's sake. Rekindle your acquaintance with your barber. Leave this." Booth waved his cigarette at the room, a gesture abbreviated by the enclosing stacks. "Come to the club tonight, and I promise you that you'll feel so much more yourself. Then go to your hospital, and go to whatever girl it is you have stashed in Soho, and come back to the club and so on and so forth, and you'll get back into the swing of things so quickly you'll wonder why you shut yourself up in the first place."

"I thought your patients were usually prescribed basketwork. That was a joke, by the way."

"You're not making this easy for anyone, you know. People are talking. If you can't be bothered, you put your friends in a rather difficult position. I thought I knew you better than this."

"Whose side are you on?" As before, Gennett's jocular tone fell flat like a tasteless pun. Booth left a little space between words before he answered.

"On your side, dear boy." The affectation, and it was an affectation coming from a man his own age, was something of a running joke between them, but today it grated. "As I always have been. If you could just see to revisiting the *Asylum Journal* piece—"

"Damn the *Asylum Journal*! If they're as cowardly as you suggest, what do we want with them? We need to strike out, the way we used to say we would back in school. Do you think Charcot was afraid of envious mutterings? There is so much—if I could just get some purchase on these ideas from the continent, about holding beliefs without knowing them, if those beliefs are frightening to us—not just to the mad, but to all of us—"

"You want to withdraw our joint papers," Booth said. All the blood seemed to have drained from his face to his neck, where the larynx bounced with repeated swallowing. "I understand. You need only have said. Without your name they won't publish, obviously—your reputation is such an asset, and with the fellows lining up to collaborate with you—if I've presumed, on the strength of our friendship—"

"Absolutely not! It's my privilege. You're worth twenty of those hidebound nincompoops, and the establishment will recognize that in time." Booth looked so genuinely distressed that Gennett steered him out to the sitting room, which cut his stream of self-recriminations off midsentence. "I've a few things left to do, and then I'll see you at the club tonight."

"It's for the best. You'll see that straightaway."

"I'm certain."

Gennett put aside his questions about that exchange as unworthy of his friend. He worked through a stack of correspondence and twice had to call the maid to freshen the fire before the thought came to him, as thoughts sometimes did, floating up full formed from the pool of concentration. He rang Booth on the telephone.

"You're not coming."

"Of course I'm coming. You're far too persuasive. No, I was wondering, how did you know I was home? Did you ring the hospital?"

"Actually—I hope you don't mind—I stopped to call on your sister. After all her effort to nurse you it seemed the thing. I don't want you to think that your friends are out gossiping about you. But your sister, you should know, is quite worried about you. I had to absolutely assure her that I would drag you out into society or sit at your sickbed all night as penance. She was most insistent. I had to guarantee that it would be tonight."

EVEN AS he watched, a cab pulled up to drop off another party at Eaton Place. He hung back to let the three women enter before he followed them up the steps.

"Ambrose!"

She looked like an actress on stage, his mother. Every lamp in the front hall was alight, and they made the marble floor glow with the warmth of wood. Ruth stood in the center, lit from all sides, in a black velvet gown. "Ernestine said you would never come. I knew she misjudged you."

He wanted to take her hands, to feel warmth and bone, but her hands were tucked away. "Mother, what—" he flailed. "I said no more meetings! What kind of charlatan has she dug up now?"

"I knew you wouldn't be angry." She smiled. Why, he wondered, didn't she bridge the gap? There might as well be a glass wall between them. "There are no men at all, my dear, and no money. It's the simplest and purest thing in the world."

The sitting rooms and parlors formed a gauntlet. Gennett tried to push his way through, but there were women everywhere. Dozens, it appeared, smelling of sherry and tea, with all the ruffling and cooing of a dovecote. He tried not to collide; he would crush them, bruise them like fruit, but just a look did that. They shrank back, wounded, but did not get out of his way. "Please excuse me. Miss, Madam, I must—please!" He must be bellowing like an animal. He had a chain of receiving rooms to go through.

Emily was in the next one. This was his mother's favorite receiving room; it should have been ringed in cozy round chairs and rose silk. The lamps were dark, and there were candles. "Emily—" At the sight of him she tried to slip aside. "Emily!" He caught up to her in the next room, darker still. He took in a vague and sickening impression of draperies, burning herbs, and an uncertain violin somewhere in the background. There, shielding Emily with her arms—as if Emily had anything to fear from him—was Ernestine. She looked how women caught at affairs sometimes looked. One could smell the fear, but see only the defiance.

Her mouth was moving, making Ernestine-type sounds of outrage blown up with air. How dare he. He would be sorry. She was intentionally blocking the door.

It was like lifting a kitten to put her aside. He had thought the door was locked, and half wrenched it from its hinges. When it collided with the inside wall draperies shook, occasional tables pushed to the walls shook, candle flames quivered. Gennett himself couldn't move an eyelash, couldn't take a breath.

On the far side of the dining table sat Lily Embly.

PART FOUR

CONVERGENCE

22

SATURDAY, OCTOBER 31,
THE DRAWING ROOM

T he doorknob had come off in his hand.

Emily had seen it happen. Ruth had still been out in the hall, but Emily had been squashed behind the parlor door while he stood, poleaxed, sucking in thick, spiced air through his mouth. "I should have known." Or, "By God, you have gall, Madam." Or perhaps just, "You!" left to trail off, menace flowing in to fill the empty space. But for God's sake, he should have said something. He had dozens, hundreds of possible rejoinders afterward, some clever, most not; more every time his thoughts strayed from work, multiplying like locusts. But even standing silent might have had its own dignity, even with the doorknob dangling from his fingers like a boule ready for the pitch. He should not have thrown it.

She did not flinch. She did close her eyes as the knob shattered on the wall behind her. Then while the other women gazed with horror at the aftermath of the small violence, she looked directly at him. He could perhaps have said something then, but there was his mother hanging about his shoulders and weeping—weeping— and this was so shocking that for a moment he tore his eyes away. And then the shouting began and he was turned about somehow, and the door behind him closed again. Emily wove between him and the screeching Ernestine. He had to steer the lot of them to move, which was like guiding a spooked horse out of a briar patch. He barked his knuckles reaching for the doorknob that was no longer there. "Get out of my house!" he shouted through the hole.

Turning, he had seen his mother's face, and known what long work it would be to overcome the words of moments.

23
Beginnings

"Get out of my house!"

Lily heard quite clearly. It was a signature quality of his voice that it could be understood as easily through a door as across a table. She admired a good speaking voice.

Her back and neck began to ache. The illusion of calm sat heavily on her now, but it had served its purpose. The remaining women were no different from any other clients, and remaining impassive in front of them was no more than reflex.

Her hostess was on the other side of the door, where the sounds of argument were receding; perhaps upstairs, perhaps out onto the street. The women twittered ineffectually along the walls. Few of her hostess's friends were matrons of comfortable position, it seemed; it was a coterie of spinsters, maidens, and a few on the painful cusp between. None seemed ready to assume charge of the company. A slender girl, perhaps twenty, crept close to Lily, but for reassurance only.

"Oh, horrible, horrible man! Ghastly! You are quite all right, I hope. But it makes no difference, does it? We can continue as we like?"

"This is quite beyond his power," another voice answered with confidence. "He can stomp and throw fits if he likes, but the spirit world hardly waits on him."

"Perhaps not, but if this is indeed his house, then I must go." Lily kept her movements even, as if her heart weren't thumping hard like a foot treading on her stomach. She hoped that deep breathing had driven the color from her cheeks. The women protested gently until it became clear that she did not mean to be persuaded to stay, but actually to leave.

"Miss Lily! Truly, you mustn't! Someone will sort out that brute. I'll fetch Miss Gennett."

A younger guest bobbed her head in timid disagreement, shifting it in a vague diagonal. "That was Mr. Gennett—Dr. Gennett, I should say. Miss G's brother."

Lily paused long enough for another to ask for her. "Is it his house, then?"

"Never mind," interrupted the brisk voice—the same pillarlike woman with a towering coiffure who had very lately been protesting the doctor's irrelevance. "Mine is just 'round the corner." She seized Lily's elbow. The others fought delicately for a place at Lily's other side.

Her name was Flora Hobbes, and "hers" was a more modest terraced house on Aldernay Street, on the border with Pimlico. Miss Hobbes's father, the winner of Lily's other elbow whispered, was bedridden, or at any rate no longer quite himself most days, and certainly in no position to interfere with Miss Hobbes. "Or with our experiments," Lily's companion added, straightening, when Miss Hobbes broke off to usher the party through her front door. They gathered in the Hobbeses' back parlor and Miss Hobbes dismissed the maid. "I'll pass the tea around, Bridget, thank you." Miss Hobbes shut the door and locked it.

The women exploded into talk. *I never! Well, could you? I ask!*

"He is not a pleasant person, this Dr. Gennett," opined Miss Hobbes, passing Lily a cup with lemon. "I have met him on several occasions and I must say that dear Ernestine's assessments are entirely confirmed! Brutish! Choleric! Every negative virtue of the self-important man, I should say."

"He was pleasant enough to me, the twice I met him," said the slender girl who had recently pronounced him ghastly. Her well-mannered smile suggested a short memory. Others nodded in agreement, though two in a corner eyed each other significantly behind the girl's back. One, with the smallest of gestures, mimed batting her eyelashes with a coquettish tilt of the head. The other tittered behind her hand. Lily had thought that the girl had a hungry look about her.

"He can be pleasant when it suits him to be. As the whim takes him, if I judge rightly, and no more studied than that," said Miss Hobbes. "But we've seen the truth of his character now, have we not?"

"A sorely underdeveloped personality," chimed in Miss Hobbes's companion on the sofa. "Such unadvanced persons are prone to rages, they say, as they apprehend their own sentiments so poorly. Much like children."

An older woman frowned. "Dr. Gennett is hardly an uneducated man, my dear, though I suppose that no one has ever cured his temper by reading books."

"He's a mad doctor," came a whisper over Lily's shoulder. This came out in an unexpected gap in the conversation and, rather than reaching Lily's ear and no further, rolled out to stand by itself in the center of the room. The good, though not excellent, teacups came to a halt in midair. Boots ranging from good to superior shifted uncomfortably on the thick mauve rug.

Lily pressed her hands to her sides to stop their shaking. She could barely keep her sagging chin up where it belonged. "He is . . . what?"

The older woman spoke again. "Dr. Gennett is a physician, but also what I believe is called an alienist, or psycho-ologist. His mother tells me that he sees patients at three hospitals, almost all with bad nerves or disturbed thinking."

"Good gracious! Imagine them coming 'round to the house!" someone exclaimed, inanely.

"He sounds a perfect saint to me," another said, "struggling for those poor lost souls day and night. Overwork taxes nerve-power and that always makes men tetchy. Dear Ruth never sees him, she says. And he certainly doesn't do it for gain, not with Herbert Gennett's fortune behind him. The father was always against it, I heard."

"The Commons would have been quite appropriate! The bar would have been acceptable. Herbert would not have minded that. Herbert had rather fixed ideas on what a young man of good family ought to be doing. When the boy wanted to go to Edinburgh instead of Cambridge . . ."

"No!"

"Cambridge medical training was 'reactionary,' as I recall. As if a gentleman goes up for training instead of an education! But Herbert put his foot down—Herbert was not a man to be gainsaid—and I'm certain that Ambrose would have come to his senses in time. But then!" Her hands folded over her breast, as if in a charm to ward off the evils of early death and willful sons.

"But no one could argue with Dr. Gennett's cures. Miraculous, I've heard them called."

"My physician says that the continental universities are distinctly second rate. They claim to be more advanced, but half of the Englishmen are only there because they lacked the connections or funds for a real school."

"Well, I daresay half of them are. But given who the *Gennetts* are, my dear, I think that we can safely say that Ambrose was in the other half?"

"He treats some very eminent personages," the older woman said, snatching back the reins of the conversation with a self-important sniff. "He was involved in the very sad case of Mr. Edmund Stone, the judge, whom I hear is still considered a candidate for recovery. I'm sure that Mrs. Stone prefers to have a gentleman physician rather than one of these thrusting low men."

"It is hardly a legitimate branch of medicine," said Miss Hobbes.

"Nearly all nervous disorders are physical in origin," added her neighbor with confidence, "and can be cured via magnets."

"Not at all! Not without a proper balance of minerals. And hydrotherapy is useless—my poor auntie should know—unless reinforced by appropriate support garments."

They were off again. Blunt darts of riposte passed each other in the air, fluttering down, targetless, in the cloud of non sequiturs. They all seemed awash in exciting new medical theories, full to overflowing with spa treatments, back supports, electrode therapy, raw-food diets, posture as the key to health. One woman's mother was having leeches applied to the bottoms of her feet and a tincture of mercury to her palms, a regimen that evidently surprised only Lily. No one asked what the treatment was for. Among them they had sufficient mysterious aches, tremors, and weaknesses to occupy a battalion of specialists, but it seemed that there had been time over long, uneventful years of acquaintance to become familiar with them all. This was perhaps why none listened but all took such trouble to be heard. Steeped as she was in the culture of drawing rooms, Lily shivered. The time beneath their nonexchanges, the trodden-down compost of days spent in talk, the same talk, burned her with cold.

The only ladies not partaking were the two lately mocking the coquette. These hovered near the door but could be overheard by a practiced ear.

"If Herbert Gennett had put as much effort into Ernestine's debut as he had into his son's schooling—"

"Be fair. A very many girls remain unmarried in this age of war and empire. Their natural counterparts have been removed from the equation." Titters indicated their opinion of whom Ernestine's natural counterpart might be; not a dashing society swain, Lily inferred.

"He could have given her a dowry in line with her new circle instead of leaving her with her birth father's fortune and no more."

"She had offers?"

"Well—say, rather, that she might have, had it not been made clear that only men at a certain level would be considered. When men at that level were conspicuous by their absence . . . for a businessman he didn't pay much heed to the realities of the marriage market."

They were interrupted by a knock at the door. "She's here!"

Miss Hobbes made a great show of unlocking the door, as if the conversation had been anything other than innocuous, if morbid. But nipping in around the door frame, tidy as a housecat, was not the expected Miss Gennett. It was Emily Featherstone, high colored with undisclosed news.

"Chaos!" Emily squeaked, dropping into a chair with unexpected looseness. Before Lily had only seen her perch on the edge as if the seat might be whipped out from under her. "It's awful, awful— Ernestine says that she wants him disowned, or something in that way. Ruth has collapsed entirely. He says it's Ernestine's fault. You can guess what Ernestine said. The housekeeper wanted to call the police, but the butler from number fourteen—he was walking by, can you believe that Ambrose left the door standing open?—wanted Ruth's doctor to sedate Ernestine! I have never—I have simply never." Emily took a slug of sugared tea, knocking it back like a whisky chaser. It was more than odd to see Emily at the center of ministering admirers, even if only in deference to her news. Lily had thought that she had the measure of this mousy aunt. Now she soaked up every detail of Emily's obvious distress. It seemed strangely free of the kind of malicious, unacknowledged pleasure that Lily would have expected from one of these doorstop women. Emily accepted more tea from her audience, oblivious to the attention.

"Is she coming? Dear Ernestine?" asked Miss Hobbes.

"Well, if she manages to avoid the doctor—I don't know that she will, she does look perhaps just a bit hysterical to me, not that I know the first thing about it. Ambrose will stop her, of course. But then," Emily was turning her teacup around in her hands in an ever-faster circuit. "Yes, he might have to leave, or he might be upstairs tending to poor Ruth. That is likely where he is now. And he'll have told Ernestine to stay where she is, but might she not slip out? But then, why need she?" Worry lines reconfigured themselves into a timid smile as she talked herself out of what she had seen. "No, they have tempers, both of them—though from where I can't say, certainly not their mother—but won't they see reason after a good night's sleep? Yes. A lot of nasty shouting, but what does that signify? Ambrose is just cross because he wasn't told. If she had, there would be no quarrel at all! It will be fine by morning, I'm sure, because they are ever so close. If you had seen them as children—the age difference meant nothing at all, and it was more touching than I can describe to see them engaged in king-of-the-castle and let's-pretend. They had their own little country, with a map and its own dialect and little stamps they made themselves from watercolors and glue! The stamps did run a bit when you licked them but so inventive, wouldn't you agree? Children must have their rows but when they did disagree—there was something about a constitutional question, and whether the queen, who was Ernestine, could overrule the prime minister, who was Ambrose—they always made up, if not by dinnertime then within a few months at least. They share so many qualities of character." With a sigh more contented than woebegone she handed her teacup back to Miss Hobbes, who was irked. Never mind that she had dismissed the maid herself; Emily was no one to be handing cups to her. "I should be getting back now. I only wanted to stop in and let you know that everything is going to be all right."

Lily caught her before she reached the door. She typically avoided speaking to clients while standing up, but Emily was very much her size. "Would you do something for me, Miss Featherstone?"

There was a flurry of curiosity around them. Lily ignored it. "Yes, of course," Emily said. Emily's eyes were focused on a point around Lily's chin.

"Would you give this to your niece?" The murmuring was building to a crescendo. The bodies around them contorted subtly in many attempts to read the print on the folded card between Lily's fingers. She dismissed the risk; the worst that could result was a great deal of puzzling over what their pet psychic was doing with a West End jeweler's card. But Emily took it without unfolding it.

"I will not be back here," said Lily.

"I quite understand."

"There is much to be done. Unfinished business sits very ill," Lily said. Emily's little smile was increasingly desperate. A man would have great beads of sweat popping up on his brow; perhaps Emily did, too, behind her old-fashioned front of curls. "I will wait for word."

Emily went, and the rest of them sat in the parlor waiting for Lily's cab, the Gennett's driver not being as on hand as Ernestine had promised. The silence was stale and brittle. They did not make small talk to her, and would not around her. They might, once she left, spring back to their usual many-sided cacophony, but somehow she doubted it.

She made a final survey of the company. In a few minutes they would fade into the choir invisible of old clients: so many and so very like. She might recall the slender predatory girl, her gossiping detractors, Miss Hobbes with her stooge of a friend seconding even her sneezes, and pick and choose those to honor with a future sitting. But only if she wanted to. She didn't have to cling to every client anymore; she had more than she could handle. Carola would not be brooding over each wayward customer before their tiny fire, wondering what had gone wrong. This time they were standing still and she, Lily, was leaving them behind.

She stepped into the cab and gave the duke's street—why should that be such a pleasure, Miss Hobbes's shocked silence? It had never mattered to her before that clients looked down on her; she expected it, used it even. Warming satisfaction warred with disquiet in her stomach as the carriage rolled away from the Hobbeses' house, another house that she would never see again, with the lace curtains twitching in the windless night.

St. Aubin, the servants said, was still dining at the club of Mr.—, a public fellow of such grandeur that an artificial cough sufficed for his proper name. (Lily believed him to be a minister of some kind, but she didn't read the papers.) Would Miss Embly prefer to be informed of his arrival? She would not. She assumed it would be very late. But might word be taken to him that she looked forward to speaking with him in the morning hours? Yes, it certainly would.

She had no idea how discreet the servants might be. They were all so fantastically polished, as unlike the hard-laboring domestics she knew as the rough planks of her flat were from these majestic gleaming floors. Perhaps she ought to be spreading bribes as she did at the hospital. (How much would it take? There was no one to ask.) If she did, she could at least measure out where she stood, to the last farthing. But they might be different, posh servants. They might be protective of a woman's secrets as a matter of policy. Or they might be loyal to the master of the house and no other. She watched the butler from the corner of her eye as he latched the door shut, silently. If St. Aubin asked him questions, how would he answer?

"Has Madam any further needs?"

"Just a light, please."

"Madam will find the gas lighting still on in the guest wing of the house. They will be turned off for the night when Madam is ready to retire."

"Oh. Ah—thank you." Ears burning, she made her way up the staircase to the east wing. Each step was as wide as a tall man was high.

The butler talked as nicely as her new clients. Real gentlemen could be a bit sloppy and slangy, even *he*, with his voice warm and clear as beef broth, even when he was shouting through a door— but it was more complicated than that, she knew. There were signals here she hadn't dreamt of, stumbling through a wood at night where the natural denizens, large and small, could see. She didn't know yet how he fitted in. But she would.

Safe in her suite she cracked a fingernail prying up the false bottom of her vanity case. In moments she had his chart spread out before her on the desk, one corner anchored by an empty candle-holder, one by her sweating hand, two by the cards, cut into two packs. She had somehow missed—

There it was.

In the tangle of celestial bodies (his was a complicated chart) there were endless signs, now that she took the trouble to search for them. A comet streaking across his eighteenth birthday. (Wasn't that when his father had died, freeing him to pursue his vocation?) A traffic jam of planets on the fringes of the fourth house, which could cloud anyone's judgment. Now that she considered it carefully, fate had designed him to fall in with the self-serving trash of alienism. Mad-houses were an occupational hazard for mediums. She knew more than a few who had gone from a profitable business to Bedlam after a complaint from a neighbor or dissatisfied client—*odd behavior, potentially dangerous*—and whatever they'd been when they went in, after a few years chained to a wall they were mad enough to satisfy. How incredible that something in her fate, and her mother's fate, rested in those soiled hands. He did not seem so lost to reason.

When she reached for her cards an irritation bit at the side of her neck: a shard stuck in her collar, a fragment of a porcelain door-knob. She worried it out with one hand while the other closed around the tarot pack. His chart curled up and fell to the floor. She could manage any strangeness if the pack were in its place.

It had always been thus. Their dingy flats, a fresh handful every year, ran together in her mind like laundry going gray in a commu-nal tub. Stuck sashes on different windows, creaks in different floor-boards, drafts under different doors. The years would have been better differentiated if they had stayed in one place. One would at least have been able to place an incident in time by the seasonal dis-comforts and advancing decrepitude of the surroundings, or at least one's height relative to the doorknob and the washroom tap. Instead, all details were lost in a cyclone of small wearying varia-tions, like a day made up not of a morning and noon and night, but the same witching hour lived over and over in different rooms.

When Lily taxed her memory it yielded up only one exception to the monotony of change. One scene: It was sandwiched in between recollections of ordinary flats, so she knew that they had not begun there. It was not her first memory, only her brightest.

The rooms had had gilded ceilings, she remembered that: yellow-painted clusters of fruit and faint vines trailing away in green. The light had hung from a great plaster rose. There had been a chair with a deliciously furry seat—velvet, she thought—that she had stroked like a pet. And there was Mama, not in her mended gowns but lovely sparkling ones, all new, and so many Lily was barely used to one before a more brilliant successor appeared. There were jewels. Lily recalled having her back thumped and, when the danger had passed, her backside thumped after she had put one of the glittering things in her mouth. She must have been two or three years old to try to eat it. Also, she would not have been punished so severely if the jewel had been a cheap fake. And then as suddenly as it had appeared the golden room was gone, whipped away from around them like scenery, and Mama in fusty black and telling her that they would be answering to a new name, the first of many. There was typically an *E* in it somewhere. Lily wondered if Mama got the new ones from novels.

There had been one very bad time (had Lily been ten years? Eight?). They lit no lamps. Mama said it was to save oil, but they also kept away from the windows, which could only be to keep bill collectors from seeing that they were at home. The tea leaves, thrice boiled and secondhand to begin with, no longer even tinted the water, and there was no coal or wood for boiling the water anyway. Lily had gathered her courage and asked the question, "Mama, why don't we go and speak to the nice man? He could give us money."

"What nice man?"

"From the golden room." Lily had described it—the ceiling and the chair and the diamond on which she'd choked—speaking faster and faster as her mother's face remained politely incredulous. "I saw it," Lily repeated. "Don't you remember?"

Mama had taken her shoulders and steered her to the table and laid the green cloth. She had taken the cards and made Lily cut them. "Lay out a pattern, any one you like," Carola had said. The Pope (in some packs he was the High Priest), and the Female Pope were there, and the Hermit and assorted Wands and Swords. Pentacles were of the kind one only wanted to see inverted, cards of wealth slipping through one's fingers and dribbling away. For them those cards were right-side-up. "Now show me," Mama had said, "where is this man, this room? I don't see riches anywhere in our past." The charts were the same. Lily had needed help with the calculations—she must have been eight years, then, for by ten she could do the figuring in her head without a slate to help—but none in interpreting what was there. No fortunes, no great affairs of the heart. Little pockets of wealth in the wake of transitory planets; Lily asked, could it be those? But Mama said, firmly, not. "I don't think the man is there, my love. Memory plays tricks."

Lily never asked about the man again. The bad time passed and there was food and they could walk past the window without even thinking about it. When her mother was out or sleeping she looked for him from time to time, but the cards and charts showed her so many other things. She grew adept, scoring victories in small disasters foreseen and avoided, and more and more it was she whom visitors asked to see. Mama was as likely to ask Lily about their twined horoscopes than the reverse. Mama could be capricious, pushing aside and disregarding auguries she did not like, preferring to speak for the departed (perhaps improving on their messages when required) but Lily took more care. The past was treacherous, deceiving and taking a different face in different people's memories. Mama could have the past and the dead. Lily preferred the future. It was so much more reliable.

Or it always had been before.

She unrolled the doctor's chart and looked again but her eyes were playing tricks. All the patterns she had seen before were obscure, while new and contradictory strains seemed to be trying to force their way through to the surface. That never happened. It was always the same to her; the correct interpretation, once revealed, never wavered. If she worked hard enough, it always came to her. But she had always before had peace, if not quiet or privacy then at least time to think, time and sleep. And Mama to confide in.

Lily rolled the chart with care and set the cards back in their box before climbing under the covers, still in her corset and hairpins, still in her boots. She dug the heels of her hands into her eyes. It was pointless to cry. The sight would return if she had faith in it, and it was impossible that fate had forgotten about her. That was not what fate did. It only seemed as though she was adrift, and she certainly wasn't alone in her particular current of destiny. The doctor had been placed right beside her.

24

Sunday, November 1,
Shoreditch

"Civilisation, which can breed its own bar-
barians, does it not also breed its own pygmies? May we not find a parallel at our own
doors, and discover within a stone's throw of
our cathedrals and palaces similar horrors to
those which Stanley found existing in the
great Equatorial forest?"

—Charles Booth, *Life and Labour of the
People of London*, 1892

The first day was quite wasted. He pounded the door of her flat until his hand was dead. "They're not here," a voice said behind him. Down the hall a thin girl stood with a gray rag in her hands.

"When will they be back?"

"I don't know." He held a penny out to her. "No, I don't know. I does their charring, but the Miss said I needn't come now."

"They? Who is they? Her husband?"

"No, only her old mum, a widow I think. Never any man as long as I been."

"Where have they gone? Why did they go?"

"Don't know. I just does the charring."

He gave her the penny. The cabdriver wanted an extra sixpence for having to wait outside in such a neighborhood, and refused to alight from the curb without it.

1st November, 1896

My dear Dr. Booth,

It is settled, then. You are his closest colleague and if you feel that he is quite himself then nothing more need be said. My doubts upon reading the draft of his most recent paper were, I am gratified to report, quite reversed by your testimonial. As you say, his tenacity is the very engine of his success, is it not? His attention has fallen upon odd targets before, and this fad will pass as others have. There is no future in Freudianism.

But you say nothing of the other talk, these entanglements with another hospital. Should we at the Kensington be concerned? When I say concerned I mean of course for his reputation and welfare, which are of course inseparable from our own, and yours particularly.

With utmost gratitude,

Sir S.H. Gov., Kensington Royal Hospital

✦ ✦

Nov 2nd

Dear Mother,

We must speak about Ernestine and her new hobby. ~~If it would not be so taxing to you~~ Please accept my apologies for the ~~accident~~ incident with the doorknob. ~~Promise me that you will not become upset.~~ It will not be as upsetting as our last chat. ~~Please forgive~~

Nov 3rd

Dear Ernestine,

The séances will end. The very idea of your moving out on your limited income is ludicrous. As your brother ~~*I insist*~~
~~*I demand*~~
~~*I implore*~~

Nov 4th

Dear Emily,

It has been so long since our last tête-à-tête . . .

⟞⟨25⟩⟝

THURSDAY, NOVEMBER 5,
REGENT'S PARK

RHEUMATISM, Sciata, Lumbago,
and Insomnia CURED by the
Malvern Hydro-Electric treatment.
Weir Mitchell's system.
Electric baths. 9 to 11, also Sundays.
—No. 66, Jermyn-street
(St. James-street end).

—Advertisement, *The Times*, November 5, 1896

Emily was waiting when he arrived. She half stood in her wickerwork chair and waved. She couldn't be wearing white . . . as he drew closer, weaving between small round tables ringed by thick, encompassing chairs, he saw to his relief that it was not so. Her skirt and jacket were pale green, made lighter by a rose pink blouse. It was her light straw hat, and her energetic waving, swinging her entire body into it, actually, that made white seem likely. White on a spinster of—well, it had to be fifty-odd—was inappropriate, however girlish she might be.

She was Ernestine's aunt, not his. As the sister of his mother's first husband, she had been a fixture of the life before Herbert Gennett, making long visits in the way of maiden aunts, for whom a week from home was a week saved on fuel. But the fuel savings were offset by the cost of transport, and the difficulties of getting someone in to look after one's pets and flues, and in persuading one's servants to accept two weeks or two months without pay (they could be quite obstinate, Emily had explained, even when one offered to help them find temporary work), and Emily had moved in permanently not a year after Herbert Gennett's death. Ruth and Ernestine had still been in mourning. In Emily's small wardrobe, however, dull colors were well represented, and by the time the black bombazine came off of Ernestine's hatbands, Emily's stay was no longer discussed as a matter of weeks or months. Emily did not, as a rule, invite discussion of any kind.

Still, he kissed her hand as gallantly as he would a debutante's, at which she colored and laughed. It was not of the same stripe as his usual courtesy. He was always polite, even attentive, but the soft jonquil fragrance of the garden teahouse, and Emily's delight and ease in it, had a strangely astringent effect on his nerves. It made him honest. Gentle teasing in private could never be the same in a gazebo, behind a silver cake stand, among one's own kind. He felt he was making a fool of her. But she did look very well, with an excellent color, and there was no reason for anyone watching to suspect anything but a treat organized by a loving nephew; if anything, a spy might draw quite the wrong conclusions about who in the family had the money. This made him feel a great deal worse, and he squeezed her hand so fiercely he thought he might have raised a spark of suspicion in even these most trusting of eyes.

"Ambrose," Emily said uncertainly.

He took a deep breath and forced it out through his teeth. He knew his voice and posture were unnatural. So he fabricated a long and tiresome journey, and in recounting this in detail saw Emily relax and sit back in greater comfort. No one ever doubted the sincerity of complaints.

"How shocking!" she clucked. "I fear that your journey was quite spoilt. I do hope that it hasn't made the afternoon seem tiresome. You look so awfully fatigued. Are you quite happy to stay? We could so easily return another day."

"Nonsense. The atmosphere is most restorative." As proof, he took a deep draught of spring air. It was more scented with ladies than flowers, but he had never been excessively devoted to the outdoors.

"What a shame it is that your mother is unwell. Would it be fairer to her to come back another time?"

If a shame, it was not much of a surprise. Ruth was prone to vapors in the late afternoon and kept about one teatime engagement in three, as Gennett had known when he had set the time. "You are kindness itself. I will return here with Mother, but I'm enjoying the air far too much to leave now. I hope I may enjoy your company along with it. I do fancy some tea. Would you indulge me and join me in a pot?"

He nibbled his way through half of the petit fours and sandwiches, as the suggestion that she order for herself made her blanch. An unwanted meal was a small price. They spoke of inconsequentialities. As the waiter came back to replace their pot of tea a second time, he allowed longer stretches of silence to open up in the conversation.

"I am boring you," she said.

"Not in the least. I had no idea that the neighborhood felt so strongly about the topiary at number twenty-eight."

"We—you and myself—we don't speak very often, do we? There is so little need. Things are going so well."

"Are they? I confess, I was most surprised at all the new pastimes that have been taken up since I have been away. We were in agreement, you and I, about the importance of family news? Your reports used to keep me abreast of developments. I had assumed that you would begin writing again if anything of importance arose. I would call this important."

"Oh. Indeed, yes!" Emily nibbled a crustless egg-and-cress, looking every moment as though she were gathering her thoughts to speak. He waited, but only to watch a preoccupied older lady consume a sandwich. Was *rabbitlike* the word for her, darting her eyes about, eating only incidentally, between distractions? He didn't mean to think of her as a generic old maid. Yet her small, rutched features (she might have been pretty in her youth, in a bland way) and her manners and her faded, fussy garments were so evocative of that type. Despite effort, he could not find them evocative of anything else.

"Emily, I wish you had told me about the séance. Now, I don't require you to stop her; I intend to speak to her myself—"

"Stop her! Not in the least! The incident with the doorknob was, well, it was regrettable, but do not torture yourself with the thought that you have dissuaded her!" Emily leaned very slightly into her words. The stiff ruffles of her jacket proceeded her and pressed delicate plates into a logjam. "You need to understand how beautiful the mystery is. This thing; you on one side, Ernestine on the other—it's so foolish, because there are no sides! Or there need not be. Spiritualism is simply the most wonderful, amazing gift that the Almighty has ever bestowed upon us. Bestowed other than our Savior, of course. Not so amazing as that. But you are so precisely the sort of person who could see that, and understand that." He coughed sharply. "Now, don't be modest! And Ruth understands too, I am sure of it, although she would never dream of speaking to you directly about it. Just the other day, just before your note arrived asking us to tea, I was downstairs working with your mother, and I put my needles down and mentioned how long it had been since we had seen you. Slightly indirectly; I believe it was in the context of when we had last had turtle soup, which was the very last evening that you dined with us. Well! Ruth simply put a hand to her forehead and sighed like you have never heard a person sigh, and she said, 'Emily, it was only Sunday.' Which of course it wasn't Sunday, either your visit or the soup, but she doesn't have the very best head for dates and things, not lately, and what she meant was that she simply couldn't say how this whole—you, your sister—could be resolved."

Emily looked at him expectantly. When he did not answer whatever question was understood, she continued. Her tone was ever so slightly didactic. It made his hackles rise. "The only thing standing between you and your sister is"—she paused to feel about for the perfect word—"a misunderstanding!"

"So perhaps I could just stroll into her sitting room, announce that this has all been a silly mistake, and we'll be friends again?"

Even Emily's faith in human nature had to balk at this. "Ah, perhaps not. Ernestine—if it began the wrong way—well."

He set down his fruit cake and tapped his lip studiously. "But this rift pains me terribly, so I must not balk at any measure that may heal it."

"No, we must certainly not balk!"

"I do prefer to be direct. But here—circumspect? No, that isn't the word. Gentle. We need to approach this gently, or Ernestine will never forgive us."

That was a mistake. A cloud passed over Emily's face, and there was nothing he could do but wait to see if it cleared.

"Nothing secretive, Ambrose, I'm sure. It's not as if—it isn't spying, our little conversations."

"But I can't think of what else to do, save barring séances altogether. It is within my power to do so, but I think that would be quite the wrong approach?"

"Oh, quite the wrong approach! No, you mustn't halt the ceremonies. Goodness, no." Her hands crept about the detritus of the tea service. "And . . . you will think me foolish to mention this, as you will have thought of it yourself, but I am not quite certain that you could stop her spiritualist activities? At your house, I mean your mother's house, certainly. But to stop her accepting invitations to other homes . . . you would have to station guards in the back garden, I suppose. It would be different if she promised, but she wouldn't give her word against her conscience, would she?"

Other invitations? "Emily, you do agree, I hope, in the importance of reuniting us in our feelings? For my sister and I to be so out of sympathy is a matter of the greatest distress to me."

Emily said nothing.

"You know how I rely on you in this. Without you I would know so little of her thoughts, and I would be uneasy. Ernestine has been . . . misled before."

"But this is nothing like that! If you learn, if you study, you will see how different it is. She cannot come back down to a lower level of spiritual development. You must move up to join her!"

Her fervor made his jaw clench, but he lifted his eyebrows innocently. "Then I must speak to her about it; only she will not meet me. What do you suggest?"

"Now, a meal, or tea—I don't think you would have very good luck there! Ernestine's good manners wouldn't let her speak of family disputes in company, and of course she won't see you at home. Is there some way to, I don't know, show her that you mean well? An olive branch, I mean. I would try to—now, I know that men do not often think of it in these terms. No doubt you will find me very silly. But if you were to, if one were to, try to stand beside her, if you see what I mean. To think of how things sound to her . . ."

"To see it from her perspective?" he said blandly.

"Exactly!" Emily beamed. "A painting term describes it exactly. You are always so very perfect in your choice of words."

Gennett waved the hovering waiter to a safer distance and topped up Emily's tea himself. "And to come closer to her perspective, what do you suggest?"

"You must expand your education on matters supernatural. That is, if you think it best." Gennett patted her fluttering hand to show that he was not offended. It was a small reassurance, but she recovered her boldness quickly. "There is reading to be done. I haven't copies myself, but I can pass Ernestine's on to you. She won't mind. Well, she would now, but she won't when the two of you are back in harmony, and she shan't know until then. But there is no substitute for instruction. When you have done your reading, I will smooth the way for you with a guide who can help." She smiled to herself, as if taken with a sudden idea, he thought. It took monstrous effort to keep his voice light.

"Who will be the guide?"

"There will be time for that. One meets so many fascinating people in these circles. I quite envy you, I do! To begin one's instruction again," she sighed like an aged adept looking back on a distant apprenticeship with nostalgia. "Truly, it is a feast stretched before you."

"I think I might wish to meet this guide soon. As you say, books are only books."

"Quite, quite. I will think on the matter. It is a shame about the last séance." She shook her head with public regret. "But a truly advanced person will not begrudge you a fresh start. And she is so advanced."

They spoke of lighter matters as he saw her home: sermons and serials she was following, what roads would be closed to accommodate the upcoming Diamond Jubilee celebrations. With some confidence established it was strangely easy to speak with her. She nodded wildly or listened with soft meows of sympathy: indeed, indeed, you do not say. Accepting, unjudging. It was like a conversation with a pet, he thought as they stopped on Eaton Terrace, two streets away from Eaton Place.

"I'll get the books to you. It may take a short while, but I will get them."

He held up a hand to stop her skipping down to the pavement. "Emily, I——" It was so strange to ask her about anything but Ernestine, really quite embarrassing. "Mother isn't involved with all this, surely?"

"Oh, but she will be! Ernestine will do her best, of course, and with your help and that of our most excellent guide I'm certain that Ruth will be on the path to spiritual awakening. Why, just a step ahead of you, I should think!"

Without preamble, Emily leaned in and kissed him chastely on the ear, perhaps having aimed for his cheek. "Please don't worry." Then she was out the door and making her way down the street. He could see epics of intrigue in her jerky gait and would have liked to shout out the window for her to act more naturally, but he couldn't recall how she had walked before.

26

Obedience

"It is not enough to be a good wife and
mother . . . you must also be an attractive
and pleasant woman. It is sometimes easy
to become pretty and agreeable to look at.
Begin by choosing, in your dress, colours
that will suit your complexion and your hair."

—Baroness Staff,
trans. by Lady Colin Campbell,
The Lady's Dressing Room, 1893

Lily was prepared to wait weeks, but it was Friday when Mr.
Eldard came 'round her room at the back and peppered the
door with nervous little knocks. His anxiety was as good as a
prearranged code.

Moments in Miss Gennett's company made Lily doubt her own
judgment. Her initial assessment had been wrong. It would never,
ever be weeks of waiting for this one. Not when it was one of those
decisions, however few, that she had the power to do something
about. Their initial meeting had been very brief. What Lily knew of
Ernestine Gennett was mainly gleaned from the notes that had
launched their acquaintance, and that mainly from between the lines.
Not a great deal—some practitioners had gone mad for graphology
and touted it as a new science, but Lily had seen penmanship vary

too drastically to consider it the key to personality. Also, she had
faked too many hands herself. Besides, all too often handwriting
pointed in one direction and reliable methods, such as the birth chart,
pointed in another. Once she had seen aggression, leadership, and
recklessness attributed to a Pisces, with a Cancerian ascendant, no
less, on the basis of a sharply angled vowel. It was suitable for a parlor game, perhaps, but not serious investigative work.

There were other things a note could tell. Ernestine Gennett's
were a study in contradiction. They came on delicate mauve paper,
scented with a heavy hand and faintly powdery to the touch.
The ink was pale. The words wanted to lift off of the page with
bile. *Dear Lily,* the last note began. *If I may call you Lily, Miss E.
I do feel as though I know you, and have known you all my life.
Your insights and <u>uncanny</u> perception convince me that your powers
over the paranormal world are everything they are purported to be and
more. How delighted and flattered I am that you are considering attending one of our <u>amateur</u> meetings at my home and lending us for a
time your renowned expertise. I myself am but a <u>poor</u> student of these
arts. . . .*

The overpowering resentment could be felt on the border, where
the writer's fingers had warped the page from pressing on it, boring
down into the blotter as she traced out flattery. The nib never took a
firm footing on the page, and paused often, the pen considering as
the words gushed. Emphasis came in odd places. Lily could hear it
when she mouthed the words: forced. False modesty. Sarcasm. Lily
ran the elegantly formed lines over her lips silently and felt an airy,
contrived gentility creeping into the vowels, and her eyebrows
arching. Sarcasm and contempt.

Establishing contact had been no trouble. With the doctor's card
in her hand the way was clear, and the ease of it all confirmed the
rightness.

The flowers Lily sent to "Mrs. Gennett, from her husband" at
the listed address returned good information. The messenger boy
had come back to her red-faced, repeating the housekeeper's admo-
nition that Mrs. Gennett was a widow and that Miss Gennett was a

thoroughly respectable lady under her brother's protection and needed no cheek from insolent boys, thank you very much. Lily gave the boy an extra penny. Where there was a spinster sister there was an opportunity. A simple letter to Miss Gennett was enough. Miss Gennett and all of her friends had heard of the celebrated Miss E, though Miss Gennett's circle was an unfashionable one well removed from the bon ton St. Aubin pursued. He need never know of it. They had leapt upon her offer; signs had revealed to her, she had written, that she should come to their home for fruitful work. The séance was arranged by post before Lily and Miss Gennett had ever met.

At Eaton Place Lily had not pressed for an extended meeting, thinking that they would have all night. All she had was an impression of pale, slightly close-set eyes and furiously intricate hair. Miss Gennett's gown had been black, as everyone's gown had been black, and when she was called away her train was so heavy with jet beading it rutched up a corner of the carpet and half-dragged it out the door with her. In her wake the tassels were churned and tangled like bladderwrack left by the outgoing tide.

Today Miss Gennett's walking suit was mint green with ivory lace at the throat. Lily was aware, somewhat uncomfortably, that it probably would have impressed her more a month ago. She would have assumed that it was her own taste that was miscalibrated. She had known very well about the dubious selections that a little bit of money could generate, but had harbored a strange idea that someone kept grander women from making the same mistakes; that their dressmakers and milliners would just stop them and tell them. No one, clearly, was telling Ernestine Gennett.

Miss Gennett suffered to have her fox cape taken by Mr. Eldard. They proceeded to the back. Miss Gennett was speaking before they had properly entered the room, and glanced this way and that as she settled, unhurried and adroit, on the smaller of the two chairs, Lily's own chair, narrow and high. She said, "Miss E, you are too good to meet me here," before faltering. She scanned the lapis blue walls. "What an extraordinary place!"

Under the disapproval, the affronted sense of what one was to expect in the studio of a medium and what one was not, was another note. Discomfort of some kind, and not the simple sort that women suffered constantly, the warm and itchy weight of convention dragging their shoulders down. There was something there, and yet it was quite tempting to ignore it. Miss Gennett was so breathlessly easy to dislike.

"It has excellent vibrations," Lily replied without thinking. That was her accustomed answer to questions about her room from divining clients—and quite true, if crudely articulated—but it flew squarely in the face of everything she said about spirits, which was that proper vibrations called for darkness, secrecy, obedience, and whatever else the stage directions required. She could scarcely remember everything she had made up. She should know what to say; cajolery was in her nature. She had Venus in the third house. Miss Gennett's rather bushy eyebrows were screwed up in a comical chevron of confusion. It was the first genuine expression Lily had seen on her. "You should see it in the dark."

"Ah, I see. It would be very different at night. Do you rent out the space in front to that funny man?"

"I only use this room. The shop is his." She hadn't thought before passing the card to Emily. It had seemed the thing to do, a pure hunch that came up from beneath reason in the service of serendipity. She had obeyed. But everyone on the street knew the name of Embly that she had been so careful not to release. Mr. Eldard might blurt it out at any moment, anything to please an affluent lady. She had an old regular coming in for a horoscope later in the morning.

"Oh! I see how very little I know of these matters."

"Appearances can be most deceiving."

Lily had meant nothing more than to fill space with a homily. But Miss Gennett blinked rapidly and took out a minute handkerchief, monogrammed in the corner with a *G,* to twist in her hands. "Miss E, you truly, truly are too good. I would not blame you if you never consented to meet with me again. The incident at my home—you could have been hurt. You could have been killed." The handkerchief began to stretch and warp.

"No one was hurt, no more than they would be by a slamming door."

"It was an inch from striking you!"

"A few feet. It wasn't aimed."

"Oh, wasn't it?"

"No," Lily said, but Miss Gennett was wrenching her little cloth and staring viperously at a spot in the middle distance.

"Wasn't it? That's just the thing to say, too. Simply watch. In two days' time no one will admit what they saw in that room. Oh, no one of us is perfect—except him, when he's coming down from the heights to tell us what to do and who to see and what to wear. He does think this! Then he keeps—I can hardly say which is worse. That he keeps a mistress on our money, or what he spends on her! Whereas I"—she sucked in air until Lily feared that she would burst her stays—"I must beg your pardon. Ours is not as other households. I am sorry if the meeting seemed a bit thin to you, a bit threadbare, but I'm on an allowance from my mother, you see, who is on an allowance from *him*. Our money all goes to grand hotels for deranged people. There's not much left for entertaining."

It was an opportunity. For an instant, Lily felt an urge to rebel and let the proffered moment pass, which stunned her. "Deranged people?"

"No one else gives a penny for his ridiculous plans. Doesn't that fill you with confidence? I have a new friend who tells me—never mind that. But I know a great deal more on the matter than I once did. And I can tell you, this is an absolute fact, half of them aren't even insane! They have committed horrible, ghastly crimes, but these stupid men say, oh, that murderer can go to Newgate, but this murderer only murders because he is mad. To the hospital with him! Perhaps he wants a nice chop for his tea!"

Again, Lily had to drag the question out of herself. "Why does he do it?"

"Arrogance," Miss Gennett said without a moment's hesitation. "Pure arrogance. He thinks he is the only doctor in the world who knows what is best for them. He wants his own way. He was always like that as a child. Wasn't this terrible and wasn't it ever so important to do something about it right away, and always dripping with false modesty as if he didn't mind the trouble or notice how people fawned over him. Worse, if you challenge him he'll say that he supposes that 'everyone undertakes good works mainly for the love of praise, but if a mouth is filled or a wound healed because of it, what is the harm in vanity?'" Miss Gennett gave a disconcerting imitation of her half brother's earnest tones. The mimicry would have done St. Aubin proud. "Have you ever heard anything so conceited in your life? No one even tried to dissuade him except my stepfather, and that only because practical medicine isn't really suitable for a family of our standing, not if one's patients are common."

Lily despaired then at the idea of squeezing another bitter drop from this sour woman, all soft and frosted with money until you reached her mean little core, which no money could reach. It was hardly Miss Gennett's fault that she was this way, as there was little in the world more calculated to ruin one's character than wealth just out of one's reach. And after this there were Miss Gennett's friends, and all their brothers and husbands, either glossy and cruel with their taproots sunk deep into the wellspring of wealth and control and privilege, or parched and furious because they could only enjoy the shade of their fellows; their roots didn't reach. And here, Lily saw, was she, about to creep into that comfortable shade. (Only for a short while, only until the bills were beaten back, but isn't that what everyone said?) Did she think that she alone could linger without succumbing to greed for permanence?

"It must have been difficult for you, this breach between your brother and your stepfather."

Ernestine gave her an uncomfortably penetrating glance. "I didn't think you'd be so interested in him."

Lily felt blood about to rush to her cheeks. Her ability to suppress blushes was much remarked upon; her mother had taught her the trick. It was a matter of outnumbering the perturbing element with other thoughts. Debt was good. A moment's reflection on how much she owed and how little time she had to repay it . . . and her face was as cool and smooth as a corpse's. She would consider later, in private, why she had flushed in the first place.

"I think that your brother is significant to this situation. Even the nexus of the predicament."

A spasm passed over Miss Gennett's face, somehow both venomous and openly, childishly vulnerable. A mention of her brother purged all other suspicions. "He is. He is the source of everything, every problem and obstacle. You *understand*—"

"So sorry!" Emily Featherstone twittered in, scattering fluffy clouds of apology. Mr. Eldard stalked grimly in her wake.

"I am so very sorry, my dear Ernestine, but the streets here can be so confusing what with the shops all changing so over a single season, and the man driving my cab was utterly, utterly hopeless. I ran as fast as I could, as I'm sure you can see from my poor complexion! Not that it wasn't an excellent idea of yours to arrive separately. To allay suspicion," Emily said to Lily in a stage whisper. "And we couldn't both take the carriage, now could we?"

Mr. Eldard's prickly discontent was so strong it had its own sound. These inconvenient women showed no sign of admiring his clever way with a cameo, or falling irresistibly in love with his one-of-a-kind jade fauns (the reticence of imitators not having put him off the wisdom of these in the slightest), which were backlogged to an embarrassing degree. Lily shut the door on him.

"I'm sure you've been having the most interesting conversation without me to ask silly questions. Ernestine is so very well informed on all matters spiritual, don't you agree, Miss E.?" Emily dabbed her chin this way and that as she addressed one, then the other, then both, deferring to each in turn. "And, well, one couldn't be much more of an expert than you, Miss E! How well you must be getting on!"

Ernestine, bored, had begun rooting through her handbag. Emily, still chattering, slipped silently to Lily's side and pressed a bit of paper into her hand. It was folded and refolded into a prickly star an inch across.

"We shan't trespass upon your hospitality any longer," Ernestine said, snapping her sequined bag shut. "I do hope——" Ernestine's face went through a series of pained contortions. If she could have put on one expression for Lily and another for her aunt, Lily was sure that she would have. "I do hope that my words have not been heard entirely without sympathy. I intend to muster another meeting of spiritual enthusiasts, this time without the danger of such rude and quite unforgivable interruption."

"We could so easily change the time to suit you, Miss E!" said Emily. "We have no engagements that cannot be altered!"

Lily supposed not. She understood that unmarried daughters of privilege had very little to occupy their time but philanthropy. With Dr. Gennett commanding that stage for himself, Lily couldn't think of what Miss Gennett had to do.

"May I be so bold as to send you notice of this gathering?" Ernestine's face stiffened further even as her voice found a less strangled note. "I should very, very much like to."

Lily swallowed. This was the opportunity. Who was she to be willful? If it was not meant to be, they would refuse. "Actually, I have an upcoming meeting of my own that might interest you. . . ."

Ernestine accepted before Lily could give the particulars. "We won't tell him, of course, not yet." She gave a tiny sphinx smile. "It's just the sort of thing he hates."

Only when they were unmistakably gone—Ernestine in her carriage, Emily in a cab summoned with extreme reluctance by Mr. Eldard—did Lily unfold the note. It was, for Emily Featherstone, a miracle of brevity. *Please keep sending letters to me only, as the servants are watching Ernestine's post. I have another meeting to arrange for you, one that you might find very interesting. Might you be available Thursday after next at about three o'clock? Send a pink envelope for yes, or a cream envelope for no.* (Why Lily could not just say yes or no in a letter was a mystery.) *How exciting this is! I will manage everything! Our very warmest regards, Emily.*

Which only went to show that there was no fighting fate. The Gennetts were unavoidable, they were foreordained. She couldn't keep away from them even if she were to try, and she wouldn't. Fate did not suffer itself to be fought.

27

TUESDAY, NOVEMBER 10,
THE KENSINGTON STAFF ROOMS

ROYAL LONDON
OPTHALMIC HOSPITAL
Moorfields, E.C.
Supported by voluntary contributions,
which are much needed.
Income 1895 decreased
Patients largely increased.
Committee had to borrow £4,000.
Contributions thankfully received by the
bankers
Msrs. Williams, Deacon and Co.,
20 Birchin Lane, E.C.
and at the Hospital.
ROBERT J. NEWSTEAD, SECRETARY

—Advertisement, *The Times,*
November 10, 1896

So I said to her, 'Madam, that's no abscess!'" The governor laughed, adding a polite round of applause with his vast, soft hands. "Ah. Hmm. Best thing I've heard all day." The junior doctors and administrators around him held their smiles stiffly. Fortunes were not made by excessive pride.

"Gennett!" the governor called over his snug hedge of syco-phants. "Do come and join us on time for once. Give us a chance, man. We might even say something that interests you." He settled down to the meeting table with his usual hearty grin. The hedge chuckled as one.

Gennett snapped shut his casebook and stuffed Aunt Emily's let-ter back into his waistcoat pocket.

"Now, Ambrose," murmured Booth, setting tentative fingers on Gennett's elbow. "Not worth a fight, now is it?"

Booth was right, of course. The Kensington was the most sol-vent of the three hospitals to which he belonged. Gennett swatted away his friend's hand.

The roll droned on—the opening statements of admissions, dis-charges, deaths in halls, the monthly shortfall. The juniors, those newly arrived and those growing stale for promotion, were straight and attentive as a hall of mirrors. Gennett could measure the crawl of seconds by the slow drip of acid in his gut, in time with the throb-bing of his head. Time was what he didn't have. The sheer volume of material to be assimilated kept him at his desk until the small hours. There was no shortcut, not if he meant to understand her—to grasp the roots of the problem, rather, and recover both his fam-ily and his peace of mind. But the nature of the reading gave him mental indigestion. Sleep evaded him at night, then lay in wait at importune times of day: at meetings, between soup and the first course at a restaurant. Concentration was as elusive as repose. And he accomplished nothing as the days passed.

Emily's latest note sat in his pocket. Emily's other coy, leading notes lay in a pile back at his flat, beneath the *Alienism Monthly* and a crumb-strewn plate, producing nothing, as his letters to his sister doubtless lay piled on the tray in the front hall at Eaton Place. He pawed through every post the moment the doorman brought it up.

He must have imagined Aunt Emily's pleasure at their secretive jaunt for tea, because he fired off fresh invitations like a lovesick swain and she batted aside every one. What he got instead was cryptic little notes on slips of cheapish stationery. *Progress!* Or, *I can say no more now—it is not the right time, but I have hopes. Focus your energies!* These stank of lily of the valley. He despised them. He despised himself, in the bad moments, for having poured his hopes into such a tremulous vessel. Yet when they arrived (never by messenger; despite the money he sent she was addicted to the penny post) he still tore them open.

This one in his pocket—but no, he would not allow himself to think it might be different. One might ask, Why would she ask if he were at leisure at three next Thursday unless she had some concrete plan? But one could ask and analyze and puzzle until one was weak with fury. He had. He pressed his hand to his chest. Through the wool and the tight silk weave beneath, soft as goose liver, not even a rustle. He wished it had a point or two.

"Gentlemen," the governor was saying, cutting through the fog of murmuring that followed the quarterly report, "I hope that I do not have to underscore the seriousness of these results. Did I apprehend your meaning correctly, Mr. Secretary, when you said *half* the income from donors as was enjoyed at this time last year?"

The secretary, who had missed a calling when he chose medicine over the mortuary service, shook his head with stage sorrow. "Half indeed. I know not what can be done to make up the shortfall."

"Whose responsibility is that?" asked a dyspeptic individual Gennett knew to be in some government post. Like the other lay members of the board, he appeared only once a quarter for meetings, and was blissfully innocent of the interdepartmental politics he trampled. "We came through three depressions intact, and now we can't keep the wards open?"

"No one gives in quite the same way in good times," the governor said soothingly. "It's a remarkable fact of the world of philanthropy."

"What do you propose then? Less light? Less heat? Less staff?"

"Less patients," snapped the secretary.

"Fewer patients," smiled the governor. Polite laughter went around again. Now both the lay members and the secretary were souring. Gennett didn't blame them, except for getting themselves between the governor and an attempted witticism, which was their own fault. Gennett himself was not exceptionally concerned. He had never known a hospital, save those that specialized in discretion for the well-to-do, that wasn't running at a loss. They always dug themselves out one way or another, usually by cutting the maintenance budget. Why the secretary and the governor were putting on this absurd double act was a mystery.

"What is to be done, then?"

"The donors will be good for it, I'm sure. Trade's got to fall off eventually. Hodge, whatever happened to that widow you were cultivating last quarter? I thought you said she was good for a new wing."

"Died."

"Damn. Well, regardless, we'll need to tighten things up until the regulars come through. What about patients in arrears?"

Booth shifted in his seat. "Do the physicians truly need to be involved in this? I feel I'm surrounded by dry goods salesmen." He spoke just loudly enough to elicit a sympathetic response from the nearby consultants, but not loudly enough to be overheard by the governor.

"Forget the accounts in arrears," barked a mustachioed senior consultant. "What are we going to do about these admissions on credit? Put a stop to it there. We never should have taken these charity cases in the first place, but we can't very well put them out on the curb like old pets."

"Indeed," sighed the secretary, "such an option would be a welcome luxury, but we are in no position to overlook savings, however small. I have taken the liberty of drawing up a short list of a few of the, shall we say, charity admissions that are at present a conspicuous drain on our books."

The handwritten list passed quickly around the table. Booth colored at the sight of it and passed it down quickly, scooting it around at the edge of Gennett's reach. Gennett knew when he was being avoided and snatched it.

"Mr. Secretary, none of these cases are in any position to be put out—"

"Dr. Gennett," the governor interrupted, "are these *all* your own cases?"

"They aren't the only charities in the hospital," muttered Booth, but again, in an undertone. He was ignored.

"At such a sensitive stage, I cannot condone—"

"Ah, but it is always a sensitive stage, is it not? I must say that I am unsure that one doctor should be assuming such a burden when it is not only he who will be bearing it," the governor said. The mustachioed senior nodded vigorously.

"Some of these cases are of the highest scientific interest," said Gennett, trying a different tack.

"Of interest to what? 'Dynamic psychiatry'?" The senior's emphasis was scathing. "Have you seen, by any chance, the most recent *Journal of Mental Science*? I suspect that a more skeptical approach is required towards these 'talking cures.'"

"None of these patients are receiving exclusively experimental treatments. But as I have argued, as not one is responding to traditional methods, what harm is there in making the attempt? In Paris—"

"Setbacks in Paris are precisely the reason for our reservations! And perhaps this discussion would be something other than academic if the funds were available."

"If this hospital and its staff are to win plaudits in the field, we must move beyond routine ailments, even if the sufferers do pay on time."

"Please, there is no need to be vulgar."

"We are talking of money. I think it's bound to be vulgar," said Gennett. Booth laid a restraining hand on his elbow.

"I don't see," the secretary interrupted, his voice rising to a squeak, "any alternative to discharging these patients unless some other avenue can be found to fund their care here or from some other source." His sentences ran together like an amateur stage performer's, tripping over himself to get to the end of the script.

"Dr. Gennett, I do believe that you have had some success in drawing in extra funds for other hospitals. St. Botolph's, is it?" A murmur ran around the table as those who had not heard of the place were enlightened by their neighbors, and those who had confirmed to one another that they had heard correctly. Sharp looks, puzzled and slightly offended, told Gennett that this revelation had not raised his stock.

"St. Botolph's is a very different institution serving a very different class of society," Gennett said. "It is struggling for the most basic resources: pay for the staff, food. Most of its patients are drawn from the surrounding area and would go without treatment if asked to pay the kind of fees demanded elsewhere."

"If an individual can prop up a ruin on the brink of collapse," said the governor, "surely he can find a bit to keep a functioning institution, a healthy institution, doing its good work?"

"St. Botolph's backers are sympathetic to it precisely because of its liabilities."

The secretary looked ready to spit, but the governor raised his hand to forestall further comment. "What a generous perspective. I hope for the sake of these patients here," he said mildly, tapping the list, "that these backers' munificence will stretch to them, too. Well, new business."

The secretary resettled his half-moon glasses on the end of his nose and they continued, to all appearances quite unperturbed. After the new business was concluded they adjourned with no further discussion of the budget. The governor dismissed his admiring junior staff and invited the seniors to shoehorn themselves into his office en masse for a quick tot of brandy. The informality was meant to foster fellow feeling. Even in the close press of bodies between the massive desk and oak bookcases festooned with pickled anatomical curiosities Gennett had space to himself. Booth, after paying his respects to the governor and the most influential board members, eased his way through the crowd to Gennett's side.

"What precisely was that? Dear boy."

"They would have gotten their way in the end, whatever I said."

"Well, they'll certainly get it now. Hodge, old man!" Booth cried out to a passing specialist. "What very good luck you've had with that new show jumper of yours. Best wishes and all that." To Gennett again he hissed, "If you yield just like that, what's to stop them next time? And what was that rot about one man propping up St. Botolph's?"

"It's been an unusually bad year. A few board members have left and they've taken their financial support with them. It's given me more of a free hand with policy, but . . . at any rate, it's temporary. I'll pull the money back out again when the time is right."

"I cannot, I simply cannot believe what I am hearing. What do you need a free hand for? You used to have this board wrapped around your finger! No one challenged you out in the open."

"They rejected eighty percent of my proposals."

"Only because you propose any mad thing that comes into your head while others are more judicious. That's just your technique. But they never—you went down fighting, invariably. You never admitted that your stupid idea was a mistake and that they were right to subdue you. No one has missed that. They attack at the slightest sign of weakness; they learn it from the patients. Look at your suit, for heaven's sake. Did you sleep under Blackfriars Bridge? Everyone is talking of you, dear boy. Everyone has noted the change."

Booth's was not a fearsome gaze such as the greats employed to subjugate patients—his usual tactic was to allow himself to be underestimated, then lure subjects into confessions—but Gennett froze as if pinned by Charcot himself. If the turmoil were not concealed as he had thought . . . what else had he revealed to the world? To her?

Booth waited, face darkening. "You have nothing to say to that, do you? Answer me this, how long do you suppose the governor has known about your, shall we say, additional involvement with that East End hospital? Yet he brings it up now. And it's not as though this place is in the midst of a crisis. They always bring out lists of patients who died and patients who complained and patients who didn't pay, but the seniors simply flog one another with them and that's that. No one is expected to do anything about it. But now they try and press you to personally support the hospital and you let them!"

"You sound as if you wish for an apology."

"I would think that you would wish for an apology from yourself—oh, listen to me. You are infuriating, that's why an apology would not be in order. I am your friend, whether or not you have treated me as such, and a man cannot run himself into the gutter and expect his friends to stand by. It affects one. It affects one deeply."

Gennett blinked, faintly amazed. "Now I'm suffering auditory hallucinations. Do you really want me to say that I'm sorry to you?"

"Forget that I said anything. I would settle for an explanation."

"I have," Gennett squeezed out. "I say this to you only out of friendship. I would not feel obligated otherwise." He would have paced a moment to gather his thoughts had they not been hemmed in with bodies and pungent leather books. Perhaps he would raise his voice—*Hark! We haven't scratched the surface of the mind; the pygmies who live about us in darkness regard us with contempt!*—and see what reaction he got from this mob of learned men. It should bother him severely that they turned their black wool backs to him. He could make it bother him as it ought, he reckoned, if he could stop seeing them as a great chattering bank of coveys, bowing to each other and then bowing again, and again, and again.

Even as he opened his mouth to speak he felt his brow furrow sorrowfully, and his hands clutch each other with anguish, and his entire frame bend with the sort of meaningfulness as would be visible from the back of the theater. "I have, of late, been suffering under a great weight. I am unsure of what I can hope to do to shift it, in truth." Worse and worse. Men did not speak to each other of these things outside of plays, or in plays spoke of them so often that, off the stage, they came out in maudlin bellows. "I think at times that I may not be able to continue."

"Come off it. You're not the first man in the world to have woman problems."

"Woman problems?"

"I thought," Booth said stiffly, "that it might be woman problems. Forgive me."

"This is my sister. This is my mother. You called on them yourself a short while ago. Did they seem normal to you?" Gennett sucked air in and out through his nose. Manly control was very little in evidence; he sounded to his own ears like either a child warming up for a tantrum or an elderly pug. Booth sipped his drink, icily distant. It was the most transparent of techniques—one they were primed for in the earliest days of practice, one that Gennett used every day—but Gennett could not resist, or at least didn't. "My mother is distracted. She thinks she has lost things, that someone has moved them. She speaks of the long dead as though they might walk through the door at any moment. And the reason? I can think of one. Like my sister, she has fallen under, fallen under the influence of, of a charlatan."

Booth looked gratifyingly startled. "Not a religious crank?"

"No, a speaking-to-the-dead sort, a medium."

Booth gave an explosive snort of which Platt would have been proud. A few heads turned to them curiously. Gennett didn't blame them; in the twenty years and more of their acquaintance he had never heard Booth release such a coarse sound.

"I beg your pardon, should I be inviting this miserable bloodsucking wretch in for coffee, such that she may prey upon my sister's ignorance more effectively?"

"A medium! You had me frightened to death. I thought it was something serious. A medium! Those ridiculous little humbugs have been fiddling about with their nonsense for years, since before we were born, and nothing's ever come of it. It's more silly than anything. They do pinch their bit of money here and there I believe, but as long as they don't get their hands on an heiress it's just the pin money going. A woman might as well spend her sou on entertainment as on whatever other folly strikes her fancy. Now a religious sort, that would be worrying."

Gennett was speechless for close to a half minute. "This is—you have no idea what I'm dealing with! This is not a crank with a crystal ball! They dig through rubbish for clues. I've read all about it. 'Mediums' stealing the fishmonger's bill and parading their extraordinary knowledge of how many kippers one prefers with one's breakfast."

"Ah, this is all new to you, isn't it? I must say, I had your sister down for a modern type—not this tiresome business with suffrage and marches and nasty little neckties, you understand. A sensible one not much for ghost stories is all I meant. Now, your mother— but my point is, I do understand how this must alarm you. I share a roof with my own dear mother and allow me to assure you, as a veteran of 'Oh, it was an unmistakable presence!'" Booth squeaked, rather cruelly, "that this needn't bother you any more than a foolish purchase from the dressmakers. Unbecoming, but not dangerous."

"Men of science have driven themselves mad over these harmless little mediums!"

"Are we talking about men of science?"

"A mind deranged by grief—"

"Ah, you are quite right; I concede that mediums—or is it media?—are not to be trusted around the recently bereaved. But your father—pardon the intrusion, old man, but he passed away ten years ago, didn't he?"

"Thirteen."

"Excellent. Well, you know what I mean. You have nothing to worry about. Why the sudden antipathy? Letters to the editor and now this? You never used to consider these spirit types more than a silly nuisance."

Gennett set his untouched glass on the shelf beside him. Daylight shone through the brandy and poured gold over a volume on leprosy. "This is an expert. This is a very shrewd, very untrustworthy confidence artist who is targeting . . . my family. Never mind why. If I am to dislodge this"—he was stayed by a sudden impulse for caution—"Miss E—"

"Miss E? Miss Lily E?"

Gennett was dumbstruck.

"My mother was asking about her. She's the latest thing. Quite the celebrity in certain circles; Mother wanted to know what it might cost to get her to the house. Rather more than pin money, I'm afraid. Only goes in for downright aristocrats." Booth narrowed his eyes thoughtfully and seemed to be scrutinizing Gennett's cuff links. "Unless it is your sister's personal estate at risk. I mean, it would be beyond crass to inquire, but I would imagine that she is well provided for?"

"This has very little to do with money. I'd offer her anything simply to stay away."

"I was unaware that fortunes could be spared so easily."

He hadn't meant to be drawn into this conversation. It was difficult to imagine a less appropriate setting and the words—when spoken, they clove together in strange patterns; their real import was obscured by extra shades and suggestions he had never meant.

"I've failed my sister. I can admit that now. This predator never would have been able to come close had I paid more attention to her mental development. Banning the séances now will only sharpen Ernestine's appetite for them, and drive her further from my protection. No, I must prove the folly of her course, demonstrate it beyond doubt. The manipulation must be"—Gennett's breath was coming fast through his nostrils again—"exposed."

Booth patted his back, as one might a restive dog.

"But thank God, no woman trouble just now," Gennett laughed mirthlessly. "If that sort of fuss turns up I don't know what I'll do."

Booth drained his glass and set it hastily on the bookshelf. "You might want to check the club register." He was swallowed up by the crowd before Gennett could question him.

"Please, not another word about Freud," a voice was saying somewhere in the throng of frock coats. "You remember the imbroglio last February about a hysteric, the Emma Eckstein case? Well, Freud let that fool Fliess at her, the one who keeps banging on about the link between the nose and the female sexual organs. 'Antimasturbatory nasal surgery,' they said. If masturbation was in fact the cause of the neurosis, I can't say it didn't help, but—"

"After surgery I doubt she was quite in the mood!"

"Well, the idiot left a meter of gauze stuffed in her nasal cavity. Nearly bled to death when they finally took it out."

Booth was somewhere in that knot, Gennett could hear him. "Freud has posited that the girl had fallen in love with her doctor—more common than you'd think, apparently—and was so crazed for attention that she willed the hemorrhage on herself," Booth said. When the group remained silent he added nervously, "although Gennett and I, on balance, are of the opinion that it was probably the gauze."

"I do say," one of the seniors mused. "He has the most extraordinary insights. Can you imagine, can you even imagine now not knowing about sublimated passions? About delayed response to childhood trauma? I think he's one of the most progressive theoreticians working today. And yet it's all mixed in with such rubbish. Freud, I mean."

"Oh, Freud," the man next to him said. "I thought you were talking about Gennett."

10th November, 1896

Dear Dr. Booth,

I do not expect that you will recall me: we met briefly at the conference on October the 2nd of this year. I spoke to you about my researches into the psychosomatic suppression of the gag reflex. By chance I spoke as well to your colleague Dr. Gennett—I met him as we were checking our coats where he generously offered to review my paper—and this is in fact the matter about which I wish to consult yourself. Is it, in your opinion, true what is said about a recent shift in Dr. Gennett's research interests? I do not pretend to be on terms of intimacy with the editors of the Asylum Journal, *but a paper just submitted (I believe that you had your own name removed as coauthor?) has generated talk, talk that has reached even my ears. I am no authority on this Austrian school of psycho-analysis and I confess that, after what I have heard, as a churchgoing man*

I cannot in conscience penetrate further. (If Dr. Gennett is, as they say, looking to challenge the whole of the medical establishment I question how the support of a lesser-known researcher such as myself could be of use to him anyway.) May I solicit your assistance in securing Dr. Gennett's agreement to leave my paper alone? With the greatest tact and respect and, it hardly needs to be said, discretion. You are noted for your discretion, Sir, if I may be so bold to say, and for your sensitivity to matters of reputation.

I anticipate a favourable response.

Your humble servant,
M. Jones

28

St. James's

Out." He stifled laughter but it oozed out the seams of his composure, like steam. "I am disappointed to find Mrs. Stone once again out." It was just on the fringe of propriety to call on a married woman; on a woman in a limbo of half widowhood, inadvisable. He had always warned her against it. "I have called these past two afternoons without luck."

"Yes, Sir. I remember." The parlor maid's hand curled white around the door frame.

"You do?" The girl was holding his eyes with a desperate intensity. He looked over her shoulder and made a deliberate study of the hall, finding nothing but Henrietta's neo-Greek columns and bronzes (such a coup to get Alma-Tadema for the décor, such a splash when the house was revealed, some ten years past). The maid's eyes were pleading when he met them again. It was unthinkable that Henrietta had made a downstairs servant her confederate, less unthinkable that the girl might have guessed. "Perhaps you do. She has been to my cl— to Simpson's, a gentleman's club, yes? This is inadvisable. You will convey that message to your mistress when she returns? She is dining with friends, I assume."

"I believe so, yes, I'm sure that's it, Sir. I don't recall which friends, Sir."

Gennett walked down the drive and took the long way around the side of the house. Outside the coach house the groom's boy was coiling up a four-horse harness after oiling. It was just past dusk. "Boy," Gennett called. "This is the Stones' carriage, is it not? A very fine one. But rather a lot of work." The boy stopped his wrapping and watched warily. "A well-paid errand might not go amiss?"

He gave the boy an envelope addressed to St. George's Terrace. "A penny for the stamp and two shillings for the labor. You should know when your mistress goes to Kensington for shopping and mysteriously returns without purchases. Simply post this on one of those days. If the, ah, message proves useful you shall have half a crown. Can you write?"

"As well as any, Sir!" the boy said, offended.

"I see. Put this in the envelope, then." He took one of his own cards and marked it on the back with the first letter that came to him, an *R*. "I'll know it." He pondered on the long walk back to the Kensington what could be the sinister hidden significance of *R*. These things were never coincidence.

GENNETT MADE it back to the hospital in time. He lingered in a dispensary as his watch ticked down the minutes and seconds to the end of the working day. At five o'clock on the dot (as he would, that was the limit of his dedication) Platt sauntered from Miss MacAndrew's room still calling instructions over his shoulder to the matron scurrying behind. "Surgical candidate, I think, but we'll see if bed rest halts the spread of the somatic abnormality. Four weeks minimum of strict Weir Mitchell treatment: isolation, massage, fattening up on milk puddings. And get those books out of her room. No stimulation, no family contact, bland and lukewarm foods only. Transfer to a sanitorium tomorrow. My assistant will give you two or three names for the family to select from. For God's sake don't give them too much choice. It confuses them." Gennett ducked behind a cabinet of premeasured purges until they passed. It had to be now. He would be seen if he tried to visit her in the long-term ward. He had to steady himself on the cabinet to rise. His own patient and he had to worry about being seen. They hadn't thought to confiscate his set of master keys, though. He bolted the door behind him and draped his handkerchief over the spyhole.

Miss MacAndrew lay like a corpse in starched shrouds. She was a handsome, sturdy girl, or had been. Now freckles stood out like splodges of paint on her waxy green skin. The foamy garland of gauze circling her throat peeped from above the sheet pulled to her chin. And beneath the sheet, if Gennett were to look, there would be a restraining coat pinning her arms to her sides, to prevent her making a noose of her stockings or a stiletto of her corset stays. If Gennett were to look. Another man might. She had been a handsome girl.

He had been satisfied for a time with muscles and nerves, cutting away disease. He took as much satisfaction as the next doctor in an aggressive cancer successfully removed, a live patient on the table and a scale groaning beneath the weight of a record-breaking tumor. But how much more satisfying—sublime, even—to hear the first words of a patient freed from catatonia?

There were no worlds left to conquer in conventional medicine. It was nearly the twentieth century and Gennett's set found no mystery in the body. Disease was half tamed and surgery scaled to the height of mythology. But the mental hospitals—those were busier than ever, choked with lost causes. Asylums filled as quickly as they were opened. Neurosis and neurasthenia, dementias praecox and otherwise, rose in a roaring wave as if the words to classify them as mad made them so. There were theories as to why. Degeneration, some said; disease and unclean living tainting the bloodstock of England, hauling the dregs of the populace down through dipsomania to criminality to imbecility, sexual excess draining their humanity out their ears along the way. It was argued that medicine should accept its limitations, sterilize the unfit, and lock up the sufferers until their sufferings have ended.

How much more noble to free the mad from their chains like Pinel, not only the chains of the madhouse but the chains on their souls? The tools of the new psychotherapy were in their hands. If they had the will and the vision, the word *asylum* would wither to an anachronism for scholars to puzzle over. Students at the turn of the next century would read old books and wonder what this *madness* could have been, rising as Gennett had risen from the blood and stench of surgery to the pure frontiers of the mind, to scour away the necrotic and perverse, leaving cleanliness in his wake.

If the mind could be clean. If the mind were not, as Gennett had been reading, by its nature primitive and crude, with conflicts and repulsive notions riddled through like knots in wood. Who could prove it wasn't? He couldn't believe anymore that one could know one's own mind, or be sure that an absence of symptoms meant an absence of sickness. And what was sickness, if every mind was steeped in filth? Illness would be to notice the filth. Health would be to stand in the cesspit and ignore the stench. The pursuit of wellness would be a quest not for truth, but for comfortable ignorance, and the prize a daily routine.

I didn't muddy my hands in trade so my son could muck about up to his elbows in corpses, his father had said more than once. He had said it on that last day, as a coda to the usual shouting match at breakfast that left Mother in tears and Ernestine smirking (her debutantehood was already stale and this did not improve her temper) and himself thundering upstairs to read his books and sulk. *Come down when you're ready to go to Cambridge!* Everything about that morning had been routine until the cry. *Ruth, my dear. Oh. I am sorry.* Then the screeching, and the doctors, and the death.

He would have overcome his father's reservations in time, he had always been sure. Medicine was not degradation but the opposite; doctors existed to elevate the human race. To be drawn to mental health, surely, meant that one was mentally healthy? Not that one had doubts?

Freud analyzed *himself.* He did it, he said, because the only mind he could fully penetrate was his own. To accept Freud's other theories—and Gennett couldn't shake them off if he tried—meant to accept that the healthy mind was not fundamentally different from the diseased. The boundaries between doctor and patient were as blurred as those between sanity and insanity. It had all been so clean until he looked too closely.

Miss MacAndrew could have been his Anna O. She could have been his star, a testament to optimism like Charcot's proletarian maenads at the Salpêtrière in Paris, raving or quieting on the great man's command.

Was there anything he could do to help her? If he were not there to heal, then he would not be a doctor. He would be a man, sitting alone in a small, locked room with a handsome girl, debating with himself over whether to lift the sheet.

November 16th

My dear M. St Aubin,

How goes our little flower in the world? I confess that without your thoughtful little notes to me (please do keep sending them with bouquets, a green thing makes the sickroom less spirit-killing) I would be worried about my darling girl. She tells me half-truths and outright lies, just like you, but between what you fabricate and she omits I get a fair idea of what transpires. Let that keep you honest. But in seriousness. I did not like the sound of Friday's session. Our Lily disconcerted by three silly women and a lapdog? If she wanted to cancel on every recently bereaved mother you will have no clients. You must be more careful of her and her nerves. She is wilful in the worst possible way, in that she thinks that she is not wilful (I hear your eyebrows rising, Monsieur, but hear me out) but rather a humble servant of fate. It does not occur to her that she sees only what confirms her chosen course, just as her clients do. Physician, heal thyself, I believe the saying goes. But what I must impress upon you is that she believes. Do not underestimate what she will do to prove her idea of the world correct, all the while thinking that she glides along like a leaf in a stream.

Keep watch on her. I do trust you, because you are not a bad man, I think, only a greedy one, and I see nothing wrong with trusting a greedy man when there is profit enough for everyone.

Mind that you do not become too greedy for anything you cannot have. Your proposition was not attractive ten years ago and it is not attractive now. (I never told her, you know. She has very little sense of humour where some things are concerned.)

Be clever and make us all rich. I did enjoy the dahlias.

Humbly yours,
Carola E.

29

WEDNESDAY, NOVEMBER 18

Timetables

> "There are a great many uneducated medi-
> ums, who sit in developing circles, and when
> they get a little spirit power they aspire for
> platform fame, and very often their qualities
> for public speaking are at a very low ebb; one
> part of the four is a little Spiritualism and
> three parts empty conceit and twaddle."
>
> —Letter from Mr. Benjamin Myers to
> *The Two Worlds,* November 1896

I sn't it exciting!" Emily whispered. "And Ernestine will be delighted, I tell you, utterly, utterly delighted. She's only been to one house party, and that was for the wedding of one of Ruth's cousins and that was years ago. Not that her own friends aren't very, very top drawer, you understand. Ernestine's father, my own dear brother, was a very well respected gentleman, if not perhaps as influential as Herbert Gennett, at least in the financial sense. Her friends simply . . . tend to be of the more independent type of young woman. Fewer domestic responsibilities."

"This is what you came to tell me?" asked Lily. "That you would be able to attend?"

"Yes!" Emily beamed.

"Emily, all your message said was to come at once. I had thought there was some kind of emergency. I broke an engagement to come here." Lily waved an arm to take in the sooty railway cars, the sooty commuters, and the rickety tea stand from which they each held a grayish cup. "Why a railway station café to tell me yes?"

"If the plan fails, it won't be due to my lack of vigilance." From someone else that would have sounded like an accusation. "How can one do too much for family?"

"We do need to be discreet, I agree. But this, and writing in the margins in lemon juice—"

"Marvelous, isn't it! You just hold the paper to a candle flame and—"

"And the entire thing reeks of rancid lemons. The postman commented on it. This is not discreet. This is . . . theatrical—" It was too late to bite it back. What a stupid, stupid word to use in front of a client.

Emily was not cowed. She gave the table an experimental thump; a shaky effort that lacked speed and did no more than rattle the sugar bowl. "My dear Miss Lily, there cannot be too much secrecy!" The tea vendor was looking over his newspaper at them. "Do you forget the words of the great Ravonsky? *The mirror of truth is best obscured from weak eyes; draw a veil over power lest it tempt the unknowing.* Oh," she said, seeing Lily's blank incomprehension, "did I have the quote wrong?"

"The great who?"

"Did you not—oh, fancy my having anything to tell you! I suspect that you're teasing me. But he is on what you might call the very forefront of spiritual exploration on the Continent, I'm told. The most fascinating man, such a marvelous lecture. I'll find a way to send the pamphlet to you safely. I must dash now. Before I am missed!"

At least she paid for the tea. Lily's return ticket cost a shilling and sixpence.

⇥ ⇥

CAROLA WAS lying on her back, her head twisted to face the darkened window. The pose looked thoroughly uncomfortable. Lily eased herself around the door frame, regretting the internal scrape of fabric and bustle that made women creak like fully laden wagons.

"Mama? I'm very late." She willed her mother not to ask how the strict visiting hours had been bent. Expensively, was the answer.

"My dear." The wheeze seemed to come from the window, not the bed. Carola did know how to throw her voice. Lily had a sudden, fanciful vision of one's gifts slipping out to run about free, exercising themselves like poltergeists, at the end of life.

"My dear," Carola said more firmly. "You have missed all the excitement, I'm afraid: two nurses, two students, one entire doctor, and he with a beard down to his belt. And what did they tell me? So I said to them, I'll find out. Tell me or I'll find out."

Guilt was not sharp, Lily realized, but spongy, smothering. "It was entirely my fault that I'm late. I'm very sorry."

"Write it down, I said, I'll sign it! A contract! They said they would observe and see how it progresses. It. What is It?"

Lily thought this grousing at first. It was as unlike her mother to rub the wound with salt as it was for her to be late; she resented it. "Mama, I can't be putting off clients, not now. And I can't tell the trains to be on time."

"Well, It is doing just fine in this hospital bed, I can tell you. I don't think It is disaccommodated in the least."

Carola's face was still turned to the window, twisted on her neck as if the starched hospital sheets were nailed to the mattress, pinning her body. She knew she was dying. Lily watched her mother's face in a series of moments. She had to look away after a glance, as if staring into the sun, and what she saw left a burning afterimage like the sun, too.

Lily was suddenly, blazingly furious that this was taking place under hospital lights. Carola was skewered by the light, every burst capillary in her cheeks thrust forward for inspection. Carola hated electric light. If Lily had her way, every lightbulb in London would be carried out to the street and smashed beneath boots, and sick women would look out into eternity in the dignity of darkness.

And then Lily saw her mother slowly return. How she came back to the present, how anyone could from the imminence of death was beyond Lily's understanding, but Carola did. Her thick neck might have creaked, it moved so slowly, but she turned to Lily. A hollow false light remained and it was all Lily could do to meet her mother's eyes.

"Tell me all your plans for the great meeting, the house party. Everything you plan to undertake with Monsieur. It is your future, after all."

SHE TOLD the cab to drop her at the corner but Mr. Eldard noticed. He stood in the doorway as she arrived, heedless of who might see him lingering like a grocer on a slow afternoon, and remained there pointedly, examining the trimmings of her new frock. "How dreadful for you to be so badly detained. I expected you at three o'clock."

"Mama is no better. I'm very sorry."

"Ah, yes. Mama. Even the most heroic of women will become demanding while ill. Though I must commend your mother, she always was admirably level-headed when it came to money and the making of it. It must be a frightful expense for you, all of these doctors and such."

"A very great burden. May I?"

"Oh, of course, do sit. You must be exhausted. Your three o'clock never showed, by the way. So regrettable under the circumstances."

"I asked her to come another time. I'll catch her later this week."

"Really? Your regular three o'clock? Well, family tragedy is a terrible thing." Mr. Eldard smoothed his necktie and returned to the back room. Lily took her place behind the displays and counted silently to thirty. Her head fell to her folded arms and she was asleep.

⇌ ⇌

"Is Monsieur St. Aubin in?" The butler led Lily to the library on the same route they always took. They never offered to let her find her own way and she never asked to.

"Lily!" St. Aubin smiled and spread his arms in welcome. The longer she spent in the house the more his adopted English manners came and went, much like his accent. "You can always knock on my door. My sitting room upstairs is so much more private."

"Do you have concerns about the servants?"

"No, it's—never mind. You made a very long day at the shop, my dear. For once I'm glad to be looking at an unbooked evening. Though I doubt my eyes will be willing to close before midnight. I did like mornings. Perhaps I'll see them again someday." He was relaxed, loose-jointed in his brocade Orientalist robe, but not with the damp helplessness of drink. Settling in his usual chair before the fire, he gave the tassel of his silk cap a twirl. "They'll have to do without you for a long weekend, I'm afraid."

"I've cleared the time."

"Don't clear it. Just take it. Don't come every time they call. They rely on you too much, and only for the dullest reasons; they are unable to grasp your unique qualities, so they take you for granted as another lump to watch the counter and play the sick nurse."

"So, only you apprehend my rarity?"

"Have I not introduced you to scores of educated, cultivated persons of consequence who apprehend it with me? The house party will be a triumph!" He forgot her for a moment, drawn back into a luminous vision that sat always at his side with the door open, ready for occupation at a moment's notice. "There will be Cavendishes," he said softly. "There will be Cecils."

"I've asked two more." Her words had the effect of finding the vision's window and lobbing a brick through it.

"You've what?" He shook his head, resurfacing. "Not one of your horoscope punters. Absolutely not."

"New clients, strictly this side of the business. And the right sort. They'll fit in." This last was a hope. She had much to learn about distinguishing varying degrees of wealth.

"Who?"

"A Miss Gennett and a Miss Featherstone. Niece and aunt. And possibly Miss Gennett's mother. They've accepted the invitation."

"Never heard of them. Why didn't—" The reproach hung in the air between them. "At which of our sessions did you pick them up?"

"They're—you haven't met them. But it's a direct referral, and they have a family acquaintance as well. They're not neophytes, I'm certain that there will be no problems."

He looked hard at her. She did her best to soften and absorb the irritation rather than reflecting it back. He was unhappy, yes. What she needed to prevent was his growing suspicion.

"What will you be doing with your free night?"

"I've barely made a start on the books you gave me."

"When you have time, my dear. When you have time. If there were one thing you would be best to master before Thursday, it would be Blavatsky, though that's only to prove you don't agree with her. Skim through a few purple passages and you'll have something to giggle over. Stuart, too. And Home, naturally, and—" She was sure that she hadn't sighed or shifted, but St. Aubin stopped abruptly. "But of course, you needn't. In fact it might be better not. Leave it to me to natter with the self-appointed experts, while you are your splendidly natural self." He stopped toying with his cap and took a closer look at her. "You are weary, my girl. You take on too much."

"I can't drop my old clients. Or the shop."

"They would understand."

"They would not."

"How is your mother?"

It was a very strange feeling when it took her unawares, like the empty drop one's gut made when a carriage fell suddenly into a rut on the road. "She is very much the same. She was most pleased with the dahlias. She would enjoy a visit from you, I think."

"A bit weaker?"

"Perhaps a bit."

"It is not betrayal to give some thought to what you will do, afterward."

They sat for some time. The fire burnt itself out and the light ebbed, but she thought she could see M. St. Aubin more clearly with every dying coal, half lying there in his dressing gown (respectably thrown over a shirt and trousers, not skin, but still a dressing gown) with long-necked cranes soaring abreast its folds in pursuit of embroidered fish, and here and there an embroidered Mandarin, fat cheeked and comical, snatching after the cranes with fingernails as long as his arms. St. Aubin's mustachios were drooping for want of wax. She could imagine, suddenly, how their future might be: the two of them on tour, returning after a tiring night to rub off their greasepaint and share a fire with the informal comradeship of the theater. He would sit as now, heedless of his double chin spilling out over his collar. She might even loosen her corset. It was at times like this, when she felt most at ease with him, that she was most afraid.

30

Thursday, November 26,

Shoreditch

"As I have said, Spiritualism and Socialism have much in common . . . and although they seem to travel along different roads, they have the same end in view—the complete emancipation of humanity, mentally and physically, from the slavery in which it has been bound for so many dark and weary years."

—P. Galloway, *The Two ISMs: Spiritualism and Socialism*, 1896

Quite sure about that address, Gov?"

The cabbie twisted around on the driver's perch to get a good look at him. This was progress, because the last two had simply refused to take him. It was the shabbiest growler in the rank, and as they pulled away Gennett made a mental note to try that one first next time.

In daylight, Lily Embly's neighborhood was nothing to shock a regular visitor to St. Botolph's. The streets were the width of West End alleys; in some cases, West End carriages. The alleys themselves were little more than gaps between buildings, drunkenly crooked, just large enough to squeeze an urchin through. When

Gennett disembarked and paid his driver—"Can't go any farther, Gov"—his shoulders brushed the walls.

Now he was sweating beneath his oldest hat, a good three years behind the fashion and too gauche in pitch for even his man Wilson to accept. They were Wilson's boots on his feet (he had not had time to ask permission but would replace them with boots newer and better). His cane was the product of a secondhand shop, a great chip knocked out of the pale stone handle. He rapped it against the undersized door to the right of the main entrance.

"Looking to rent?"

The man appeared at first to be some kind of dwarf. Then Gennett noted the hump between his shoulders, straining against the confines of a woolen waistcoat so old it might have dated back to the days of health; to Gennett's eye the deformity was acquired, not congenital. A tape measure worn to illegibility hung around the man's stringy neck, which seemed to confirm the diagnosis. The pointed inquiry in the man's eyes told Gennett that an assessment had been made of him, and more quickly.

"Not to rent. I am here about a young lady whom I believe until recently resided upstairs." He had no plan except to improvise with as few specifics as possible.

"What's your business?"

The man might know St. Botolph's, which was hardly calculated to provoke a friendly response. He didn't want the neighbors spreading rumors that the girl was mad. Gennett raised his black doctor's satchel (his own and polished like glass, but that could not be helped at short notice). "I'm rather out of my territory here, I'm afraid, but I've come about a patient—"

"Ah!" The man stepped aside smartly and ushered Gennett inside. Gennett evaded the door frame but cracked his head on the first beam. "Watch the old head there, Doc. You won't blame me for being suspicious, I hope. Plenty of odd fish around here, wanting this, wanting that. Especially where old Carola is concerned. There's been a pack of right toffs coming and going of late, and one been coming back in the day. You'll pardon me, Doc, but for a moment I thought you was him!"

The man led him through a narrow room set up like a workshop, skirting low benches heaped with bits of cloth. These were crossed with chalk like the stuff his tailor used to mark his jackets but looked too small to be complete garments. Small, dark females sat hunched here and there, needles darting in and out like dragonflies, impossibly quick, and at the door an even smaller girl was lugging in a basket of more anonymous pieces. The shopman stopped to give her a few coins. Both of their faces were jaundiced.

"Funny way to get the news, but those two like their surprises." They had come through to a tiny room under the stairs. Judging by the ledger books and slips of paper stabbed onto spikes, it was the shop office. The man generously waved him toward the straight-backed chair on the far side of the table, beneath the highest point of the sloping ceiling. Himself he shoehorned deftly into the corner like a magic act in reverse. "How is old Carola, then?"

"Truth be told," Gennett said cautiously, "I was looking for Miss Embly. Miss Lily Embly."

The shopman sucked in his breath. "That bad, is it? I won't argue with that—the daughter should know first. They haven't a soul else to call kin. Least none as will own up to it." He frowned sourly at this. "And I've looked. I must say, I'm not sorry to see you. Such worry we've had, and our Lily not been seen for weeks." His accent was a curious admixture. For the most part it was native down to the idiom, but a foreign, possibly Bavarian note came through in perhaps one sentence in ten. His manner was easy, as befitted a meeting of equals. Gennett surmised that the "doctors" of his acquaintance were apothecaries of the lowest type. "When will she be back?" the man asked.

"Quite impossible to say in these cases. Might I have a look at the flat?"

"The flat? Whatever for?"

Gennett tapped his case, inventing at top speed. "I came here to find Miss Embly because the matter is quite urgent. I had hoped to consult her regarding her mother's medication, what she might have been taking—before her recent, ah, decline. But if I might look myself," he shook his head compassionately. "Her mother is not capable of helping us with these questions. I could not possibly enter her flat without your approval, of course."

The stairs were as Gennett remembered them: warped and treacherous. The flat was not. His vision of an occult bordello faded like a dream the moment the shopman opened the door.

"Is this all they have?"

"Our Lily cleared out her best clothes quickly enough. And the carpet's gone to the pawnbrokers with I don't know what else."

It was like a half-emptied attic. The theatrical leavings were difficult to imagine as part of the everyday furniture, yet they must have been. Gennett skirted a stuffed owl and brushed his fingertips against the ornate wooden frame of an enormous mirror. A grand mirror in the sitting room? (At least, he thought it was a sitting room; the other room was nearer to the door, but it had a huge bed in it.) Perhaps it had been to the pawnbroker's and back already. Or perhaps it was too decrepit to be worth the effort of hauling it. The frame looked gnawed and the glass was speckled as a plover's egg. The signs of poverty pricked his conscience as if this were the home of a decent woman instead of a thief—and thief she was, of confidence and confession and trust. He should be glad to see that crime did not, evidently, pay. He should not feel like a bully.

He found what he needed on the windowsill. Tiny bottles— quite an alarming number—in green and blue and amber and clouded white, square-sided and round, catching the last of the afternoon light like a collection of ornaments. Many were empty or long since dried to nothing, but there was more than enough left to kill a grown man. Archaic things: aconite, quassia, paregoric, and oxide of zinc. Most were in scarred bottles labeled with a single word, most likely the product of cut-price local quacks. The contents were apt to be powdered milk. But two had a label he recognized: McCourt Brothers, a large and professional establishment just off of Upper Street in Islington. Why should they go there for common drugs—unless these were new prescriptions, left behind by the daughter before she had fled? There were not so many hospitals in Islington. If one had patience, one could check them all.

The shopman was close behind him, scrutinizing Gennett more closely than the bottles. "Found what you need, then? Care to take it along?"

"Just the one. I'm finished here."

The shopman stepped smoothly in front of the door. "I couldn't be more pleased to have been of help. Now, between friends, what would you say to being of help yourself? I can see how you might not want to speak of Carola, that's fine. But I would dearly like to see the old girl myself, particularly if she, as you say, might not be on the mend, and I'll be blowed if she didn't forget to tell us where she's at! She and I have fallen behind a bit, you might say. Though if you know aught of Lily, that will do."

"I don't—" Gennett stopped and reached for his wallet. "Sir, is it even possible? You have been generosity itself while I have forgotten the other half of my errand." The shopman's hands twitched as Gennett counted out notes. How much it would be he had no idea; a tenth of Mayfair rates? A twentieth? He hadn't brought small change, which was foolish. "Mrs. Embly has been highly concerned about her rent. She spoke to me about it. Before she became too incapacitated to speak, of course." His explanation was becoming increasingly ludicrous, but the shopman accepted the cash. The stack was up to about a quarter of the Mayfair rent for a flat this size. Gennett hoped the man would give them a few months credit.

"Sir, you are too good." The shopman shuffled the stack like a euchre dealer with cards. With his hands full of notes he was unimpeachably gracious. "I knew our Lily would come through for us. If you see anything she might like to have, you go ahead and take it to her, right?"

Gennett was about to reiterate that that wouldn't be necessary when his boot struck something caught between the darker floorboards in the center of the room where a rug must have lain. It gave with a papery crunch. Bending down (and somewhat dirtying

Wilson's trousers) he tugged loose a square of heavy paper, now somewhat crushed on one side. It was painted with a faint figure on one side like an oversized playing card. The shopman was peering over his shoulder so he slipped it into his pocket to examine later. "Only this. It appears to have been dropped."

"I might be able to give our Lily a bit of leeway next time, if you'd be so good as to help remind her when the rent's due," the shopman said, clattering the locks shut with fine keys like fishbones. "Not too much, mind. And I can't keep telling their clients to try back later. If I let again—and I'm not saying I mean to, mind—I won't want a lot of barmy fortune-chasers needing their palms read."

"Palms?"

"Well, astro-logical future-reading, what your dreams mean, anything that pays the bills, I'd say. This ghost lark did well in its time, but I think Lily needs to get her mum back to basics, don't you agree? Bottom's dropped out of ghosts." Their bargain seemed to have put them on terms of intimacy. The shopman all but threw an arm over Gennett's shoulders as he continued in a confiding tone. "They're show people. That's the way to understand 'em. 'Fortune-telling family' sounds like a witchlike sort of knack, but it's just the same thing as folks on the stage." The shopman whistled a few bars of the latest Marie Lloyd toe-tapper, in case his audience was too elevated to have heard of music halls. "Born in a trunk, was our Lily. Always moving around, and grown-ups for playmates and a crystal ball for a plaything, I don't doubt. Didn't know them myself in those days but the type's nothing special. Never a day of school in her life. Knows everything there is to know about her trade but ignorant as a baby otherwise. And the friends the mother had about! Bohemians. Big characters in threadbare clothes. Warps a child, all that adult company, and going to bed at dawn." (This as if Gennett hadn't seen the rows of child workers in the man's shop.) "Can't make a girl a good wife without a kitchen to raise her in, I always say, but"—he chuckled unpleasantly—"not such call for that as I can see."

"She is not . . . spoken for?"

"Our Lily? Strewth, no. Not that there haven't been a few interested, but Carola saw them off right quick. She's a good little earner, that girl, for all she can't cook."

The shopman led him down to the street. Before shutting the workshop door he turned, though the scene was regrettably public, and added, "You can take a message from me to our Lily if you like, just a favor from me to her. If she's all set up and flush now she might want to send a little message to Bettering. He's been 'round twice a day lately."

The name Bettering was oddly familiar. "Why is he coming by?"

"Oh, she'll know. Folk who cross Bettering, you don't see them again, unless it's washing up on the riverbank at low tide. But between you and me, seeing as you're such a compassionate fellow"—he winked, and again Gennett wished they weren't doing this in the street; an urchin peered at them before slinking away into the nearest alley; might he be bearing news to some unknown master?—"there ain't no Mrs. Embly. Never was. It's Carola Essenkova around here, though I daresay a mile east it might be something else again."

"Lily Essen—"

"You miss my meaning, friend. Lily Embly. A one-off, you might say. Do tell her I said hello."

31

FRIDAY, NOVEMBER 27

Consolidation

"I have only acted the part of an amanuensis and endeavoured to write down as truthfully and as carefully as I could, the words given to me by the Spirit Author himself. . . . The Spirit Author Franchezzo I have frequently seen materialized, and he has been recognized on these occasions by friends who knew him in earth life."

—Transcriber's Preface to *A Wanderer in the Spirit Lands*, by "Franchezzo," as dictated via mediumship to A. Farnese, 1896

L ily sorted her undergarments into four piles: pack for weekend, keep to hand for everyday, store, discard. Everything else was settled. Her new gowns were still wrapped securely in their tissue paper from the dressmakers. The duke's housekeeper had put aside most of what she needed for a long weekend at a country house well set up for guests, all at St. Aubin's behest, covering for Lily's ignorance of the protocol. She would be handed off to a lady's maid attached to the house itself when they arrived. "Much more typical to bring one's own, of course," St. Aubin had explained, "but servants do chatter. Best not to let them go gossiping where it might get to the wrong ears. And there's no worry as long as one lets one's hostess know in plenty of time—which I've done for you, of course—and doesn't neglect to tip." Her undergarments, however, she kept as sacrosanct as her slates, her wires, her charts, and her cards. More secret, really, because St. Aubin was welcome to comment on the latter. His willingness to involve himself in the former was both unwelcome and worrying.

The shopping expedition had been a pleasure at first. Just the look of the boutiques, the gorgeous piling on of velvet and trimmings was a jaunt through Aladdin's cave. She had witnessed such a childlike glee in others at the sight of Mr. Eldard's wares, but jewels were too familiar to excite her. She had never expected ever to feel such a quickening of materialistic delight herself. And so much else had been clear at last: her clients' talk of French fastenings and Bruges lace (no better than the stuff from Nottingham, but more satisfying to the acquisitive sense) and tea consumed during the fitting, a girl hovering with a saucer whenever the right arm was to be moved, and "those insufferable shop assistants" whose obsequiousness they clearly adored. St. Aubin came along. He had a highly specific vision of her ideal appearance. He gave instructions directly to the proprietress.

"An unbroken column of color, for height," he had said, holding up swatches to Lily's cheek. "Too bright. A rich shade but not gaudy. Bold fabrics. Brocade. Eastern influences. But keep it close, to flatter the figure." Gowns were chosen with scant input from herself.

"You'll not need so very much for one visit," he had told her the morning before, in private. "One traveling outfit—what you have now might do for that. One morning ensemble to appear in after breakfast. You could wear that for luncheon as well, with a different blouse for the second day. You shan't need shooting garb for now. At least two tea gowns, for after luncheon, and two more elegant gowns to dress for dinner. And then for the evening sessions themselves"—she had dropped her fork in alarm, scattering egg across the tablecloth. St. Aubin had laughed.

"Surely they can't expect me to—I needn't appear at all during the day, I—"

"And act like a servant instead of a guest? I think not. This is
what fine ladies do: They buy frocks, and change frocks, and eat tiny
little bits of food so they can fit into their frocks, and then buy more.
And never mind about the cost. Dressing for dinner isn't what it used
to be; you'll be able to reuse quite a few of these, perhaps even keep
them until next year. It's an investment. In the meantime, enjoy!"

She had worked up a grin to pay him back in a small way for all
the trouble he was taking. He grinned himself to conceal his disappointment. In the gowns? At her unease at being served? Perhaps
only that she was not quite so delighted to be in the sweet shop
at last.

Enjoy indeed. Her one remaining corset was patched with wire.
Her old camisoles were crisscrossed with patches where the stays
wore through; she was in the habit of wearing two at once to protect
the bodices of her gowns. But St. Aubin had asked—asked her
directly, like a mother, like a husband in a one-room cottage before
whom privacy was irrelevant—and she had said, firmly, no. Any
solution to the underwear problem could not include him. The
"pack for the weekend" pile consisted of a single chemise, too large
and never worn. The discard pile consisted of nothing.

There was a knock at the door. She threw a voluminous petticoat
over the tatty lot of it, then for good measure a blanket over that.
"Yes? Enter."

It was not the housekeeper come to invade the last corner of her
domestic competency. It was a housemaid. "There's some men
wants to see you, Miss."

"At the door?"

"Er, at the back door."

"I am not in."

The girl was back in minutes. "I can't find Mr. Graham. He's the
butler, Miss." She was perhaps twenty and serene in the protocol of
the house, flummoxed by these spiritualist visitors who so often disrupted it. "They won't leave. He, the big one, he knows you're here.
He says he's been watching the house since you came home this
morning—he described the carriage. Miss, you might want to speak

with him. He says if you won't—I don't know what this means, mind you," she added nervously, "but if you don't see him, he'll go to the hospital?"

Lily paused only to smooth her skirts, leaving her hair as it was, weary from a long day in pins. Transmitting threats would be unthinkable for most guests. There was no one in the house unclear on her difference from most guests.

They were waiting at the tradesmen's entrance, incongruous as the proverbial beggars in the house of the king. They looked sinister as ever together, the looming boss in his optimistically undersized clothes and the shriveled little underling appearing less a man than a toadying boy. "Inside, please," she said.

The servants averted their eyes as Lily searched for a private corner. She had never been downstairs before. She had held it in her mind as a possible refuge if the public grandeur became too much, but the kitchens were more alien to her than the grand foyer. Vast trestle tables gushed out in every direction, some freshly scalded, some laden with dead birds. Copper pans shimmered overhead like the fruit of a monstrous tree. In an alcove a sugared folly three feet in height awaited the hand of the specialist confectionery chef for completion—this was for every day. This was no hearth, but a factory churning out the grand life for consumption upstairs. She led her unwelcome guests to a nearby stillroom and shut the door. How they had found her despite her precautions she didn't know, and she schooled herself not to speculate. She had underestimated them. Her concern now was exactly how dearly she was going to pay for that mistake.

She had meant to keep them standing but both settled down into hard chairs without hesitation. There was no possibility of playing them off against each other. They were as seamless and symbiotic as an old married couple. They were unlike other East End operators. Everyone knew that.

"It was you who bought the debt, then," she said. "What on earth made you interested in us? What we owe is a pittance by your standards."

"You're running with a grand crowd these days. We hear about you from the strangest fellows and we think, what a lot is happening with our Lily, what a dark horse she's turned out to be. Then I asks around the neighborhood. I see you owe a grocer here and a stationer there and, oh, quite a few quack doctors, and I think, how untidy a bird can be with money. I'll take on the debt myself, a spot of consolidating, and then she can pay me the lot. Convenient, like. It seemed a right clever investment. We've done a bit of work on your new pal. And what a hostess you are, Lily," the larger said, dragging out her name like the punch line. The smaller, predictably, sat quietly. An observer unfamiliar with their double act would suspect him of inattention.

Lily's brow knit in confusion. "New pal?" St. Aubin was somewhat changed, but she would have expected people to recognize him.

"I can think of some polite conversation for a lady to make," the larger continued. "You could tell us about your cracking new digs; you forgot to fill us in before you cleaned out your flat. Your landlord's right curious about that, by the way. Or we could talk about the cost of living. Everyone has something to say about that." He lifted a crystal ashtray, half cleaned, from a countertop and spun it around in one of his huge hands.

"Where I stay has no bearing on the agreement. You'll have your money, and all the interest due. I'll earn it even quicker if you learn a bit of discretion. Showing your face here doesn't do me any good."

"That's the last thing we want, queering the pitch for you. We've been discretion itself. If you only knew the lengths we've gone to and the slack we've cut to keep your little show on the stage. But then you stops going to your regular haunts and that makes a man nervous. We think you need a bit of reminding as to your outstanding obligations."

"I have the money. It's just tied up right now. Next week—" She stopped to breathe and slow her words. She wouldn't believe herself if she were listening. "I have a very large, very important, very lucrative job over the next few days. We've sunk everything into it—"

"We?" piped the smaller, but she continued over him.

"—but the returns will start coming in next week. You may hold me to a payment."

"Say we want a payment right now? Get it from your fancy man."

"My—" Shock would not help her here. They wouldn't take it for anything but weakness and pretense. "You've known us for ten years, for God's sake. The entire neighborhood knows us. You know our business."

"I find that I don't know you as well as I thought I did." He flipped the ashtray in the air in a spinning arc.

"I'm not a whore."

The larger's hands stilled, but the smaller stepped in, unabashed. "We've seen 'im. Three times to yer own flat 'e's been, and we've seen 'im. And followed 'im up north, too. Came out of your flat an' led us right to yer Mum Thursday night. How'd she like a visit in hospital, eh?"

"I will not hear this." She stood. The larger rose slowly to his feet and the smaller, glaring with fierce affront, was forced to do the same. "You'll have your money, just as I said. Go elsewhere for your satisfaction."

The larger nodded pleasantly, the very reverse of the smaller's ugly sneer. "Just so. As an old friend, I'll let you call this a last notice. Friendly, ain't it? Balance—"

"A payment, I said."

"—next week. And now we know where to reach your old mum should anything go astray." He wiped away the smears his fingers had left on the ashtray and set it down with perfect delicacy. "Beautiful thing, that. Good day. We'll see ourselves out."

"And that man at my flat—" Lily stopped short. They had reached the hall and a scullery maid's cloth-swaddled head had appeared in a doorway. It was as mortifying to have an interview terminated on their schedule as it was to have it forced on her in the first place. "The man you've been following. You know Monsieur St. Aubin. He looks rather different and his hair is dyed but it is him. He was the only one you saw."

"Was he now?" He looked surprised for a moment, but pleasantly so. A smile was lost in the massive face. "Well, some say you know just about everything, Miss Lily. So I'll leave it at that."

November 27th, '96

Dear Professor St. Aubin,

Please find enclosed payment as agreed. I was shamed that you should even suspect that I might have flouted your instructions, I wouldn't dream of putting filthy lucre directly into our dear Miss E's otherworldly hands, but perhaps you could reconsider about that private session? It was so very stimulating to attend a session with Eva C, I will never forget it, and Miss E is so much more gifted and intriguing than she. Perhaps we could meet to discuss the matter again. I remain unsure as to the aspect of my proposal that was disagreeable to you. Perhaps a clarification of the sums would be of interest. My club is as always open to you.

Your committed colleague in the study,

Mr. –

32

ISLINGTON

It was true: There were not so many pharmacists in Islington. Checking each one was not so tedious with the aid of a telephone, especially when the boy minding the counter at McCourt Brothers had been so helpful. Gennett's brief visit Thursday evening had confirmed that the patients' roster at the Victor Cranwell Memorial Hospital included one Carola Essenkova. Now he took his satchel, but also a suit of severe grandeur, his silver-handled stick, and a topper that brushed the ceiling of the carriage.

One senior doctor on staff at the Cranwell had recognized his name and was there at reception to meet him. The man gripped Gennett's hand in both of his and plied him with invitations to discuss his article on the special difficulties of treating phobias in the elderly. By the shiny enthusiasm on his face he actually did wish to discuss dynamic psychiatry rather than connections and preferment. Gennett squeezed the man's hand with sincere regret.

"Another time, perhaps, if I'm fortunate. My business today is most pressing. I am, in fact, looking in on one of your patients for a friend."

"A related case?"

"Just a personal matter."

The doctor supervising—if that was the word—Carola Essenkova was a relic with the beard of a biblical patriarch and ears that almost bent under their own weight. Gennett was reminded of a

lop-eared rabbit he'd been allowed for a short while as a boy. A small
lapel pin seemed to indicate that the man was a veteran of the
Crimea; it swam in and out of sight beneath his beard as they walked
to a distant ward, Gennett moderating his steps to match. His guide
was not talkative, but Carola's case was evidently at the stage when
there was little more to say about it. "I'll not trouble you further. My
thanks." The elderly doctor departed and Gennett entered the room
alone.

"Mrs. Essenkova?" He rapped the door for courtesy and let himself in.

Asleep was his first thought. It was morning, but every bulb in
the room was blazing, giving the room that incandescence that felt
so unnatural indoors. The white walls reflected and it was almost
enough to make him squint. But despite the brilliance the humped
figure in the bed was not propped up, had no reading or knitting or
letters. It was still as a corpse. She couldn't have taken a bad turn
now, just when he needed to speak to her. It would be too cruel.
He hurried to her bedside. He was leaning quite close when her
eyes flipped open. She was not asleep, not in a swoon, and not
disoriented—certainly not disoriented. Her eyes huge and icy
brown—seemed to take him in all at once like a camera shutter. He
jerked with surprise. It was instantly clear that his moment of weakness had not escaped her.

He turned to reach for the pine chair and the glassy feel of its
back, machine made and slick as tin, helped turn aside the influence
of those eyes, half freakish and half familiar. By the time he sat facing her, satchel at his feet, he was himself again. His hat he rested on
his knee.

His composure was not steadied by her appearance. She was
short in stature—the whimsical peaks of toes beneath the blanket
were far from the foot of the bed—but the narrow mattress was an
insult to a woman of her bulk. Under her stiff bed coat her shoulders spread out like the back of a sofa. She had no neck to speak of
and her eyes, ringed by majestic bags, bulged like poached eggs. She
was in extremis. Even as he noted her waxy skin and wheezing (the

heart) and yellowed eyes (the liver), he found himself wondering, This isn't what Lily will become?

"May I have your wrist, Madam?"

"You don't look like a doctor."

"There are all kinds of doctors." This seemed enough answer for her as she rolled her arm upward for his inspection. He was accustomed to suspicion from patients, a threadbare front for their unease. But her response had been calm, not querulous. Her pulse was thin and quick but that had little, he suspected, to do with him.

"I've been seen by not a few. Like ants they were coming, one before lunch, one after, a raft at teatime. But not for the last week, no. It's once a day now."

She let that sit in the air. She was composed, in spite of the pain her various conditions were undoubtedly causing her, and she watched. Not intently, not with expectation—simply watched, calmly. The urge to break the silence was excruciating. He counted to keep from blurting something out. When she finally spoke there was perhaps a note of approval in her voice. "And what does it tell you, my poor wrist?"

"No surprises. Your case is continuing much as one would expect. I wouldn't prescribe any changes to your regimen."

"My case. I take it that you mean my health. You know of my case?" Her voice was pleasing, rising and falling in expressive waves, but rough. He wondered if she was that rarest of creatures, a female smoker.

"I know a bit."

"And where have you come from to brighten my poor room?"

"Just now I've come from Shoreditch." Her pulse quickened; he didn't need to be holding her wrist to tell that. More care would be needed. There was no small risk of frightening her right into an attack. But while there was fear in her eyes some other emotion was keeping abreast of it, and that was what gave her the strength to raise her heavy shoulders to a half-seated position. He helped her to shift the bolster to sit up.

"Don't take this the wrong way, young man, but you do not look much like a student of the uncanny."

"And you are such a student."

"I answer questions. Do you have questions for me?"

"I do, but not that kind."

She favored him with another surveying look, stroking from his glossy shoes to his hair. Something about the timing was incongruously sensual. "She's not here. You've missed her."

He was frozen for a long moment while a clock—a clock?—ticked on the windowsill. "Mrs. Essenkova, you are guessing."

"What of it? I'm right."

He slumped down to rest his elbows on his knees. His hat dangled briefly from his fingertips before bouncing to the wood floor. "I don't know why I've come—"

"You have the look of a man who needs a drink." She stretched to the edge of her limited range of movement to pluck two tumblers, in cheap molded glass, from the bedside table. One she handed to him. She tipped the contents of the other into a basin concealed beneath the bed, swirled it clear with water from the ewer, and drank down this residue with a grimace. "Well?" she said, looking at him expectantly.

He stared in bafflement.

"Impossible," she said under her breath. "Pass me that," she added more clearly, pointing to an ancient cracked suitcase tucked behind the bedstead. Flipping open a side pocket, she drew out a silver flask that proved its provenance by its tarnish. "You're the first doctor I've seen in a long life who didn't carry a drop on him. Or you're too clever a sponger for me." She poured them each two fingers of something clear and odorless. "Let us talk of my girl."

He stopped his glass halfway to his lips, then set it down. "I have a specific purpose, Madam. I very much hope that you can help me."

Carola rested her own glass on the shelf of her wool-covered lap, hands folded primly. Her eyes were hot with displeasure.

"Your daughter is Lily Embly, is she not? The medium." Carola gave a weak shrug in affirmation; he knew he would get no more. "I must speak to her."

"And yet you have come all this way to speak to me."

"That is only because she has left the addresses at which I have met her in the past. I must speak to her and it seems that I must convince you to do it."

"Ah." Carola sipped her liquor. "Will she? Agree to meet you, I mean."

He frowned thoughtfully. "I do not know. I——"

"Oh, you do!" Carola laughed, displaying small white teeth. "She may be reluctant, but you will surely convince her. The matter is too great to be trifled with! But come." At the hard line of his mouth she softened. "I am too . . . lighthearted for a serious thing. Forgive me. Perhaps I can help you." She patted his hand like a comforting granny. Her hand was bluish and already cold.

"Madam. This is indeed serious, but I suspect that I have caught us both in a misunderstanding. If you suspect some . . . personal dimension to the business I am to discuss with your daughter, I can reassure you. All it is——"

"Ah! I never pry into my girl's business. You may keep that to yourselves."

"You will help me to arrange a meeting then?"

"I didn't say that. Come, come"—she gestured to his glass—"you're a waste of a good warmer as well as, may I say, not the most straightforward chap."

The first sip made him sputter. It wasn't gin, it was vodka, and overproof. Carola was finishing her glass. "This is not the best thing to be combining with your medication."

"What is it going to do? Kill me?" Her eyes snapped up to his. The obscure power they had held in that first look had returned. He could feel all she had left borrowed from the future and brought to bear on him now. "How long do I have?"

"They have not told you?"

"They won't even tell me what it is that's wrong. They tell my daughter, in child's talk. 'It's like a puzzle, we have to figure her out.' 'It's like a recipe, we have to put in the right ingredients.' I overhear them, but never at the right time. Then Lily goes away to read her cards."

"Cards?"

But Carola was struggling for a more upright position and that small effort was exhausting her. He took her shoulders and lifted her into place. Her arms trembled like the shanks of a spavined horse.

"She believes everything the cards tell her. She does whatever she thinks the cards tell her to do, that and the charts. Oh, I see your thought: Miss E who finds truth through the spirits, but also Lily who finds truth through the stars? Only the very naïve think there is a contradiction. It's not religion, you know. But Lily does labor so to be consistent."

She fell back onto the bolster, wheezing. "But she does not always do what is best for her, you see, what is practical. She sometimes needs persuading. You see?" The terrible eyes were shut. "I know that I am dying."

He made a decision. "My belief," he said slowly, "is that it is indeed your heart, but not only your heart. Your liver is failing as well. I suspect cancer. There are treatments, some more credible than others, but what might slow the progress of one will only aggravate the other. What they are giving you now is primarily to make you comfortable."

"And how long?" It was a croak no louder than a whisper.

"Very difficult to say. Some cases—"

"Tell me what you would tell my daughter."

"My best estimate is weeks."

She sank backward into the bolster, the buckwheat stuffing grinding like gravel under her weight. "Thank you."

They sat for long minutes. Now and again feet or a rattling cart would pass in the hallway.

"I shouldn't, should I?" she said at last, passing her fingers over her flask. She poured out the last measures into his glass before he could protest. "I've always been able to hold my drink, you know. Never a cause for worry, even from my Lily. She could worry about the sun coming up in the morning. That's the Russian way, both."

"You are from Russia? She is as well?"

"The Russian way, that's an expression." Carola's face was terrible. Light words passed over it like gentle rain over a landscape ravaged by fire. "A proper little sphinx, she is. So closed up in her chosen course. But why should she be curious when she knows best about all things?" She addressed him without looking at him. He prayed she would not. "Will she agree to speak with you? The truth, please; you have such a talent for it."

"She will." He was sure of it, suddenly.

"But she has not approached you."

"No. But——"

Carola laughed weakly. "Of course not, no. It must be put in her path, or she'll die of hunger at the stable door. But she does choose her own way sometimes, you know. When is your birthday?"

"She asked me this."

"As well she should." That seemed to settle some lingering question. She continued with greater energy. "And she can tell me, I take it. Very well. You may leave your suit with me, young man. If you are honest, you may expect to see her again."

Pressing a dying woman made him ill himself. He thought, horribly, of his mother propped up in a metal bed, and then morbid imagination supplied an interrogator, tormenting her with questions. He pushed it away. "I am sorry, but I must see her soon. It is not for me that I ask."

"You can wait together then, whoever you are."

"I could wait here."

Carola's eyes snapped open. Her goodwill had vanished.

"She must visit you every day. The hours are in the early afternoon?"

"Not today. She's gone away, you see. Off in the country."

"Leaving you alone?"

"For work," Carola smiled. Her anger had vanished as quickly as it appeared. "You'll have no luck with that tactic, my boy; she'll never be back here again if I don't wish it. What a pity that you spoke instead of staking out the door."

He stood and settled his hat on his head. With a grimace he tossed back the remaining vodka. "Madam." Just as he reached the door she spoke.

"What a fool I am! That's precisely why you said it!"

33

Espionage

"Where do you think you're going?"

Lily's hands shook as she fought with the display-case locks. She had stood at séances for three-quarters of an hour with a feather balanced on her black-gloved finger while the punters gasped at how the spirits held it, in midair and motionless. "I have to be at King's Cross in forty minutes."

"And you're shutting up my shop to do it?" Mr. Eldard said.

"You're late. It would only have been closed for a few minutes."

St. Aubin had laughed at the very idea that closing the shop early required an apology. "My girl, by Monday we'll be made for life." The locks chattered in protest but gave in the end.

Lily's hissed argument with Eldard was interrupted by a hard, staccato knock on the front window. Lily thought the glass would break before she had fished out the front-door key. "We're closed," she started to say, but the tall figure in black slid past her into the shop and shut the door.

"This is number nine Abingdon Street?"

It was a woman, a lady, with brilliant red hair showing through the gaps of her stylish but enveloping hat. She pulled aside her veil to study Lily more closely. The lady's face was exquisite, with classical lines at odds with the suspicion in her narrowed eyes. The scrutiny passed over Lily like a gust of cold air.

"You are certain?" The lady thrust a slip of paper under Lily's nose. It was one of Mr. Eldard's cards, frayed and smelling of an ashtray. Lily thought she could see the imprint of crude writing on the reverse. "There is no residence at this address? And you are . . . no, never mind."

At no point had the lady's voice wavered from the courteous, and hauteur was nothing unusual for a woman of her class. Lily couldn't explain what made her hackles rise.

"I require information. Where is your employer?"

Mr. Eldard nearly did himself an injury scurrying forward. "Whatever you require, Madam!" He was unlocking the case with his best jewels. "Run along now, Lily."

"Lily?" The lady gave her one more inquiring look, as if reconsidering something. She was a stunning woman. "Yes, I will stay. Mr. . . . . Eldard, is it? I think that we could have a very interesting conversation."

27.11.96

Booth,

I cannot accept your last response. I need your help and not for my own sake. I am as dumb as Cassandra—no one will listen to me when the evidence is everywhere. What will it take for them to see the danger posed by spiritualists? Must I lay it at their feet? My voice alone is not enough but so help me if you will not add your voice to mine I will find other means and you will in time see what your hesitation has cost us.

Gennett

34

St. James's

He rode west struggling to convince himself that he had made some progress. Whatever Carola said, the hospital was a strong lead. He could speak privately to the administration; there had to be a contact address. He could bribe a clerk to intercept her post. It might be best to wait until she made up her mind as to whether or not he was a good prospect for her daughter; he knew how crudely she misinterpreted his interest. It didn't matter for what reason they thought he was searching (he didn't fool himself for a moment as to what the shopman had thought by the end of that visit). All that mattered was the finding and the time.

Two notes awaited him at St. George's Terrace. One was from his mother. The other was addressed in his own hand and enclosed his own card, marked on the back with an *R*.

THE PARLOR maid kept him waiting on the stoop while she swallowed and sweated under her cap. "Mrs. Stone is not at home, Sir."

"I believe you will find that she is."

Henrietta was ill prepared to meet him. Time had been found to choose a becoming gown and slippers to match, but a coat was slung over a chair in the corner, an affront to the crystalline order of the rooms, and a pair of boots left a halo of dust on the rug. Her cheek was pale and her eye unwholesomely bright.

"Please," he said softly, "give me some explanation." He didn't need to fight against his voice. He had gone through anger and emerged on the other side, to a still quietness where violence and temper no longer traveled together. He might in a fury be gentle. Or perhaps, if his arm might rise to strike of its own accord, it would be as silent and peaceful as a bird's wing stroking the air.

"Give me one moment. If you sit, I will welcome you properly."

"My dear, you have been twice, twice that I know of, to my private club, and I know not where else, making a spectacle of yourself much remarked upon. Your coachman says you've been many times to Kensington High Street. Why there, if not to my flat? I risk coming here to reason with you and you are absent, and ignore my messages. Twice I have come to your home at night and found you elsewhere—"

"Unwell, only! I will throttle that minx of a maid if she said I was out when I was only upstairs in a swoon."

"—and I fear that I am becoming such a liability to your reputation that I must terminate our association. With the greatest regret."

Her eyes bulged over their dark circles. She was motionless but hummed on the verge of explosion. His hand reached behind for support and found a chair back. He had never grasped quite how much of Mrs. Stone's appeal came from her poise; how could he, when he had never before seen it about to slip? It was as if a figurine from the mantel sprang to life and bounded down to smash itself against the firedogs.

"I was worried for you," she said at last.

"Worried?" Insulted, perhaps. Skepticism must have been more evident than he intended, for she rushed on.

"You have been so cold, so strange! I confess, I went by your flat—not your family home, not that." She shrugged helplessly. "I know that I should not have. The charwoman let me in. But I found that you had been ill, and not told me! I went by your club, then—"

"Henrietta," he interrupted, "you didn't go through my desk, did you? You didn't take anything?"

She burst into genuine tears, tears that made her face red. "I feared that you were dying! Forgive me!"

There was no way to avoid putting out an arm of comfort. She fell upon this like buoyant flotsam from a wreck and scrubbed her face into his wool sleeve. "Hen . . ." It would be delightful to believe her, weeping at home for fear of his health. He didn't know whether to despise his coldness or his weakness. Better to be one than a contemptible half of each.

"Hen, please. I wanted only to end this . . . insincerity. I can stand lying to the rest of the world but only if we can be honest with each other." She wept harder. To deflect questions? "I cannot stay. I will be back; very soon, we may speak for as long as you like and decide—"

"Don't leave me!" She was suddenly off his sleeve, twining about his shoulders like a vine. "Stay. Your little project: I've seen her with my own eyes, haven't I? I will make you forget her. I will be a much more engrossing project than she." The redness of her face mattered little when she was kissing him so fiercely, too close to see.

His rush of response was like a tap thrown on full. But this was not his Henrietta, not his composed, aloof, queenly beauty, his chaste idol. That was his preference, not waifs or victims. His feelings for women of that type were strictly protective—

An eggshell barrier cracked. Henrietta's cornflower eyes ran together with gypsy-dark ones. Pity and desire did not crowd each other out, but merged, lifting on a welling of sodden animal heat, spilling over the boundaries of decency to enfold a good woman present and a bad one absent in undiscriminating lust. Not unlike, an uninvolved corner of his mind commented, seeing that a hunk of meat is rotten but wanting it regardless. The revulsion he felt was mainly for himself. He stood, dislodging his mistress, who slithered to an undignified heap on the floor.

"I will come back. When I return all will be in order, you will see."

27th November

I know that Ernestine has written and given you all the Details but I could not go away without a few words, even if it is only until Monday. You'll know from your Sister where to write, should Work permit you. Do be certain to take some Rest and Refreshment; we see so little of you, and we do worry.

    Your loving Mother,

    R.G.

35

BELGRAVIA

The cabbie was unable to drop him directly at the door of Eaton Place. There was another large carriage perched on the curb, its doors thrown open and roof crowded with parcels. The Gennetts' manservant was trudging up the steps with a crate. He set it down and stood smartly at attention as Gennett passed, taking the steps two at a time.

"Afternoon, Sir."

"What in hell is this?"

"Just back from the station, Sir. Miss Ernestine and your mother, with Miss Emily, Sir."

"Where to? What's this rubbish?"

"They packed a bit more than was needed, I believe. Miss Ernestine saw what Miss Emily had in her baggage and said they wouldn't need half of it. Miss Ernestine wasn't best pleased, I think, but that's for no one but you to hear, Sir. Sent back everything excepting wardrobe."

Gennett dropped to his knees and unbuckled the straps of the crate the servant had set down. The man cleared his throat and took a sudden interest in the roofs of the houses opposite while a passing woman, arms laden with baskets, looked curiously at the gentleman pawing through luggage on the pavement. Why hadn't he turned first to the note addressed in his mother's hand?

It was books. Dozens of volumes, some worn but most so new the leather squeaked when he flipped through them. There was Helene Blavatsky, Daniel Douglas Home, *Beyond the Door*, *Through the Mirror*, someone called Ravonsky. Emily had been threatening to lend him that one.

"What about the next box? Give me that one."

A crystal ball and a Ouija board (even he recognized that), some flimsy thing labeled as a "planchette," and, bizarrely, a bulging sack of lemons. This last he held in his fist as he ran up the stairs to his mother's rooms.

"To the house of a friend, in Hertfordshire," the housekeeper said, fiddling with the half-folded towel on her arm. "They've left the address in the usual place. I thought that Miss Ernestine was to gain your approval?"

A crystal ball, and all Lily Embly's predictions of ruin coming true.

He stood in the first-floor drawing room with the lemons dangling whimsically from his hand, not unlike the china doorknob (his mother had replaced that, he saw, with plain brass). Plain and homely metal in place of brittle artifice. He hadn't convinced them to turn away from superstition. They wanted proof—Freud was correct. It was not sufficient to reason out the weakness of a theory; words could not be fought with words. They canceled each other out, thesis and antithesis both thin as smoke. They would listen when he had proof. He would expose the fraud, expose *her* in the most public manner, and they would see.

"Hey there!" he called to the manservant, now nearly finished with his unloading. Gennett heaved up one of Emily's hastily refastened boxes by himself. "Back in, I'm afraid, and back to the station. Stop by St. George's Terrace on the way; I'll have my valet deal with my luggage. And then," he added, tossing the crate up to the roof, "give yourself a few days off. The other servants as well. You shan't be seeing any of us until next week."

PART FIVE

CONJUNCTION

36

The Grand Entrance

Ah! The country. Could anything be more refreshing?" St. Aubin tugged the window down a notch farther and sucked in lungfuls of air. It was, Lily conceded, very clean. She could think of no reason for him to comment on it, unless as part of some secret regimen to inure her to dull conversation before they reached the séance site. After two hours of his ramblings she felt that chat with a duchess over Papillons versus Pomeranians would be enthralling. "It does remind me strangely of the country around Rennes. I have an uncle who breeds horses there."

She tried to discern some resemblance to France (never seen, but described by her mother as blessed) in the sodden landscape. It looked like a painting to her, brown around the bottom where carts sunk in as though in quicksand, gray around the top, scratched into fragments by bare black branches. It was all too bleak to be real. Weeks ago, when St. Aubin had put it to her, a journey of a few hours had sounded effortless; it often took her longer to get across London. "What are they doing out there?" she asked now, pointing to the slow figures wading through the clay.

"Oh, some kind of farming work, I expect. Tilling?" He ran it over his tongue like the name of a foreign capital, read of in the papers but never pronounced. "This was all the duke's land, you know, before he sold off plots here and there for those vulgar little 'country houses' on two-acre tablecloths. These all would have been his folk."

"It's raining."

"It's England. If they didn't work in the rain they'd never work. I daresay they'd enjoy that arrangement. I don't think it reminds me so forcefully of Burgundy now that I think about it. Do tell me that you haven't some inconvenient sentimental bond with the English countryside. I quite approve of London, but for the rest—one can do better. Now, Nice . . ."

He was off, eulogizing all the places they would go when this party launched them into the highest reaches of "the international brotherhood—and sisterhood, naturally" of open-minded students of the paranormal. "Once you've caught these, we're ready."

"Abroad?"

"Or wherever you like, of course. And while your mother is . . . still unwell, we can remain in London for a large part of the year. Here's the station now." He declined to meet her eye while they collected their bags from the porter and found a boy to cart them to the station entrance. "If it hadn't been for those damned connections, we would have been in time for dinner. Our driver should be along any moment."

Outside the station muddy green rolled away in every direction, a farther distance between buildings than she had ever seen apart from Hampstead Heath. The small outcrop of houses nearby was new to the point of raw. Beyond that she could see the spires of the market town bounded by a moat of brown nothing. In London there was always another church, another clan, another nation across the street. If one fouled the nest with just one clump of houses here, she wondered, where did one go?

"Any moment now," St. Aubin said, checking his watch again.

THE HOUSE was a disappointment, but a large one. Brick (any dreary old thing could be made of brick, Lily thought) flew out in every direction, sprouting east and west wings. The windows were all the same window, stamped and stamped into tedium. It lacked the grandeur of the nicer department stores.

Stepping out of the cathedral-high front door to greet them was, not a butler or maid, but a tall young man in knee breeches and a wig. He opened the carriage door and bowed low, his sprightly powdered pigtail pointing at the sky. "Footman in livery," St. Aubin said in the faintest of undertones, guiding her up the steps with a hand on her elbow. "Same duties as a footman in tails."

The entrance hall at least had marble. Their footsteps rang out like pealing bells. The chandelier above them was the size of a German Christmas tree. "Electric," St. Aubin murmured. In other company he would have added, as he was doubtless thinking, *vulgar*. He disdained electric as thoroughly as Carola did.

Another powdery youth, perhaps more important than the silent one outside, appeared to greet them. He had strong white teeth and splendid calves. "This way please, Miss. Milady will be pleased to receive you in the morning room."

St. Aubin trailed behind them through a passageway that seemed half glass, so many windows had it facing out onto the park. The room itself was more conventional: the same side tables and wallpaper as one would find in Islington, only larger and garnished with marble and gold. Lily counted *one*, *two*, *three* after the footman departed and their hostess appeared.

"Miss E!" A large soft hand fell on either side of Lily's chin. She was pinned in unsubtle rose fragrance. "You are exactly, precisely as we imagined you. How pretty you are! And you," she tittered demurely, "must know who I am even before I tell you!"

Lily disengaged the hands firmly, settled her own on her hostess's shoulders and kissed her on each cheek. "I think anyone would see that you and this house belong together, Lady Maude."

Lady Maude Stubbs laughed with delight. "You are wonderful, wonderful! I like you more than anyone I've ever met. When will you be ready to begin? The guests are at dinner but we will settle you with a meal upstairs; the late hour is not a difficulty. It may even give you more time to prepare. Do you think—tonight?"

"We wish to settle ourselves first. Afterward I'll begin surveying the rooms individually to determine where the vibrations best converge."

"Surveying! May I watch?"

"It would be dull. There is nothing to see."

The footman reappeared at some hidden signal. "Ring if there is anything at all that you require. I will be seeing to my guests. Monsieur St. Aubin," she added as an afterthought. Her fingers, which looked as though they might squeeze like jelly if subjected to a strong grip, touched his in a flabbily genteel greeting.

The footman led them a dizzying distance to the east wing. The room was on the second floor.

"Splendid," St. Aubin said, turning to the room next door. "We'll take our meal in my sitting room. She—"

"Sir, your quarters are upstairs. I am . . . not sure that the suite includes a sitting room."

"No sitting room?"

"The party this weekend is considerable."

St. Aubin opened Lily's door. "I quite understand. Serve us in Miss E's sitting room. That is all."

THEY ATE with a maid in attendance and sat afterward with the door to the hall open as was proper. Maids swept by at intervals with linens or buckets of coal. They were both thoroughly practiced at preventing their words from carrying.

"They only dress like that for a large formal gathering, you know. The footmen. Otherwise they look like other upper servants. Don't mention anything about their costume." St. Aubin leaned forward to light a cigarette with a stick of braided straw lit on the fire, a basket of which sat on the hearth for the purpose.

"Of course not."

"And remember what I said about the luggage. Do your own unpacking, but don't draw attention to it; you'll make the maids curious. If they search the trunks they could find the compartments."

"I shall remember everything you've told me."

"Good." He made as if to stub his cigarette out in a saucer on the mantel, but stopped himself and tossed it into the fire instead. "I think it might be just as well if you cased the rooms downstairs yourself. I have so many things to deal with I may remain upstairs. Lady Maude will very likely turn up to vex you. Tell her I'm busy." He stopped a pair of maids in the hall on his way out, asking them to see to the dishes. They would report, if asked, that he had left the room and when.

There was much to do, but she closed and locked the door instead of going downstairs. There were tables and desks in profusion around the sitting room, bedroom, and dressing room, but she chose the vast bed as a surface to spread out her cards. The counterpane was tight as a drum.

Ten of Pentacles, Ten of Swords reversed, Queen of Cups, the Wheel of Fortune. Her heart rose up into her throat as she laid out the pattern more quickly. The cards were crooked and sloppy when they should have been even. Strength, Three of Wands reversed . . .

She sat and stared dumbly while the mantel clock ticked away her time to prepare downstairs. It was . . . entirely conventional. It signposted imminent opportunities with some risk attached, the need for calm and shrewdness, but an optimistic prospect of success. Her stars had been saying much the same for the past week. No matter how long she studied there was no upset, no meetings, no showdowns, no Page.

37

The Opening Sally

onversation died when Lily slipped in around the reception-room door. She had been sitting upstairs in her least elaborate new gown, listening to the maids rush back and forth, frittering away the minutes until she might join the company without being too early. She had misjudged badly.

They were ghastly. They were a multitude, and this was only the female contingent. The silence lasted two breaths before bodies filled her plane of vision.

"Miss Lily!"

"Miss E!"

For a moment she thought it was going to be like her first séance with St. Aubin, waving arms and demands, but it was only Lady Maude being excitable. The rest of the crowd that had gathered so quickly melted away, heads turned sharply at the sight of a gauche knot. Conversations sprang up from nothing as two neighbors, seeing the possibility of a scrum like the unwashed crowding around a champion at a boxing match, banded together to conceal their interest. Lady Maude, perhaps sensing an unspoken rebuke, became instantly cool and indolent. "So, so charmed to see you. Do allow me to introduce you to my sister-in-law, Mrs. Cummings."

Tall but in profile resembling a trout, Mrs. Cummings pressed her hand with perfect dispassionate courtesy and began a discussion of the weather. Lily's pulse gradually slowed to a normal pace. Perhaps there was something to be said for patrician manners.

She was introduced in turn to each guest. Some were spouses and companions along for the house party. They would not be joining the "spiritual work," as Lady Maude put it. Her husband, Mr. Stubbs, was one of these (Lily had seen him in passing; a look at his small eyes and red-veined nose made Lily glad that she wouldn't be required to rouse him to new planes of being). The rest were serious practitioners. There was a large contingent of Theosophists. A Miss Lawrence was exceptionally fierce in her convictions, pinning Lily to the mantel for long minutes while she outlined her plan to build a School for Theosophical Meditation in some receptive village nearby.

Around the periphery Lily caught sight of St. Aubin kissing hands and touching elbows before departing to join the men. Most of the greetings were warmer than Lady Maude's, some even distinctly friendly. In a corner she saw what she was looking for. Disengaging herself from one cluster of talk, she skirted others and made for the two women talking only to each other. "Miss Gennett." Lily stretched up on her toes to kiss Ernestine's cheek.

Ernestine froze, then clutched Lily's shoulders with strength enough to bruise. If it had been her choice rather than heeding signs, Lily would have felt very cruel for dropping her here, the odd woman out of every conversation.

"Oh, Miss Lily. I've been—isn't it a lovely party?" Ernestine's giggle had a hysterical edge. She had surpassed herself with a spring green ruffled confection that gave her skin a malarial hue. Emily Featherstone was in white and stood out among the guests like a pigeon in the company of raptors.

"So many leading individuals who have come to work for mutual advancement!" said Emily, evidently moved to tears. "When so many others have simply given in to Mammon and hopelessness!"

"Mother is upstairs," Ernestine added flatly. "The journey was too tiring for her. She's only here because she was good friends with

Lady Maude's great-aunt, before she died, of course. She doesn't want to bother with all of what we're here to work with and discuss." Ernestine clamped her mouth shut in a thin line. It seemed that Ruth would be staying upstairs for as long as Ernestine could engineer it. Lily murmured the expected pleasantries, then offered to introduce them to Miss Lawrence, who on her single subject would be both unsnobbish and conversationally infallible.

"Do sit," interrupted Lady Maude, gesturing toward a davenport.

Perhaps the hostess meant to join her there, but Ernestine was quicker. "Don't let her order you about," Ernestine whispered. "Sit by me. You can tell me who that ridiculous Frenchman is and how he seems to know you so well."

THE HOUR with tea stretched like taffy to impossible lengths. Lily couldn't imagine why St. Aubin hadn't warned her that she would be on her own. Half the social activity here seemed to be split, men here and women there, and the women didn't stop plying her with questions. She was leery of answering alone. St. Aubin was the one who knew these people and what they wanted to hear.

"Lily, what was the result of your *divining* this evening? Were the vibrations correct? Which room shall we choose?" Lady Maude had leapt ahead to a footing of Christian names, but Lily doubted that she would be calling her hostess plain Maude.

"Divining!" cried the drab woman who was, improbably, the granddaughter of a duke. "Are we going to have our fortunes told? How marvelous! Harold said it was just going to be spirit hands and things."

Lily's throat could not have closed more rapidly had a pair of spirit hands materialized to strangle her from behind.

"Not fortune-telling," Lady Maude corrected in a tone likely reserved for cockroaches and communists. "Miss E has been *examining* the house I should say, *spelunking* for the kind of sympathetic vibrations that a séance requires. Spirits shan't pop up in any old spot. It is all much more scientific than that." She laughed suddenly. "Really, Miss E telling fortunes like a gypsy at a fair!"

A few of the women looked askance at that. Lily wondered how many had detailed astrological charts tucked away under their beds at home.

"Miss E," asked another woman, one who had been attempting to catch her ear for a quarter hour, but without the energy for success. Her face was drawn and mournful. "Can you reach the souls of the departed?"

"Sometimes."

"Have they described heaven to you? Tell us, what is it like?"

At that moment a footman appeared at the door. "Another guest arrived, Milady."

"Nonsense. They're all here."

The footman crossed to Lady Maude's chair and murmured into her ear for a long moment. Her brows lifted in an expression of not-unpleasant surprise.

"Oh, well. Send him up, then."

In the buzz of speculation over the identity of this mystery guest the doleful woman's question was forgotten. Lily's relief lasted almost a minute.

38
Mute Sentries

He walked into the room as if he owned it.

As if he owned the place! was one of the most damning indictments that Carola could deliver on a man, but when the thought came to Lily it wasn't a judgment. He simply seemed to her eyes to be proper and right. His suit was creased and travel stained, almost shabby beside the elegant white tie of the men in the dining room, but it was the women who looked out of place. Their jewels, even the dainty tiara adorning the brow of the duke's granddaughter, were reduced in an instant to trinkets.

His manners seemed very proper, too. Before even his sister he approached Lady Maude with the most disarming smile. "Lady Maude. I have not had the pleasure. And now, I fear, due to my appalling luck on the roads, the pleasure truly is all mine. You must have long since despaired of my arrival at a tasteful hour—"

On he went, through an amusing tale of his travel misfortunes, well supported from beneath by a trestle of compliments for Stubbs Hall and its mistress. When he finished his recital she was fluttering happily on an updraft of praise.

"You are far too good, sir! As if you could ever be an unwelcome addition to the party! Everyone," Lady Maude said, clapping as if every eye in the room were not already fixed to the center ring, "may I introduce Mr.—Doctor, I beg your pardon—Dr. Ambrose Gennett. Doctor, I entirely forgive your sister for not mentioning that you would be joining us."

Across the room Ernestine went blotchy red but said nothing.

"Not mentioned? I would welcome such an alibi! The truth is that I told her I would write to you myself, and then failed in my correspondence as much as I have in my transportation. Can you forgive me?"

Lady Maude's coy wave of the hand indicated that she might.

Lily felt as though a steel spike, plunged from the top of her head to the base of her spine, had fixed her to the cushion. She could feel Ernestine quivering with rage beside her. This could not be happening. The cards had said nothing.

"The men are in the dining room," Ernestine blurted out at last, her voice harsh as a parrot's caw. "You'll not want to waste any more time here, I'm sure."

"They'll be in in just a few moments, Dr. Gennett," said Mrs. Cummings.

"He won't want to miss any talk of shooting. That's what he's here for. Shooting."

Lady Maude now had her eye fixed on Ernestine. Ernestine, rather than qualifying her statement, returned the look. The other women watched the standoff with ill-disguised avidity. The doctor walked between the combatants and broke the deadlock.

"My dear sister is determined to spare me embarrassment, but this is quite impossible. Lady Maude, I most humbly request that I might join your group of spiritual explorers."

Lady Maude beamed and had opened her mouth to give assent when Emily interrupted. "Ambrose! I knew you would come around!"

"I am but a curious student, Aunt Emily, but if our hostess will allow—"

"It's not her decision." Ernestine was actually shaking now. "It's Lily's séance. Ask Lily."

Gennett was instantly on one knee before the davenport. One

hand he rested briefly on his sister's knee, for comfort or in apology. Then he took up Lily's right hand. To the watching women it would seem a very correct address to a woman not of his acquaintance. "May I?" he asked, holding her gaze. "There is nothing at all worse than an interloper." His eyes were as hot and dry as his hands. He might burn her alive.

"You are here now." She made herself smile. The cards had said nothing. "Who am I to argue with fate?"

39

Sparring Partners

"All I can say is that when I lived in London, things happened in my house quite as strange and convincing as anything I have read. There was no mystery made about it, either. Most wonderful things happened both in light and dark séances. . . . The company assembled were mostly scientific and literary people, not easily imposed upon."

—E. B. Jackson, *An Hour with Modern Mystics,* November 1896

Those of the party with a thirst for ghosts, or no particular grudge against pheasants, were laying in a good morning's sleep to set against a long night. Gennett hadn't heard a human sound since the footman had left with the remains of his breakfast tray. It was a very fine day, poor news if she was holding out for a dark and stormy night. The ground behind the house was still saturated from previous storms. Gennett's steps released a bloom of rural scent from the mud and hay, a clean mulchy funk.

"Whatever is favorable!" Maude had said last night when he asked what time the spirits were expected. "It is so very much like sailing, so dependent on currents and prevailing winds, though of a different type. We hope for the proper conditions to make contact tonight. Miss E will keep us informed." He had forced his lips into a smile at that. Of course she will keep you informed, he had thought; she will proceed the moment her props are in place and you're all too drunk or exhausted to think clearly.

There would be no confrontation. Instead, he would lay bare her tricks and techniques before witnesses. When the great and the good turned their backs Ernestine would do the same.

Maude's house looked no better by daylight. He found it curious how much was missing when one wiped out the delicate intricacies of taste. He had always thought that the flip side of good taste was vulgarity, piquant and memorable as the Wife of Bath, each gaffe unhappy in its own way. Now he found himself in a wilderness, missing the target of elegance, yet failing to strike anything else, bumping gently to rest in a flat plain of *ah, how nice.* They hadn't the excuse of inheritance, either. In an interesting reversal of the traditional pattern of trade dowries propping up gentle names, Lady Maude Stubbs held the blue blood and her husband the money. She was on the robust side for a true aristocrat, but came from the horsey, hearty set rather than the dissipated, though a bit domesticated to be riding with the hounds. Her skin reminded one of the soft and fragrant children in Pears' Soap advertisement. Without such democratic good looks she would surely have had to content herself with a smaller fortune than Oliver Stubbs's.

What Maude was doing getting her fingers into this rot was beyond him. There were a thousand and one problems lying in wait for such a mixed marriage, but he hadn't heard of the Stubbses suffering any one of them: Their money had survived the financial chaos of the past decades, neither had been caught out in a dalliance, Oliver Stubbs had proved adaptable to his new milieu and not too much of an embarrassment in society, no extremely bad relatives had turned up. What it was in Maude's life that made her turn to superstition was yet to be discovered. Fortunately, answers to most of his questions might be found in the same small hands.

EMILY ANSWERED the door, or rather peeked around the edge after Gennett's knuckles were well exercised. "Oh!"

"You were expecting someone else?" He made to open the door but she stopped him with a tiny cry of horror.

"Oh, no! I'll meet you in the conservatory. Just give me a moment."

"Aunt Emily, what do you have in there? Strange men? I would like to speak to you, whatever is the matter?"

"Downstairs!"

He obeyed with very poor grace. At least she didn't keep him waiting for long. Nor did she offer any observations on the fineness of the day or the loveliness of the Stubbses' plants as she settled into the cane chair opposite him.

"Ambrose," she said, not waiting for him to begin. "This is not how I would have planned for your training to advance. I am over-joyed, utterly, that you have given the search such precedence in your life, and I'm absolutely certain that Ernestine will be overjoyed too, once she"—she stopped to mangle a handkerchief. Gennett was still too surprised by her sudden boldness to interrupt. "I had meant for you to meet with Miss E, truly I did. It was all arranged, but for *after* this gathering. You would have learned so much from her and then when you met Ernestine again that would have proven that you were not the enemy."

"I am not here to meet Miss E," he snapped. Emily had been planning a meeting? "Nothing could be further from my mind. I am here to save my sister. To save us both from the pain of estrange-ment, you understand."

Emily continued as if he had not spoken. "But simply— barging—Ambrose, she is so angry."

The excitement of a crisis drained from her face. He was unpre-pared for the guilt. Why should he feel so when he was working entirely for Ernestine's welfare? But he had to pause to shake off doubt, and this made him slow to reassure. "I would not have chosen this either, Emily, but it is the only way. I had thought to regain her confidence slowly but we have made no progress." His words sounded unsatisfying even to himself. "She grows more hardened against me by the day. If I must—this is bound to be painful, is it not? It is painful to me." He gathered momentum. His thin words filled up from beneath. "If I am to show her, prove to her that I am not her enemy, and she will not yield me an opportunity, then I must—push a bit. But any means that lead to a rapprochement are for the best."

How easy it would be to say these things about other people. Or to say them years after any of it mattered; he could state a theory as it came to him, warm to it as he warmed to intriguing trains of thought in a hospital meeting, then take up another theory and try that out as well. No one would think him dishonest. It was only here in the present that simple truth must be spoken for the first time and perfectly, untainted by rehearsal or calculation.

He reached out and took Emily's papery fingers between his own, pressing them as he had Lily's supple hands the previous evening. Since then his wits had thickened from a quick stream to a slurry. Words, ploys, options gathered faster and faster on his tongue. They choked him.

Emily took his hand in both of hers and squeezed. "I will help you. It is difficult. It is like a birth. But to help you both, you and Ernestine, to expand fully into spiritual awareness, it is worth any amount of pain." She smiled at him gently, benevolent master to pupil. He resented condescension even from those who had something to be condescending about. It was his own fault for flattering her. He was reminded of the proverb—or fable?—in which a shepherd gives a frozen snake a place to thaw by his fire, and receives suitable reward.

"To help us both? What does Ernestine need to do?"

"She is—oh dear," Emily freed a hand to tug fretfully at her lace collar. "I suppose you could say *blocked* or not moving forward

properly. . . . I am putting this so badly. But frustration and unhap-
piness in one's life . . . she doesn't want to discuss *ideas* the way she
did. She talks and talks about how important it is that we continue
and—forgive me—how much you will hate our doing so, but she
sounds so cynical sometimes, and she never has a moment for her
reading or exercises, only for letters to this new friend, Morris or
something like that." The mentor was quite gone. Emily was
shrinking back into herself as she continued, flushing and stutter-
ing. "You will help her?"

"I will do my best to bring her back to the truth."

"The truth, yes."

"It will mean so much to Mother, will it not?"

"Ah, yes. Ruth. When we are all united in our pursuit of the
study—I was meaning to tell you, when I said that Ruth was on the
path to her epiphany along with us? I may perhaps have been just a
touch optimistic. She is more —"

Rustling broke out from the direction of the door, followed by a
savage clacking of heels on marble. Gennett and Emily watched
together as a pair of town shoes, glowing like onyx, sauntered out
from the shade of a dwarf palm. Behind the vanguard were crisp
trousers, a vibrant waistcoat, and a jacket well suitable for an afternoon in a continental spa town, somewhat out of step with Hertfordshire. Settled atop these like an afterthought was a face that
looked as though it had once been rounder, the jowls dragged down
and deflated. The thick waved hair and pointed beard were as black
as the polished shoes.

"Hello!" Emily called out. "How are you this morning, Mr.—
oh, I'd forgotten that Ambrose missed dinner and hasn't met you.
Monsieur St. Aubin, this is my nephew, Dr. Ambrose Gennett.
Ambrose, this is a colleague of Miss E's, an expert on psychical
research. Well, you will have much to talk about!" She looked back
and forth between them expectantly, then with puzzlement, as they
stared at each other. "Much to talk about!" Puzzlement turned to a
child's anxiety, the fear of having angered the adults. "Well! I am so
overdue for my, ah, walk, and—"

"Are you indeed, Miss Featherstone? How unfortunate when I have just arrived. I shall very much look forward to seeing you at luncheon." It was the voice that Gennett remembered. St. Aubin's was trained to an extraordinary pitch, every note spaced out in beautiful, sonorous artificiality. Awfully high toned, but it retained enough of a generic continental filter. Otherwise it would sound like imitation of his plummy hostess, or mockery.

"Quite! Good-bye!" Emily skittered off, and the two men were left scrutinizing each other's cuffs and watch chains. Excepting the slight otherness of St. Aubin's attire—an effect surely calculated to keep himself a touch separate from the merciless English pecking order, and one that Gennett was forced to acknowledge as sound strategy—Gennett could not find a weak point. He kept calm only because Wilson made certain that he had no weak points himself.

Perhaps St. Aubin had given up waiting him out, or perhaps he had only been planning his opening sally. "I was informed that there had been an unexpected guest. I confess, I had imagined that your kind took a bit more care with your intrusions. Another one so quickly?"

"Intrusions? Well, I'm sure that I'm not too proud to be tutored by the experts." Childish, that, but he thought he saw St. Aubin twitch.

"You would do best to depart before I inform Lady Maude of your recent improprieties. It would spare her the embarrassment of having you removed."

"That would leave me so little time to tell her of the two of you."

"She won't listen to fanciful stories, I daresay. Not about her invited guests."

"She is free to confirm the fanciful stories herself, then. I can tell her where to look. Mr. Eldard's shop, for one, is quite convenient to Victoria Station. And the Victor Cranwell hospital is not such a journey if one has enough reason to venture to Islington."

This all sounded very hollow to Gennett, but St. Aubin stood with a frozen sneer and the rebuttal never came. Instead, the Frenchman (if that was what he was—his complexion had an olive cast) settled himself into Emily's vacated seat. "You are a doctor, Miss Featherstone says? Of what?"

"A medical doctor."

"You are very amused by a simple question."

Gennett's smile, a sincere one, skinned back now over his teeth. "Nothing so—dramatic, I am afraid. I am a doctor of the most usual kind, an alumnus of the most usual universities. I am smiling simply because, very early in our acquaintance, Miss Embly asked me the same question."

St. Aubin ducked his head to fish a cigarette from a flashy case. He settled it into a long ivory holder. "And you told her what? That you sought to plumb the mysteries of the spirit world, but are regrettably untidy with your engagement calendar? What a pity that you did not explain yourself more fully; she might have asked you here."

"She asked my sister."

"Ah! Well then!" St. Aubin waved his cigarette still unlit. His free hand fished messily through his waistcoat pockets. "As good as being asked oneself."

"You misunderstand. She—"

"I do admire you physicians," St. Aubin continued. "Such a worthy trade. But also such a scientific one, no? Tap my knee, listen to my lungs, all is revealed. Cut up hanged men. And I know well how tenacious you can be. I wouldn't want a timid doctor! No, I would want one who would not be told, who would not stop until he was satisfied." Here he would clearly have taken a drag on his cigarette for effect, but mimed one instead. "But you must realize that this fine doctorly approach cannot serve you here."

"When you disparage medicine you wrong our common ancestor. You are aware of Franz Anton Mesmer?"

"The Study has progressed somewhat since Napoleonic times."

"One hopes. But the fundamentals of hypnotism remain the same. I'm not too proud to say that we share your debt to 'animal magnetism'—we merely took the high road, employing his techniques to heal instead of rob. One might say that spiritualism is the bastard cousin of my profession, a degenerate branch of a noble family tree. That's how I recognize your base manipulations for what they are."

St. Aubin's laughter sounded quite genuine. "Bravo! Your schoolmasters must have been very proud of you, young man. It must have taken hours to read all that."

"My education was stronger on science than shell games."

St. Aubin gave a barking laugh. "Science? Do you think I do not understand science? No, I do not believe that I could tell you the Latin names for *ear* or *foot*. I have only lectured to the Psychical Society of Paris and the Senate Subcommittee on the Study of the Supernatural in the United States of America. These audiences were full of little men in frock coats who could tell you the Latin names of five varieties of phlegm, I should imagine. Half of them still believed in phlogiston but each one was an expert on what is impossible."

"They understand mechanical physics. Pulleys. Wires."

"Every profession has its parasites; the more complex the arts, the more fed upon. Do you expect to be tarred by quacks selling penny cures in the gutter? I think not."

"I would if I were one of the quacks."

St. Aubin had given up on his matches. He waved the cigarette holder like a conductor's baton, punctuating, then sweeping dismissively through Gennett's rebuttals. "I give you too much attention. What are you here for, but to vex my associate? I regret even to speak such coarse words, but that appears to be your language—she is a medium, Sir, of the highest order. She is not a housemaid to be chased up and down the stairs by Monsieur." Here was the perfect pause for a fierce exhalation of smoke. St. Aubin glared majestically as through a cloud. "You may chase her up and down the country if you like, you will not have your way. She has friends. They—we—will not stand for it."

"You should regret to say these things, Sir. They are slanders that a gentleman will not brook."

"Slander is that which is untrue. But what of it? You will not be brought to account by me, or at least not by me alone. A wise man pursues only his enemy, and bothers not with those who are merely not his friends."

"Shall we not be enemies, then?"

"Neither of us would gain by it."

"Very well. Answer me a question, then, as a sort of friend. What do you mean to do here? What phantoms are you pursuing with the Stubbses?"

"We will," St. Aubin said, shifting through a series of pompous attitudes, "be attempting to make contact with other planes of existence."

"Specific, ah, souls?"

"We can but attempt. It is not so simple as pulling a lever. It is not, as you might say, an exact science."

"When you attempt, then. What will you do? How will you invite them to communicate?"

The older man smiled pleasantly. "Wouldn't you rather be asking me about Miss Lily? Come, come— the worst I will do is refuse to answer you. Unless you are merely casting about for after-dinner conversation. If you are, I fear that your opinions of the supernatural will not interest her greatly. What do you wish to know?"

Rather, Gennett thought, tell me how much you know already. Now that the chance was upon him he was strangely reticent. He looked up and around to the wide spatulate leaves of the rubber trees in their white porcelain pots. Was that tropical soil inside, sailed in from hotter climes with their parcels? When they outgrew the pots, were they bequeathed larger ones and yet more foreign soil, or consigned all at once to Home Counties clay? The conservatory was as large as some ballrooms and destroyed perspective. In its corners, parted only by the clearest glass, English shrubs appeared to mingle with the birds of paradise. "How much do the two of you charge for a session like this?" he asked.

"Charge? Oh my, what a commercial mind you have. Miss Lily and I are seekers of truth. Very few have the gifts, sadly, so we give selflessly of ours. Our fellow seekers, when they are persons of means, help to support the cause in other ways."

"They support generously?"

"For the furtherance of a gift such as Lily's, they do indeed."

"Why is she so badly in debt?"

St. Aubin coughed, a dry hack. "You are both crude and mistaken."

"Carola Essenkova is willing to accept my help. She has very little time, you know. Cancer and heart disease both. Whatever you think of my intentions, you must realize—"

"Carola!" He perhaps had a reaction now. St. Aubin did not appear to sweat or color quite as other men did—his surface was so glossily artificial. The flushing was something like a flame illuminating yellow wax. "Do I know that you have anything but a name? I do not."

Gennett took from his coat pocket the druggist's bottle from the Shoreditch flat and set it on the table between them. Beside it, on impulse, he laid the faded paper he had taken from the floor, snapping it down like the playing card it resembled. The youthful figure, holding a round goblet or cup above its head, was bisected by a fold that threatened to crack it in two.

"Allow me to tell you something about Carola," St. Aubin said. "She has nothing to do with her daughter's work, and I can categorically assure you that what she says and what she believes have never in a long life crossed paths. She has been a good mother in her way, particularly to a child who was, you might say, thrust upon her. Carola has been many things to many men in her time. And now she is an old woman dying quickly and will grasp at whatever straw the good doctor has to dangle before her. You are a busy one, by the way. What did you threaten her with?" The wax was cool and opaque again. "She has, as you say, very little time. It can have no possible bearing on the daughter, whatever deal you have made with the mother."

"What deal did you make?"

And that was a reaction at last. The shadow of fear that crossed St. Aubin's face came and went in an instant, but it was there. "Miss E and I are colleagues who assist one another. We go where invited.

You may be sure, Doctor, that no amount of agitation on your part will bring us to you."

"I want only for her to stay away from my sister."

St. Aubin laughed. "Done!"

Gennett blinked. Just like that? "You guarantee that she will not be involving my sister in any further séances?"

"Your sister? The Miss Gennett at dinner? Oh, dear—we would certainly never involve her. We work in rather—different circles, you see. We—"

"Not you. Lily. Will she or will she not be prowling around? If you book her appointments, kindly do not book any more in my home."

"In your home?"

They must have been an amusing sight for any passing servants: two sleek men with all their sophistication gone, gawping at each other with open mouths.

"The séance in my drawing room. You didn't know about it, did you?"

"I must bid you good day. The time has quite escaped me." St. Aubin picked himself up quickly, but with mannequin stiffness. He tapped his holder against the rim of a plant pot and tucked it, complete with unburnt and badly mangled cigarette, into his breast pocket by rote.

"Where is she now?" asked Gennett, but St. Aubin was already halfway out to the hall. The house had roused itself as they had spoken. Assorted feminine hands sought to waylay Gennett while St. Aubin, unmolested, made haste up the stairs.

"Mrs. Cummings!" Gennett greeted the lady to his left. She smiled warmly. "How well you look. A pleasant morning, is it not? I have spent it in search, but you are just the person to help me. Would you know where I might find Miss E?"

When he remembered the bottle and the card it was too late. Both were gone.

40
The Dress Rehearsal

Lily's night had been long but the moments would not string together. When a loud rapping came on her door in the morning she opened her mouth to speak, but nothing came. Her thoughts rolled around the ceiling like marbles.

"Come," she forced out at last.

After weeks in the duke's house she was accustomed to servants bringing her breakfast. Fried meats and mushrooms were hardly as attractive at an early hour as a proper hard roll, but the tea would be nice. The first hard step told her it was not the maid. She jerked up from the pillow, quick as prey.

"Hssst!" Ernestine hissed for quiet as she shut the door behind her. "It's all right. He's with Emily; she can pin him down for hours. We must speak. We'll get you dressed. The grounds are better than here. Anyone could be spying. Don't call the maid! I'll help you."

Lily's was not a complicated toilette, but she wasn't sure that she had ever accomplished it so quickly. Ernestine lacked expertise but was brutally efficient with what she did know. She chose a day dress and settled Lily's stays while Lily compressed her armfuls of hair into rolls held with combs.

"Oh, forget your hair, you can't do it yourself. The forms are impossible," Ernestine said, searching the dressing table for the horsehair frames over which most women arranged their hair to achieve fashionable amplitude. "Your maid can sort it later."

"It's done."

Ernestine led the way downstairs, jabbing a look over her shoulder every third step, for watchers and to be sure that Lily was still following. The gardens had been put to sleep for the winter. Lily had seen engravings of grand gardens, and the dwarf emulations that her suburban clients sometimes affected: bright quilts of flowers bisected by paths, sculpted hedges, stone vessels perched on plinths. In this one the urns full of nothing were marble and six feet high, and matched with marble benches and a great gray fountain full of dolphins and fat little boys. The fountain was dry and in place of flowers were low swaths of growth in dull purple. It looked like a graveyard with strange headstones.

Once away from the house Ernestine straightened her back and slowed to a less frantic pace. All of these gentle people, Lily thought, even those consecrated to the city, seemed absurdly reassured by the outdoors. It stood for something to them ancestrally, or aspirationally. Lily felt exposed. The cold worried at her thin jacket.

"Now," Ernestine said. The cold seemed very salutary to her. It brought her down from the boil to a state where she could speak without sputtering. "We require a plan. *He* makes plans. He will have the better of us if we do not do the same."

"For?" Lily was shivering. Her thoughts were rolling again.

"He means to ruin you." Ernestine stopped and turned to face her. Lily was level with her chin. "He means to *ruin* you. He will sabotage this gathering by any means necessary. He will expose—"

"There is nothing to be exposed."

"Oh yes, I forgot." Ernestine rolled her eyes. "But he can still be highly disruptive. Simply by sabotaging the necessary conditions of peace and silence he could prevent a materialization, could he not? If he can't find—what he can't find to expose, he can invent. He could plant things. People do all the time to someone they resent, don't they?"

"He would not lie."

"Oh, wouldn't he! I find your view of gentlemen charming, but perhaps uninformed by experience! If you had ever exchanged words with him that did not involve a flying doorknob, you would know what he can be like."

They walked again, in the constrained lady steps that the garden seemed to have been laid out to accommodate. "And so," Ernestine reiterated, "we require a plan. Let us begin with this: Go nowhere alone. Stay by me whenever possible. Do not speak to him if you can possibly help it, and if you must, then only on the most trivial subjects. He will confuse you, and then goad you into saying things that you did not mean, and then repeat a twisted version to others."

Lily nodded in acquiescence. She could, she admitted, envision that. "What if he does not mean to be avoided?"

"Well, quite. I have thought about this carefully. In addition to remaining by me—for heaven's sake, don't bother with Maude's lot for protection; some of them have unmarried daughters—I've charged Emily with keeping him well occupied." Ernestine smiled a very thin and vinegary smile. "By evening he'll be a master of the dotty little bits and bobs she's stuck together into a theory of the universe. Believe me, there is no possible way to stop her."

"What about . . ." Lily trailed off. "I have preparations to make. Maude expected a session last night; I can't cancel again. And what about tomorrow?"

"Let us concern ourselves with getting through tonight. Tomorrow we will get you back to town and you need never see him again."

The wind was rising and it grew too cold outdoors even for Ernestine. Their absence would soon be noted. Whatever else they had to say would need to wait for another quiet moment.

"About *him*," Ernestine said briskly as they turned back to the house. "I am of course very sorry that he has turned up here, but you must see that that's not my fault."

"Of course not. There was nothing you could have done to prevent it."

Lady Maude's butler caught them in the foyer. "Miss E, Dr. Gennett has been inquiring after you. If you would care to wait in the blue room, I'll fetch him."

"Inquiring? What a pity," said Ernestine. "There's no time at all to see him now before luncheon. Do come, Lily. There's barely time to dress."

"EMILY!" ERNESTINE hissed. Her aunt was caught just before whisking out of sight around a corner. Emily crept back into view. "Where is he? Why aren't you with him?"

"I couldn't stay. Monsieur St. Aubin came and it was just too awkward. I did try."

"With Monsieur St. Aubin?" Lily asked.

"Oh, you really are useless!" Ernestine snatched Lily's arm and piloted her past a series of oak doors. "Hurry!" Emily was left to trail behind as they slipped through the last one on the hall.

"Keep to light subjects; don't overtax her. She's not strong," Ernestine muttered.

It was a guest suite, somewhat less spacious than Lily's own, decorated in the same bulbous, gilded style St. Aubin called French Revival. A gray parrot whistled and clucked as they entered, swinging his domed cage on its stand. By the fire a gray-haired woman turned to blink at them. "Don't get up, Mother," Ernestine said, although the woman had made no move to do so. "You remember Miss E?"

Mrs. Gennett nodded. Ernestine motioned for Lily to join her on the sofa by the fire. "What a pleasure to meet you."

"Mother, you met her at the séance."

"Of course, I recall perfectly. Are you an acquaintance of my son? He—"

"Mother, Miss E would scarcely wish to discuss him! Did you manage any breakfast after all? Are you sure that you should be sitting up?" Ernestine seemed almost to forget that Lily was there, so intense was her focus on her mother. Mrs. Gennett submitted to the cosseting without rancor.

"I hope that you do not think me rude, not coming down to breakfast, but the journey was so fatiguing, and my daughter was most uncertain as to whether it was wise. She feared that I would tire myself and miss dinner. Dear, should we go down for breakfast after all?"

"Mother, it's midday now. And you must avoid overexcitement," Ernestine said, "and should keep to gentle conversation, I think. Emily, I'm sure that you can think of something appropriate." Emily blanched under Ernestine's gimlet stare. "I will be back shortly. I am sure that you will be occupied here until luncheon—you may even decide to have a tray sent up rather than bother with the crowd downstairs." She gave Lily a significant glance, passed one more Gorgon look at Emily, and departed.

"You do look very well, Miss E," Mrs. Gennett said. Lily knew that her toilette was careless and her face drawn. "I would not forget meeting you! My daughter is prone to these small mistakes, I fear. She is forever bringing 'round new faces and thinking she's introduced them already."

Lily had met Mrs. Gennett in the hall of her own grand home. Mrs. Gennett had worn a black velvet gown and diamonds at her throat and the gaslights had drawn warmth from the marble and oak, bounding the hostess in a halo like a golden egg. She had pressed Lily's hand and told her she was welcome. It had been so clear then how Mrs. Gennett had fitted into the pattern: Lily's very next reading had featured the Queen of Cups.

Away from warm light it was clear now how much had been a glamour of evening. She was an oldish woman, tall, gone stringy rather than stout. Lily noted the long nose and chin that had marked her out at once as one of his; those had struck her instantly on their first meeting. Now, in thin blue morning Lily looked in her eyes. The likeness ended with the color.

"And now she tells me that the meeting tonight is to be a supernatural one," Mrs. Gennett was saying. "Please do not mistake me, I bear no grudge whatsoever against the spiritualist profession—the spiritualist cause, I mean, it is all rather beyond me—but I think that a gathering of this type may not have been what my son would have wanted."

"But he has changed his mind?" Lily asked as lightly as she could.

"We would never have come without his approval! My daughter told me that she had spoken to him and that he declined to join us." Her forehead creased with vexation; by the smoothness of her brow this was a rare occurrence. "But Emily thinks that she may have forgotten to tell him about it. I cannot imagine how the muddle occurred."

Emily, rather forgotten on a hard chair in the corner, leapt in with a diversion. "Ruth is the most fortunate of mothers in that her children are so singularly devoted to one another. Ernestine is, of course, the daughter of my dear brother—Ruth's first husband— but since she was adopted by Herbert Gennett immediately on their marriage, it has not made the slightest difference in the children's intimacy. . . ."

Emily blundered on, hurling privacy to the winds. Mrs. Gennett held Lily's eyes without the slightest trace of humor or hidden meaning, or indeed any idea of indelicacy in such things being spoken of to a stranger. She was perhaps one of those who classed the medium with the lady's maid and let their tongues run on accordingly.

". . . there was one time when perhaps a cloud seemed to pass between them, but if you consider it properly, this was hardly the case. Ernestine is the most generous soul and more moved by the spirit of philanthropy than most others can grasp. She is frequently misunderstood by more worldly women. But last spring there was the possibility of trouble from this; swiftly averted, of course. A person whom we had thought a gentleman came into our circle of acquaintance, a clergyman of some sort, in the missionary line. Ambrose had lately moved to a new establishment in Knights-bridge, which you will agree is very fitting for a bachelor, and we did not feel in the least bit neglected as his attentions to us remained the warmest that can be imagined. Only, at this time his work with his hospitals—he is selfless in support of these!—was more demanding than usual. Otherwise he would have made a point of making his sister's friend his own." Emily paused and sat looking at Lily as if she expected her to finish the story.

"Where was I? Yes, this new friend. He was, I have said, in the missionary line, or perhaps I should say involved with a missionary society, and these societies are of course obligated to raise funds for their good works, so of course he met many ladies of both conscience and fortune. But even among this very select group his admiration of Ernestine was so marked that I did wonder if there might be an announcement on the way. When I"—she darted a look at Ruth, who was looking at the ceiling with a puzzled expression—"when Ambrose was told of it he wrote to this missionary, and he might not have struck the best note. Of course the missionary took this for disapproval. Then of course he had to depart abruptly. It was the disapproval of the head of the household that made it impossible for a man of taste to linger, not anything Ambrose might have said about Ernestine not having much money of her own. I still believe the entire thing to have possibly been a misunderstanding."

"Your daughter blames your son?" Lily said to Mrs. Gennett.

Ruth thought for some time before answering. Her words came slowly as if gathered from the furthest reaches of recollection. "He believes that had he become involved sooner, the . . . misunderstanding could have been avoided. I am sure that he is right. And the missionary man, the sum he left with in the end was very insignificant, I believe." Mrs. Gennett smiled. "Altogether it demonstrates how devoted they are as siblings, does it not? But really, we should go down to breakfast. Lady . . . Lady . . . our hostess will wonder at her lazy guests."

Lily had been consulted in cases such as this. If the spirit were already wandering, desperate clients asked, could they not make contact before death? Use the Ouija board and the planchette to communicate with Father, who spoke only of his schooldays and no longer knew his sons? She could recognize it now in even the early stages. She also knew the signs of a daughter who would not yet allow herself to see. Did *he* realize, she wondered? Did he see his mother with a doctor's eyes or a son's?

Lily was pinned by those blank eyes. A woman like this could decline so far before the change was noted; her mind nipped and bobbed from infancy like a dwarf tree, expertly pruned to restrict it to the scant space accorded. There was no ripple to hint of movement beneath the surface. Lily found herself drawn to look harder, to prod and wheedle and provoke, to deny the awful nullity. Little wonder that Ernestine and her brother papered over their mother with their feuds and then raced around her in their own snarling endless battle. Anything to avoid looking, and falling in.

Lily snapped her gaze away and stood. "Mrs. Gennett, I believe it is midday. Your daughter has ordered a tray for you. Shall we go down to luncheon, Miss Featherstone?"

"Should we," Emily swallowed. "If Ruth is taking a tray up here?"

"I prefer company I think." Lily caught herself and smiled to forestall offense. "A wider company, I mean. A bit of noise can be refreshing."

"Oh, quite." Mrs. Gennett smiled. No offense was taken. "Emily, when is Ambrose coming by? Did you see him this morning?"

"Ah, I believe that he may be busy. He is working, I think."

"Work, even here?" Mrs. Gennett almost frowned before favoring Lily with another delicate smile. "You see his dedication! He does like to *know* about people, you see. To solve them. And there is always more to be done. If it were medicine of the usual kind, he would simply treat the ailment and send them on their way, but these poor unfortunates never seem to find an end to their problems. It appears necessary to become personally involved. How sad that he cannot just heal them and be done with it. I'm sure that would suit him better."

It was a reduced and mainly feminine company that gathered in a bright room with views of the grounds broken into a thousand tiny vistas by the panes of leaded glass. The shooting party was being served out in the field. Lily could see a string of servants bearing picnic hampers away into the distance.

St. Aubin was working the far side of the room as she and Emily took their seats next to Ernestine, whose mouth was shocked and tight at the sight of them. Lily let Emily take the buffering chair. Their hostess was not yet present; the other guests left a space beside Lily. St. Aubin settled several seats to the left, neatly outside the hostess's sphere of conversation, without giving them so much as a glance. Lily scanned the room discreetly, Emily less discreetly. Where was—

He entered with Lady Maude. They were laughing together like old friends. Lady Maude's hand floated between his shoulder and his elbow in a most familiar way. "Here she is!" said Lady Maude. "You have been scarce this morning, Lily! Doctor, you sit here next to—no, by your sister; Lily may sit next to me. Don't let her slip away again in the next minute. I need to give the housekeeper her instructions."

"I'll keep an excellent eye on her."

His sleeve brushed her hair as he took his place at the table. That curl sent a tremor down to her scalp. Plates were laid and glasses brought by servants, the hands of the clock on the mantel made their circuits; all Lily could think of was that tingling patch on her head, buzzing every time he egged the company to another round of laughter. The urge to rake at it with her nails was over-whelming.

She took in his appearance with the smallest glances, watching him in morsels. She was practiced at observing without seeming to. The ridges on his fingers were deeper; he had been gripping a pen fit to snap it in two. There were threads of crimson in the whites of his eyes. She had been anticipating their meeting for so long—anticipating a resolution of the pattern of which he was a part—that the differences leapt out at her like footprints on snow. He was changed. Haggard, but harder and sharper as well, and angry. She had to look down at her plate for a moment to master her irritation.

He was rich, and a man, and had his sister's fortunes and Lily's in the palm of his hand. What cause had he for anger?

The food came. It was lunch things: made dishes and casseroles, galantine, cold meat pie. They talked of the roads. The rails. Town was so inconvenient, but then so was the country. Several of the women had seen a certain play at the Apollo; what did Dr. Gennett think of it? One had attended a lecture by a disciple of Mr. Ruskin's at the National Gallery, asserting, as she understood, that the English were in danger of losing their instinct for their own land-scape, and thus their racial vitality. What did Dr. Gennett think of that? He said far less than some members of the party, and nothing exceedingly controversial, yet they hung on his words.

"Very much so," he was saying, in response to a question on the terrible increase of whooping cough among boarders at a parish school. "I suspect . . ." (they rose at attention in their chairs) ". . . but indeed, the expert opinion . . ." (they quite abandoned the busi-ness of eating) ". . . hardly at all!" (they relaxed back against their chairs in satisfaction at the conclusion of the anecdote). She half expected them to applaud. And it was trivial chitchat. He was a mas-ter, she was forced to admit that. Across the table, the fixed state of St. Aubin's smile, waxen, suggested that he too was chewing over this unpalatable fact. Or was it something else? She watched him: St. Aubin simply sat, attentive, sometimes exchanging a few words with his immediate neighbors, scarcely venturing into the conversa-tion at large. He often looked in her direction but never met her eyes.

"Lily, you are very quiet!" Lady Maude laughed.

Her fork clattered against her plate, horribly loud. She was sure that she hadn't dropped it. "I am listening."

"What, not whispering with Miss Gennett? We will have to do better if we wish to pry you from your new friend!" sniped Mrs. Cummings.

"We—well! Well!" the Theosophist Miss Lawrence picked up and set down her glass of elderflower cordial several times. "We might speak on topics of more general interest! Is it not curious, all of us gathered here for a single purpose, and not a word said about it?"

"Quite!" nodded Mrs. Cummings. "Dr. Gennett, what do you think of it all?"

He had the grace to laugh at that. "Miss Lawrence is quite right, but I am hardly the person to rectify the situation. We require the expert's opinion. Miss E," he said, addressing her directly for the first time, "what are we about?"

"We are here to explore." She was, in fact, attempting to formulate something to add, but this fell behind the pace of luncheon conversation, and another guest cut in.

"Indeed! We are here to explore, to . . . look beyond . . . make contact!"

"Speak to ghosts?" he asked, all innocence. "I'm afraid I'm still stuck at what my nanny told me, that souls went up to heaven. Where are they when you speak to them?"

"Oh—not heaven!" the guest exclaimed. "It is . . . making contact, looking beyond . . . Monsieur St. Aubin could describe this so much better."

So summoned, St. Aubin roused himself from his quiet retirement by the curtains. "It is somewhat more complex than that, Doctor. Your flippancy belies the seriousness of the question. This is what we all ask, having seen things—'undreamt of in your philosophy,' I believe the saying goes. Where do we go when we die?"

St. Aubin paused for a sip of wine, and Lily could hear him swallow.

"The Bible tells us that we go to a place called Heaven or a place called Hell. Unless we are not quite so good or quite so bad as that, and then we go to a place called Purgatory. And where is that? And for how long do we suffer there? So we go to Purgatory, a sort of . . . null place? In-between place? Unless we were pagans, at least noble pagans in the Homeric tradition, and then we go to Limbo, a place about which we know even less. Unless we die upbaptized, and then we go . . . where?" He gave a majestically Gallic shrug. "Your priest will tell you that these are things beyond our ken; what you tell your daughter when she asks if her puppy Rags is in Heaven. It is, perhaps, not so different from our knowledge of God's will: limited not by a 'lack of hard evidence,' but by our capacity to understand. We aspire to transcend this rude and ignorant sphere. Earlier generations may have desired comfort. We desire . . . illumination."

No one had a word to say. Lily was aghast. They never spoke of religion; the barrier between spiritualist and spiritual beliefs was too fluid, and the risk of slighting Christianity too great. What could be driving St. Aubin to flip up the skirts of the ladies in attendance she didn't know. Any comment that brought them back under cover of the innocuous would be welcome, however inane—Lily risked a swift survey of faces. The meal was ruined, but as to which of the men was at fault . . . opinion was divided, was all she could say.

"Well!" Miss Lawrence exclaimed, tossing down her napkin. The relief at some break in the tension was palpable; she could have recited the alphabet and been applauded for her initiative. "I find it greatly refreshing to hear some informed debate on the subject! Most scientific persons—Dr. Gennett, you will not, I'm sure, be offended if I say that most are better known for their grasp of the proven than their curiosity about the unknown! It is so marvelous to meet a doctor of medicine who is not so closed-minded."

"It is lack of courage in their convictions," Lily said. Her voice was low and the table fell silent to better attend her words. "They do not question because they dare not. It takes great courage to ask if one is wrong."

He glanced at her there. She expected derision, but the look on his face could almost be taken for fright.

Lady Maude caught her in the hall as they exited. Ernestine still clove faithfully. Lady Maude gave her a sharp look as she tried to pull Lily aside. "A very interesting discussion, to be sure, but we are no further on the arrangements! Now, which room? I will have the housekeeper arrange whatever you require. A large table, certainly—that would suggest the Egyptian room, which also looks very delightful in low light, and has the most cunning entrance for service, so unobtrusive. So the Egyptian room will do nicely?"

"I must speak to Monsieur St. Aubin first. I presume that it will do very well."

"Speak to him again? You have had days to speak. He must be very awkward about settling things. No doubt you find it very inconvenient. Perhaps I should speak to him now." She summoned a maid with a tilt of her chin. "Bridget, put Monsieur St. Aubin in the Egyptian room for me. Give him a cigar if you must. Oh, and Doctor," she said over Lily's shoulder, "I am about to bereave your sister; can you amuse one another for an hour or two?"

Lily spun to find him directly behind her. If he stooped, his chin could be resting on her head.

"I know how you wanted to speak to Lily, but we'll put you together later."

He smiled down at Lily. "Depend on it."

St. Aubin was examining the windows when they arrived in the chosen room. Any proffered cigar had been declined. He had one of his usual French cigarettes in the holder and was peppering the air about him with short puffs of blue smoke. He usually smoked slowly. Something about this seemed to irritate Lady Maude even further. She strode up to him—as much as ladies were ever seen to stride—with steel in her posture. Lily didn't doubt whom she blamed for the wreck of the meal. "Well! Have you any objections? I would never proceed without the approval of the experts, but I do not think I need to tell you how splendidly the *objets* are set off by candlelight. And the servants' access—"

"It is the vibrations—" He was overcome by coughing, stray wisps of smoke thrown aside like oil on disturbed water. "I beg your pardon, Lady Maude. Forgive me. It is the vibrations that will determine the suitability of the venue."

Lily was shocked; Lady Maude seemed to be trying to work out whether he had actually had the temerity to interrupt her. "Lily,"

Lady Maude said with a cautious sort of hauteur, "has said that this room will be ideal."

Lily shook her head. "By your description, Lady Maude."

"You are here now. Is it?"

Yes or no? But St. Aubin was back at the window, smoking more furiously than ever. Lily was, in an instant, shot through with rage. Anger was alien to her—it was pointless, it smacked of arrogance. Yet for a moment it drenched her like hot brine. It burned in her eyes. Fury passed as quickly as it had come but left her shaking and weak. It had cut channels through her and these filled with fear. "I am sorry—"

"Paul!" called Lady Maude. Suddenly there was a footman easing Lily onto a chaise, assisted, with her own hands, by Lady Maude. "Be careful! She's had a terrible turn. Lily, can you hear me? Fetch salts!" Lily had the confusing sense that she was being given errands, but it was only Lady Maude ordering the servants. More footmen were summoned. "A restorative, please!"

A glass of brandy appeared under her nose. Proffering it was St. Aubin.

"Pray do not be alarmed, Lady Maude. Miss Lily is extremely sensitive. I do not think it likely to delay our gathering. In fact, I suspect that this room will be very suitable. I shall remain with her if you wish."

Nodding, Lady Maude retreated in search of the housekeeper. As soon as she left the room St. Aubin dispatched the remaining footmen for hot water, cold water, strong spirits, until he and Lily were alone. "We have a few minutes," he said in an undertone. "Will you be all right?"

"I'm sure." She was not sure.

"Then," he came closer and his face warped, became beastly. "How dare you. After all I have done for you, you ungrateful— how dare you."

Now she wanted the anger back. Anything that would lift her off the chaise and help her defend her dignity; but she was so cold. She shifted her head as if to shake it: no.

"I have denied you nothing. Now I cannot believe a word you say. You are your mother's daughter after all."

"I did not know. That he was coming. I am sorry."

"You held a séance for him, though? How much money had you planned to amass behind my back? On my back, I should say. Do you think you are anything without my techniques, my contacts? Do you think you deserve anything but to be ejected from this house and sent back to the sideshow where you belong?"

"I never held a séance for him!"

"At his house?"

"For his sister—she is here, she is the one I asked, her and her aunt. He knew nothing of it." She fought to breathe. Her lungs had shrunk down to papery nothing.

"You have never met with him? No favors, no encouragement?"

"I spoke to him once. He stopped me outside the shop. I never gave him my name. I have told you this."

"Why does he call on your mother at the hospital?" He was watching her face, and his relaxed by degrees as she took that in. "But you did not know that. I can see that you did not know that. He is a doctor, who knows what his resources are? I have been—" He checked himself. "You have been very foolish. You have kept things from me, and I cannot protect you when you are not honest with me. He is a man of means and he can ruin you as easily as he kicks a dog in the street. You must tell me everything, now. You said that you met him at a train station. How did you come to be such great friends with his sister that you drag that gauche woman to a fine house to embarrass you?" His hand darted through a circuit of his pockets. She shrank with dread from what he might produce to frighten her. She glimpsed a little jar, and a dirty card shape of colored paper . . .

A maid was upon them almost before they heard her approach. Truly, the servants' access to the room was exceptionally discreet.

"Poor girl!" Lady Maude was all solicitude, fluttering over her as the housekeeper unbuttoned Lily's cuffs to expose her wrists for chafing, St. Aubin and the footmen having been swiftly dismissed.

The warm compress on her forehead had been soaked with cut lemons and this real smell, this hard smell, drove nails through the bottled roses that had been hanging about her since she had entered the house. The housekeeper was massaging her wrists in tight and even circles. She wondered if other people might find that motherly. " . . . you are so extremely sensitive," Lady Maude was saying. "Upstairs and a long rest, I think. Do you agree? Of course you do. Now, I do have responsibilities to my guests, but if you need me, that is not to be considered. Someone else could sit up with you, however."

Lily couldn't sense what response was wanted. It was as though a glass bell had been dropped over her head. It didn't help that she was trying to read their faces upside down. "Someone else could sit up with me?"

"Anything for you, my dear. Not that"—Lady Maude came as close to a sneer as her cultivated lip ever would—"that man, though."

Lily had a terrifying moment (she was glad to be lying down) before she made the proper connection. "Monsieur St. Aubin. No, not at all. I'd prefer not to see him this afternoon, actually. Too tiring."

And so she found herself upstairs in her rooms, installed in shoe-less, loose-stayed half decency on the divan, with the "very restful" Mrs. Cummings in attendance. Lady Maude had graciously released this sentry indefinitely. Mrs. Cummings was interested chiefly in her soldier son—living, fortunately—and asked no awkward questions. Indeed, no questions at all. Lily dozed in a fearful half stupor to the accompaniment of young Reginald's daring exploits in the Sudan. She had begun to dream when a firmly shut door sparked her back to wakefulness.

Ernestine was shooing out the aggrieved Mrs. Cummings. "Of course I told Lady Maude. She's expecting you downstairs now, you mustn't keep her waiting. Ugh!" Ernestine added in a whisper as the door shut at last. "I really do feel sorry for you. Nasty old cat." (This was quite unfair, as Mrs. Cummings's failings were, if anything, in the dull and bovine direction.) Ernestine wedged a chair beneath the door handle with the deftness of long practice. "You're quite safe here. I won't leave you for a moment."

Lily was chasing after the last footsteps of the dream Ernestine had punctured. He was in it, and her old street in Shoreditch, and a carriage with horses that clattered like pots and pans as they galloped by. It could be significant. "Ernestine," she said weakly, "I need you to leave me for a moment."

"Leave you! He'll be up here like a shot." Ernestine's eyes narrowed. "You don't need to . . . make preparations, arrange the room, that sort of thing? I'll help you. I'm not so naïve as Maude, you know. Just don't let Emily see. She wouldn't understand."

"Ernestine—" Lily broke off and pulled her compress back down over her eyes. Argument was futile. She hadn't cast the tarot last night—her thoughts had been too disordered, and she had taken it for granted that she would be able to do so today before the séance. How on earth did one find a moment's privacy at a house party? Everyone went from chat to chat to chat like an endless gorging meal of light talk; there was never a respite, only a pause between courses. "I only wanted a moment alone. But it's not important." It was odd that she could, under such a testing gaze, but Lily was drifting back into leaden sleep before she knew the dream was upon her.

41
Suspicions in Context

In a drawing room with particularly regrettable paneling he found a writing desk with stationery (embossed with *Stubbs Hall* in oxblood).

> *Dear Ernestine,*
>   *A great deal could happen this evening, or nothing at all. For Mother's sake speak with me before this goes any further. I will not lie to you.*
>   *A.*

He summoned a maid to deliver it. "If she's not in her room, try that of Miss E—I say, how are you referring to her belowstairs? It must be a bit out of the ordinary."

"We call her Miss E," the girl shrugged. She was sturdy and rather good looking, though her teeth weren't going to last her much longer. She didn't seem intimidated by private conversation with a gentleman.

"It must be a funny thing, waiting on a psychic."

The girl laughed at that. She was really very pert. "I should say, Sir. Knowin' what was on the breakfast tray before you lift the lid. Ain't brought her own maid, neither, but she doesn't want much helping in the morning. They can be strange in their ways, these foreign ladies."

The note went; his sister did not appear. So be it.

QUICK READING was one of the most useful tricks a medical man could cultivate. Still, it amused Gennett, in a grim way, to see his training put to such use. Emily's trunk of books sat open in his room upstairs and Wilson was well occupied carting volumes up from the library; Lady Maude had an alarmingly comprehensive collection. Besides Crookes and Podmore he now had Emily's *Nature's Divine Revelations* and a few volumes by Daniel Douglas Home. These he listed beside the works of Robert-Houdin and the other rare stage magicians who had published their techniques, keeping in mind that if he were a stage magician, he would probably not discard the habits of a lifetime and reveal the whole tedious truth. These he cross-referenced where possible.

The result was, at the end of his black case notebook, a thick sheaf of notes capped by a loose table linking triggers to tricks. If he heard the word *materialization,* he would look for concealed objects; but *manifestations from the spirit world* often included *ectoplasm,* which could be nearly anything. It could be smoke, wax, cotton soaked in phosphorescent paint, but most often gauze, packed in the medium's mouth or nose to issue forth as proof of otherworldly contact. There was a young woman he kept reading of, one Eva C, who drew dazzling crowds for her "unique materializations." What tricks could there be up her sleeve when her leotards were too snug to conceal a pocket handkerchief? A gentleman might be invited from the audience to inspect her shapely person before she produced her uncanny extrusions, which the spirits sometimes directed to the most unexpected orifices. . . .

He reviewed his crib sheet at regular intervals, adding here and there as a fresh trick came to him, pausing to shut his eyes and breathe sharply through his nose when anger shuttered his vision with black.

Clairvoyance:	*"Mind reading"; assistants in audience*
Materializations:	*Concealed objects, gauze*
Ectoplasm:	*Same*
Clairaudience:	*Gramophones, noisemakers, asst. concealed on premises*
Levitation:	*Wires (obvious)*

The shame of it, using psychological techniques like burglar's tools! Mesmer's children, indeed. He would, he hoped, know where to look when the time came. It was all quite clear on paper. It was only looking at *her,* soft and resigned, as if she were the passive victim of circumstance and not the puppeteer, that matters became confused. What precipitating event in her past had warped her sense of morals and propriety? Freud believed that neuroses came from sexual assault in childhood later repressed . . . she would not even be aware of the event that molded her. . . .

He pushed that thought from his mind. He had not been able to interview her alone and that meant scarce data; he regretted that. But the balance of probabilities was that she was indeed the mistress of her own actions, and therefore responsible. Everything had been mingled and confused since that morning at the station; what more proof was needed that spiritualism ate away at truth? Clarity was wanted and clarity was what his plan would bring. Yet that was her primary gift (an odd word to choose but that was what his mind supplied): to cloud reason's eye.

The first bell rang, announcing the hour to dress for dinner. He turned the page to make a last note. He had thought this was a fresh notebook. He had forgotten how recently he had wanted a separate place to set his thoughts, away from his official casebook.

Bnkr.—1 session succesf. Memories: fraud, concealment, exposure (consistent w/traps). Progress simlr to MacAndrew girl. Mst avd simlr result. Try suggestion: nxt session, "forget" casebook, have notes tkn by asstnt hidden behind door. See wht Bnkr says when thinks not being recorded . . .

Gennett tore out the pages and went upstairs to dress. The butler caught him in the foyer. "Post, Sir. Forwarded from your own household, I believe."

Gennett hadn't had time for the post in weeks, and now his valet wanted him to catch up while away—

Dr. Gennett,

Our patience is wearing thin. Please do not think that by ignoring us you will cause us to disappear. We continue to follow your affairs with interest; as, we believe, will others when informed of your clandestine dealings. Respond as previously specified.

H. Bettering

42
The Rules of Engagement

arling!" Lady Maude kissed her on both cheeks. "You are so pale! Surely the rest refreshed you? If you have overtaxed yourself . . . I could not bear it, having led you to exertion." Lady Maude's eyes sparkled as if with tears. Each absence seemed to elevate Lily further in her hostess's esteem, and by extension, the esteem of the party. That, or it was the sherry. Lily stretched up on her toes. The fragrant Valkyrie saw her purpose and stooped to accommodate. Lily kissed her in turn, two little child-pecks.

"Well enough. You are very kind."

Amber sherry was pressed into her hand, in a showy glass bristling with facets. She supposed it might revive her somewhat. It was as sweet as apples, but it stung; she had bitten her tongue. It was surely only seconds ago when Ernestine was shaking her awake. "You didn't hear me when I called," Ernestine had explained, looking for once repentant, perhaps a bit alarmed. "You are sure that you are well enough?" It had taken them both, plus a press-ganged maid, much too long to bundle her into her best gown, the garnet silk. Laces had snapped. Buttons had popped free and bounced under the dressing table. Her hair was a horror. They had been the last two down to the drawing room.

No tarot cast. Not even the dream found again, only a clinging slumber that still had a chill limb coiled around her neck, even as her pulse jumped and shuddered. They had been wrestling with her evening slippers when a footman had brought up the post. "Forwarded from your household, I think, Madam. The rest was for Monsieur St. Aubin." Mother's doctors, she had thought at first, but the jerky handwriting was all too familiar.

Miss Embly, it said, *please do not insult me by showing yourself on my premises again. The lady wronged by you has explained matters to me. . . .*

On it went, sheets of tirade, patched where Mr. Eldard's pen bit so savagely as to tear the paper. His meaning came to her only gradually, building up like filth on the hem of a gown as she waded through the accusations. *A most refined lady, clearly of the highest character, Mrs. Stone*—had been to the shop. Her insinuations had told him all he needed to know about Lily's "new clientele." *Given your low connections I should perhaps have foreseen such brazen deception, but I confess that your sordid harlotry with Mrs. Stone's gentleman friend, a physician and a man of some standing as I gather, is shocking in the extreme, though it does explain your cruel neglect of your responsibilities to me, as well as the gaudy new finery you so shamelessly paraded in my presence. What reason but kindness has this lady to share with me a tale so injurious to her gentle sensibilities?* Lily *could expect only the loyalty she had shown* him, and he *would no longer permit his good name to shelter such wantonness. . . .*

Her clients. He was spreading these lies to all comers, turning her divining clients against her, telling them she was a kept woman in terms as crude as those used in the duke's kitchen—and of course, of course. Her great round creditor and his stunted little friend had found her at the duke's. How would they have known the address, if not told it by Mr. Eldard? And Mr. Eldard would be angry enough to do it, if he believed her a whore.

Now the women were greeting her with soft willow-wand hands on her arm, the men with whiskery kisses. Everyone knew of her bad turn and was very sorry. "And how lovely you look, even so pale," Maude whispered in her ear. A credit to her hostess, the tone said. "But we are so selfish, you shouldn't be on your feet."

The hands guided her down to a chair and the company drifted by in its tides. Men drifted more than women; bees from flower to flower, some half-remembered verse reminded. Young drifted more than old. Significant persons—they seemed more real and solid, rooted to the carpet like lavish trees, disdaining to notice when their conversations had broken up. They sipped and lasted until another arrived. Ruth Gennett was one of these.

Ernestine and Emily: They at least were not mysterious. The one was perched stiffly on the edge of a chair and the edge of a conversation, having been shaved from Lily's side by the crush of powdered bodies. Emily had clearly managed to make a few friends in the interim and was talking animatedly with Miss Thompson. She felt sure of these two. Not that they would be true to her, but that they would be true to themselves, and all that was needed was to grasp their natures. A Scorpio and a Pisces with not many surprises between them; any questions that were left were for the cards to answer, and they had. The cards had brought them here. The cards had brought them all here, so why was she concerned? The Page was what told. There were cruel cards in the pack but she had not drawn the Devil, the Tower, the Ten of Swords. Or the Judgment. She was meant to be severed from her old clients, her old life. It was fate. Eldard and her creditors were the illusion. Reality was here. It was merely complex.

He was at the mantel, swinging an untouched glass from his fingers with supreme confidence. That was the way with Leos. The white collar and tie of his evening attire were like a mirror, framing and reflecting to beam his effervescent spirits to the farthest corner of the room. Leonine charisma with a Gemini's silver tongue, yet a Virgo's attention to detail, plus Aquarian whimsy and puckishness: His was a complicated chart, but one that she could picture when she closed her eyes, so carefully had she committed it to memory. She

could see the Moon, the silent side of the character, the deep footprint
of the Ascendant leaving its mark in the birth hour; Venus defining
the cast that love would take in a given life, Mars shaping the passions.
His was Mars in Sagittarius. It was the number of conflicting influences that made him unpredictable.

And yet. The cards had said nothing. He should not be here.

She had been watching the wrong spoke of his chart. Whatever
planets he had in the third or twelfth or fifth houses he had the sun,
Leo's planet, in the house of reputation and the public self; that was
where the root of it lay. He had the sun in the tenth house and was
therefore what he seemed to be.

She was aware of a faint noise in the background, turning over
steadily beneath the conversation. An insect sound, beetlelike yet
mechanical in its regularity, ticking over signs and where they had
led her. The reading, her mother's accident, the train station—
tick—the café, taking his card, writing to Miss Gennett—*tick*—
coming here. Ticking doubt.

Ding!

She nearly dropped her sherry. But no, that was only the last bell,
summoning them in to dinner. "Here at the back, Lily. You're by
me," whispered Lady Maude, as couples formed up behind Mr.
Stubbs in order of rank. "You needn't be worried about feeling faint
at the table. Every eventuality is provided for."

Lily was not surprised when the doctor's warm hand fell on her
elbow.

43
Thesis and Antithesis

ady Maude was chattering in his ear; he should make light conversation, wrap the talk around her if he couldn't manage to draw her in. But Lily did not look up at him (up close, so white, with bruise-blue circles beneath her eyes) and he could think of nothing to say. He smiled at Maude and wrapped his hand over Lily's before hers slid away. She had accepted his arm without a word, yet she would not be supported. She had given him more of her weight than this on that first walk together on Kensington High Street.

Maude's dining room was as he expected, Limoges and Baccarat, impeccably expensive, great crystal things here and there with expansive curves, imposing and featureless. They passed from polished wood to a thick Turkey carpet on their way to the table and the small hand tightened on his arm. His gut swam, as if the floor had just dropped a few feet beneath him, just when he needed to be resolute and cold. There was a knife in his back. The hand on its haft might not be that of a stranger.

His first reading of the blackmail letter had left him blind and gasping for breath. *Her.* And yet, when he considered, was it logical? Whatever her crimes, he did not think that Lily could know of Henrietta or the financial situation at St.

Botolph's. And if she meant to profit from his family, how did it serve her purpose to damage the family by destroying his reputation? She might be a pawn of the blackmailer. And if she were a pawn in this, how much agency did she have with regards to the rest?

He could imagine any member of his circle as behind this blackmailer "Bettering," any member of this decorous company, now settling down to read the menus handwritten on gilt-edged cards. In his heated imagination the amorphous Judas sat down at the table and tried on faces. A friend's face, now; a pretty woman's. His conscience protested: They were loyal, however strangely they had been acting.

Conscience protested again: Who had been acting more strangely than he? And he was quite innocent.

It would be a start if he knew what he was being blackmailed about . . . but no, there was only one realistic possibility. The hospital finances, the setbacks with Coffley and Miss MacAndrew, the frank neglect of his responsibilities there (he would change, as soon as this disaster was dealt with he would give them all the attention they deserved) were what sprang to mind, but what were these compared to an affair with a patient's wife, however chaste? Someone from St. Botolph's? He couldn't imagine anyone there knowing of Henrietta. Platt? It would never occur to him that the Soho trips were for anything but whores. Even Ernestine didn't have a name to put to her pinched letters and jeweler's bills.

Ernestine sat between two uninspiring gentlemen, one of whom was making desultory conversation to which she declined to give even the scant attention it deserved. He caught her looking at him.

Not her, surely not, surely not.

THE DOCTOR settled her into her chair like an invalid. He had been to the hospital to see her mother. Or St. Aubin had said he had. She would have to ask. But to hack in with a question so crude seemed impossible when everything about them was submerged in carpeting and wallpaper. He glided through the money like a fish.

He sat to her right, Lady Maude on his other side. He began

immediately to chat with their hostess. On Lily's other side was the Hon. George again, who turned to her and remarked on the unusual weather of the morning. The Hon. George was not a natural observer (excepting the meteorological) and would not notice her shallow breaths.

Soup emerged. It was greenish and tasted like warm milk with butter.

"The thing with shooting is that the best wind is—do you shoot, Miss E?"

"No."

An explosion of brass laughter struck her ear; she couldn't keep from turning. Lady Maude was just withdrawing her hand from his arm and covering her mouth with belated decorum. "Oh, Dr. Gennett, I'm sure not!" How had she thought Lady Maude refined? Orange-girls knew better than to fawn so over a man.

Lily turned back to find the Hon. somewhat put out.

"Whereas, the wind in Hertfordshire is so often—are you familiar with Hertfordshire, Miss E?"

"No."

No one else seemed bothered about finishing the soup, though when she looked more closely, everyone seemed to be not finishing the same amount. She made herself eat it down to the level of the others. A hand in white cuff came down to take it away. She had to find her tongue if she meant to get through this dinner. She lifted her chin and tried to think of an appropriate question. "Are you often in Hertfordshire, Mr.—"

She was talking to the back of the Hon.'s head. Everyone at the table had simultaneously swiveled and entered into a tête-à-tête with the person on their other side, men looking left now and women right. She turned herself and he was facing her.

"We'll all turn back again after the next course, and so on," he said quietly. "And don't look so offended. I wouldn't say so if anyone were listening. Speak softly and look calm and say *that* and *you know* instead of something specific." He was not smirking or sneering or laughing at her; she didn't know what she might have done if he were. (Thrown her wine in his face? Stabbed him with a fork?) He was utterly grave.

"Is it so important, what we have to say?"

"Oh, isn't it? I think it might be."

A new plate was set before each of them, this one with slices of pale fish fanned out under a bright ribbon of yellow sauce. She waited for him to finish his thought. As the silence stretched out she felt a giggle trying to force its way up on a rising cloud of hysteria. "We can snap at each other if you like, but people will talk."

He found his voice quickly, and favored her with a polite smile for anyone watching, and cold eyes. "You don't need any instruction in making them think what you want them to think. Practice makes perfect. Are you enjoying Hertfordshire?"

"I always enjoy the country, thank you."

"Always. This is your first trip."

Now her heart was thumping to make her see stars. Everyone else was polishing off their part-consumption of the fish; she forced down a sliver before the plate was taken away. And then—oh, impossible!—he had turned away. It was weather through the next course, molded meat confections festooned with garnishes. When they turned back she was ready, but by his redoubled composure, so was he.

"You would not speak so to anyone else at this table."

"Indeed not—neither an assumption nor a liberty, I hope. I do try to give my fellow creatures the courtesy they have given me."

"It is ugly."

He sighed at this. "It is very ugly."

She found his sudden air of martyrdom irritating and humorous in equal measure. "But that is not your fault. You are deeply wronged. It would be beautiful if it were up to you." She had never in her life spoken so, not to her mother, not to St. Aubin, not to her most self-deluding clients. She always said what was best for them to hear. Sometimes what was best for her, not them, but only when a kindness was beyond her means.

Lily watched his eyes flick across the table to Ruth Gennett's

seat. His mother ate her morsels at a refined pace and allowed conversation to be made with her. His anxiety for his mother tainted the
air like smoke. He didn't understand, then, that there was nothing
he could do. She would think of some way to tell him, once she was
away from this table and able to think. Could that be her purpose in
his life, to give him that information, whatever his purpose in hers
proved to be? The significance of their connection was so searing. It
hummed beneath every word.

"You are—at another time you might be correct." He spoke
through gritted teeth, as though he were fishing the words up from a
dark and unexamined well, and it pained him. "I am no different
from anyone else. I am no wiser, though I like to think myself infallible, as anyone does. But I do not say that I am right, or that I have
been right; I only wish to correct my behavior and do my best for
the future. If I apologize to you, will you leave us alone?"

Their mutton was taken. Weather through a pineapple sorbet.

"It must be very nice to be a man." They waited patiently for
their plates. The roast—at last, at last. Surely they would be given
longer for the roast.

"Now I find myself asking for clarification, if it is not importunate to ask."

"A man with money, I mean." Did that word catch a few ears?
She could feel prickling looks from somewhere. She gave him a
warm smile as close to real as she could manage; let them think he
was joking with her the way he joked with Maude, and that *money*
was a naughty aside. This new frankness was trickier than she
would have thought. "If one does something, it is because one
wanted to do it. But I am only being facetious. Truly, you judge
yourself very harshly. We manage just the smallest corner of our
affairs; after that we hope. Surely you did what you thought best?
And if you are, as you say, not so unique, surely others did as they
thought best as well?"

He nodded as if she had made a mildly clever point. "Were it not
so ludicrous I might say that you were offering to forgive the tres-
passes against you."

She watched his hands tighten on his knife and fork. Surgeon's hands, she supposed: smooth but hard and deft as a juggler's. The doctors she knew had clammy fingers like herrings. She could still feel the heat of his palm on her elbow when she shut her eyes. "You did offer to apologize."

He sliced and consumed his pheasant with mechanical speed. She was suddenly ravenous but could not force a morsel past a hard knot in her throat, could not even manage a mouthful of wine. "It was fate," she said, her voice half choked.

"What?"

"What else brought you to the shop? What brought us here? Don't be vicious to me when it's no one's fault."

"No one's—" He ducked his face into his wineglass before hissing, "That was not an accident. I searched. Is that what you call fate?"

"We met. You were drawn. I was drawn. That is fate."

"I had you followed. I paid. That's how I found your flat. Don't look so stricken, for God's sake. You found my family through the card I gave you, I expect?"

"That is—" She thought of him skulking around her neighborhood, the talk that would cause. Her creditors had claimed to have seen a man. She had assumed that was St. Aubin and thought no more about it. "Who did you pay?"

He was not listening, but looking directly at her, indecorously at her, through narrowed eyes. Others at the table were beginning to flick glances in their direction. "You forced yourself into my home. If that is your idea of fate, what else have you been up to?"

Lily bit her lips to keep the panic in. She had a sickening hunch. "Tell me, who did you pay to find me?"

The roast pheasant went, but no one reversed into conversational pairs. Lily and the doctor were silenced. Rather, all present looked out to the center of the table, peering around the epergne, awaiting Lady Maude's signal. "Absolutely," she was saying to the man on her right. "Very tolerable in the spring and appalling at any other time of year. Don't you agree?" she tossed out to the table at large. "German spas. Quite superior in their way, but I would not be found in one before March."

"Without a doubt. I have always preferred the French approach—"

"My cousin was quite scandalized by the low standard of dining in a spa town in—no I believe that may have been Belgium."

"I met a medium at a spa in Germany," a round-faced man broke in.

"Did you really, Cyril?" Mr. Stubbs asked.

"She was . . ." Cyril struggled for words to frame it. "Extraordinary. She listened. One never exhausted her patience. I daresay nine-tenths of what I said was tosh but she listened to all of it and then listened to the spirits, too, of course, and advised me on what to do. She said I had a blazing affinity for home and suggested that the Lords might not be the best place for me and by God she was right. I packed it in and haven't looked back since." His face was suddenly fresh and boyish: pink, sheepish, proud, touched.

"Blimey," said Mr. Stubbs, efficiently dispatching any air of religious mystery.

Beside her the doctor set down his wineglass. She could sense him tensing as if for a leap. "There are a great many mediums currently practicing in Germany, I believe."

"It must be some feature of the geography or atmosphere— concentrated natural energies, I think I have heard it called," said Lady Maude.

"A concentration of something, I'm sure," he murmured.

"I have wondered," Lady Maude said. She stopped to consider, or perhaps give the company a chance to admire her; certainly no one interrupted. They spoke when addressed, giving Maude the appearance of a bell-ringer, selecting this size and that from her orchestra as the note was required. "I confess I would not have known you for a student of the occult, Dr. Gennett. You are known to be an exact sort of man. How did you come to be involved?"

He looked down, a calm and reflective gesture, although Lily saw the tendons of his hands taut as piano wire. "I would take 'exact' as a compliment—perhaps that betrays a dogmatic streak—but if I were flattering myself, I would also say that I strive to be open-minded."

"Not curious?" The teasing note was back in Maude's voice. The dining room seemed at once smaller, more intimate, and far more dangerous. "And it seems a bit wicked, all the conflict with your work."

"On the contrary. It is intimately connected with my work."

"Exposing frauds?" asked one of the gentlemen. "I have heard that most of them are mad, these middle-aged spinsters who have visions and such. Soured virginity, that sort of thing."

"A great many of those have no ill intent whatsoever, nor any conspiracy to deceive. This is what fascinates me. Are you familiar with what is called the power of suggestion?"

Lily reached down to grip the knobbly gilded shanks of her chair. They bit at her fingers like handfuls of thorns.

"A subject with a very strong belief—an irrational, extreme belief, I should say—has extraordinary ability to sway others with the strength of her, or of course his, deranged conviction. In severe cases one sometimes sees hysterical symptoms catching around a ward like mumps. But not only in the obvious manner, the level of conscious belief in something intangible or abstract. It can extend to physical phenomena. Say a medium—or in this case, a delusional hysteric who believes herself to be a medium—sees something out of the corner of her eye. She turns to look. Her audience, hypnotized in a sense by her conviction and personal charisma, not only believe that she has seen a ghost; they firmly believe that they have seen it, too. Or a sound—she says she hears it in the distance, or coming from a sealed casket, and so it does. But then, this type of primitive misdirection is also used by stage magicians, so it can be most difficult to determine who is innocent."

"Innocent?"

"Innocent of deliberate deception. Though it is deception just the same."

"But," interrupted the same gentleman, "this would only apply to women. Not very difficult to identify them!"

"None of this is the least bit simple, I think. But that is one theory." He drained his glass. "A reasonably insightful individual can speak as though she is on familiar terms without knowing one at all, like a paranoiac. Have you ever spoken to a paranoiac? They guess at this and guess at that until by chance they hit a mark, and then you wonder, how on earth did they know that? They can seem positively supernatural. They mightn't even realize what they're doing."

There were many uneasy expressions around the table; perhaps, like Lily, they felt the undercurrent as well as heard the words. Emily in particular was gazing at him with wounded bewilderment.

"Well!" Maude rose, and the company with her. "We will leave you gentlemen here. Perhaps you can summon up between you more restful conversation."

THE WOMEN took their leave. Gennett specifically did not watch her go out, though he surveyed both Ernestine (stiff-backed with more resentment than usual) and Emily. He would have to speak to Emily. If she kept staring at him like a dog whose tail had been stepped on, someone would be curious. He wanted their attention on Lily. He couldn't say whether he had sown any doubt, but perhaps he had persuaded a few to watch more closely.

Reasoning with her had been a spectacular failure. Thinking about it made his hands tense into claws again, his stomach knot. ("Brandy, thank you," he said, taking a cigar from the humidor the butler held out for his selection.) She looked so very helpless, drained and wary—though he was hardly one to romanticize ill health—and her skin was taking on something of the lit-from-within quality he associated with consumption. Perhaps it was only exposure to that St. Aubin that made her seem waxy and unreal.

So helpless, and then like a wounded cat if one took pity and came close. So sly and crafty, behind that air of dreamy abstraction. He could see past the way she flattered, following his every movement, devouring with her eyes as if no other man could fascinate her so. It was baffling how the others seemed oblivious to the seduction. She reeked of it. Why hadn't he recognized this before? ("Indeed— most despicable, the current government. Gladstone's rubbish shan't be cleared in a day," to which Mr. Stubbs nodded approvingly.) That was his mistake: to give her a chance to explain herself. To even entertain the possibility that she was redeemable brought the fog of confusion back down on his head. He took pity and wrenched it by the neck.

IT WAS unlike other nights. The ladies did not circulate through various clusters of talk, but clung together in one amorphous band in the center of the room. Lady Maude had Lily's hand again. Ernestine was on the other side. "Is it time yet? Should we go to the séance room, do you think?" one asked. All turned to Lily.

"The gentlemen," she said.

"Quite. They shan't take more than three-quarters of an hour; I'll send word to the butler."

Tea was produced. There was no sign of breaking up or even pausing before the men arrived, and by then it would be much too late. "Might I . . . I feel a bit . . ."

A divan was cleared and the invalid Lily laid out with maximum ceremony.

"You mustn't move, not a muscle, until you feel stronger." Lady Maude continued in a poorly disguised undertone, addressing the other women, "She is extremely, fantastically sensitive. This morning, in the Egyptian room—where we're going to attempt contact— I wanted to know if the vibrations were strong enough, and she fainted dead away the very moment she stepped through the door. It is so staggeringly charged that she can barely stand in the face of it!"

"Could I be . . ." Lily faltered. The women gathered close, perhaps expecting Delphic pronouncements ahead of schedule. "Could I be alone? For just a moment."

And so she was on another divan in a tiny retiring room just off the main one, with a cold cloth over her eyes and a watchful matron guarding the door. No other exits. She was not going to be slipping away to check the room. She was about to walk into a session cold, which she had never in her life attempted. If St. Aubin had altered any of the predetermined arrangements . . . though they had always planned to adjust them specially to suit the space . . . but he would know that she was going into it blindly and keep deviations to a minimum . . . but after the accusations he had made earlier, who knew what he would do? The cold compress dripped water down her neck, slithering fingers that made her shudder and then streaked her red gown with black.

THE MEN spoke of this and that. Few beyond the fool spouting nonsense about Germany—Cyril something, or something Cyril—seemed to have any concern for the séance. Gennett did not attempt to turn the conversation again until St. Aubin rose from his silent withdrawal, murmuring apologies. "Not going already, old man?" Gennett asked pleasantly. "Where are you off to?"

"I prefer to review my preparations in advance rather than keep my host and hostess waiting. If you will excuse me."

"A fine idea, I'm sure. I'll help." A ridiculous suggestion, but the important thing was that the other guests see how badly St. Aubin took it. His expression was eloquent.

"You are too kind, sir. I could not possibly impose."

Cyril rose. "I would be most obliged—so very interesting—unless of course my presence would somehow disrupt the proceedings."

"Disrupt?" Gennett said. "What trouble could an intelligent observer possibly cause—to an honest practitioner, of course, but we have ceased our discussion of frauds—by his mere presence?"

Cyril looked startled. "The spirit world is most delicate, Sir. I understand that you are something of a neophyte in these matters, but have you not heard how they thrive in conditions somewhat different from our own? For example, only the gentler end of the spectrum, the deep blue and indigo—"

"Like photographs," Stubbs interrupted. "You do know how photographs have to have the dark until they're cooked and done, or else they wash out and you can't see a thing. Maude told me."

Gennett found himself shifting backward. He checked himself before reaching for his brandy; he was drinking too quickly. "I have heard that theory. As the visibly dimmer end of the spectrum, blue to violet, is in fact the higher in energy, I do wonder why this would be helpful."

"Forget the lighting. Don't you scientist johnnies like a bit of privacy when you work? Making up experiments, that sort of thing?"

"Nothing in science is secretive. A man who can't stand scrutiny is no scientist at all."

"They do call them operating theaters, don't they?" another man supplied. "Anyone who likes can come in and see them sew a chap up. And they do those lectures."

St. Aubin spoke again. "But your own patients, Dr. Gennett? Is it permissible for a man outside the profession, a man such as myself, to sit in on one of your . . . sessions? And watch you cure the insane? Or would your patient prefer to speak to his doctor and his doctor alone?"

The men drew on their cigars. Gennett missed the saucer and tapped his ash out on the white damask. "You compare two unlike situations."

"To be sure, to be sure." Stubbs took the deep draw of the uncluttered conscience. "No offense meant, I'm certain. I was thinking, I've never seen this electricity and all that, what? What I mean is, I see the lightbulb and so forth, but why it's a bulb instead of a flame I don't know, and I certainly don't see what it is that electricity does to make a telegram run to India. But at our last little gathering a little girl ghost dropped a garland, a beautiful white garland of flowers on my sister's lap, out of nowhere! And there was a violin playing in the air and so forth. Amazing stuff. Amazing as a telegram, almost."

Cyril cleared his throat. "Monsieur St. Aubin, would it be all right if I accompanied you for your preparations? Dr. Gennett, would you join me?"

The men exhaled and watched. Gennett thought of a pride of lions, idly watching an antelope pass by because they were not hungry just then.

St. Aubin sat back and cocked his head in the gentlest gesture of regret. "Our time has gone in talking, I fear. If we do not make haste, the hour may pass us entirely, and there will be no spirits tonight. I will prepare myself as best I can."

Cyril tipped back the remainder of his brandy. "Pass us by? Send a footman for the ladies this instant. We should go to the room now."

"But Monsieur St. Aubin will wish to speak to Miss E first, won't he?" Gennett said blandly. "To tell her that not all preparations were made?" Gennett saw a wash of suspicion in a few eyes, he was sure of it. But St. Aubin was already shaking his head.

"No need." St. Aubin signaled the footman. "Please inform Lady Maude that we are as ready as we shall ever be."

THE BUTLER knocked and the ladies snapped to attention. Lily was back in the main room propped up with cushions and hot watered whisky. She had never drunk so much in one day in her life. "Ah, the gentlemen," Maude said. "Straight to the Egyptian room, do you think? Well, where is Monsieur St. Aubin, then? Find him. He can meet us in the anteroom. Everyone!" Lady Maude clapped her hands. Her eyes were feverishly bright and her laugher climbed the scale. They filed toward the door in a disorganized fashion, some of the men looking about for a place to set their half-finished brandy. "Take it with you, for goodness' sake. Come along now!"

Mr. Stubbs came to offer Lily the support of his arm. She had scarcely spoken to him. He was large and slow of speech and regarded her from afar with oxlike eyes, and mild interest without curiosity. Lady Maude was a Virgo with strong Leo influences (which partially explained her affinity for the doctor) but Lily hadn't cast Mr. Stubbs's chart. Why hadn't she cast it? "Who are you hoping to reach, Mr. Stubbs?"

"Maude has quite a list. This queen Cleopatra would make quite a show, I think. I'll put my money on her."

"What do you think of it? This business."

"A very nice diversion for the ladies." He didn't qualify or apologize, and there was no malice in it. Lily found his flat-footedness refreshing. Perhaps that was the attraction for Maude as well—that and the money.

In the dark of the hall a hard grip fastened on her upper arm; she jumped.

"It's only me," hissed Ernestine. "Mr. Stubbs, I'll take her. What did you think of that performance at dinner?" Ernestine demanded. Lily motioned for her to keep her voice down, forgetting the darkness, but Ernestine brought her voice under control without prompting. "Get him thrown out if you can. End the entire thing as quickly as possible and then come back to London with me. Now that you have Maude's approval you're someone to society and he has no legitimate grounds for objection." They were coming to the room. Ernestine broke off and hurried on ahead. For a moment there was no one fighting for her arm or her ear—but then there was another at her elbow, with bird-light and brittle hands.

"Lily, I just don't know! It makes no sense!" Emily whispered. "I must confess something to you. I had meant to say nothing—he asked me to say nothing, but you must know that there is a plan afoot. He is here to make peace with his sister and he means to do it by accepting the mysteries of the spirit world at last! He has been studying! I simply cannot explain that horrid, horrid stuff at the table; he is not usually so stupid! Oh, bother, there's Maude." Emily detached and fled.

"Lily, he hasn't left you to struggle on all alone! Oliver, really. Are you trying to sabotage this séance?" Lady Maude swept back out to the hallway, wrapped her arm around Lily's shoulders, and led her into the lighted room.

44

The Rules Suspended

It was one of those theme rooms for which the gentry had developed such an appetite in the previous generation. The only illumination came from candles in curious lanterns (Moroccan, if anything) of pierced copper, but in the rough diamonds of light he could see wall hangings in geometric patterns, a round mahogany table, stiff-backed stone cats, and above the fire a bust of Nefertiti, its eyes painted like a tart's. The wallpaper was William Morris. Maude was guiding Lily to the seat closest to the fire. "No," Lily said, "the chair opposite." Her voice was cat's-tongue rough; now she sounded as though she'd been beaten up, as well as looked it. "If I sit with my back to the fire, how will you be able to see me?" Nodding all around, Gennett saw. He also saw that the seat with its back to the fire was taken by St. Aubin.

"Doctor?" Maude, less warm to him than she had been before his remarks at dinner, still motioned him to a choice seat beside her own.

"Thank you, but it's wasted on me. I'll just be observing." He took a chair at three o'clock to Lily's twelve, and St. Aubin's six, the better to see them with. Ernestine, not bothering to consult the hostess, stalked to the chair farthest from him—that was at nine o'clock. She gave him the lady's stare: glancing baleful looks once per minute. His mother took the next chair. He marveled at how breeding allowed her to behave as if she were insensible to the atmosphere. Emily sat between them, an imperfect eight o'clock, squeezed in on the distended quarter of the table. The other numbers filled in; he hardly cared how.

"Thirteen," Miss Lawrence said. "I suppose it was twelve before you, Dr. Gennett, but I'm sure that will be lucky in its way. Won't it be lucky, Miss E?"

"Thirteen can be an auspicious number, as can twelve."

THIRTEEN WAS a terrible number. The Zodiac twelve had been the plan from the beginning. Lily stole a glance at the interloper. The hard front of his white shirt did strange things with the lamplight—a mirror, bathing the chin in light; a severed head in white tie, burning. He joked pleasantly with his neighbors but he was burning.

Her séance state was coming on now—the lightness and the rising feeling, porous to sensation, carrying. But there was something different in the mixture. She stretched her fingers, counted breaths. What was it? If only Maude would stop talking.

St. Aubin caught her eyes. His face was as unreadable to her as to the others, his special-occasions monocle a round silver coin. She knew he was looking at her. He could be signaling. She should have spoken to him, she should have found a way, if only to apologize. For what? Anything. She would apologize for the fall of Man if it would get her through this sitting and out of this room, if it would extinguish the doctor and take him away. She couldn't stop thinking of his hands. Would Maude never be quiet?

"Is everyone ready? It is very important that you concentrate. And listen to Miss Lily, but concentrate, and do not break the circle—ignore distractions, but leave yourself open to impressions and sensations, and messages . . ."

MAUDE WAS gabbling on. Surely this wasn't how the show was intended to begin, with amateur patter before the performers were released on stage? Gennett saw glances sent back and forth. Maude's cheeks were pink and her breast rose and fell faster as she blathered on about Egypt; she looked on the verge of a fit. "Oh, dear—join hands! It is very important that you join hands!" So that was what she meant by not breaking the circle. It was the worst after-dinner speech he had ever heard.

Gennett fought to keep his face respectful and attentive while his feet were busy under the table, feeling along the floor for pedals, levers, wires. Damn these hard evening pumps; he couldn't feel a thing. There! Something was there. It was . . . Mrs. Cummings's foot. "I beg your pardon." She gave him a look to quell rowdy boys in church.

Damn his shoes and damn the darkness—he couldn't read the faces across the table well, let alone search for wires. This was not going to be as simple as he had hoped.

". . . and in the third dynasty, under the great mystic Imhotep, it was foretold that a great queen would arise and rescue Egypt from her isolation—"

"Indeed, Lady Maude. Such was the power of their affinity for the eternal." St. Aubin's rich, round amber tones seemed to come from behind them and around them. Gennett had underestimated that voice. "A power that endures, separated from us by the thinnest of barriers: a veil, mere gauze to those with the gift of seeing. Shall we see through it tonight? Let us direct our minds. Let us concentrate."

Let us pray. That was where the voice was from, not the theater; not even the operating theater where Gennett had been taught to imitate that tone of absolute authority. He would lay a bet now as to where St. Aubin had trained. But knowing was not the same as resisting. Gennett's back twanged straight, his head bowed by itself. He felt shame for his frivolous, wandering thoughts. But it was all shrewd artifice, nothing more, nothing more. . . .

St. Aubin had taken control at last. Lily pushed the panic back down beneath her feet. It would be all right. He would not betray her, he would not.

"Is our guide here? There is a spirit to whom Miss E is a firm friend, one Mar . . ."

He was on to a spirit-guide story. Not so scientific as their usual approach, but safe. This was to be their triumph, and now they were bailing water to try and get it into harbor in one piece. But she shouldn't let herself be distracted by his share of the work; she needed to concentrate, reach her state. Stop floating to the surface. Stop looking across. . . .

No pedals under the table? That meant wires, or hidden assistants. Air currents could betray a hidden passageway or trapdoor. Did he dare to light a cigarette and watch where the smoke drifted? He did not.

St. Aubin was rolling out golden words in a long, shining tail of narrative, childish rot about a slave girl in ancient Egypt, but the sitters were rapt. Maude was quivering with excitement. Ernestine looked, amazingly, distracted from her ire; his mother, puzzled; Emily, halfway to a state of religious ecstasy. Lily was white as death.

He knew that she could be making herself shiver, could be hyperventilating to make her fingers blue, her eyes feverish. She could have doped her own drink after dinner: opiates, stimulants, sinister unclassified Eastern drugs. Belladonna in her eyes to make them black and wild. Wax to make her lips look wet. He had seen every kind of self-hypnosis and hysterical suggestion, just as he had heard preachers, madmen, carnival barkers, ghost stories. Aside from nerves—yes, aside from that—there was no earthly reason for the hair rising on the back of his neck, or the sweat, or the fear.

Then she screamed.

They all jumped. She jumped. "Miss Lily," St. Aubin intoned from the far end of the table, "are you well? What is happening? Are the spirits attempting to make contact?"

SOMETHING WAS happening, certainly. Her hands were numb and her head was buzzing, heightened awareness magnifying small sounds to overpowering booms. The currents were flowing through the joined hands. All this was typical, part of opening herself to the influences, how she had always known that there was more to it all than fraud. Something was happening and then the guests would take it as whatever they wanted. But now—her breath came shorter and faster. The cards had failed to warn her of his arrival. His chance appearance at the shop had not been chance at all. If fate was not fate, she couldn't be sure of anything. Might this feeling not be just what the doctor had described at dinner? Mightn't it be madness?

SOMETHING WAS happening. It was as if a live circuit were running through the clasped hands around the table. Gennett could feel buzzing and numbness in his arms, and sweat. Some exotic scent— spicy, resinous—wafted up from beneath the table. (No, from the fire, surely; a fragrant combustible St. Aubin had thrown in the fire without him noticing.) And a sound: low rustling, almost a hum. Insects? His ankles twitched as if beetles were already crawling on them. How were they doing it?

"Miss Lily, what do you see? Is Mar with you?"

She cried out again. Gennett began to shake in sympathy. She was—she appeared to be—in anguish. Her eyes were crushed shut as if denying the unbearable. "She is here," Lily whispered. In the faces around the table he saw awe and horror and dismay but also titillation. They wouldn't be looking for wires.

"What tidings from our friends on the other side?"

Lily made a piteous noise, a not entirely decorous moan. The men leaned in closer. "I—"

"Everyone, concentrate!" St. Aubin barked. "Send every ounce of your psychic strength across time."

Gennett's hands were squeezed violently on both sides. The scent, the smoke, the grating, buzzing noise all climbed to a desperate pitch. Some of the women began to moan in sympathy. He was sweating like a pig. How were they doing it? Whatever their stage effects, this panic was as real as the scream clawing to escape his throat.

"What do you see?"

"A man and a boy," she said, her voice a soft moan of agony. "No, two men. One large, one very small—ah!"

COULD SHE doubt it now that her visions were nothing but her own fears blown up with air? As she cried out, the image, which was surely nothing but her creditors calling after her debts, caught fire like a paper lantern and burned away.

"That must be the boy pharaoh, her brother!" Lady Maude cried out. "Do you see *her*?"

"Lily, who is Mar showing you? Is it the Queen of Egypt?" She knew St. Aubin well enough to hear the panic in his voice. The dizziness was turning dark and frightening. The only response she could muster was to whimper in pain. "Mar!" St. Aubin shouted. "Do you hear us? Will you give us a sign?"

A SOUR gong. Gennett was not the only one to cry out. There was—there was a giant brass gong hanging in the air over the table, the mallet before it priming for another strike. It had to weigh seven stone. How in hell was it suspended in midair? How?

"Mar! Tell us if the queen is near!"

The table shuddered and rose. *There were no levers beneath it.* The insects were chattering—he could feel them running over his feet in swarms, asps twining around his ankles in the baking desert heat—

"Yes!"

Gennett's hands were in the air, the circle broken, the table swinging up in slow motion where he had struck it with both fists from beneath—but it was not he who had spoken. Emily was on her feet, knocking the other guests aside, waving her arms in the air. "I am she! My eyes are open now—I am the queen reborn! I am Cleopatra!"

Maude gaped, the table upended, somewhere strings were twanging and snapping and the gong swung crazily by one corner of its frame. Formerly hidden wires dangled obscenely. A rogue noisemaker brayed from its hiding place, now hopelessly out of sync with the script. St. Aubin disappeared in an explosion of flash powder. Lily was gone.

45
The Last Open Door

She heard feet pounding by. If she breathed, they would find her. If she spared a thought for what had just happened, she would start screaming and never stop.

It was a tiny retiring room just off of the sitting room the women had gone to after dinner, a room for fainting, bad turns, spells. A basin and compress sat on a table beside the divan. There were no other doors. Lily stood in a corner—not crouching or cowering or hiding, just standing—in the dark. He shut the door behind him. There was no light save the pale moon seeping in around the curtains. "I will not tell them you're here," he said.

"You can."

"I will not. You can escape, I'll help you. I understand now. All that in the room . . . it was real to you, wasn't it? You never meant to deceive? Say that you didn't."

She was not too far gone for scorn. It was the only readable emotion on her chalk white face.

"I can give you money. All you need do is go. Never trouble us again." He was pleading. He felt, somehow, that it was not quite too late.

"You wouldn't. Why should you?"

"I have already helped you. I paid your debts at the hospital for your mother's care—I didn't tell her I paid, but I did. I paid your rent. I have helped you and I will help you again if you will only go."

"You . . . what?" Her thoughts were bobbing on open sea and now the last bit of flotsam that might buoy her up spun away. There was nothing to lose now. "You paid for me? To my creditors?"

"To your landlord. He was about to take your flat from you."

It was delicious in its way, this anger that dashed her senses out. Giving it vent was freedom. "You went up and paid for me. We have worked—we had a reputation, no one could touch us on that. And now you've paid for me and made me a whore!"

Now she had her fists on his chest and her nails on his face and it felt wonderful.

SHE WAS having a psychotic episode. She was so small it should be far less trouble to catch her wrists—her fingernails raked his cheek and it burned, far more pain than it ought. He would injure them both restraining her. He had his arms around her and her clawing fingers were at his chest. He pushed her against a table.

Now SHE had his lip in her teeth. It felt better still.

HER MOUTH slid over his, oiled with coppery blood. Her heart was rattling like a bird in a cage against her corset—now his hands in place of the corset—her skin was smooth and hot and very slightly musky, maddeningly sweet—why—

THE DOOR opened.

PART SIX

ECLIPSE

46

"It is almost a definition of a gentleman to
say he is one who never inflicts pain."

—John Henry (Cardinal) Newman,
The Idea of a University, 1852

He rolled in before dawn when the bakery boys were still passing their burdens to sleep-dulled maids. He would need to
reach his mother and explain, but not in evening dress with
the shirt studs torn off and blood on the collar. Wilson would—
God damn it, Wilson was still at the Stubbs Hall. He had with luck
been given time to collect his master's clothes.

Gennett hadn't been thrown out. Eviction had been understood.
Anticlimactic in its way, tucking his clothes back into a semblance of
order before walking out past the blank faces. Some had turned
while he struggled with buttons, conspiring to give him some parody of privacy, but others had not, Stubbs among them. (Disgusted,
but not, he fancied, surprised.) That was how he knew that this was
not going to be simple. God knew where a carriage had been found
at that time of night but it wasn't the Stubbses's.

He climbed the steps with a drunk's care and unlocked his door.
His evening shoe skidded on a square of greasy paper. It was an envelope. He looked around him in puzzlement, but his post—weeks of
it, unopened—sat where Wilson had left it, in a reproachful stack by

the door. This bore no stamp, no name or address; any ink had been smeared away. It stank but his hands were already dirty. Inside: no name, no salutation, only a half-literate hand on foolscap: *We do not bluff.*

He stood staring while the day grew no younger, while Ernestine would be filling their mother's ears with poison. Eventually his eyes trailed back to the foyer table and the basket of post. Letters from colleagues, letters from friends, bills. A half-dozen letters in the same envelopes and addressed in the same hand.

October 30th, '96

Dr. Gennett,

I regretted your indisposition yesterday noon, and regret more that I have not heard from you since. I can only surmise that your excellent servant is not as meticulous with calling cards as he is in guarding his master's privacy—but this last is the supreme virtue in a servant, and always to be valued most highly. It is in fact on the subject of privacy that I and my colleague wish to speak with you. It is a matter of some urgency. We will be most grateful for your swift reply—as, I am certain, will you.

Best regards,

Henry Bettering, Esq.

Gennett turned out the tray by the door. Three cards from Bettering, one badly creased as if by a tussle at the door. How many more were submerged in the chaos of his office he could not say. The tone of the letters suggested very low tolerance for frustration. *Some urgency ... to your advantage ... limited patience ... indisposed to accept rudeness.* Then a shock like icy water:

November 27th, '96

If you wish your relations with Lily Embly to be made public, by all means continue in your current course of flagrant disregard. Consider this warning to be your final one. Your arrogance is astronomical. Should you invite it upon yourself, be assured that its reward shall be more than commensurate.

"Final warning," was the thought that surfaced first through the gray wash that threatened to engulf him. Then, "made public" to whom?

47

Character

The butler's reaction told her everything she needed to know. "Is Madam quite certain? We were not prepared for your return; I fear that you might find the reception wanting. I would be delighted to ascertain whether an alternative accommodation could be found." Blocking the door he said this, drawled it in his put-on toffee voice while she stood on the stoop.

"You misunderstand. I am here to collect my belongings, which is the work of a quarter hour. I am sure that your staff would prefer not to be involved in my packing." And he let her, for once, lead herself upstairs.

Someone hadn't waited on the packing. As she came close she heard thumping and rustling from her suite, no attempt at disguise. She stole up the corridor on her toes, gripped the knob, and threw the door open in a rush.

St. Aubin was throwing her new gowns in a trunk. He glanced up at her without slowing. "You took your own sweet time."

"You left me. When I went upstairs after the séance you were gone."

"I divined that we had outstayed our welcome. Hadn't you? The servants' entrance was quite as discreet as advertised. Besides, I knew you could get yourself out without help."

"They threw me out," she said. Her hand was still on the knob, for support, and he was moving on to her hairbrush and toilet articles. He shrugged, wrapping an alabaster box she didn't think was hers in a wool shawl. "Did you hear me? They threw me out of the house!" They had done more than that. Maude had slapped her. Ernestine and Emily had abandoned her without a word. The duke's granddaughter and the others had merely stared as she tried to cover herself with the remains of her dress, the way they would stare at a Hottentot Venus paraded for a shilling a peek. Her shoulders burned with the effort of keeping straight in the face of it. She had never known that she had so much pride to lose.

"What did you expect? You've ruined us, you do know that." He moved on to the drawers. "My dear, I have been in this business since before you were born. I rode out the bad years and I saw every huckster with a white sheet do his best to destroy the reputation of the profession, and I have never seen any quite as stupid as you."

"That is enough," she croaked.

". . . but despite the fact that you are the worst fool in Christendom, I am prepared to give you one more chance. I have ever been too softhearted for my own good. If you think that you have learned your lesson and have had a bit of proper obedience knocked into you, pick something up and make yourself useful. There's a train to Dover at twenty past ten; we'll just catch the ferry to Calais."

"I can't go to France with you!"

"My dear." He gave her a sneer of miraculous power; it made her, in her current state, feel more degraded. "I do think it's a bit late to be worrying about your honor. Never mind. I'll marry you as soon as we reach Rouen. You'll just have to keep up appearances until then." He seemed to take her shocked silence for assent. Men never expected their proposals to be rebuffed. "Good. Take one of the smaller boxes and get it past the butler. There's a growler on that side street to the left."

"What about my mother?"

"She'll accept it. I realize that her hopes had risen of late, but when she hears that you're not likely to get a flat and a suite of emeralds out of your gentleman, I'm sure she'll reconcile herself. She was ever the most practical of women."

"I can't leave her."

He looked at her then and seemed about to say something that wasn't quite so vicious, but then shrugged and turned back to the vanity table.

She leaned on the doorknob until it must, surely must, break—then she could throw it. It would shatter behind his ear, or it could even be caught and thrown back. It could, it might, it needn't. Nothing need happen at all. The future was a black maw that swallowed her signs and reasons. It was only she, stringing together portents without admitting the intervention to herself, who made a pattern of it. And all to conceal a tawdry thing like lust.

"You can take all of that. Give me my share of the money and I'll go."

"The money." He packed faster. Any trace of softening was gone. "You have a most primitive idea of finances, my dear. One must speculate to accumulate. Existing obligations must be met first—"

"You didn't say you were in debt!"

"—and given all I have done for you, laying out my attention and connections quite selflessly, you really should be paying me!" His voice rose to drown her out.

"We earned it together."

"If you wish to accompany me, you may. That is my final offer." He was nearly finished. The valuables had been reduced to small and easily carried packages. What was left had been cunningly rearranged; one might not notice how much was missing at the first or even second look.

"Mr. Bettering says he's calling in the debt, Mama's and mine. He wants his money today."

"Then you had best make your arrangements without delay." He tucked the various packages discreetly about his person. "Oh, yes." At one pocket he paused to draw something out to make space. "There is something here for you; from your erstwhile paramour, in fact. He meant to give it to you himself, but the best laid plans, eh?" He dropped a small parcel on the bed. "Good day."

Inside was one of Mama's medicine bottles and—

Scratched, creased, blotted, cracked in half, her Page of Cups. Her old, lost Page, of whom she had made so much. The last of her faith in fate burnt up and blew away.

⟞⟞ 48 ⟞⟞

Monday, November 30,
the Kensington Hospital

> "I owe my results to a new method of
> psycho-analysis, Josef Breuer's exploratory
> procedure; it is a little intricate, but it is irre-
> placeable, so fertile has it shown itself to be
> in throwing light upon the obscure paths."
>
> —Sigmund Freud, *Heredity and the*
> *Aetiology of Neuroses,* 1896

I simply wish to know—"

"That is not important at this time, Dr. Gennett. It is a source that we take seriously, and I will remind you that you are obli- gated to answer our questions. This is not yet a formal inquiry but you will not want obstructiveness to damage your case further."

The governor sat in a long row of directors and depart- ment heads, all Gennett's seniors. Behind him, fanned out in wings, sat an audience of his contemporaries. This should be taking place in a private office, not a spare operating theater. The added humiliation made the outcome of the meeting a matter of little suspense.

"Then I request that the allegations against me be clarified. I can hardly explain if I don't know where the misunderstanding arose."

The governor gazed down over his glasses like a headmaster. It was a comic note in the midst of grave undertakings. Gennett felt a manic giggle welling up in his gut, of the sort that had been popping up often in the last few hours. He suppressed it for now.

"The substance of the matter," the governor continued, "is possible improper relations with patients under your care. Do you care to elaborate?"

Gennett could do no more than shake his head.

"A young woman of disordered mind, whom you approached in the vicinity of another hospital with which you are affiliated—"

"That was—this woman is not and never was a patient of mine!"

The interruption was a terrible mistake. The governor retreated to stony disapproval. Another director, an old-fashioned prude with no head for analysis, whom Gennett had never liked, sprang forward into the breach. "I believe that you do understand the nature of these allegations, Dr. Gennett. Did you not present yourself at this unfortunate woman's home in the character of a physician?"

"There is also the matter," drawled another, "of curious after-hours visits to this hospital, one St. Botolph's. We have another letter here from a patient, a Mr. Coffley—not a patient of yours, that is significant—alleging that you came to him to perform strange and degenerate experiments in dynamic psychiatry. Nocturnal visits have been confirmed by the night porter—"

"Not female patients! I spend time with my patients as their cases demand; this is occasionally outside scheduled treatment hours."

"Ah yes, treatment. You are well known for your progressive approach. Many of the innovations you have proposed here have been rejected as excessively experimental. I presume that this St. Botolph's has fewer objections." He affected a casual glance at the papers before him. "Is it true you are the primary financial backer of St. Botolph's?"

"Now wait—"

"Not forgetting the subject of female patients," snapped Gennett's hidebound opponent, glaring briefly at the other questioner, "is it true that you have been linked, shall I say, to the aforementioned woman, in a social context? That she has been seen at your home?"

"And what is this rumor about the wife of yet another patient paying calls at your private club? The wife of a patient whom you yourself committed?"

"This is insane! This is entirely twisted—what am I accused of!"

Murmuring at the back was cut off by the governor. Suddenly benevolent, he waved back the questioners and folded his hands. "Dr. Gennett, I hardly need to remind you that your conduct of late has been, shall we say, erratic, and the course of your research frankly degenerate. Concern has been mounting for some time. On a personal as well as a professional level we must agree that you are unfit to respond to charges. Let us suspend the inquiry until such time as you are more yourself. Gentlemen."

The senior board began to gather papers and chat.

"Sir! I've had no opportunity to answer these . . . I don't want to call them charges. I cannot let my colleagues walk out with a distorted pack of rumors—"

"There will be ample time to discuss it. For now, Dr. Gennett, you may consider yourself at leave."

Gennett was left to wait while his contemporaries filed out by the main door. Only a few glanced at him as they passed. One face remained resolutely askance. With a start, Gennett realized this was Booth. He took a step closer. "Booth, what—"

Booth glanced up in alarm and wedged himself into the departing throng. No one looked up at Gennett again.

49

Departure

The lockbox was gone. The clock, the quilt, the lamp, all brought from home, had been taken as well, so Carola knew. They had sat for hours in the dark and Carola had not yet asked about St. Aubin or the great enterprise. How long they would sit was something the doctors would not answer. *Tonight? Perhaps, perhaps. I wouldn't leave her side if I were you, young lady. But tomorrow? Quite possibly. No one can say.* Carola was propped up on an extra bolster to ease her breathing. Each draught of breath was an epic that drained them both; each took longer, and when it had come and gone at last and left its snip of relief, the room was colder. Lily sat on a stool with a shawl around her that she pulled closer as the moon rose.

Carola spoke from time to time. "Is it getting colder in here?"

"Yes, Mama, a little."

"Take another blanket, then."

"I don't need it."

"Take it, I'm roasting."

"I'm fine." Lily answered her as briefly as possible. This was her last chance to answer, or to ask any of the questions that had been left to lie between them over the years. But to speak them aloud would be to admit that this was the end. The breaths were not the epics, really. Within each there were a score of moments that rose, and then came to the crisis—she would say—and then fell away, dead. She had not.

In a way it had always been thus. The two of them, sitting, the unfinished things around them almost comforting, a great warming web of expectations not yet met. With so many promises yet to keep, how could they part? With no success, no men, no change to come between them, they had been safe.

"I didn't sleep a wink last night. For that damned consumptive next door. Gone, now?"

"I don't know, Mama."

"Lily." The wheezing grew heavier. She was gathering herself. "Lily, what will you do?"

Lily quailed.

"Answer me."

Lily took a deep breath to answer but it came out in a ragged ladder, gasping up the scale.

"My girl. I'll tell you. Don't run out on the debt. It can't be much, but not much is enough to catch up with you." A pause to rest. "St. Aubin risks it too often. Don't bind yourself to him. Learn, but put him off if he wants more."

"What," Lily kept a grip on her voice, "did you think he wanted?"

"Anything he could get. Don't give it to him. But let him think you might. Do you know, that man thinks he has a deal with me? He took a fancy to you once, and men never learn to give those up. It feels like losing. He wanted something of value in return for his teachings. So I let him think. But I never promised, and nor should you. Same with your hoity-toity doctor." She laughed without air, a kind of feathery putt-putt. "Not sure what. But he's good for something."

"No, he's not."

Carola was giving her the kind of look where dark didn't matter. You could almost smell that look. Maybe it had always been down to that, all Carola's imbroglios, quick rises and heroically slow declines: paper propped up with that look. You could taste something real and that made you patient with the paper. "Don't rule him out yet. But . . . that's not the problem."

Lily shook her head, a blanket denial, of everything. "I'm all right." They had found her at the duke's but perhaps they had been bluffing when they'd said they'd found Carola. She didn't know when they intended to collect, either. Except that it would be soon. "I made a mistake. I made many."

"You need to be on the move," Carola said. "It's all gone very wrong, hasn't it? Is there any chance?"

"No."

"You can't be delaying here, then."

It was the time, if ever there had been a time in her life, to grasp at the yes, affirm. I will never leave you. She would say it. She would . . .

The moment passed away. The real answer hung between them.

"Go. It will wrong-foot them." Wrong-foot them because what kind of woman would leave her mother to die alone? That was left unsaid, too.

"I'm a disappointment to you."

"My dear." Carola's hand curled up to beckon: Come. It was clear even in the darkness. Lily dropped her shawl and curled tight to her mother's side in a ball. Carola's icy hands stroked her hair. Cold lips kissed. "All children are in some way. I am a child as well."

Lily ran back from the omnibus stop; a hack would have alerted her entire neighborhood. (Her old neighborhood—she had to remember that she'd likely never see it again.) There wasn't much left in the flat, but the scraps would do if one knew where to sell insignificant things, which she did. On saucers and ribbons and bits of cloth she could make Southwark. Then from across the river, to the coast? That was a problem for later. She took the stairs with a burglar's grace. She was very good at slipping past the landlord and his piecework slaves. No one would know she was here. The door gave at her touch before she'd taken out her key. She wasn't quick enough; the hand that reached around the frame had her by the arm. Then other hands had her by the throat.

"You're trouble enough for six, Miss Lily," said the great round one. "You didn't think you'd fool old Bettering, did you? Hope you said good-bye to your mama. Won't be seeing her again."

The little shriveled one and the other men laughed and then the beating began.

50

Tuesday, December 1, Eaton Place

GEORGE PROCTOR, age 46, was charged
with loitering, supposed for the purpose of
committing a felony . . . the prisoner then
said, "it is my luck. I've only come out of
prison from doing 12 months for loitering."

—*The Times*, from the "Police" column,
December 1, 1896

He loitered on the street corner, walked past. He'd walked from Kensington to Belgravia twice yesterday only to turn back, not quite ready to admit defeat. But there could not be another night of wandering the streets. Besides, his mother deserved an explanation, now that his disgrace would make them all social outcasts together.

Resolved, he turned at last for the house. As he mounted the steps two men in drab coats detached themselves from the background and hurried to block him. The shorter of the two touched his hat in a parody of deference.

"Police, Sir. A moment of your time?"

THEY DECLINED brandy and so Gennett was forced to do without. He would have given blood for it. They sat still as choirboys and watched Gennett's hands shake. Outside the morning room door were the servants and Ernestine.

"Gentlemen," Gennett began, "I would be most grateful if this business could be conducted away from my family home. The upset to the ladies—you know how easily ladies can misunderstand."

"Quite, Sir," said the shorter of the two detectives, nodding in agreement but doing nothing to comply.

They were working to unsettle him, Gennett thought, pinning his shaking fists against his knees. That is what he would do in their place.

"We had to meet you somewhere, you know, and since you never went back to your flat last night—no need to confirm that, we already have. Not much point in waiting for you at the Kensington hospital. Since you've been suspended, I expect you won't be much there in the future."

"Perhaps you could tell me the nature of your business?"

"The nature of our business?" The detective was rankled by that. Another mistake to throw in the pile. "That's something you'll have to help us with, sir. It's a very curious business, this. We know what it is that's happened, but we'll need you to explain it."

Gennett shook his head in confusion. If obfuscation was the latest thing in interrogation techniques, it had yet to filter down to the academic journals. The shorter seemed ready to wait him out, certain that he had found a mousehole and given enough patience a mouse would appear, but the taller intervened.

"It's about a Miss Lily Embly."

"It is not a police matter."

Their eyebrows shot up. They meant to force him to say it. "It was not—I understand that there were, different interpretations but that was a misunderstanding. It was a mistake, but a mutual one. We're both paying for it now."

"Paying," said the taller.

"It was mutual, our . . . convergence. It was not an, an assault." Both fixed their eyes on his cheek. He had forgotten the scabbed-over scratches. Oh, God. "Why are you even here? You were tipped off, weren't you?"

"Our sources are not your concern."

"That's what my hospital board said! I am being—I would not reveal this to anyone but the authorities, but I am being black-mailed. A man called Bettering, or who calls himself Bettering. I would not pay him and now appalling lies are being spread."

"About your relations with Miss Embly?"

"Yes!" Gennett waited for them to apologize and offer their help, but both consulted their notepads with grave concentration.

"But you were involved with Miss Embly."

"In a certain sense. I wanted to help her—I didn't know her rep-rehensible profession, then—but my sister is entirely potty about the supernatural and I never consciously pursued, or consciously accepted that I was pursuing, because I fear that I was—it's very complicated. This Bettering threatens to misrepresent it, that's all."

Their eyes dropped from his cheek to his grubby, slept-in suit. "You look most unwell, sir."

"I've been walking all night. I was most upset by these develop-ments, as you can imagine."

"I see. Where were you last night between the hours of eleven and three?"

"What?"

"Mr. Gennett, have you seen this morning's paper?"

Sharp knocking came from the hall door. "We're not finished, Mr. Gennett," the shorter warned, but the door swung open without an answer. Booth and Platt stormed in still in their topcoats, Ernes-tine trailing behind.

"She rang him at the club," Platt said shortly, jabbing his thumb at Ernestine and Booth in turn. "Some unearthly nonsense about police. Didn't want me to come, either of them, but can you imag-ine Maurice Booth facing down Her Majesty's finest? Now then," he said to the detectives, "you two can shove off."

The shorter detective was too stunned at the impertinence to speak. The taller was more composed, but clutched his hat in both hands, creating an unfortunate resemblance to a tradesman explaining himself to the master. "This is an investigation, Sir."

"Investigation, my foot," Platt barked. "Some girl, isn't it? She should have her father 'round if she feels hard done by, not the police. You're being made a fool of, man. If Gennett's told you it's settled, that's the end of the matter."

"They mean to ruin us!" wailed Ernestine. "They'll rip our family name to shreds!"

"If you take the word of some cheap floozy over that of a gentleman, I am profoundly shocked," said Booth.

"It's this Bettering!" Gennett shouted. "It's a plot of his, all of it!"

"Mr. Bettering?" Mrs. Allen the housekeeper appeared from the hall. "The Mr. Bettering as was here last week? He was a great round man with wee spectacles—and a nasty wee lad in a flat cap at his elbow—he said you would know him. I didn't like his voice, Sir. Should I have let him in after all?"

After all. Gennett felt the room begin to rock gently back and forth in his vision. He was back in the smoke and shouting of the Spitalfields tavern, his tongue sour with beer. No mystery at all as to how Bettering knew of him, nor coincidence. They were entrepreneurial blackmailers; they fostered scandal the better to profit from it. Lily was mildly famous in her neighborhood, he had found. They had known it was her Gennett sought from his first description in the tavern, and then served her to him like a poisoned apple. A grating noise in the background, manic giggling, puzzled him until he realized that it was his own. "They guessed, or rather I told them, I suppose. Did all of you know? Was it scrawled across my face all these weeks?"

Ernestine tried to shush him, the alarm in her face mounting to terror.

"Oh yes—how must it look to the policemen! All the time I was following that woman with one thing in mind!"

"Dr. Gennett admits his association with one Miss Lily Embly," the embattled taller detective barked, "who has been the victim of a terrible crime. Our informant was highly specific, though we'd rather he hadn't told the papers as well as us." He drew from his jacket the morning edition of the *London Daily Graphic*. On an inside page under a headline in screaming bold—GENTLEMAN KILLER—was an ink illustration in the most lurid Gothic style. A dark girl, her dress torn indecently, cowered in terror like Nancy in an illustration from Dickens, but instead of Bill Sykes, her tormentor was a leering beast in monocle and topper, Dr. Jekyll in tails. "We don't take our marching orders from Fleet Street, mind you, but if her lover here didn't do her in, then I'd like to know who did."

HE WOKE very gradually. The curtains were drawn but he could hear faint heralds of the end of day: maids lighting lamps in the hall, traffic on the road fading to a carriage now and then. It was so very calm and restful to remain with his arms flat at his sides, his clothes loosened. The tourniquet on his arm lay slack now, but he knew that his present repose was owed to morphine. He did not much care. He could just remember falling into a fit: dropping to his knees, raving; incoherently cursing Bettering, Ernestine, himself, all present. A form of shock, really, compounded by lack of food and sleep. How it must have looked to the policemen. He found that he did not much care about that either.

He could hear them in the next room: Ernestine and Booth, conferring, bewailing the same regrettable facts. (Booth should give Ernestine a bit of morphine, Gennett wagered.) They weren't troubling much to keep their voices low.

"We must. It's in most of the papers for the evening edition. The police can't be made to drop it now." (That was Booth, soothing or wheedling, depending on one's interpretation.)

"It's abominable, Maurice!" (This was Ernestine.)

"I know. Disgracefully impertinent, the lot of them. For a good family to be treated in such a manner—"

"We were a good family!" Much sobbing followed. "It's no better than having him in prison!"

"It's much better. It's only temporary. Just keeping him out of the way long enough to let this pass out of gossip and then the entire thing can be dealt with properly, quietly."

"Why now? Why can't we wait? I only met with you to share information, to stop my brother being such a fool. I never meant— so drastic—I need to think about it."

"If something turns up . . . they won't find any real evidence against him, of course; it's unthinkable that there would be any- thing to find. I'm not certain that they can even bring a case before they've found a body. . . ."

No body? Gennett thought.

". . . some blood and a missing girl and a landlord who claims to have seen Ambrose earlier in the week, that's all. It doesn't make for a murder. The newspapers may print libel by anonymous letter writers, but the police have only this informant's word that the tart is even dead. But you know how these vulgar little beasts are. They're loving this, getting their hands on their betters. They'll charge him the moment they conjure up a pretext and then it will be too late."

No body? Only blood, and reports of a violent struggle, and more slander of the kind that had poisoned the hospital board against him? She could be alive. He felt rents opening up in his pain- less apathy. Perhaps he should get up after all. He rose unsteadily and put his ear to the paneling. He could hear them clearly now.

Ernestine was bawling. "It's only temporary!" said Booth. "Don't say anything to Platt until they arrive."

Were the police coming back already? Gennett couldn't think, couldn't even stay crouched by the wall. He slid to the floor and let his spinning head rest. The damage was done; was there any point at all? How long he sat there before the slamming door in the next room woke him he didn't know. It was Platt, and a troupe of thud- ding feet.

"These ruffians say you sent for them! I won't have it!"

"Be reasonable, Platt. It's for the best."

"You're a damned sly bastard, Booth! Don't think I don't know what you're up to, you and Miss Gennett." There was rumbling and low shouting, and a woman's shrill cry. Then Platt's voice rose to a bellow. "You'll keep him out of police hands by putting him in a madhouse? While you two manage his money? If he's half a mind left, he's already out of this house! If he hears me, he'll be running now!"

Then scuffling and slamming doors. There was only a moment to be befuddled, or the morphine told him it was only a moment before men in coats, orderlies, streamed in to his room. They found him by the wall and lifted him into the strait-waistcoat like a toy.

Platt was there in the doorway. "You bloody fool!" Platt shouted. "Why didn't you run?"

[EPILOGUE]

Thursday, June 10, 1926

Are you certain you wouldn't prefer the lift?" the orderly asked. The boy was perhaps twenty-five, sound and handsome as a recruiting poster; his courtesy was of habit and training. They made them like this now; they had since the War. Every lad on the street seemed to be square of jaw and straight of spine, the working-class tall and striding as the aristocrats, each one smart as a tin of paint. Their manners were store-bought.

"I don't see why you need this murderous linoleum. Couldn't get a grip with pitons." His cane scrabbled across the step in emphasis. His hand was unsteady on the rail. The boy took his elbow.

"In my day—" He winced as he said it but pushed on rather than apologizing. "In my day an asylum was judged on its construction. Stone floors, tile. None of this linoleum. False economy, I call it."

"Hygiene is our main concern," the boy replied.

Their halting procession of two dragged up more stairs, down corridors, through doors mute with white paint. The door they sought was identical to the others but set apart, in a corner of the top floor: the penthouse suite, he supposed. The boy slid open a panel at chin height, revealing a loose grille of wire. "It's really more correct to call it a sanatorium," he added. "Ambrose?" the boy called in to the room. "It's Dr. Platt here to visit you."

The patient sat by the window in a chair that wrapped around his sides. He was made like a bed with blankets tucked in cleanly around every limb. Not a corner had been disarranged by movement. He didn't turn to see who it was at the grille. His face was framed against the sunlit window—a huge, beautiful picture window—and the sharpness and sameness of the profile struck Platt like a kick to the chest.

"Are you all right, Dr. Platt?"

"Fine." He tried to brush the orderly away but his hands were shaking. He snapped the panel shut. "His hair. What the devil happened to his hair?"

"That's the shock treatment, nothing to worry about. The patches look a bit odd but sometimes the hair grows back completely. Not often with the elderly patients, though. How do you know him?"

"How do I know the elderly patient? We were . . . at medical school together. Went to the same clubs."

"Did you know him when he was writing? His monograph on the sexual origins of superstition—that was incredibly early for a Freudian approach, 1896 or something—our chief clinician says he was assigned it at medical school." The orderly glanced back at the door with a sort of proprietary pride. "He was one of the early adopters. It must have been quite something to know him."

"He was off on a bloody goose chase. Antispiritualism, not psychoanalysis. You'd laugh yourself sick at his cures. He would have got back on track, of course, given time."

The orderly looked disgusted, but not with Ambrose.

With horror Platt felt his eyes growing wet. That came on him now, sometimes. The orderly took his elbow to guide him to a bench. Platt slapped his hands away. The orderly stepped back with irritating speed—confident, indulgent speed. Platt knew what he was to this boy. Another sodden Victorian, paying now for a lifetime of repression, pitiable. "You can go now. I'll ring when I mean to depart."

"You know I can't leave you alone with him, Sir," the orderly said.

"I'm not here to have a chat about the weather! I have news. It's family business. A man needs to be told these things in private." The orderly's even look was withering. Farther down the hall something on rubber wheels screeched like a cat as it rolled out of earshot. "I know that he might not understand what I say."

"He certainly won't understand what you say. He won't know that I'm in the room. He probably won't know that you're in the room. Didn't you say that you're a doctor?"

"It's only—you can sit in the corner. Keep quiet."

The orderly gave him a yet more restrained smile—they were so awfully like nuns in their resignation, modern staff, when the old ones were like prison warders in a Hogarth engraving—and unlocked the door.

"Hello, then, Gennett. It's been a long time, longer than it should have been. I'm dead sorry about that." Platt made as much to-do as possible with settling in the wicker visitors' chair, passing his coat to the orderly, propping his stick in easy reach, but eventually he had to meet the patient's eyes. He knew, he knew he should not misinterpret that look. The man didn't know who he was. Ambrose hadn't known him the last time he had come, six years ago, and he had declined since then. And yet, the look was not vacant. It seemed broad yet penetrating, leveling differences, bathing all things in the same sympathetic regard. How could it be so gentle without understanding? And if he did not speak . . . in truth, he seemed an unworldly mystic for whom speech was an irrelevancy. How blissful it would be to go away believing that: There had been no decline, simply a rise to the blessed impassivity of a holy fool.

"Gennett, I have some rotten news. Your sister . . . I don't know whether the hospital told you . . ." Platt shot a look at the orderly, who looked baffled at the mere idea. "She's died. Influenza. In a woman of sixty-five one can't be surprised. I believe that her health was good before that." Or it had been when Platt had last heard of her, when he had come years ago with news that Ruth Gennett had died. The patient had been lucid enough to understand at that point. The resulting collapse was, his doctors said, fair proof of that.

The patient gave no reaction, only watching him steadily, as if Platt were a painting on a wall, or a window. The orderly caught Platt's eye and wagged his head significantly.

"Well, that's a sad task done," Platt said. "She left her affairs in a wretched muddle, as you might expect. No will; that would be far too considerate. The executor—that's your solicitor's son, now; she never changed firms—the executor is knocking back claims from the most absurd directions. Maurice Booth's people want money. Did you know he had any people at all? They're just as you'd expect: mean little spongers with airs. Coarse as fishwives. Anyway, he lasted, what, two years after the wedding? I wager he was glad to go after that. Spent as much as he could, but I doubt he had much joy of it, luxury on Miss Ernestine's purse strings." Platt swallowed a hard knot of bile. "But that's only news to the scavengers, isn't it? They think it was a straight bribe, the family fortune for having," Platt shot a stealthy look at the orderly, who did not appear to have made the connection, "for having signed his name at the bottom of the order. They forget how much she gained from having an M-R-S gracing her calling cards. She would have taken any man she could dominate. Old maids can't be society hostesses, though I doubt her galas and benefits raised for charity a tenth of what she spent on party decorations and gowns." The orderly wore an expression of mild interest. This was after all idle gossip, perhaps of interest in the tearoom, but academic in the question of the patient. What matter was it that Mrs. Booth (née Gennett) would no longer be authorizing treatment? One of the few things on which the executor had been briefed was a suitable proxy. The hospital governor—the office, not the man—would have authority as well as funds, and could be relied upon to find innovative therapies for Dr. Gennett's singular and curious manner of illness.

"What is the current regimen?" Platt hissed to the orderly. "You mentioned camphor as a convulsive agent?"

"The shock treatments? Oh, that was highly salutary, but it was the leucotomy that made the real difference. Are you aware of the new technique? It's surgical. He hasn't had a violent episode in almost a year. He used to fly into fits, accusing himself of murder, demanding to be punished—that's when he wasn't wheedling with the doctors, trying to argue himself out, as if those episodes never happened. Nor the periods of catatonia. Complete denial over the seriousness of his condition. So now it's mainly the hydrotherapy, and the enemas, and insulin injections when necessary. He's very calm now."

"Yes, I can see that. What about restraints, punitive reconditioning?"

"Good heavens, no." The orderly looked scandalized. "Well, earlier in his illness, perhaps, but that's entirely discredited now. His family never balked at employing the most progressive experimental treatments. No expense spared."

"That's guilt," muttered Platt. He hadn't meant to be overheard.

"Guilt? Quite possibly. Many of the families suffer from it. Purely displacement, of course, and relegating suppressed emotion to the id. Entirely sublimated."

Platt turned back to the patient and flushed. He had been determined to address Ambrose directly, not speak about him as if he wasn't there. But looking into those eyes . . . "My lads are doing well. Finished at King's, both of them. I was looking forward to having them invited to my club, but it's closing. Not enough new members, they say. I say the new lads in the profession have ideas above their station, think they can do better. Er, our roses are coming along very well this year." The sun was coming out from behind the clouds and a yellow pane of light, broken where the bars crossed it, fell on the patient's face. Pink scalp caught the light like polished coral. "Does he have any post?" Platt barked to the orderly. "I used to read his post to him sometimes. Have it fetched."

There was little enough. Platt flipped through the meager stack, scrutinizing the faded postmarks. "Where is the recent post? Some of this is years old."

"This is all of it." The orderly's glossy patience was flaking off. "You can go look in his file yourself. All correspondence is kept for five years and then discarded. Read to be certain that the contents will not disturb, of course."

"He has read these? Or they have been read to him?"

The orderly's shrug was answer enough.

"I'm aware that your time is valuable. Please feel free to leave us," Platt said briskly. The orderly folded his arms and set his jaw. Platt started at the beginning, two thin missives from 1921, from admirers, students of psychology. Was it common knowledge where such letters were forwarded? Platt wondered. The next was a surpassingly dotty missive from an "Aunt Emily," writing, it seemed, from New England. One look at the contents tempted him to crush the letter up in a ball and hurl it out between the bars. Another look at the postmarks, however, indicated that if he discarded all her letters, there would scarcely be enough to fill a quarter hour of reading. The grim orderly was settled in for a long wait. With trepidation Platt began to read aloud.

"*Lily Dale, New York State, January 2nd, 1922,*" he read.

"*My dear Ambrose,*

How much has happened since I wrote last! I still feel keenly the absence of any response from you to my letters, but with the help of my most excellent *advisors of the soul have overcome any petty wish to withhold my own comfort and communication. I understand well that your energies are devoted (quite rightly!) to recovery, and not to correspondence. Your sister has made her opinion quite clear! But I shall continue to write. If she were open to the influence of the angelic voices that counsel me to place warmth before cold caution, how differently she would feel!*

Life in the commune is more splendidly nourishing than ever, and our happiness grows daily. Occasional nuisances in the shortage of fuel or comestibles are as nothing to a body of spiritualists, whatever your sister might say! (Though a small token of friendship, whatever pittance of the household budget could be spared now that I have renounced any claim to personal property, would be accepted by the commune with the highest gratitude.) Only last week we succeeded in making contact with the seraphim of the sixth level, and my husband (though he passed into the spirit world one hundred and sixty one years ago, I know him through our spirit contact more intimately than I know any living person, and we are bound now by the most solemn oaths and will dwell together in perfect happiness when I myself pass over—O happy day!) says that more such miracles are to come . . ."

Perhaps the letters might be less ridiculous if read in any voice but his. Platt struggled to find the beginnings and ends of unruly clauses, crying *O!* in gravelly baritone. Now that he had begun, he could think of no way to stop. 1923. 1924. Incredulous, indifferent, and oblivious, the three of them picked through the minutiae of the elderly Emily Featherstone and watched the yellow pane glide down to the floor. "*July 29th, 1925,*" Platt read. His voice was hoarse and papery. Emily's stationery was little better than newsprint by now.

"Happy birthday, my dear nephew! It is an auspicious time for us all. Good things come in threes, as you know (this number being well known in its mystic properties by Rosicrucians), and apart from this happy anniversary, we have just completed a superb materialisation . . ."

Platt stopped to rest. The guard looked no nearer to cracking. Ambrose just looked. He could go on a little longer, just a few more pages, and then think of some way to exit. *Perfectly awful to see you, old chap,* he could say, *I'll have nightmares about it. Shame I came all this way to see whether now that your jailer is dead you might be up for release at last and what do I find, but you've grown into the prison! Quite rum, but then you always were.* Platt cleared his throat and continued. He didn't know what he was saying until it was on top of him.

". . . and then, dear nephew, what do you think happened? I had the most extraordinary meeting with Miss—"

(and later he was sure that for just an instant before he blurted it out he knew)

"Miss Lily Embly."

The orderly actually looked up. Ambrose was still—he had been still since Platt walked in, the same sort of tranquil paralysis. Why shouldn't Platt keep reading? If it provoked a ghost of a reaction, would that be such a terrible thing? The orderly's eyes narrowed. Platt hurried on.

"Ahem! Frog in my throat. Anyway: *Miss*—I said that already . . .

"I and many of my brothers and sisters in the Study were down in New York City to attend the public demonstrations of a renowned psychic (his busy schedule made it quite impossible for him to accept our hospitality on the Commune, much to his regret). I was walking down Fifth Avenue, and there she was! Someone less trained in the connectedness of events in the universe would call it an amazing coincidence. I cried out, 'Miss E!' and rushed to her side as quickly as I could without losing all my leaflets. I knew her at once, of course (I have an infallible memory for auras) but she was much changed. Older, naturally, but also rather cautious *and* pinched, *if you understand me. I am afraid that her lovely profile is not well served by a broken nose. It took her some moments to place me (though everyone agrees that the Study keeps me amazingly youthful) but when she did! The frisson ran through her like a crashing wave! I could see her shake, and her eyes were like saucers, and her face was white as salt. I thought she would swoon in the street! A man was passing and he must have thought so too, as he offered her his arm, but she cried out at that, and turned from him and took my arm and hurried down the street. Then she laughed aloud! I am very accustomed to seeing strong emotion, so I was not disturbed by her wild look or her laughter, and I confess that I was most gratified that she was so affected by seeing me again. I found a diner at which we could rest and ordered coffee (tea being horribly difficult to obtain here). I asked her why she was carrying on so about the man in the street who offered to help her, but she promptly began to question me on my life and the Commune, and the man was obviously quite forgotten. She was keen to hear all my news, and since so much of it concerns the family in England, it is natural that the conversa-*

tion came around to that—my thoughts were quite of you, and I took care to express your current difficulties of health in a circumspect manner. I do not believe that she had any idea of what has happened to our family since"

(this was crossed out.)

"She was rather agitated and I fear that I at first gave her the impression that you were in prison, on account of that strange misunderstanding when she departed from our circle, and I was forced to give a more frank account of your whereabouts. 'It has nothing to do with you, my dear,' I explained, 'as we always knew you were not dead.'

'How did you know?' she asked.

'Because I tried so many times to contact you, my dear! If your spirit were in the next world we would have found it! I have made certain that Ambrose knew that, too.' I fear that this did not entirely reassure her. In fact, she put her face in her hands. I asked her what work she pursued now, but it was not a welcome answer—she has in fact abandoned the Study, she says! 'With your gifts? But what do you do instead?' I asked her. Her answer was most unsatisfactory—evasive, I think. She lives now in the borough of Queens and, if you can believe this, works in a psychiatrist's office! 'Not a doctor's assistant, not really' is how she put it to me. 'I talk to people, women. They feel better afterwards.' Whatever kind of work this is, I fear that it must not be a lucrative sort. Her frock was a very old and drab one and her hat was very sorry indeed. We spoke for an hour or more but I fear that I learned very little of her life, not even how her face and hands came to be so damaged (the latter are as knotted and knobbled as broken sticks). 'I was in London for a while, after. Working off a debt,' she looked very grim as she said that! 'in places you wouldn't know. I tried France for a few years. I made my way here. What does it matter how?'

I replied 'I think it matters a great deal! Things are not always as they seem!'

She grew very queer indeed at this. She looked very much as though she might laugh, but also that she might cry out in pain at any moment. I took her arm and begged her to say no more if it pained her. But she laid her hand on my wrist (I have great red marks where she squeezed!) and said, 'But they sometimes are. They are sometimes exactly what they seem. They are sometimes—' She set down her coffee then and took my hand and spoke so slowly and so clearly that I remember every word just as if I'd written them down at the table. 'However tortured the rationalisations we prefer, the thirst of one human being for another can be so—humbling—but I preferred to think it fate. And then mad desire. Anything but a fortress built on the back of a whim, and all to defend a single false impression, an illusion of significance in random events. How much easier to say there is no coincidence, and certainly no mistakes, and carry on to our destruction in defence of . . . how shall I put it? My idea of myself. One will sacrifice anything for that.'

'Sacrifice?' I asked her, but she did not answer me. She said, 'If I could tell him one thing, it would be that.' "

Platt met the patient's eyes. "Gennett?" he said. "Ambrose?"

THE ORDERLY locked the door behind them.

ACKNOWLEDGMENTS

IN PUTTING my name on the cover, I'm taking credit for the expertise and generosity of many, many people. Allison McCabe is the most brilliant editor this book could have had. I suspect her of actual clairvoyance, given her ability to see the story as it should be and work small miracles to get it there. The team at Crown—Steve Ross, Jenny Frost, Kristin Kiser, Donna Passannante, Christine Aronson, Dyana Messina, Shawn Nicholls, Heather Proulx, the superb designers—met every obstacle with ingenious solutions. Esmond Harmsworth and his colleagues at Zachary Shuster Harmsworth have been tireless champions, and Esmond an ever-heartening presence in our particular publishing foxhole.

The late Victorian period is a joy to research. The wealth of primary sources, particularly pamphlets and periodicals, is available to the (extremely) casual scholar, thanks to the work of archivists, librarians, and, increasingly, unpaid enthusiasts with Internet connections and a desire to preserve. My great thanks to the British Library, particularly its Colindale newspaper annex, the Cambridge University Library, the Wellcome Institute archives, and the inexhaustible patience of the staff therein. Likewise, www.spirithistory .com, www.spiritwritings.com, www.victorianweb.org (created by Brown University, supported by the National University of Singapore), and innumerable other sites, many of which have already come and gone like the ephemera they catalog. Curious readers could do much worse than to look here for more information on spiritualism, psychiatry, and the constantly surprising intersections between. For an introduction, overviews like Peter Gay's *The Freud Reader*, A. N. Wilson's *The Victorians*, and, for matters domestic, Jennifer Davies's *The Victorian Kitchen*, are very readable places to start. Anyone interested in the history of Western psychiatric treatment owes it to himself to consult the works of the late Roy Porter, particularly *The Greatest Benefit to Mankind* and *Madness: A Brief History*. Readers will note the liberties I've taken for the sake of time frame: items from Freud's London lectures to the positions of the planets to the entire career of the celebrated Eva C have been reshuffled for the characters' convenience. The remaining errors are entirely my own.

Absurd numbers of people contributed time, advice, and patience. I wish I could call Mr. Shields and Mrs. Gully by their given names, but it's hard to call them "Jim" and "Frieda" when I recall how much they taught me in high school about good books and high standards. Lan Samantha Chang, Tim Barbash, Graham Joyce, and Kathryn Hughes were inspiring writers with whom to study. Noshua Watson, Sarah Schoenfelder, Oriole Henry, Clare Littleford, Pip Nall, Jill Van Velzer, Hugh Parnell, Alan Mitcham, Nyki Blatchley, George Johnson, Kristen Eglinton, and Miranda Seymour did everything from reading drafts in progress to helping me find space to write.

Without my parents, Bryan and Jeanne, my brother, Jack, and my grandmother, Dayle Dietz, I would never have been able to begin. It was my outrageous good luck to grow up next to my father's insight into the past, and to my mother's grasp of human nature and (I doubt this is unrelated) fit-inducing sense of humor. I cannot express my thanks to my sister, Dr. Shelby Dietz. She critiqued so many drafts, talked through so many quandaries of plot and characterization, and never for a second gave up hope that we would one day reach the goal, namely that someday she wouldn't have to read this book anymore. She was remarkably calm when I told her I'm writing another one.

For my husband, Bryan Donoghue, thanks are inadequate. How one person can provide so much optimism, inspiration, commiseration, understanding, good humor, and plain faith is beyond me, but fortunately not you.